"An-mal" Crackers

Survival of Three Divorced Women

M. E. Pickard

5/8/12
To:
Debbie
With Love &
Best Wishes
M E Pickard
"Naomi"

Wasteland Press
Shelbyville, KY USA
www.wastelandpress.net

"An-mal" Crackers
Survival of Three Divorced Women
by M.E. Pickard

Copyright © 2011 M.E. Pickard
ALL RIGHTS RESERVED

First Printing – February 2011
ISBN: 978-1-60047-540-5

The following novel is fictional. Names, characters, descriptions, places, and incidents are the products of the author's imagination, or are used fictitiously. Any resemblance to persons living or dead is entirely coincidental.

NO PART OF THIS BOOK MAY BE REPRODUCED IN ANY FORM, BY PHOTOCOPYING OR BY ANY ELECTRONIC OR MECHANICAL MEANS, INCLUDING INFORMATION STORAGE OR RETRIEVAL SYSTEMS, WITHOUT PERMISSION IN WRITING FROM THE COPYRIGHT OWNER/AUTHOR

Printed in the U.S.A.

For Marion and Single Mothers

"Come In From The Rain"
Well, hello there
Good old friend of mine
You've been reaching for yourself
For such a long time
There's no need to say
No need to explain
Just an open door for you
To come in from the rain
It's a long road
When you're all alone
And a girl like you
Will always take the long way home
There's no right or wrong
I'm not here to blame
I just want to be the one
Who keeps you from the rain
From the rain
And it looks like sunny skies
Now that I know you're alright
Time has left us older
Wiser, I know I am
And I think of us
Like an old cliché'
But it doesn't matter
Cause I love you anyway
Come In From The rain,"

-Carole Bayer Sager/Melissa Manchester

ONE

"What's this?" He asked as he opened his mother's bedroom bureau drawer.

"What the ----- Oh, my God! You don't know, do you?"

"Is it what I think it is?"

"What do you think it is?"

"A vibrator?" "What the hell she doin' with a vibrator?"

"Well, Dah, Derek! Maybe, she neeeeeeeededed it."

"Jesus, Cheryl, Ma?????"

"I just can't believe she kept it. After all these years!"

"What? All these years?"

"It was supposed to be a joke, a birthday joke. I knew that her boss at Sim-U-Flight gave her one for her birthday as a gag gift. The story goes that she was sitting in for Laurie, the receptionist, while Laurie was on vacation, and Bob came out into the lobby when half the Army was there. Bob was always a jokester and he wanted to be sure that the soldiers would ask to see it."

"Anyway it wasn't wrapped but was in a brown inter-office envelope and when he gave it to her, she knew it was probably something of a sexual nature. When she worked for him they used to share Friday morning coffee breaks in his conference room reading the weekly edition of *Screw* newspaper. She told me that Nixon's caricature was in many of the editions picturing him coming out of a toilet bowl."

"So what happened?" He asked.

"She didn't want to open it in front of half the U.S. Army but they teased her until she pulled it out of the manila envelope and held a box in her hand containing a vibrator. They all had a good laugh over it and she brought it home and threw it in her bureau drawer."

"But funnier than that was shortly after, she had gone to bed, was sleeping, and was awakened by a noise in the middle of the night. This was after our parents divorced. Thinking that either the furnace or some other expensive appliance was broken, she tried to follow the noise going up and down the hallway until her search brought her back to her bedroom and over to the bureau where, while listening, she realized the noise was coming from the top drawer. Upon opening it, she discovered that the vibrator somehow turned itself on and was humming away. She sat on the edge of her bed laughing til tears rolled down her face. "

Her son Derek and daughter Cheryl were talking about their upfront, in your face, spit-it-out, feisty, seventy-somethin' year old mother, Marie. The two children were in their mother's home trying to put her personal documents and possessions together after Marie suffered a heart attack. Although she was every bit as described as above, she was also loyal, sensitive, truthful, creative and loving.

Loving to a fault some said. Before heart disease started curtailing her very active life, she used to laugh while remarking, "I've been around the block and around and around and around. Guess I could say I have round heels." No truer words could be spoken of her, especially by her for indeed she had been around in the lovin' arena. That part of her life adventure was cause for much sorrow and pain for those who loved her and for whom she loved dearly, but I'm getting ahead of myself and will get to that part of her story later.

TWO

    Marie Maxwell was born on Christmas Eve, 1935 in Forty-Fort, Pennsylvania to caring parents. Her father, Mitch, worked for the local utility company; her mother, Marion, was a stay-at-home housekeeper, but in those days wives didn't work.

    She had two older brothers, Mitch, Jr., who was thirteen years her senior, and Danny, who was nine years older than she. Her sister, Margaret, was four years older than she.

    Mitch, Jr., although very intelligent and witty, was also the clown in the family. His body was small framed. He probably only weighed a hundred twenty-eight pounds on the day he married at twenty-seven. He grew a moustache to give the appearance of a man his age. His clothes were impeccably chosen: wing tipped shoes, argyle socks, creased slacks, white oxford button down shirt and his signature bow tie. With his coal black hair and moustache, he was suave and debonair. His buddies called him "Sharpie."

    Could that man dance: tango, jit, ballroom, polka. You name it, he could do it or if a dance was foreign to him, he'd invent a step to go along with the music. Believing himself a Gene Kelly, he also taught his sisters how to dance and how to appreciate music including classical symphonies.

    Danny, on the other hand was the serious one. While they looked alike - dark eyes and hair - his body shape was larger than his older brother by twenty pounds. Though intelligent, he wasn't witty - he was studious.

    Before he was born, Marion, one time on a lark, went to see a gypsy fortune teller. The room she was seated in wasn't at all like that pictured in old movies: crystal ball, draped curtains surrounding the room, darkness with only candles lit to see, and the gypsy woman dressed in flowing clothes with bright shades of purple, and yellow turban tied around her head.

    No, she was dressed in street clothes; looked like your next door neighbor. She didn't even take Marion's hands in hers when she told her, "You will have pain and loss in your lifetime. I see two marriages and a son who will become a Catholic priest."

"Oh! No," Marion said. "That can't be. I'm not Catholic," and she tried to hide her doubt in what the gypsy told her.

"This will happen," she told her. "Trust my words, and in the meantime, enjoy the life you have now."

Danny started singing in high school and he was still singing the day he passed, many, many years later. He fashioned himself like Frank Sinatra. When he sang, he sounded just like Frank and although he pictured a life of show biz, fate took him down another direction into ministry. His seriousness was essential in helping his mother raise his two small sisters after a divorce between his parents

Margaret's "nose got broken" the day her mother brought Marie home from the hospital. The difference in those two girl's personalities was apparent from that day on and for the rest of their lives. Margaret would enter the convent.

Margaret was just four years old when Marie was born, and was the apple of her brother's eyes: sweet, quiet and even as a child, she was contemplative. The brothers and sister all looked alike, dark hair, dark eyes. Then into their lives was born a blue eyed, light-haired baby girl full of piss and vinegar who got all the attention. The "baby of the family" would ask years later, "Did you see who put the basket on the porch the night I was born?" It was a family joke for Marie looked just like her father.

The sibling rivalry between the two sisters was more profound in the oldest of the two, from their elementary years through adulthood into their senior years, and almost cost them total estrangement. Unaware to her, Marie's sister was jealous to the point of sometimes desertion.

The Maxwell family came to be known as "Maxwell Circus" cause every one of the kids had to be center stage elbowing each other off the platform in order to be the next performer. They were all gifted in music. Marie sang in darkened smoky jazz bars from an early age until she had children. Then her singing was to her babies.

Mitch and Marion enjoyed their life together until Marion felt something was missing. Her decision to convert to Catholicism in her thirties brought pain and anguish to her family that had damaging consequences for the rest of their lives. While the religion itself was not the problem, she became fanatical over it and tried to pull her husband into it with her.

THREE

"What's this?" Marion said to a neighbor after picking up a silver medal off the ground while hanging out laundry.

The Italian neighbor looked at it and replied, "Oh! That will bring you good luck. It's a miraculous medal. See, the Virgin Mary is on the front."

"But what are the words written around her?"

"Mary conceived without sin, pray for us who have recourse to thee!" said the neighbor. The neighbor couldn't tell her what the words meant. She didn't know.

Marion took the medal into the house and kept repeating the words. Her interest in those words peaked until she remembered that there was a Catholic church nearby and called for an appointment with the priest.

Fr. Derkin answered the door and invited her into the rectory. He held the medal in his hand and said, "Mary is the mother of Jesus, so she had to be without sin and if you pray to her, she will help you."

"I want to know more about this. Would you give me instructions?"

"How do you think your husband will react to you wanting to become a Catholic? Are you getting along with him? This is a very difficult religion to live by. I will instruct you but you must search within to see if it is for you. Come back next week and we can begin."

When Marion told her husband, he remarked, "Sure, what harm can it do. Go ahead."

Near the end of her instructions, Fr. Derkin said, "Now, about birth control. The faith you practice now allows it. Am I correct?"

"Yes, Mitch and I have spaced our children four years apart with the help of birth control."

"Do you understand the church cannot condone the use of artificial means to control birth and that it is a mortal sin to do so? Would your husband agree to stop practicing birth control?"

She fell silent.

"I'll ask him."

She waited until after supper that evening to spring it on him saying, "I'm ready to be taken into the Roman Catholic Church, but there is one thing we have to agree on beforehand."

"We? What we? I'm not entering into an agreement with the church. Even though I don't attend services, I'm a Methodist and have no intention of changing, so what's this all about?"

"According to the doctrine of the Catholic church, birth control is not permitted and is punishable by the loss of my soul into hell forever."

"Now they're sticking their nose in the bedroom of my home and I will not allow it, and no, I will not agree to it."

Marion knew she would never be able to talk him into accepting it and hoped she could find another way to deal with it.

"Well then, father said that because you are my husband I cannot turn you away from me, but that I could not actively participate in sexual intercourse and be a member of the church."

"Which means what?"

"I can't participate."

"So you're telling me that you would have to just lay there?"

"Yes."

"This has gone far enough. If it is your decision to remain on this ridiculous path and enter into a church that takes personal choices away from you, you tell father whoever that your husband does not agree and is moving out of the bedroom." That said, he went to the bathroom, cleaned up, went out the door and headed to the VFW. From that day forward until the marriage ended, this became his evening ritual. The only thing Mitch insisted upon was that he bring up the boys Methodist and she could bring up the girls Roman Catholic.

They spoke to each other when needed about the children, household expenses, important issues, but never slept together again. Marion took it to another level when she started burning votive candles in front of a statue of the Virgin Mary. No one ever knew for sure but it's possible she was praying for her husband to convert.

After a hard day at pounding the streets reading meters, Mitch came home early one afternoon to find the house empty. Searching for his little girls, he ended up going into the cellar where he found a lit candle and no one there. Returning from the cellar he was provoked to the point of exasperation. Then, he heard the sound of children's laughter coming from the backyard.

Upon opening the screen door, he saw Marion sitting on the top step.

"What the hell are you doing up here with a candle burning in the cellar?" he asked. "You could start a fire. And what's all this burning of candles in front of a piece of plaster? Have you gone mad?"

Not expecting him home so early, Marion became afraid. She'd forgotten about the candle and intended to blow it out and hide it before he came home.

She got up and turned around to step into the kitchen when he noticed a silver medal on a chain hanging around her neck. She slid by him and into the kitchen. When he realized that it was a medal Catholics wore, he pushed her against the wall, ripped it off, threw it on the floor and charged out the front door. He didn't know his two little girls were standing outside the door, noses pressed against the screen with tears running down their cheeks.

"Mommy, why is daddy so mad?" Marie said.

"He doesn't understand why I wear the medal of Mary around my neck and seeing it made him angry," Marion said.

Margaret stood in the corner sobbing quietly, afraid to move. And that was the first time of many times to come, she couldn't hold it and peed her panties.

The next morning, when Marion was in the kitchen making breakfast, Mitch came into the room and asked her where the medal and chain were.

Timidly she answered, "It's broken. I have to get it fixed."

"Give it to me and I will get it fixed. Early this morning, upon awakening, I heard a voice, from where I do not know, that said, "Let her go!" so I won't stop you from pursuing this again."

From that day on, he never brought it up again, never tried to dissuade her in her search for her religious belief, but the marriage was broken never to be revived again.

Danny was sixteen when this happened, in high school and beginning to date, but his life was changed as a result, and he had to step into the shoes of father and husband to help his family, something he would do for the rest of his life.

No matter what age, divorce takes a tremendous toll on a family and so it was no different with the Maxwell's. The difference was the way the two little girls handled their loss throughout their lives.

Marion's religious fanaticism had become overwhelming for Mitch, and he could see there would be no end to the burning of candles, not to mention pictures of Jesus and His mother on the walls throughout their home. He worried about his wife's mental health but knew it was impossible to try to do anything about it. She was a very good mother to his children, but he couldn't help wondering what went wrong between the two of them, and caused her to adopt a belief that was so foreign to him.

Because a practicing Catholic is not allowed to divorce, but a legal separation is acceptable, Marion contacted a lawyer in an attempt to start proceedings for a separation from Mitch. Although he never tried to stop her from practicing her religion, there were still bitter words spoken between them, so Mitch moved out when the fighting became too much to tolerate and rented a room. Neither Marion nor Mitch recognized that their daughters heard them fighting and how badly it affected them and would throughout their lives.

FOUR

Shortly after Mitch moved out, Marion became sick. Her stomach was distended and she couldn't keep anything in it. Throwing up throughout the day caused her to dehydrate. Arriving home from school one day, Danny found his mother in a weakened condition laying on the couch.

"Mother, what's wrong?" he asked.

"I'm sick, Danny. So sick. I can't eat. The nausea is lasting most of the day now."

"We need to call Dr. Kessler," he said.

At the same time he was dialing the doctor, Marion slipped off the couch and on to the floor.

"Mother!" he yelled, dropped the phone, ran to her, knelt down, and cradled her head in his hands.

"Hello, hello" came a voice on the phone. "Is anyone there?"

"It's my mother, he yelled. "She's passed out and on the floor."

After placing a pillow under her head and laying an afghan over her body, he was able to reach the phone and talk to the nurse who was on the receiving end of the line.

"Did you say on the floor?" she asked.

"Yes."

"Who am I speaking to?" the nurse asked.

"Marion Maxwell's son."

"Can you drive her to the hospital?"

"I'm sixteen, don't drive and we don't have a car," he said.

"Where is your father?" she asked.

"My parents are separated. He doesn't live here anymore."

"OK, try to remain calm. I'll alert the doctor. He is at the hospital near your house and will come right away." She rang off.

Danny sat on the floor next to his mother rubbing her hand and talking to her.

"God, Mom don't die now. I don't know how to take care of two little girls and Mitch isn't here to help." Marion's oldest son, Mitch, had moved and was living with his grandmother in upstate New York.

Danny hadn't time to notice that his sisters were wrapped in each others arms and huddled in the corner at the end of the living room, crying .

When Dr. Kessler walked through the door and recognized his patient, he was aware that she was gravely ill. Upon examining her, her skin was gray and clammy. Her heart rate was slow. He put his stethoscope in his pocket and turned to the young boy and said, "We have to get her to the hospital now. Is there someone nearby who can drive her?"

Opportune at that moment, one of Danny's friends, Stan, had just pulled up to the curb in his automobile and while walking up the sidewalk, Danny ran out the door and said, "Thank God you're here. My mother has to be taken to the hospital and I had no way to get her there."

Having been a school friend of Danny's from elementary through high school, Stan had known Marion for years, but looking at her now, he hardly recognized her. She looked so frail.

As they entered the house together, Dr. Kessler was finishing up his examination of Marion. Upon turning to leave, he saw Danny down on one knee with his arms around his sisters and heard him say, "Don't cry girls. I have to take Mom to the hospital, but I'll be right back and take care of you. Margaret, take care of your little sister til I get back, OK?"

His sisters were sobbing uncontrollably, but he didn't have time to stay and console them.

He picked his mother up off the floor, tightened the afghan around her body and went out the door, shutting it with the toe of his right foot.

Dr. Kessler called ahead with instructions, so, upon her arrival at Mercy Hospital, Marion was taken to x-ray. By this time, the pain was so severe that she was in and out of consciousness most of the time. Morphine was injected into her IV hookup.

The times when she was lucid she cried out for her little girls, "Are they OK?" she kept repeating.

After an internal examination and upon reading the x-ray, the doctors conclusively agreed that she had a uterine tumor. Malignant or benign could not be determined without exploratory surgery.

There was no one else to discuss her diagnosis with but her sixteen year old son. The husband had not been called, so the doctor called Danny into a waiting room and gave him the bad news.

"Your mother needs an operation and somebody has to make that decision. If we don't operate, she will die and if we do, she could die anyway. If your mother doesn't consent to surgery, is there someone who could help you or give permission to operate?"

"I don't want to call my father even though they are still legally married. There's too much bitterness and I don't think she would want him to know about this. How long can we wait before deciding?"

"The surgeon informed me this must be decided very soon. Too many complications can erupt if we don't. Even at that, it's risky. She's malnourished, her weight is so low and she is very weak. If she rallies and is coherent, we'll ask her what she wants us to do. Go home and take care of your sisters."

"If she stands a chance of dying, I want my sisters to see her before. Can I bring them to the hospital?"

"Although children under the age of twelve are not allowed in the hospital rooms, I'll get permission for your to bring them. I'm sure you are aware of the need to keep from them the discussion we have had."

Danny went into his mother's room, stood by her bed, gazed down at her and took her hand. The drugs had numbed her senses, so she wasn't aware of his presence.

And so he closed his eyes and prayed aloud. "Father in Heaven, I love my mother and beg you to heal her. If this is not to be, please give me the strength to make the right decisions for her welfare and the welfare of my sisters. You know there is no one but me to protect all three of them now and I am only sixteen. Please hear my prayer and help me. Amen."

With tears blinding his eyes, he pulled up a chair, sat down, and put his forehead on the edge of the bed, when he felt his mother's hand leave his own. She placed it on the top of his head and said, "Don't cry, Danny. I'll be OK. How are the girls?"

Regaining consciousness gave him hope that she may be able to make the decision for her care. "I was just about to go home and get them - bring them to see you."

"They don't allow children in the hospital, do they? I must be in bad shape if they'll let the girls come to see me."

He had no choice and told her what the doctor had said.

"Go home and get them. I want them to see that I'm OK."

When Danny stood up to leave, he saw the surgeon and Dr. Kessler enter the room.

Not believing it fair to ask a boy to make this difficult decision for his mother, the surgeon said, "Mrs. Maxwell, has your son told you that you need surgery or you will die, but you could still die if you do have it. You have a tumor in your uterus that must be removed as soon as possible."

"Is it a cancer?" she asked.

"We won't know that until we open you up," the surgeon replied.

"There is no decision to make," she said. "I will have the surgery. I will survive because I have two little girls depending on me," she said.

"We'll schedule it as soon as possible," the doctor said and the two doctors left the room.

His sisters were waiting on the couch holding hands when their brother came home.

"Girls, I'm gonna take you to see Mom," he said.

Mercy Hospital was within walking distance of their home so early in the evening, Danny and his two little sisters walked down the street and around the corner past the Fairmont Ice Cream Shop their mother took them to for butter pecan cones and headed toward the front entrance of the hospital.

While walking down the hallway, holding his sisters hands, Marie became frightened, started crying, broke loose and started running toward the exit.

"Stay right here while I go after your sister," he said to Margaret, but she had started crying also.

"What's the matter, Marie," he asked her.

"I'm afraid to see Mom. Is she dead? Did God come and take her away?"

"No, she's waiting to see you, give you a hug and kiss. Come on honey, take my hand and we'll go see her."

He coaxed her to come with him back to where her sister was waiting.

Marion had a bed in a semi-private room. The curtain to her bed was pulled, she could not see who was entering, but she could hear footsteps approaching.

Seeing the curtain drawn, Danny became fearful that her health might have taken a turn for the worse, so he was hesitant to open it.

His sisters stopped dead in their tracks. He took two steps, drew back the curtain, and saw his mother laying there, arm extended, hand opened.

At least she was still alive, he thought.

"Where are they?" Marion asked in a weakened voice.

"Mommy?" said Marie. She ran to her mother's bedside and what she saw scared her to the point of withdrawal. Her mother was laying on her back. Her gray hair was uncombed, her skin was chalky and her eyes were glazed.

"Don't be afraid, honey. Come here and let me see you."

Gingerly, the sisters shuffled toward their mother's bed and afraid to take her hand, just stood there staring at her.

"Why are you here and when are you coming home?" Marie asked.

"I have to have an operation to make me well again. Don't you worry. I'll be home in a few days."

"Who's gonna take care of us then?"

"You remember your Aunt Myrtle, don't you? Danny called your Gramma and talked to her and your aunt and Aunt Myrtle is on her way here."

"Will she play games and give us candy?"

"Sure, she loves you both and will take real good care of you."

Marion started tiring and told her son to take the girls home but not before giving them a kiss. She wasn't sure if it would be her last, but in her prayers that evening she prayed: "Dear God, not for me, but for those two little girls, I beg you to let me survive the operation tomorrow. They've lost their father and only have a young brother to help, so I need to get well to raise them."

The tears welled up in her eyes and ran down her cheeks, but she was able to fall asleep.

In the middle of the night, she woke and saw a vision at the end of her bed she believed to be that of Saint Mother Cabrini. She was smiling at Marion and in her mind Marion heard "Don't worry, you will live." And with that, the vision disappeared.

FIVE

Aunt Myrtle stepped off the train and onto the platform and searched for her nephew. Myrtle wasn't the prettiest of the four daughters born to Mame and Jerry Collier. Her arms were big, the fatty tissue extended off the underside of them and her legs were quite large which made them appear to look like that of a pool table. Her gray hair was done up in curlicues and her face was puffy. She wore black "nun" shoes, and her stockings were thick and black with seams running down the middle of them.

She had been married once but couldn't seem to accept the responsibilities of a wife, so she left her husband and went to live with her mother and father. No one ever knew if the marriage had been terminated by divorce or there had not been any legal action taken to dissolve it.

Marion had said many times that Myrtle was "odd." Even the two little sisters witnessed funny behavior while she stayed with them. She hummed and talked to herself all the time. Marie would laugh at her; Margaret didn't dare, but somehow their aunt never recognized that the joke was on her.

Myrtle turned when she felt a hand on her shoulder to see her young nephew, Danny, standing behind her. He appeared to be tired, his face serious with worry about his mother.

"Aunt Myrtle," he said.

"How is she?" she asked.

"She goes to surgery tomorrow morning. The doctors believed it better to wait until you got here before operating in case she doesn't survive," he said with tears in his eyes.

"Have you told your father?"

"No, I thought it best not to. There's been so much discontent between them. I didn't want to upset her and she didn't even ask if I had. I'll tell him after the operation."

"I think that's a good idea. No one knows what happened between them. The family living a distance, I guess your mother didn't want to worry us. Do you want to talk about it?"

He told her about his mother becoming fanatical after embracing Catholicism and how it caused painful emotions for the children.

"Do you have any idea why she became so obsessive over this religion?"

"No, I have no idea what happened to take her in this direction. They seemed to get along fine until she embraced it, but I wasn't home a lot of the time - off on my bike to cheerleading practice and out with the guys to Carney's Soda Shop. The girls took the brunt of it because being little, they couldn't wander too far from home. The times I was around the house the fighting and yelling was pretty bad."

Danny picked up his aunt's suitcase and they left the train station heading toward the bus stop.

Aunt Myrtle started humming some unknown melody as soon as the bus started pulling away from the curb. She didn't stop until their block approached and she got off the bus.

Danny's sisters were in school when they arrived so it gave the aunt and her nephew time to get acquainted and explore the triplex the family lived in.

The living room was wood floored; the furniture consisted of a horsehair sofa and chair. There was a worn rug on the floor and a stand alone lamp aside the couch. An arch-shaped dial radio sat on top of an end table. A small stand in the entrance to the dining room held a telephone; its numbers read 21118, a phone number Marie would remember the rest of her life.

The dining room had a large wooden table and six chairs at which Marion and Mitch sat at either end. Aside the wall was a dining hutch that held assorted dishes and pictures.

The wooden kitchen table, which also seated six, was painted green with red circles around the bottom of each leg. A black cast iron coal burning stove that Marion cooked on was next to the back door. In the corner of the kitchen was a small gas hot water heater that had to be lit with a match.

The door leading to the cellar was behind the chair where Mitch used to sit.

It was decided to remove the dining room furniture and put a hospital bed in the dining room, because it was expected that Marion probably would be too weak to climb the narrow stairway leading to the upstairs bedrooms and bathroom.

"I'm thinking of staying downstairs and sleeping on the couch as to be near Marion when she comes home from the hospital. Then when I think it's OK, where do you want me to put my things?" Myrtle said.

"For the time being, I'll carry your suitcase upstairs to mother's room and you can use her dresser drawers. Margaret shares mother's bed with her and Marie still sleeps in her crib alongside the bed," Danny said.

They decided to go to the hospital before the girls came home from school. Myrtle wanted to talk with her sister before the surgery in the morning.

Danny filled her in on what to expect while walking down the hall of Mercy Hospital, telling her about his mother's thin and emaciated body. Myrtle had done convalescent sitting for the elderly and was aware that she could find her sister in a deplorable condition.

Upon arriving in the hospital room, Myrtle was shocked to see a woman lying in bed she hardly recognized. Still, she tried to hide her distress.

Marion's eyes were closed and she appeared to be sleeping but she heard the footsteps entering the room, opened her eyes and said, "Oh, Myrtle, thank God you've come. Now I can go to surgery without worrying about Danny and the girls. Thank you for coming to help us."

"How could I not. You're my sister."

Although Myrtle wasn't one to cuss, she said, "And where the hell is Mitch? What's going on Marion? Mother and I thought you had a very good marriage. Now this separation and illness. Wouldn't you want him to be at your side for the children's sake?"

"No. It wouldn't have done any good. He found out I was in the hospital, and not knowing how bad my condition was, he came to see me last night. Myrtle, he asked me for a divorce. Said as long as we weren't getting back together, he met someone else at the VFW and didn't think it appropriate to be seeing her while married."

"A divorce? When you're laying in bed getting prepared for an operation? This is unbelievable. Has he been around the children? I mean at least seen them or taken care of them?"

"Not that I'm aware of, but I don't think Danny would tell me and I can't be laying here worrying about that."

"Well, don't you worry anymore. I'll take care of the girls for as long as need be and let Danny do things a sixteen year old needs to do. Get some rest. We'll be back early tomorrow morning before your surgery."

Aunt Myrtle and her nephew left the room together. While walking down the hallway toward the exit, she turned to him and said, "I know you're very young but I can't help trying to control my anger at your father. Did you hear your mother tell me that he came to the hospital?"

"Yes, I heard all of what she said."

Then he looked at his aunt and even though he tried to hold them back, tears welled up in his eyes.

She put her arms around him and together they stood in the center of the hall crying for neither of them could believe that a person could be as cruel as Mitch.

"These things come back on one, Danny," she said.

And while not wanting to wish his father any harm, he secretly couldn't help himself for wanting his father to get a taste of what he was doing to his mother.

The girls were home from school when they walked through the door and they ran to their aunt and wrapped their arms around her waist. Joyfully, they said at the same time, "Welcome, auntie."

She took the older of the two by the hand, picked up the little one and sat on the couch.

"I'm here to help while your mother gets better, so don't worry about who's gonna take care of you, OK?"

"Daddy called a little while ago, Marie said.

Myrtle had to mentally shove her anger away for the little girl's sake and asked, "What did he say?"

"Oh, he wanted to know if we were OK and I told you were coming. We both got to talk to him. He said he loved us. I love him too. Did you bring us any candy?"

"Let's go to the candy store right now. What would you like to have, lollypops, candy corn, bubble gum? We'll get them all."

The candy store was on a corner a block away. Myrtle held Margaret's hand and Marie skipped down the street ahead of them. She waited at the corner and looked both ways before crossing as her mother had taught her to do.

In the early hours the next morning, Marion's family arose. Not wanting the girls to be upset even though they knew their mother was going to have an operation, Aunt Myrtle and Danny remained as calm as possible although they both were extremely anxious.

The surgery was scheduled for 9:00 a.m. so there was enough time to ready the girls for school before leaving for the hospital in time to see Marion before she was placed on a gurney and wheeled into the OR.

Upon arriving at the hospital before nine a.m., and before entering her room, they took a minute in the hallway and said a short prayer which Myrtle led, "Lord if it be your holy will, please see Marion through this traumatic experience - give her courage and strength to get well and watch over her. For her two little girls please give her back to her family. We ask this in your name, Amen."

The hospital staff was prepping her for surgery when they entered the room, taking her vitals and inserting an IV into a vein they had trouble locating. She had been given a sedative so she was groggy but aware enough to realize family had arrived.

"How are the girls?" she asked in a tired voice.

"Mom don't worry about them," Danny said. "We got them off to school and Mrs. Baker has offered to greet them when they come home this afternoon. How are you feeling?"

"Tired, but ready," she replied.

"We have to take her to the operating room now," said a nurse. You can walk with her down the hall and as far as the OR doors. There is a waiting room across the hall from the operating room where you can wait for her surgeon until her operation is over."

Walking beside her, Danny held his mother's hand. As she was slipping into a state of becoming unconscious, she squeezed his hand and said, "You're all they have now. Take care of them."

No one could envision, not even he, on that day that he would step forward many times in his life to take care of and help his sisters.

Her hand fell away from his when the doors to the operating room opened and she was wheeled through.

They walked to the waiting room and tried small talk, tried reading a magazine, and finally said nothing at all. Occasionally, one or the other would get up and walk down the hall and hurry back again to see if there was any news.

Although it was three hours, it seemed like forever before the door to the operating room opened and Dr. MacDonald walked toward them while removing his hospital mask.

"Well, she pulled through," he stated. "But the next seventy-two hours are critical so she will be in post op most of the day."

"What did you find?" asked Myrtle.

"She had a tumor the size of a grapefruit in her womb. We believe it was benign. However further testing will be necessary to be sure. We'll know in a couple days. She kept asking for Danny before and after she went under. Are you Danny, her son?"

"Yes, I am," he replied.

"Although she probably won't be awake enough to realize it, I'm gonna have you go and see her but only for a couple minutes. I think it will help her emotionally come around. If you'll come with me, I'll see you to the recovery room."

Upon entering the post-op area, what Danny saw sent chills throughout his body. Although he didn't understand all that was going on to save his mother's life, he did focus on tubes in her nose and an IV in her left arm. Her eyes were shut and her head was elevated slightly.

As he approached her bedside, she moaned, slightly opened her eyes, and recognized him.

"Is it really you?" she asked.

"Yes, mother," he replied. "You made it through and things look good for your recovery. The girls are fine, in school and Aunt Myrtle and I will be in the waiting room, so rest for now and we'll come see you soon. I love you, mother."

She tried to whisper an I love you back at him, but her strength was fading. She closed her eyes again turned her head and went back to sleep.

"I think it was good that she recognized you," the surgeon said. "She'll be out of it for a few hours. Why don't you go and get something to eat. Come back later in the day. As I stated before, she isn't out of the woods yet. I don't want to alarm you with what we watch for, so why don't you leave that in my hands. Go to your sisters."

Walking down the hallway of the hospital the two of them, aunt and nephew, breathed a sigh of relief and each said a silent prayer of thanksgiving that Marion had made it through the surgery.

They arrived home just before the girls came home from school to find Mitch sitting on the front porch.

Myrtle walked by him. She couldn't stand to look at him, but Danny stopped for a second to ask him what he was doing there.

"Why didn't someone tell me beforehand that your mother was in such bad shape?" Mitch asked.

"Would that have stopped you from going there to ask for a divorce?" Danny replied. "She told Aunt Myrtle that you went to see her. What the hell's the matter with you, dad? Have you no shame? How could you be so selfish?" Danny asked.

"I didn't know she was so sick, or----"

"Or what?" You'd of waited?"

"And who is the woman you met at the VFW? It didn't take you long to find someone did it?"

"Now that's none of your business, son."

"I'm not proud to be your son. I'm asking you to get out of here before the girls come home. I have enough on my mind telling them about Mom without you interfering - making things worse."

"I have a right to be here and see them. I'm not going to ----"

"Daddy!" yelled Marie running up the steps and into her father's arms. Scared, Margaret held back and remained in the background.

"How's my girls? Come here Margaret and let me see you."

Sheepish she edged toward her father and when he held out his hands to welcome her, she ran into them.

"When are you coming home?" Marie asked.

"We'll see, but for now, it's important to help your mother get better. I'll come and see you as often as I can. We can go for ice cream. Would you like that?"

"But why do you have to go at all?" Marie asked. She couldn't leave it alone, but then she was so young and couldn't understand what had happened to her parents.

"Your mother and I aren't living together, so I have to live in another place, but it doesn't stop me from coming to see you. Do you both know that I love you?"

"Yes, daddy!" said Marie.

Margaret held back again and said nothing.

"Margaret?" Mitch said.

Hesitantly, she turned her head away and whispered, "Yes."

Mitch left the two little girls sitting on the glider swinging on the porch when Danny opened the screen door and stepped out. His father hadn't noticed it but he had been listening to the conversation through the door.

"Supper's ready" he said. Aunt Myrtle made your favorite chicken and mashed potatoes."

The doctors were amazed how fast Marion was getting her strength back, but she remained in the hospital for six days after her surgery.

On the seventh day, her son came again with his friend to drive her home.

After he was given a list of instructions for her convalescent care, he lifted his mother off the bed into a wheelchair and wheeled her down the hall toward the exiting door.

His buddy had pulled up to the entrance door and had the motor running.

Danny again lifted her up into his arms and placed her on the back seat of the car.

They didn't notice that Mitch was watching from around the corner of the side entrance of the hospital with tears in his eyes.

Marion worked hard to get her strength back, but in spite of all her efforts, she was still weak, so it was decided between Marion's mother, Aunt Myrtle and Danny to move Marion and her daughters to her hometown in upstate New York to stay with her mother.

The Laurel Line train pulled out of the station on time that Friday morning. It was difficult for Danny to say goodbye to his mother, aunt, and sisters but he held it together until the train rounded the bend and headed north toward Suttonville, New York.

Danny was left to make arrangements for the moving of the household furniture that would be stored in his grandmother's garage. He still had to finish high school so he rented a room at the YMCA, until graduation and before joining his family.

He made no attempt to contact his father during this time - his anger was still too difficult for him to deal with. Plus his father was not paying child support and Danny knew that trying to get it from out of state would probably be impossible, but he couldn't worry about that now.

In order to pay for his room at the Y, he had to find a job after school. He needed to be able to bike himself both to classes and to work, so the search became difficult and then a friend told him about a position at a nearby gas station. They needed someone to pump gas in the late afternoon til closing at 9:00.

He didn't mind working at the gas station - at least it was income.

SIX

The train pulled into the station in Suttonville on time. Myrtle had to help her sister get off and make it to the waiting car their father was driving. Mame, their mother, was waiting at home.

The old house on 6 Cedar St. was a gift to Mame and Jerry from Mame's parents. It consisted of two stories and a large attic that could be turned into a small apartment. A large door opened into the threshold of the hallway. French doors opened into the downstairs living area. On the first floor there were two bedrooms, kitchen, dining room and living room as well as a bathroom. In the kitchen was a gas stove with four burners located to the side of a small oven. Mame had no refrigerator, but there was an ice box on the back porch. A rug was folded on top of the ice box that could be rolled down over the two doors on the front of it to keep the sun from shining on the box. The top door held chunks of ice delivered twice a week and bottom door stored perishables.

The living room had two sofas in it, one where Pa slept. There was a cherry wood radio hutch with matching chair where Pa sat and listened to the Marine marching band while playing the sweet potato.

A two car garage behind the house had a dirt floor.

The first floor of the house had a closed-in windowed porch. A Morse chair, day bed, tall lamp, end table and throw rug were the only furnishings.

The same entryway to the downstairs had steps ascending to the second floor where another apartment with three bedrooms, living and dining rooms, kitchen and bath were. A veranda above the downstairs porch was open aired, had two wooden cushioned rocking chairs and overlooked the grapevines and plum trees Mame attended.

Upon arriving at her mother and father's home, Marion breathed a sigh of relief. Although she was tired, she talked with her mother while the girls told their grandfather about the train ride and how Aunt Myrtle had sang "Bye, Bye, Blackbird" throughout the trip. Marie laughed and said, "Pa, she's funny isn't she?" Pa was the name

Marion called her father, so the grandchildren did also. No one dared call the grandmother "Mame" to her face except Pa especially when he was upset with her.

After registering the children in the nearby school, the six family members tried to settle down to living with one another. Marie slept on one of the sofas in the living room curled up with her mother. Marion's sister, Ruth, took Margaret to live with her temporarily.

Shortly after moving in with her parents, and in the middle of the night, Marion was awoken by Marie's scratching.

"Mommy, s'quitors are getting me," she whispered to her mother. Upon turning on the light on the end table Marion was astonished to see little white bugs all over her daughter's arms and legs and she let out a yell that brought her mother running into the living room to see what happened.

"Look at her, mother," she said, "She's eaten alive. These look like bedbugs to me. We need to get some DDT and spray the house and kill them."

"They'll be no spraying of that poison in my house," Mame said. "She's just scratching. I don't see anything." and she turned to walk away.

Marion grabbed her mother's arm to stop her, to make her look and realize something had to be done, but Mame got angry and said, "I said NO poison will be sprayed in this house and if you don't like it, move out. I don't understand why you left Mitch anyway. Didn't he pay the bills, take care of you?"

So now the truth comes out, Marion thought. It was a mistake coming here. Her mother didn't agree with the separation, accepted her returning home out of pity. But then too, Mame was a "Johnny Bull" of an Englishwoman: stern, strong willed, a woman who had to have things done her way. Poor Pa was a gentle man who put up with his wife's ruling hand by retreating to the cellar to concoct various salves, plumose and liniments to sell door to door in the neighborhood.

Once a week on Fridays, Mame walked to the savings bank to check on her accounts, so Marion thought it would be a good time to get to the hardware store and purchase DDT. When she arrived home Marion didn't see Pa and then realized he was in the cellar mixing his concoctions. No one else was home. Myrtle had gone out with her girlfriends. Marion unwrapped the paper around the metal can that contained the liquid pesticide. She held it in her hand and, pointing it toward the ceiling, starting pumping the plunger through the cylindrical shaped device that moved the DDT through it.

What Marion didn't expect was the chemical smell and fumes that permeated the rooms as she moved through the living room, into the dining room and eventually through the kitchen. She tried to fan the cloudy spray with a towel, but it didn't help. She waited. The smell remained even after a half an hour.

"Oh, no," she thought. "For sure this odor will not be gone before mother gets home."

She heard the front door open and saw her mother come through the living room. "What is that smell?" her mother asked.

Marion stood in the dining room, spray can in one hand, towel in the other. "I sprayed the house, mother. I cannot let my little girl go on night after night getting eaten up by bedbugs."

Mame's face became red with anger "I warned you not to bring that poison into my house. It's time for you to find other living arrangements. Maybe your sister will help you. I can't have you going against my authority." And with that, Mame pushed past her daughter, went into the kitchen and pulled the slider door between the kitchen and dining room closed.

Never believing her mother would turn her out, Marion went out on the porch, sat in the Morse chair and cried. "So much loss," she said to herself aloud, and for the first time, her faith was shaken in her decision to convert to Catholicism.

There wasn't a lot of conversation at dinner that evening - it was downright quietly disturbing. Needing help desperately, Marion decided she would have to call her younger sister, Ruth, who was married to a professional man.

"Ruth, I need your help," she said. "It was a mistake to move in with mother. There's just too many people living in one house, in cramped quarters."

"What about the renters upstairs?" Ruth asked. "I mean for family, I think mother should ask them to leave so you can move in."

"It was brought up and she said she needed the rent they pay. I'm not able to pay that much and with not knowing if Mitch will ever pay child support, I can't promise mother that I will."

"OK, well, look we can help some. I'll drive over tomorrow after the girls go to school and we'll look for a place. In the meantime, I'll search in the ads of the newspaper for availability. Look, Marion, I don't want to get into this with mother so why don't we say I'll be there at 9:00 in the morning. Wait outside for me to pull up and we'll head out and see what's available. "

Marion didn't sleep well that night.

The next morning she was sitting on the steps in front of her mother's house waiting for her sister. Her mother and she had not spoken since the altercation yesterday and she felt very sad.

"If it weren't for my girls, I wouldn't care about anything anymore," she thought. "Lord, please help me find the strength to go on and get them raised," she begged.

She heard a horn honk and looked up to see Ruth pull up in her new Buick. Marion hurried down the steps and jumped into the waiting car her sister was driving.

Pulling away from the curb, Ruth said, "I think I might have found a place on Timberland Road, Marion. It's across from a park where the girls can go play. They even have a merry-go-round and zoo, but it's what is called an furnished efficiency, so there is a kitchen and combined living, bedroom. Shall we go look?"

"Why not," Marion answered.

The apartment was located two miles from Ruth's home in an old house on Timberland Road. The landlords, the Martindale's, lived upstairs and in the in back of the efficiency apartment lived the landlord's mother, a very elderly lady.

The furnished apartment had a tiny kitchen painted granny apple green that had a small refrigerator and gas stove in it. There was linoleum on the floor. In between the kitchen and living/bedroom was a door that slid shut much the same as the door in Marion's mother's house. The combination room had a large bed and a day bed with a kerosene heater to the side of it. There was a door that led out and onto a porch that overlooked an empty hilly lot where two trees stood, on which a wooden slated swing was hooked.

"The rent is paid weekly and is twenty-eight dollars," Mrs. Martindale said. "Do you work?"

"I'm searching for a job now and expect to starting working at the 5 & 10 cent store soon," Marion answered.

"Well, I'm not sure ---," and before Mrs. Martindale could say another word, Ruth pulled out her wallet and offered a month's rent in advance to her.

"I'll be responsible til my sister is on her feet," she said. "Do you want me to sign a lease"?

"Are you Dr. Robert's wife?" she asked.

"That's right, I am." Ruth replied.

"Oh, well then that's OK. I trust that you will take care of the rent should your sister have a problem."

Ruth dropped Marion off at her mother's house. Marion had a sad feeling. Her mother's back was to her when she approached her in the kitchen. She wasn't quite sure how she would take the news about moving, but suspected it would be welcomed.

"Mother, today I found a furnished apartment for me and the girls and we'll be leaving by the end of the week. It was good of you to let us stay here and I appreciate it. Can we forget what happened and return to being mother and daughter? I'd like a hug if that's OK."

Mame turned around and with open arms walked toward her daughter and said, "I'm sorry Marion. With so little space and three family members living in it already, I think that you and the girls moving in just overwhelmed us, but I'm happy you found a place to live nearby. Your furniture was delivered while you were gone. I had it put in the garage. It's not in my way and can stay there until you're settled."

"Oh, no," Marion thought. I didn't think about where it would be stored when Danny packed it up, but stored in a garage with a dirt floor, it will be exposed to all kinds of bugs, mold and God knows what else.

But she didn't tell her mother her thoughts cause she knew it would provoke another confrontation with her, so she bit her tongue and said "OK."

SEVEN

Margaret was in junior high school and would attend the same school, but Marie was still in elementary and would have to switch schools and would have a three mile walk to her new school. The side road leading to the main street was desolate with very little traffic on it, so it gave Marion concern for her daughter's safety, but she had to find work, so another prayer was sent to heaven pleading for the safety of her daughters and again her faith was shaken.

"What have I done to my girls, Lord? Show me the way. Please protect them from harm and send their guardian angels to watch over them."

Long distance rates were considered excessive by Mame, so conversations between Danny and his mother were kept at a minimum - once a week on Sunday morning when the rate was low. Not wanting to worry each other, neither one of them wanted to tell the other how things were going. It was rough for Danny, living at the Y, working nights and going to school, but he suffered though it knowing it wouldn't be long before graduation and he would be joining his mother. She told him about the apartment but not about what precipitated the move.

Although there wasn't much to move, mainly clothes, Ruth came to help her sister. Together they loaded the car, said goodbye to Mame and drove to the new apartment. The girls seemed to take it all in stride, like a new adventure. Upon driving up to the new residence, the roar of a lion and the music of a merry-go-round could be heard.

"Ma Ma," said Marie. "Is that a lion?"

"I think so and did you hear the merry-go-round?"

"Yes, could we go to the park and see?"

"After we settle in. Margaret did you hear the music?"

Margaret was not happy with either of the moves because it took her away from her friends. She pouted, didn't answer her mother, and turned her head. She would carry this displeasure toward her mother for the rest of her life.

The park gave the younger of the two much happiness. Being the precocious little girl she was, she befriended Mack, the merry-go-round operator and the men who attended the bears, lions, and monkeys. Running across the road after school, she could be found with her nose pressed up against the fence housing the animals, then riding the merry-go-round before returning home.

Even though Marion was weak from her surgery, she got a job at the five and dime store downtown. She had to walk a mile to the bus stop to catch her ride to work. There were times after school when Marie would walk to town to wait for her mother to get off work so she could ride the bus with her home.

One time after arriving at the bus stop near the apartment, Marion was so weak, she had to sit down on a bench. It started raining and they had no umbrella with them, so Marie ran home to fetch one, and ran back to the bus stop and helped her mother walk home.

After her girls went to bed, Marion liked to sit on the porch and look at the stars. One evening while sitting in the rocking chair she noticed a light on the hill above the park. Upon standing up, she could see a cross burning and became fearful. Believing that the Klan hated Blacks, Jews and Catholics, and thinking they knew a Catholic had moved into their territory, Marion ran into the house, locked the door and sat on the edge of the bed. The anxiety she felt caused every nerve in her body to feel electric and once again she prayed.

Marion couldn't afford a phone. Her messages were relayed through her sister. Her prayers were answered two days later when Mame called Ruth and told her the upstairs renters had given notice and were moving out. Mame wanted her daughter to be nearby and safe, so she offered Marion the apartment at a reduced rental rate.

Upon being told the good news, Marion was thrilled. She knew her son would be graduating within the month, would be moving in with her, would gain employment and could help her pay the rent.

Marion was amazed when she opened the garage doors of her parents' home. The furniture stored on the dirt floor was in good condition and she breathed a sigh of relief that she wouldn't have to fumigate all of it, just the mattresses and box springs.

Her older son, who had been living in a rented apartment on the west side of town, decided that he too could help out by moving in the three bedroom with his family above his grandmother's residence.

Marion was ecstatic to have her family together again. She fussed over them, cooking, cleaning and watching them grow into a happy, fun loving gang of characters. Danny was working for and with his older brother at a drafting and design company and attending night classes at the local college. Margaret was in her senior year of high school and her younger sister, Marie, was in eighth grade at a junior high.

As mentioned before, Mame was a strict, opinionated matriarch who had boasted that she had never been to a doctor, had used old wives remedies for all her ailments including Lydia Pinkums which had, some say, a high percentage of alcohol in it, so it was not surprising when Mame had a stroke at eighty-two and could speak only enough to insist that she not be taken to a hospital. A hospital bed was set up in the living room where she lay for two weeks before dying, leaving Pa and Myrtle to fend for themselves. Of course with Marion and her family living upstairs, a lot of decision making was easier because of the three of them, Marion had the most ability to do so.

He loved to read tea leaves - Pa. They either didn't have tea bags or didn't use them. Being that Mame was a hundred percent British (she used to call England the mother country), she probably wanted to brew her own tea. She had bone china tea cups in which to serve the beverage. After drinking it, Pa would gather the grandchildren around him. "See the leaves at the bottom of the cup," he'd say and would go on to make predictions of what he saw in the formed leaves to which Mame, before passing, would look at the ceiling and roll her eyes.

It was becoming more noticeable that Pa was having trouble remembering. When Mame was alive, his license was taken away from him because he kept forgetting where he left his car and the local police spent time searching for it. After the third instance of returning it, the Suttonville police requested he give his license up. Mame agreed, took his license out of his wallet, gave to the officer, and sold the car.

One of Marie's favorite things to do was to sit on the porch with her grandfather. One day he looked at her and said, "That woman upstairs makes good apple pie." to which Marie said, "What woman upstairs?" to which he became agitated and repeated himself, to which Marie said, "Pa, that's your daughter." "It is? Well, she sure makes good apple pie." And he kept on rocking away.

At the end of her shift, Marie ran up the stairs to tell her mother what happened. "Ma, Pa called you the woman upstairs. Doesn't he know you are his daughter?"

"Don't pay any attention to him," Marion replied and continued with her household chores.

Although it wasn't discussed very often, hardly at all, there came a time when something had to be done about his "condition." A knock at the door brought Marion facing a neighbor who reported, "Marion, your father is walking down Saxon Ave. in his pajamas, bathrobe, and wearing slippers, tipping his straw hat to passersby saying "How do."

Marion rushed past the neighbor down the stairs down the hill and found her father walking along the street acting exactly as described by the neighbor.

"Pa, where you goin'", she asked.

"Oh, I don't know," he answered.

"Well, I was just coming back from town. Can I walk with you back up the hill to the house?"

Even though Pa was easy to get along with, questioning his actions since his condition started would make him angry, so Marion knew she had to gently get him to agree with her to escort him home.

At this point, a family meeting was called. It was agreed that Pa would need constant monitoring during his waking hours. Shifts would have to be assigned. It was also revealed by Marion that her father had what was then called hardening of the arteries and couldn't help what seemed to be an alarming change in his personality.

Myrtle took the evening shift because she lived with her father. One year later, early one morning, she yelled up the back stairs for Marion to come quickly. "Pa's gone," she cried.

Upon arriving in her father's bedroom, Marion discovered that her father was dead - had died in his sleep. She offered a silent prayer thanking God for His goodness in taking her father as he slept.

EIGHT

Shortly thereafter, Mitch, Jr. met his future wife, Jeannie, and brought her home to meet his mother.

Jeannie was not of the same ethnic background as the Maxwells, who were of Scotch-English descent. She was Lithuanian and had been raised in the cultures of that background. She had a heart of gold but either liked you or didn't, and if she didn't, she could become cold in that she would treat one as though they didn't exist. In her family were three brothers and three sisters, she being the middle child. Her father worked in the shoe factory, was a little guy who could speak very little English, and who liked his booze so much so that most of the time he was content drinking vodka and smoking cigarettes which caused emphysema and eventually lung cancer, but he enjoyed one last cigarette in his deathbed hours before his demise.

Her mother towered over him both in height and weight, so when told that he constantly beat her up, it was difficult for Mitch to understand how. Given that this culture married for life, Jeannie's mother stayed with her "abuser" until his death taking care of him through his many painful cancer treatments.

Mitch and Jeannie married and within three years had two sons: Justin and Mark. Even as a little boy, Mark was always into some kind of mischief or another - falling out of trees, riding his scooter down a hill and smashing into the rear end of a car for which he had to have eye surgery. It wasn't known at the time if he would lose his sight in one eye or not. It seemed that a black cloud hung over his head all his life. It remained there until his life was snuffed out at an early age.

Marion didn't have to worry financially since Danny was working for his brother and Margaret was a secretary working in the defense industry making good wages. Marie was now in high school not applying herself as well as she could have. She was having too much fun much to the chagrin of the rest of the family.

Cheerleading for her church basketball team was taking a lot of her time so studies fell behind causing her marks to be in the Cs and Ds. Togetherness in the family evolved as a result of the tough times in years gone by.

"One can't break into the Maxwell circle," became the mantra of those who married a Maxwell.

The jealousies she felt upon the birth of her sister would haunt Margaret for years to come and into her old age. It became so serious when she started working and buying classy outfits that she bought a metal wardrobe and put a padlock on it so Marie couldn't "borrow" her clothes after she left for work and before Marie went to school.

Realizing she couldn't afford to buy Marie stylish school clothes, Marion was beside herself with her daughter's sibling rivalry and interfered asking, "Margaret, why can't you let your sister wear some of your clothes occasionally."

"No, she won't take care of them like I do," Margaret replied. And that was that.

What Margaret didn't know was her younger sister had watched from a few feet away as Margaret turned the dial of the combination lock, removed it, and opened the doors. Marie's eyes were good enough from that distance to memorize the numbers. So school mornings after Margaret went to work, Marie opened the closet, rummaged through her sister's trendy clothes, picked an outfit and wore it to school.

After a stint in the army, Danny again got a job working for his brother. He contributed to the household by giving his mother half of his paycheck each week, but he felt a calling in another direction. It was time to share he thoughts with his mother.

"I want to enter the seminary and become a priest." he said.

"Where did this come from?" Marion asked.

"While I was in the army, I was taken into the Catholic church. This yearning has been with me for a long time. I've discussed it with Fr. Flanagan and he has agreed to sponsor me. He called the seminary in Buffalo and offered to subsidize my family contribution to you until I am ordained."

"I don't know what to say," Marion ecstatically answered.

"I am so proud of you."

"I'll be leaving in the fall for the seminary, mother, but will be home on holidays and for the summer, so I can take over at those times by working."

The fall tree colors were in variable shades of red, orange, yellow and maroon on the morning the Ryan's picked Danny up to drive him and Joe Ryan to the seminary. After a hug and kiss goodbye, Marion stood in the doorway and watched as the Oldsmobile turned the corner and headed for the interstate.

The expression on her face was one of pride for so many years she wondered if she had hurt her children by divorcing their father. On this day, she knew she had done the right thing, knew that the day she found the medal in the backyard, guidance from above had placed it there for this moment.

Although she was skinny, Marie wasn't an ugly one. Brown hair and blue eyes were her focal point, but her personality her asset; she was vivacious, bubbly and fun to be around. She had a quick action of funny remarks, and her sense of humor was such that most girls her age didn't possess.

In tenth grade, she met a young man, John, thought she was in love and was sure they would marry. There was a lot of heavy petting goin' on between them, but she called a halt to anything more.

Her junior year brought her first love disappointment when John came to her and said, "I have to quit school. My mother needs my help financially, so I'm goin' to work for my brother, Paul, who is in the produce trucking business."

"You know Paul doesn't like me. I'm so afraid he'll talk you into dumping me," she answered.

"Nothing could do that," he replied.

Her suspicions proved accurate when shortly thereafter, John quit his job and joined the air force. He took his basic training at a base near Syracuse, New York. Upon completion he had a week's leave before reporting to Biloxi for radio training school.

Her heart broken, Marie wasn't sure if she could ever live through this loss even though he promised they would marry one day after her graduation from high school.

Two nights before John had to leave for Mississippi, they decided to celebrate by going to dinner. John had borrowed his brother's car and the night was heavy with happiness. After dinner while holding hands they climbed up the stairs to the apartment, entered the living room and had a surprise waiting for them.

"Danny!!" Marie screamed, "What are you doing home from the sem?"

"Mother called the rector and said there was some family problems with you concerning the possibility that you might run away with John, so I just want to talk to both of you."

"Oh, God, no, I'm so embarrassed. How could she do that to me?" And with that she ran into her bedroom, threw herself across her bed and sobbed into her pillow.

Danny didn't move toward the bedroom to console his sister; he was insistent on talking with poor John and John didn't dare move toward that door. It just wasn't the thing to do, so John sat there and faked listening to his possible future brother-in-law's advice.

"John, I'm sure you know that dragging a wife around from base to base is not the thing we want for my sister. Don't you agree?"

"Yes!" *Jesus, I need to get out of here.*

"So I'm sure you understand why my mother called me home to straighten this out. Right?"

"Yes!" *Now can I go?*

"OK, well now that we are in agreement, I'll talk to my sister about it. Why don't you call her tomorrow? You'll see her before you go to Biloxi?"

"Yep!" *I'm outta here!*

And with that John hurried to the door, took the steps two at a time and ran out the front door.

Marion didn't like John much. Quitting school caused her to wonder if he was dependable, but more than that he wasn't Catholic - was Russian Catholic, so to her thinking, he's not Catholic and she was gonna make sure her girls married one.

After John left, Danny went into the kitchen to talk with his mother about the meeting. Sobs could be heard coming from Marie's bedroom, so after a discussion with his mother, he went to the bedroom door, knocked and asked her to come out. With red tear-stained eyes Marie opened the door and stepped out and walked into the living room where her brother sat waiting.

"What the hell is with her?" she asked.

"For one thing, she's going through her change which causes a lot of emotional and physical problems," he answered. "You've witnessed the terrible headaches she gets - has to go into her darkened bedroom with a pail to vomit into. This is hard to say to you but she's worried about you getting pregnant."

"Pregnant? I've never even thought about having sexual intercourse mostly because she always seemed to trust me so much that I couldn't break her heart. What good did that do me?"

"I only have a couple days before returning to the seminary. It's very rare that a seminarian is allowed to go home, but in this case, the rector believed this to be an emergency after talking to Mom, so I need for you to understand her concerns, and she needs to be OK with this."

John called to say goodbye and to see her one more time before leaving for Japan where he would be stationed a year which made Marion very happy. He didn't want to come to the apartment so they met at a restaurant.

"A year is a long time." Marie said. "How am I gonna live without you being here and what my mother did? Tell me you don't hate me for that. God what was she thinking?"

"No, I don't hate either one of you. I love you and we will marry when I return from Japan. I'd give you a ring now, but I know your mother would not allow it, so we'll just say we're engaged to be engaged. OK?"

"I guess." And she started to cry. Thought it was the end of the world for her and she was losing him.

"I love you too and will write every day," she answered.

The last thing she remembered after they left the restaurant was walking home, kissing him goodbye and then descending the steps as he turned around, waved, and was gone.

It took a few days but mother and daughter found harmony with each other and as time passed, the Maxwell household became peaceful again.

NINE

Marie's senior year was filled with activities and although she was faithful and did not date anyone she had a lot of boyfriends that she and her girlfriends palled around with.

The drinking age at that time was eighteen. Although her friends could pass for eighteen, she could not, so she borrowed an older friend's birth certificate and went to the bars where she could connect with the band and sing jazz. Progressive jazz was the popular music, with Stan Kenton being the top musician, so she bought his records and fashioned herself after his vocalist, June Christy, and did a pretty good rendition of imitating June.

The popular drink in those days was sloe gin and as long as she could prove age requirements, she was served. Of course, the bartender could care less. After all, she had proof.

One morning, the door to her bedroom opened and her mother stood by her bed, hands on hips yelling for her to come out of the bedroom immediately.

"Geez, now what!" Marie thought. She was hung over from drinking sloe gin with her friends, smoking cigarettes, dancing and singing the night before.

"Who is Patricia Pinto?" her mother asked.

"What?"

"You heard me. Who is she?"

Her mother was standing at the kitchen table. Noticeably, the contents of Marie's purse were spilled all over the table and her mother was holding a document.

"Oh! Shit. She found the birth certificate."

"Is your name Patricia Pinto?" her mother asked.

"No."

"Then why do you have her birth certificate?"

The one thing Marion could not stand was lying and her daughter knew it, so she replied, "So I can get served at the bars."

And with that she insisted on Patricia's phone number, dialed it and talked Patricia into coming to the house to pick the certificate up.

Patricia was older than Marie by five years and was of Italian descent. She had a solid build, dark eyes and hair and was very buxom and didn't look a thing like Marie. "You know I could get you in trouble for loaning your birth certificate to my daughter?" she asked when Patricia came to the house.

"You'll have to promise never to let my daughter use it again or I'll keep it and call the police."

Saying nothing but the words of a promise, Patricia took her birth certificate and got out of the house as fast as her legs would carry her.

After his training in Mississippi, John had a furlough of two weeks before being sent to Japan. Marie and John spent every minute they could together before he left. Letters expressing their love were sent and received for months before the one that arrived telling Marie not to write again. Upon reading it she sobbed uncontrollably, her world devastated. Her marks in her classes at school suffered as her despondency continued until one evening when she got a call from the air force base in Japan.

"I'm sorry honey," John said. "It's just that I'm so far away for so long a time that I thought it better to break it off for your sake. It just doesn't seem fair to ask you to wait for me for two years. Do you forgive me?"

She was ecstatic and forgave him on the spot telling him, "I'll wait for you forever."

Correspondence continued until another letter arrived from him breaking it off again.

This time her mother stepped in and asked, "Is this the way you want to spend your life? Someone who can't make up his mind if he loves your or not? And what of a marriage with him. Would he leave and return because he couldn't decide what he wants?"

"No, mother," she answered. "I think I'll have to accept it as the end of us."

Dating again wasn't difficult for Marie. She had a lot of friends, both female and male, but in those days it was friendship that was important. Sex before marriage was taboo, condoms were the only birth control used and they were forbidden in the Catholic church even in marriage. Even though her girlfriends and she discussed it, sex was discouraged by parents who felt it better to scare the bejesus out of especially their daughters by stating, "You'll go to hell if you do!"

At age eighteen, graduation was on her mind the following year. She had taken a commercial course in high school with shorthand and typing being her major subjects. Unless girls came from wealthy families, they couldn't afford to go to college. Even those who could go usually took teacher or nurses or "catch a rich husband" courses. It was generally accepted that after high school girls should find a job, find a husband, get married, and have babies and so it wasn't any different for Marie.

Friday nites were spent at a bar called Jake's where girls sat in booths and boys sat at the bar while the jukebox played music for a nickel a record. "Rock Around the Clock" was a favorite among the latest songs playing but trying to get a guy up to jit was next to impossible.

It was on one of these Friday nites that Marie met a girl who would years later become her best friend. This friendship would grow as close as two sisters without the sibling rivalry and would change their lives forever. Her name was Jackie.

Five girlfriends, Rose, Irene, Josie, Laurie and Marie, were sitting in a booth at Jake's Bar and Grill, drinking beer and talking about some of the guys at the bar. The jukebox started playing "Rock Around the Clock."

"Let's jit." Rose asked Marie. "If you think any of those guys are gonna ask any one of us to dance, you're dreaming. They don't want to make a fool of themselves cause they don't even try to learn to dance, so we might as well dance with each other."

Homosexuality was a word no one ever said nor for that matter even knew it existed, let alone what it meant, so it wasn't thought of as being gay (which meant happy in those days). Boys and girls did some slow dancing, but two of the same sex slow dancing wasn't okay.

These girlfriends came from different "wards" or sections of the city and knew each other by way of attending the same high school. No one drove a car so they pitched in and pooled their money to hire a taxi to take them from their respective residences to honky tonks which lined a street called Herley St. where ethnic cultures of Polish, Slovac, Russian, Lithauanian and Ukranian citizens lived.

Some girlfriends from a neighboring high school were sitting in a booth opposite Marie's group and struck up a friendly conversation that evening.

"You guys seem to like to like bumming in our neighborhood," Joan said.

"Why not, there is no scarcity of places to hang out. I mean we counted and there are twenty-five bars on this street, let alone the ones on side streets which we don't frequent. Is there a problem?" Rose asked.

"No, just remember the guys are from our ward and we kinda like to reserve them for ourselves." Joan answered. "So if you have designs on them, we wouldn't like that."

"Don't worry about that. We're just here to have fun," Marie said.

The music started up again, all the girls got on the floor to jitterbug, but the one called Jackie, who was very attractive, had naturally blonde hair, was very neatly dressed, and who stood out from the rest of the gang.

Graduation was filled with parties, partying and more parties. Marie hadn't heard from John in a long time and accepted the fact that the romance was over.

There was a lady who lived across the street from her who offered to speak for Marie to her boss at a legal firm in the downtown area. The interview went well with a lawyer who was a partner in the firm.

She was told that she would be working for two lawyers who did real estate searches and closings and that her salary would be $45.00 a week which in 1954 was a goodly amount of money. She had to give $10.00 a week to her mother for room and board and after deducting that amount, had $28.00 left for herself to spend as she pleased.

Her first extravagant purchase was a mooton lamb fur coat which she bought from a local furrier on credit and paid for weekly. Not having a car or license to drive left her and her friends with the only transportation - walking - to where they needed to go although bus service was available during the day. They continued to chip in for a taxi if there were enough of them going clubbing to afford it .

Her job at the legal firm wasn't going too well as she didn't proofread her typing, thought it was OK when there were errors, and was reprimanded for it a few times. Legal descriptions of properties had to be exact with every t crossed and i dotted.

Six months into her employment, she was called into the office of the man who hired her.

"I'm going to have to let you go," he said. "Your typing has too many errors in it, has to be done over too many times by another secretary and the firm cannot afford to keep you on."

"You may not know this, but Mary has been retyping your mistakes and although she hasn't complained, she needs to concentrate on her own responsibilities."

"I've let this go on longer than I would have because I know that you help your mother financially and wanted to see your employment through to six months so you could collect unemployment."

"May I suggest you search for employment in an industrial environment where exactness isn't essential. Good luck to you. You are free to collect your personal items from your desk and leave. And oh, by the way, I will give you a reference so you can find another position."

She was shocked, never realizing that this could happen to her. Running to the ladies room crying, she heard footsteps behind her and turned to see Mary trying to catch up to her.

That caused more embarrassment so she hastened her pace, opened the door and hurried into the room.

"Wait, wait!" she heard.

Tears running down her face, she turned and looked into Mary's eyes and said, "Did you know?"

"I just found out before he let you go and begged him not to fire you. I didn't mind helping you out if we could have had a get-together to discuss it, but he was adament. The legal occupation for some is a very high stress field because of the need for preciseness."

"I do think that it would be better for you if you could find a position in a field that was not so exacting."

There would be many more disappointments in her employment experience, but there would also be one to be grateful for that would lead her to her search for happiness.

Walking home that day, she didn't know how to tell her family. She was afraid she had disappointed them but decided the best course was to tell them the truth and move on.

Marion wasn't awfully surprised when her daughter came through the door in late morning that August of '54. Having lost her father at eight, she knew her daughter wasn't as disciplined as the rest of her children. She also knew her daughter had a liberal, independent personality that could cause her problems with supervisors.

Feeling rejection, she went to the state unemployment compensation office and signed up for unemployment the next day. After filling out the paperwork, she was directed to a resource counselor who interviewed her in an effort to help her find employment.

"We have a position for someone with your qualifications at an auto supply store. You could still walk to work and I think you would fit right in. Let me call them and see when they can interview you," the counselor said.

At the interview, she was asked why she left her last position. "Working in the legal profession is not what I wanted, especially wills and deeds," she replied. She didn't know what else to say and didn't want him to know that she had been fired.

She was hired and started working for the ABC Auto Parts Co. the following Monday. Although the position didn't take advantage of her secretarial skills because it entailed keeping track of parts coming in and going out, it was more than sufficient enough to keep her in the style of living she enjoyed - clubbing with her friends.

TEN

One particular Friday night at Jake's she noticed a guy she had not met sitting at the bar with some fellas she knew. She couldn't tell how tall he was cause he was sitting, but did notice that he had dark wavy hair, hazel eyes and although his nose was slightly large, he was the handsomest guy she had ever seen. There was no lettering on the suede gray and navy jacket he wore.

Boldly, she walked up to the bar, tapped Len on the shoulder and said, "How you doin?"

"Oh, hey, OK, and you?"

"Good, and who's your friend?"

"Oh yeah, this is Steve Trotsky," he replied.

Turning to him he said, "Steve, this is Marie."

"Hey, Marie," Steve replied, "How are you?"

"Great," she answered.

While she was standing there the conversation between the men moved to going hunting.

Although she had never held a rifle in her hands, she said "I know how to hunt."

"Really?" replied Steve with a knowing smile on his face.

"Well, then why don't we go hunting this weekend? Where do you live? I'll pick you up."

After giving him her phone number, she went back to the table to tell her friends.

"Can you believe I'm goin hunting with that handsome devil over there this weekend?" she said to no one in particular.

"You don't know the first thing about hunting, can't even hold a gun," Rose said. "How you gonna fake this?"

"I don't know, but I'll find a way. It shouldn't be too hard to shoot in the woods," she replied.

The next morning, Steve drove to a wooded area near a state park and they walked for a long while.

"How far do we have to go before we see a rabbit or a deer?" Marie asked him.

"What's a matter?" he asked. "You getting tired already?" He knew she had never hunted and was playing along with the game she was trying to pull off, although he had to give her credit for trying.

"No, I've done this before," she replied.

There appeared to be nothing in the area to hunt, so he walked her further into the woods searching for game.

He was ten yards ahead of her, heard her yell and turned around to see she had fallen over a downed log.

He helped her up, leafs and dirt all over her clothes, and it looked like she was about to cry.

"That's enough of this charade," he said. "It's obvious you have never hunted before, but I gotta give you credit for trying to pull this off. Time to go."

Realizing she had been caught in her pretense she became quiet and was embarrassed. They decided to go home and she said nothing to him which was rare for her.

When he pulled up to her house, humiliated, she jumped out of his car and ran up the twenty steps leading to the home. At that point, she wasn't sure she wanted to see him again, but he rolled down the window and with a knowing smile on his face, yelled, "See ya!"

She didn't turn around, but opened the front door and stepped into the hallway. With her back to the wall, she slid down it, sat on the floor, and started to cry.

"Why the hell I ever thought I could pull this off is beyond me," she thought. "Now I'll never see him again. He must think me an idiot."

Embarrassed, she forgot about the whole situation in a few days and continued working at the auto parts store, but was anxious about going back to Jake's the following Friday nite with the girls.

On Wednesday evening following the weekend hunting outing, she received a call from him.

"Marie?" he said.

Knowing who it was, she answered, "Yes!"

"It's Steve. What are you doing Friday night?"

She thought her heart would jump out of her chest, it pounded so hard.

"Nothing - why?"

"Well, I thought we'd catch a movie if you want."

"Sure, I'd love to."

She couldn't get her mind off his call and wasn't very efficient at work the next day which caused her boss to call her into his office and reprimand her. The fact is that Marie hated the job which made her all the more resentful. This caused her to make too many mistakes since her employment with the company. It didn't help that her co-worker, Jane, a brown nose, hoping to be promoted, reported every inaccuracy she made to their boss.

"I've called you in so we could have a talk about your performance which hasn't been up to par since the day you started working here," he said.

"This is the one and only warning I'm gonna give you. It's your choice. Either shape up or I'm gonna have to let you go. Do you want to tell me why your performance is so poor?"

"Oh! Shit!" she thought. *"Not again!"*

Knowing it was a lame excuse, she replied, "Well, I seem to be having trouble with Jane who is constantly looking over my shoulder, making me nervous, causing me to not be able to concentrate on my work."

"Be that as it may, Jane is one of my best workers, one that I rely on, so I'm sure that she means no harm correcting your work when she feels it necessary. Wouldn't you agree?"

I ain't gonna get nowhere with this, she thought. Wonder if she's screwing him too.

"Yes."

Steve called again that evening to ask her what she was doing and if she wanted him to come get her.

They went to the Slovak Club located on the street where he lived and to which he was a member. Sitting at the bar drinking a beer, he told her that he was unemployed.

"I had been working for a film making company wrapping rollers, a very boring job, and they laid a bunch of people off, me including, so I signed up for unemployment. It's rough out there job wise and I don't know when I'll work again."

"Ya know my brother started his own business recently. Do you have any drafting experience? Maybe he could use you. Do you want me to ask him?" Marie said.

"Why not, sure, what's his name?"

"Mitch. I'll call him and ask if he could use you and let you know."

Her brother interviewed him and realized he had an aptitude for drafting, so he hired him as an on-the-job trainee, a military veteran's government sponsored training program.

In the meantime, the job for her at the auto parts store didn't last long. Two weeks after the first reprimand, she was called into the office again and given her "pink slip".

"I'll sign for you to collect unemployment," he said. "Your work just isn't up to par, so you can clean out your work area and leave now."

How to explain this to her family. Two layoffs in a year?

She left the auto parts shop and walked home to tell the family it had happened again.

"Mom, I just don't understand why I was let go," she said. Jane has been looking over my shoulder since the day I started working there. It's all her fault."

Marion knew deep in her heart that her daughter lacked discipline, but did not comment. Instead she calmed her down with, "You'll find another job, honey."

When her sister, Margaret, came home from her job at General Power Corp. that evening and was told of Marie's unemployment, she too realized that something was wrong. Marie was downhearted, so Margaret suggested a way she might gain employment.

"They're hiring at General Power and I know the supervisor who is doing the interviewing. I think it would be a good idea to go there tomorrow and fill out an application," she said.

The next day, she slept in and didn't get to the plant until late morning. Filling out the application she thought, *"I'm a shoe in with my sister working for the manager of engineering."*

Waiting to be interviewed, she felt quite confident about gaining employment until the door opened and through it stepped a tall, gray haired woman in a business suit, who would become her supervisor. Her name was Ellen Ryan.

"A woman boss?" she thought.

With her right hand extended, she said, "Hello, I'm Miss Ryan and would like to interview you for a position of temporary services secretary in the engineering department.

"Temporary! What the hell does that mean," she thought.

"In engineering, we have ten supervisors who need extra clerical help when their secretaries are either out sick or on vacation and that's where the position I am filling will come in. Eventually, one of those supervisors could choose to hire you should the need arise, but until then, you report to me and work for them. When there is no need, there are other duties to be performed in my department. How does this sound to you?"

"Wonderful," Marie lied.

She couldn't quite picture herself working for a woman when the last position she had caused her dismissal because of one.

"Well, you couldn't get a better recommendation than having your sister work here. I hope your standards are the same as hers cause she is a top performer in this company and very well liked."

"We'll give you a shorthand and typing test and I'll come back and talk with you again after you complete them."

Testing makes everyone nervous but she was scared because it was especially important for her to pass so as not to disappoint the family again. When she completed the test, she had more than allowed typo errors, but the examiner who knew her sister passed her.

"We need to schedule a physical for you before giving you a starting date," the tester said.

To backtrack a bit, Marie and Steve were dating every week on Friday nights usually catching a movie or stopping at the Slovak Club. Fearing for her daughter's virginity, her mother had asked her not to see him so frequently and set dating rules for her - no more than three times a week, so Marie would go out, supposedly with her girlfriends, call him at the club and after parking at round top - a parking wooded haven for dating couples whose hormones and testosterone were at peak levels, she'd have Steve drop off around the corner from her home.

Entering the second floor apartment where she lived one evening, her mother was waiting for her. "Was that Steve's car I saw going down the hill?" she asked.

Knowing how much Marion hated lying and if caught, the consequences would be harder than telling the truth, her daughter, answered, "Yes!"

"Didn't I tell you you could see him only three times a week?"

"Yes, but mother we haven't done anything."

And that was the truth.

"That's it then. You're gonna have to get married. I'm not going to worry about you getting pregnant."

"But mother," she replied. He doesn't have a job, is collecting unemployment and can't afford to buy me an engagement ring."

"I kept the ring your father engaged me with, so he'll only have to get a new setting," her mother said.

The next evening, while sitting in his car, she told Steve about her mother's order to which he replied, "I think we should get married, so tell her I'll take it to a jeweler and have it set."

"Yeah, but she wants us to get married as soon as possible, like within a couple months, and Danny won't be ordained and able to marry us."

"It's OK," he replied. "That's what we'll do. But we have to wait til November cause that's when my last car payment is and we'll need money for the wedding and to get an apartment."

She hadn't worn the engagement ring to her interview nor did she tell Ms. Ryan that she was getting married the following November which, when she showed up for work the next Monday with ring on finger, caused her supervisor to question her.

"I notice you're wearing a diamond ring on your finger," Ms. Ryan said. "Does this mean you're getting married?"

"Yes, in November," Marie replied.

Being Catholic herself, Ms. Ryan realized that it was highly possible that Marie would be leaving shortly after that for pregnancy, so she asked, "Do you plan on having children?"

Roman Catholics in 1955 did not practice birth control as it was considered a mortal sin, so she knew that Marie probably wouldn't be employed for a lengthy period of time which also meant she would have to train another secretary within a year, and that annoyed her.

Sensing the displeasure in her supervisor's voice, Marie thought *"Oh no, not again with another woman,"* but she answered, "Yes, but not immediately. My fiancée is on-the-job training, not making much in wages, so we'll have to wait before starting a family."

Ms. Ryan's face showed irritation, but she said nothing.

"Let's take you back to engineering and get you oriented, introduce you around to the employees you will be interfacing with."

Steve wasn't Catholic, was not baptized, so when the date for the wedding was set, they contacted the priest at the church she attended on Sundays.

"Are you sure you want to marry into this family?" Fr. Mullen asked holding a smile on his face. "You are in for a bumpy ride for the Maxwell's are not your average family. "

After realizing that it was meant to be a joke, they relaxed in chairs offered to them by the priest. Steve liked him immediately.

"Let's see now," the Fr. Mullen said. "You don't have to practice Catholicism to be married, and I won't try to talk you into it, but there are some instructions you will have to take before the wedding."

"I think that it would be a good idea if I did become Catholic," Steve said. "Any children born of our marriage should probably have a religious foundation.

There were three months before the wedding date, enough time to give instructions to him, so father gave him a catechism and told him to read the first four chapters.

"It's a very difficult religion to live by but also a beautiful one to die by," Fr. Mullen said. "If you should decide at any time not to continue with instructions, I won't push you."

When he went to the rectory for instructions, Marie went with him. She hadn't paid that much attention in religious education classes her mother made her attend when she was in school, and found the information she gained while listening was beneficial for her as well.

The biggest concern she had was the fact that her brother had not been ordained yet, was in the final year of his seminary studies and would not be ordained until four months after the planned wedding. He could not perform the ceremony but her mother would not relent in her decision to have the wedding before that date.

Danny could, however, take part in the ceremony as a deacon, but that would mean a solemn high would have to be performed with three priests officiating.

With little money for the ceremony the family offered help with such as the flowers, wedding gown, and wedding breakfast after.

She had lost a lot of weight before her wedding and had to have her wedding gown taken in three times. Marie weighed eighty-nine pounds on her wedding day. That day in November was crisp and sunny. She had asked her older brother to give her away. Her father was not invited to her wedding.

The aisle was long - it seemed like forever walking down it holding on her brother's arm, but when she reached the altar, she saw Fr. Mullen, Fr. Webber, and her brother standing at the altar waiting to greet her.

Her brother, Mitch, handed her over to Steve who stood by the altar railing waiting for her. She was shaky and without words, he calmed her down.

When it came time for communion, Fr. Mullen turned to Danny with the chalice held out and said, "Give your sister and her husband communion."

Danny was shocked to believe that he, an unordained seminarian, could touch the host and offer it to his sister, so while placing it on her tongue, he found his hand shaking while his sister's mouth was also doing the same and at the same time she started to cry. Emotions ran high that morning. The joy of the moment was overwhelming.

Because the was solemn high, the ceremony took over an hour. She thought it would never end, but the joy of her brother's participation was so awe inspiring that she relaxed.

The brunch was held at a local hotel immediately after the wedding for the family and a few valued friends after which the couple headed to the parking lot to embark on a honeymoon at Lake Ontario. As they were pulling out of the lot, they noticed Danny running toward them. When Steve stopped the car and rolled down the window, his brother-in-law stuck his head in and said, "Now, ah, be careful OK?" "I mean, Steve, be careful, alright?"

With a knowing smile on his face, he answered, "Yes, I will."

"What was that all about?" the bride asked.

"Oh! I'll tell you later," he answered.

It was a four hour drive. The hills were alive with colors of orange, red, yellow and henna - the temperature in the 50s and the couple settled into their first day of married life.

On her wedding night, she chose to wear a flimsy see-through baby doll nightwear. Being modest, she went into the bathroom to change clothes, and when she came out, he was already in bed. Although he slept in his boxer shorts, he had purchased pajamas for the wedding night realizing that she might be embarrassed if he had not.

After entering the bed, they began to kiss while he started feeling her body, which was responding to his touch. She felt inept not knowing what she should do and he recognizing this said, "Look we can wait for another time. Let's just go to sleep." He turned over and attempted to sleep, but it was difficult.

Feeling neglected, she tapped him on the shoulder and said, "Maybe we could just hold each other?"

Turning toward her, he pulled her close to him and wrapped her in his arms.

It didn't take long before nature took its course for his member became hard, and while kissing her, he started to slowly guide his penis into her.

Not experienced in sex, she asked him, "Is it in yet?"

He tried hard not to laugh, kept his chuckle inaudible and answered, "No" to which she started crying for her awkwardness in not knowing.

His penis became flaccid - he knew he couldn't perform at that moment and faking being worn out told her they would try again after a good night's sleep.

A good night's sleep came to an end in the middle of the night when turning toward each other, they embraced and attempted again to have sexual intercourse.

She knew what to expect this time and gave herself to him willingly, exploding in an orgasm which surprised both of them.

"What are you crying for?" he asked.

"I never knew I could experience anything like that," she answered. That was such a fantastic feeling that it took my breath away. I'm crying for happy."

Because they had no money for furniture, it was suggested by a family member that they rent a furnished apartment. They found a second floor one-bedroom near the plant that, although small, was clean, had relatively new appliances, and was affordable.

She didn't have a license, didn't own a car, so he drove her to work each day and picked her up at days end.

ELEVEN

In February, her brother was ordained along with twelve other seminarians in a cathedral near Glaspell, NY. The Maxwell family was gathered for the ceremony to witness their son and brother declare his vows of poverty, obedience, and chastity as he lay prostrate before the diocesan bishop, after which Fr. Danny Maxwell put on his priestly vestments and descended the steps in front of the altar to give his blessing to family and friends.

His father, Mitch, arrived just before the ceremony began and took a seat in a pew alongside the rest of the family. When it was time for the blessing, Mitch, along with the rest of the family, walked up the aisle and knelt at the rail. Standing in front of his father, Danny placed his hands on the top of his father's head and said, "Receive this blessing in the name of the Father, Son, and Holy Spirit. Amen." His father was so overcome with emotion that he broke down crying and had to be helped back to his seat by his oldest son, Mitch, Jr.

In the first four months she was in engineering, she worked for four department heads before taking a permanent job with technical writers.

The writers were just what she wanted to know as the "fitting in" feeling that she needed, as they were not as concerned with perfection as most engineers were. She typed rough drafts that were corrected before being turned over to final typing, then to printing.

The ladies rest room had an anti-room that had a chaise lounge in it. One morning, Marie came into the lounge area and decided to rest a bit, sat on the chaise, put her feet up and fell asleep. When she awoke, she realized she had been there for a half an hour.

Upset with herself, she returned to her work station when she saw her supervisor, Mr. Miller, standing in the doorway of his office looking at her.

"Oh, crap!" She thought. "I'm in for it now."

Figuring that honesty is the best policy, she approached him.

He invited her into his office, shut the door, and asked her, "How are you feeling?"

"I don't know what's the matter with me," she answered. "I keep falling asleep. I have had anemia in the past. Maybe it's back again. I'm sorry, Mr. Miller. I'll get an appointment with the doctor and get it checked out."

"OK, well let me know how it turns out," he said. He had a big smile on his face and she thought that odd when she had just shared a medical problem with him.

After a physical which included blood work, her internist recommended she see an obstetrician. Her menstrual cycles had never been within a twenty-eight day timeframe, even went to forty-two days, so she wasn't surprised when she missed a monthly.

A valued family friend, Maria Hennessy, suggested her OB/GYN, so Marie made the appointment and saw him the following week.

"Good morning, I'm Dr. Wagner," he said as he entered the examining room. He was a fatherly sort of physician who appeared to be in his fifties. He had gray hair, and wore glasses. In his hazel eyes was a smile that was infectious. It calmed her anxiety the moment she looked at him for she was concerned that she might have a serious disease.

After the internal examination, he told her, "I think you are pregnant, but it's too early to tell (they didn't kill rabbits in 1956) so I'm gonna ask you to return to be sure.

She was ecstatic! Steve was waiting for her in the car when she left the doctor's office.

"He thinks I'm pregnant," she said excitedly.

"Are you sure?" he asked.

While they both knew where babies came from and didn't practice birth control, they were surprised, and he did not tell her he was concerned about the financial loss of her having to quit working. He was still in the on-the-job training program and wasn't making that much.

"The doctor made an appointment for two weeks at which time he expects to be able to confirm the pregnancy."

She expected it, but didn't get morning sickness which made her wonder if the diagnosis could be accurate. She did however, notice that her breasts were sore and seemed to be getting larger. She used to joke that her bra size was 28AAA. She wore falsies, even stuffed socks in her bras when she was a teenager.

She returned to Dr. Wagner and after another internal, he determined that she was indeed pregnant. She was overjoyed and rushed out of the office to her husband who again was waiting in the car.

"So what do we name him?" she asked.

"You are?" he asked.

"Yes!" she answered. "My due date is estimated to be mid-October . He gave me a bunch of pre-natal vitamins and made another appointment for one month from now. Said to keep working cause that would be good for me, and seeing as how I have no health problems, I can pretty much remain active. So what about a name?"

"Boy or girl?" he asked.

"Boy," she answered. "I've always liked the name, Derek. It sounds beautiful and at the same time strong. What do you think?"

"I like it too," he answered.

"Derek it is then," and from that day forward baby Derek was the reference to her pregnancy.

When she told Mr. Miller, her supervisor, he smiled and said, "I knew you were pregnant."

"How?" she asked.

"Cause every time my wife was pregnant, she was tired and fell asleep."

"So that's what the grin was about when I fell asleep in the ladies lounge," she said.

"Yes. When is your due date? You know company policy is working until your sixth month is complete."

Knowing that in order to receive maternity benefits, Marie had to be employed six months before, she lied and gave a due date a month later than predicted by her doctor hoping her doctor would sign the date which he was agreeable to.

Morning sickness never occurred in her pregnancy. She felt better than she had in her twenty-one years - full of life, full of energy, that amazed her and her family.

She felt the first movement at three months and was overjoyed that God and she had been a part in creating a life. She bought five maternity dresses that she wore to work and one peddle pusher outfit for leisure.

Because she was so thin all her life, her mother was concerned that she would not be able to deliver the baby vaginally, so in her concern she asked Dr. Wagner, "Will I have to have a caesarian section? My mother is worried about my ability to birth the baby."

"Ah! Mothers," he answered. "Do you trust me to take good care of you?"

"Yes," she answered.

"Then in believing that, don't worry about your care and tell your mother not to either."

She didn't gain a lot of weight even though in the evenings, while watching television with her husband, she indulged herself with hot fudge sundaes, chips, and popcorn thinking how funny it was to be able to use her belly as a table top and although she had smoked for years, she had no desire for a cigarette during her pregnancy and didn't light up. Liquor wasn't kept in the house; well, maybe a beer now and again.

She was all baby - looked like a beach ball was placed inside her maternity top for that was the only part of her body that gained weight.

Her last day at work was in August. The tech writers threw a baby shower for her, gave her a playpen.

Spending her remaining pregnancy making baby gowns on her sewing machine, she looked forward to the birth of what she prayed would be a baby boy - Derek Robert.

Her sister, Margaret, had believed she had a calling to be a nun. Shortly after Marie left the company, Margaret gave notice that she would be leaving to enter the convent. She favored an order that supported wayward teens and had traveled to New York for an interview with the mother general (a kind of CEO of the order).

Margaret entered the convent in September of that year leaving her possessions to her sister, mostly consisting of her clothes. It seemed strange that the belongings she held so dear when Marie was a teenager were so easy to release now.

TWELVE

Marie was at her mother's apartment on a Saturday in September when the need to use the toilet was necessary before taking mother for groceries. When she walked out of the bathroom, she told her mother, "I can't stop peeing and don't know why." It was certainly too early for the birth, so she was afraid something could be wrong with her baby.

"I don't know," her mother answered, "but I think you should call the doctor."

Dr. Wagner returned her call immediately and advised her to go to the hospital without delay. "Don't go home, not even for your toothbrush. Your husband can bring it to you later. I believe your water has broken and you are getting ready to deliver," he said.

"It's too soon," she cried, looking at her mother and husband.

The ride to the hospital took ten minutes and while he was getting her admitted, she was whisked away to the maternity ward.

"Are you in any pain?" the nurse asked.

"No!" she answered. "I just can't stop peeing."

"That's the amniotic fluid, not urine," she answered. "You're gonna deliver your baby. We'll keep you comfortable until you deliver. The doctor has called in orders and will be in to see you soon. I'll have to give you an enema just before delivery to clean you out, so that your bowels don't move during delivery which can cause infection."

Two hours after getting settled in the maternity ward, the pains started. She rang for the nurse and said, "I'm having pain but it's in my lower back. Aren't the pains supposed to be in front where the female organs are?"

"Many women have labor pains in the low back," the nurse answered. "It's nothing to worry about. Dr. Wagner's orders were to give you a shot of Demoral when they started, so I'll prepare one and be right back."

"Where is Dr. Wagner?" she asked.

"Don't worry, honey." He'll be here in time for the birth." And with that she left for the nurses' station to prepare for the injection.

It didn't take long for the shot to take effect. She started to feel slightly unaware of her surroundings, light headed, and although it didn't take away the pain, it didn't seem to matter that she had any.

She dozed for a while and when she opened her eyes, Dr. Wagner was standing by her bed.

"How's the pain?" he asked.

"It's starting to get worse," she answered.

"I have ordered a pain medication every four hours to help get you through, but in the meantime, I have a pleasant surprise for you. Look toward the doorway."

When she turned her head and looked up, she saw her mother and brother standing in the doorway, smiling and throwing kisses. Her brother had his priestly garment, a stole, around his neck and blessed her with the sign of the cross.

"I cannot let them in the room," the doctor said. "Cannot risk an infection. They'll be waiting outside and will see you when the baby is delivered."

At first, the doctor thought the brother was the husband until he noticed the roman collar on his neck.

"Where's my husband?" Marie asked.

"Right outside pacing the hall," he answered.

When four hours had elapsed, the pain was much worse, so she received another shot of Demoral which put her in a fuzzy state of mind, and again although she knew the pain was there, it didn't matter.

In all, she received four shots of Demoral before her delivery. It was time for the enema and as if the labor pains were not enough to contend with, the enema was dreadful. All she remembered was the overhead lights as she was being wheeled down the hall into the delivery room.

The push - stop pushing orders being given to her by the staff were very nonstop and she followed them automatically.

"The baby's head is visible," the doctor said. "Just one more push and we'll see your baby."

The last thrust she gave permitted the birth of her son at 10:16 that Saturday evening on October 1st twenty-two hours after her water broke. She didn't remember anything after being told that she had a son until she was wheeled out into the hall and saw her husband waiting. He smiled and said, "I told you it would be a boy." The orderly wheeled the gurney aside the nursery so she together with her husband could look at their new born son.

Two insurance policies allowed her to spend five days in the hospital - one from her job and one from his. The fact that she delivered early worried her that they would not pay due to time limits of her employment, but there was no problem.

She decided not to nurse her baby; didn't think she'd have enough milk, was always so small breasted, but there was another reason she didn't, didn't even know why at the time which will become clear much later in this story.

It's hard to tell just who he looked like at birth, although it was becoming unmistakenly apparent in a couple days that he favored his father.

The family was overjoyed at the birth of the new family member; Marion gazed down at him through the nursery window while Danny stood beside her.

The Trotsky's bought inexpensive furniture and rented a second floor two bedroom apartment that a friend's father owned. It was an old wood framed house with a cellar where Marie washed clothes using the old wringer washer machine her mother gave her that belonged to her mother for years.

After coming home from the hospital, Derek had his nights and days mixed up insofar as sleeping. His bassinette was next to his mother's side of the bed so she could hear him, but he cried every two hours all night long and drank only an ounce of his formula at a feeding of his two ounce-filled bottle. This kept his parents awake most of the night, much to the consternation of his father who one night got angry, got up and swearing, shoved the bassinette into the adjoining bedroom and slammed the door.

This was the start of discord between the couple that would last throughout the marriage.

Marie was in shock as she got up screaming at her husband, ran to the adjoining bedroom, picked up her son and went into the living room to rock him back to sleep.

"Don't cry little one," she said while crying. "Ma Ma will take care of you." She started singing, *If you go out in the woods today, you're in for a big surprise, If you go out in the woods today, you better go in disguise. Cause every bear that ever there was, will travel there for certain because, today's the day, the teddy bears have their picnic.*

Once he settled down and fell asleep in her arms, she placed him back in the bassinette and went to bed alongside her husband. She couldn't help wonder what just happened, so she got up, went into the living room, sat in the small rocker and cried.

There was no way her husband could not have heard her weeping, but if he did, he didn't get up to comfort her or to apologize.

He went to work the next day, left before she awakened from her sleep on the couch.

She needed to wash diapers, so she made sure her baby had his bottle and was tucked in his bassinette before going down two flights of stairs to the cellar to wash. As she was placing the baby clothes into the washer, she heard a noise in the walls and couldn't make out what it was. Little tap, tap, taps, up and down the walls. She dismissed it and went back upstairs to check on her baby, then back down to the cellar to hang out the diapers after running them through the wringer.

Steve came home from work and never mentioned the baby's crying the night before. They went to bed, but not before she made sure the baby was secure in his bassinette in the attached bedroom. She didn't want any more problems with her husband about the child's two-hour feeding needs, so she made sure she slept lightly so as not to awaken Steve.

She slept so lightly, that she heard the tap, tap again up and down the bedroom walls.

"Wake up," she said to her husband.

"What?" he asked irritably.

"Listen to that noise in the walls!"

"Oh, go back to sleep," was his answer.

But she couldn't and wouldn't sleep, so the next morning she called the landlord who said he'd be over during the day sometime. He guessed it could be mice, but before he came and while she was fixing lunch, she opened the drawer that held a breadbox with a loaf of bread in it.

"Oh, my God!" she exclaimed.

Half the loaf was gone. Noticeably the bread had a frayed edge where it had been pulled away and eaten.

Shivers went up and down her spine realizing that whatever it was was getting in the apartment, possibly into the interior of it, and she became terrified for the safety of her baby.

She showed the landlord the half eaten loaf of bread when he arrived.

"That looks worse than mice," he said.

"Oh God," she cried. "Not rats. I have a little baby here."

"I'll put rat poison pellets down in the cellar. That should take care of 'em."

The landlord placed the pellets in ash trays around the cellar. Twice a day he came back to check and had to fill them up each time.

Marie made up her mind they would have to leave the apartment and started searching the paper for another one.

She told Steve when he came home from work that evening and vowed not to leave her son unattended, so she had to do the wash in the evening.

Steve had an sexual appetite that was exciting and all right with her before having the baby, but after the birth, she was tired in the evening following a hard day of caring for her child, plus she was experiencing anemia and low blood pressure.

The newspaper had many ads for apartments, but one caught her eye on the south side of the city, near her mother. It was a third floor two bedroom dwelling and although there were many steps to climb, the rent was within their means.

After moving into the apartment, the couple decided that Marie needed to get her driver's license. Steve had no patience teaching her, yelled at her most of the time while she tried to learn, so she found a girlfriend to help her. She passed her driver's exam on the first try. Now she could drive her son to doctor's appointments and have some independence getting around without asking her husband to drive her everywhere she needed to go.

She had always wanted more children; they didn't use birth control, so when Derek was six months old, she was pregnant again.

Again she was ecstatic and informed her husband.

"I think I'm pregnant again!" she exclaimed.

While appearing that he wasn't disappointed, he was concerned about finances.

"Do you think it might be a girl?" she asked.

"When you plant sweet potatoes, you don't get radishes," he remarked. "I know what I'm doing and I'm sure it will be a girl."

Marie befriended Ellen, the wife of tenants occupying the second floor, a woman who had one baby and another on the way, so it was important to schedule washing of laundry which was done in the cellar.

The landlords, a middle aged couple by the name of Wilson, lived on the first floor of the building and asked her tenants to only wash on certain days because of the water bill.

"This is impossible," Marie said to Ellen. "We not only have our laundry to wash but the baby's diapers as well."

"I have an idea," said Ellen. "The Wilsons go out every morning to help their daughter in her corner store. We'll just have to watch for them to go and run down on prearranged times to get the wash done."

"I think it would be a good idea to wait a length of time after they go to be sure they don't return possibly having forgotten something," Marie said.

"Sounds like a plan to me," Ellen replied.

So the friends set up a time table to get their laundries completed while the Wilsons' were away. It was nerve wracking never knowing if they would return at any given time before the wash was finished.

"Oh! Shit," exclaimed Marie one day while she was hurrying up the stairs to her apartment. She heard the outside downstairs door open, quickened her pace and rounded the corner of the stairway before Mrs. Wilson entered the landing.

"Are you doing a wash on a day you're not supposed to?" Mrs. Wilson asked angrily.

Caught in the act, Marie 'fessed up that she had and tried to explain that it was impossible to keep a schedule with a baby who needed diapers washed.

Not deterred, Mrs. Wilson reminded Marie that she had a time set for laundry and if she waivered from it, she would have to find another apartment. Marie said she would comply realizing that her family would have to find another place to live.

Her pregnancy was a healthy one even though climbing the stairs to launder clothes became cumbersome as she gained weight but she didn't complain - she so wanted this baby, hopefully a girl. She still used the wringer washer her mother gave her and hung out her clothes as they had no money for a new washer and dryer.

Her husband was working as much overtime as possible in an attempt to balance the finances. The payments on a second hand car they owned were becoming too much for their budget, so they sold it to his brother.

Her son's feeding schedule had settled down after six weeks at which time he slept all night. He was a beautiful chubby, hazel eyed, toe headed baby who gave his parents no worries. Many were the times when taking him for a walk in his stroller, she was stopped by a passersby to look at her baby.

"What a beautiful little girl!" remarked the strangers, which made her mad because he was always dressed in baby blue, to which she answered, "He's a boy!", an indignant declaration.

Marie's mother lived within walking distance in a one bedroom second floor apartment. Marion helped her daughter every day during her second pregnancy by walking Derek in his stroller to her apartment where she had set up a crib in her kitchen. She loved her little grandson but had a feeling that his father was not very affectionate toward him; however, she kept her opinion to herself for years until she could no longer be silent. She shared it with the family then her daughter who had noticed it also, but didn't want to accept it.

Marie loved to walk to her mother's. One day during her seventh month of pregnancy and wearing wedgies, she twisted her ankle and fell in front of Marion's apartment house. She let out a scream and her brother, Danny, who was visiting his mother heard it, ran down the stairs, picked her up and carried her up the stairs into his mother's home. He set her down on the couch and checked to see if her ankle could be broken. After examining the ankle and gently turning it, he was sure that it was just lightly sprained especially because it wasn't swelling.

The pregnancy continued without any more mishaps. She was thrilled to think of the possibility of a girl baby being born in the winter.

The couples search for a name proved taxing because every time Marie came up with one, Steve knew a "slut" with a name like that and it wouldn't do for a daughter of his. The name was chosen serendipitously when her sister, Margaret received her final vows at the convent located north of New York.

Upon arriving with her brother and mother to the convent to attend the ceremony, Margaret ran to greet her sister with open arms and a hug, saying, "Wait til you hear the name I'm taking with my vows. I need to go get ready, but I'll see you after at the reception." And with that, she disappeared down the hall and into a room.

"But, wait!" answered Marie. "I have good news for you too."

When a postulant (studying to be a nun) is taken into their order, the ceremony begins with the postulants who march down the aisle and into the chapel holding a candle whereupon she will prostrate herself in front of the bishop vowing to give up her worldly possessions, to remain celibate, and to obey her superiors. As a postulant, she is given a name of a saint chosen by her beforehand.

And so it was that after reciting her vows, the bishop said, "Henceforth, you shall be called, Sister Mary Cheryl" at which point Marie started crying. Her baby's name had been chosen for her.

THIRTEEN

Marie's healthy pregnancy continued with no problems and she joyed in taking care of her baby son as her belly grew. Again she did not put on weight - nearing the end of her gestation gaining only seventeen pounds.

She felt a cramping in her back one evening and thought, "Oh, Oh! This is early." She remembered her son's birth being early by two and a half weeks and was concerned that it would happen again, but this time, it was a month early. She called her doctor and he advised her to go to the hospital should the pain become stronger. Waiting a couple hours, the pain increasing, Marie decided to head to the hospital. The only insurance policy they had was her husband's insurance. They knew that a visit to the hospital meant a deduction from it.

She was admitted to the maternity ward and waited for her doctor to come. The nurse who cared for her had a puzzled look on her face when she commented, "Honey, I don't think you're gonna deliver yet. I think it's false labor, but we'll see when Dr. Wagner arrives."

Sure enough and because she became pregnant so soon after delivering her son, her uterus hadn't had time to fully heal, so after examing her, Dr. Wagner sent her home claiming that it was false labor.

Her concern was for the child she carried, not for herself. She trusted her doctor and went home to wait til the "real" labor began.

Around her due date in the middle of December, once again, she started cramping. "Surely this is it!" she said to her husband, and she called the doctor. Once again, he told her to go to the hospital and she did only to be told again it was false labor.

"I could force labor," Dr. Wagner said. "But you haven't gained much weight and you're carrying a small baby, so I'm sorry to have to send you home again."

Crying, she exclaimed, "Oh! Please. How will I know when to come back? When the head's hanging out?"

"Don't do that. We'll make sure that the next time is THE time and I won't let you go through admittance again til I'm sure you're going to deliver."

So home she went once more downhearted, tired and disgusted. That night the baby inside her was so active that she couldn't sleep, so she propped herself up on two pillows. Her husband heard her whisper, "Go to sleep little Cheryl."

Two and a half weeks later on an evening when her husband worked overtime, the cramping started again, but this time she decided not to do anything about it immediately. She was past her due date and wondered if the child would ever come, but when she went to the bathroom to void, there on the toilet tissue, was a red, plug like blood stain.

The doctor's answering service told her to remain by the phone after she had told them she had already gone to the hospital twice with false labor. It wasn't ten minutes before her call was returned by Dr. Wagner. "This is it!" he said. "What you saw was the mucous plug. I want you to go to the hospital now."

She called her husband. He helped her down the two flights of stairs to the old Pontiac he was driving, but after he placed her in the passenger side and went around to start the car, it wouldn't start.

Frantically, she started crying. He knocked on the downstairs neighbor's door and together, they got it started with the help of jumper cables.

She felt like it was "old home night" when she arrived at the hospital for the third time. Orders were left by her doctor to prep her for delivery which meant one more time of shaving the vaginal area and one more time of an enema.

In the fifteen months since delivering her son, it had been decided by obstetricians that too many pain relievers slows the labor and causes unneeded wear on both the mother and child, so she was given one shot of Demoral when her labor pains were strong. She was fully aware of her surroundings as well as her pain, but knew it wouldn't be long before she would deliver her baby - a girl.

Sharing a labor room with a woman named Ellie, who was in labor with her first, she felt it important not to scare her, so she kept her painful labor cries at a minimum, but at some point neither one of them could contain the contractions and out of desperation they started laughing at the seemingly rhythmic, "Uh, Oh's" they shared in pain.

They both had the same doctor who was called at the appropriate time by the nurse to deliver the babies. He decided that Ellie would probably deliver first so had her go to delivery room 1 and put Marie in room 2.

When she was placed on the table, Marie's water broke, she crowned, the nurse called to the doctor who had to step over the water which was running from under the table and was flowing to the door.

"Well this baby might not have wanted to leave the hangar, but she's ready now," he said.

As she looked up into the reflector, Marie was aghast at what she saw.

"My God," she exclaimed. "Is that me?" She was fully dilated and saw the crown of her baby's head.

"One more push," her doctor said.

That push birthed her daughter, Cheryl Anne, into the world and at that moment she felt the hand of God touch her. It was 4:03 on the morning of December 29[th.]

"Put her on my stomach," she said.

"She hasn't been cleaned up yet," her doctor said.

"I don't care. I want to kiss her."

The nurse placed the baby on her mother's stomach, raised Marie's head and she kissed her baby girl for the first time. The baby was covered with a Vaseline like covering that babies "wear" while in the womb.

The baby was then taken to be cleaned up before placing her in a glass bassinette that was wheeled alongside her mother. When she brought her back and placed her in the bassinette, the baby kicked off the blanket she was wrapped in, her little legs moving up and down, forward and backward. It was then that Marie noticed a little strawberry birthmark on the inside of her daughter's left calf that was the same shape and color as the one on the inside of the calf of Marie's right leg.

The birthing of her daughter required the doctor to help by performing an episiotomy to make the birth canal larger. While stitching her, and after giving her a shot of Novocain, she asked him, "What are you doing that stings so much?"

He explained the need to help her deliver the baby and that he needed to stitch the area where he made the incision.

"Stitch it all up," she said laughing. "We got a boy and a girl and that's it. No more babies."

"I'm sure your husband wouldn't appreciate that," he answered.

Her husband was waiting for her when she was wheeled out of the delivery room.

"I told you it would be a girl," her husband said. He beamed with pride. "A baby two days before the new year. Thanks for the tax deduction," he jokingly said.

Her family was overjoyed with the news of a girl baby. She was the first granddaughter and niece. Marie's brother, Danny, came on New Year's Day with fourteen dresses of which she could choose two for the baby. She chose the tiny pink and white checked with the white lace trimmed collar.

Money was tight that year of 1959, there being a recession. Steve had to take a pay cut to continue working in her brother's company or face unemployment which meant no health insurance, so like the rest of the employees, he accepted a ten percent cut in pay.

They knew beyond the health insurance he carried at work, that they couldn't afford for her to stay in the hospital as long as she did for their son. Three days after the birth of her daughter, she had to go home, but when the bill came, $70.00 was owed of which they couldn't pay.

She was sobbing when her Danny came to visit her in her hospital room. He asked her why and she replied, "We owe $70.00 beyond the maternity insurance. The hospital won't let me go until it is paid and we don't have the extra money with which to pay it."

Her brother stepped into the hall and took out his checkbook. While using the wall to write upon, Danny wrote a check for $70.00 to bail his sister and niece out of the hospital. "I'll take it to the billing department," he said. "Call Steve to come and take you home while I'm down there and we'll get you out of here straightaway."

The desperate tears drying on her cheeks turned to ones of gratitude for the brother God gave her as she dialed her husband's work number and told him to come get her and the baby.

Her mother was waiting with her fifteen month old son, Derek, at the apartment when she arrived home with her daughter. She wanted her son to get acquainted with his sister, so without removing her coat, she sat on the sofa holding the baby in her arms.

"Come see what I have brought you, honey," she said to her son. "A baby sister."

He toddled toward the baby and with his right index finger pointed at her and said, "Baby Sia." His grandmother standing behind him was fearful that he would hurt the baby and said loudly, "Oh, No! Don't poke the baby's eye," at which point Derek sat on the floor and cried.

"Mother, how could you yell at him and scare him? He's just a baby too. Take Cheryl." And she handed the infant to her mother, picked up her crying son and held him close to her chest while walking with him and said, "Don't cry honey. Mommy loves you."

"Baby Sia! Baby Sia!" he was sobbing - his head turned toward and tiny hand pointed at his sister.

Cheryl was a good baby, waking up once a night for feedings. That surprised her parents because her brother's all night need for his bottle had worn them out for six weeks after his birth. Marie had recognized that possibly he had been hungry and decided to mix a teaspoon of baby cereal with her daughter's formula twice a day, which kept the infant satisfied - "a sticking to the ribs" so to speak.

One morning after Marie put her babies down for a nap, she decided to relax by soaking in a bubble bath. Upon finishing and drying off, she wondered what an episiotomy looked like if indeed she could see anything at all. She took a hand mirror and placing it between her legs spread the vulva and while she did not see stitches, she noticed a space which seemed strange to her.

Calling her husband at work, she said, "Something's wrong!"

"What do you mean?" he replied.

She explained how she used the mirror to see the episiotomy and saw a space.

"Call the doctor," he said.

"Hello, could I speak to Dr. Wagner please?" she said after dialing the doctor's office phone number.

"Could I help you?" asked the nurse.

"No, this is too personal. I need to speak with him about this."

"He's with a patient. I'll have him call you back. Is this an emergency?"

"No, I just need to talk with him. It's very personal."

"OK well he'll call you back when he is free."

A few minutes later, when the phone rang, she anxiously picked it up. After identifying himself and asking her what the problem was, she said, "Oh! Doctor, I took a mirror to see what the stitches looked like and saw this space in my pelvic bones and I'm afraid I didn't fully close after I had the baby."

"Well, how big is the space?" the doctor asked.

"Well, it's about an inch and a half long from front to back and a quarter inch wide. What's the matter with me?"

Her doctor had to stifle himself before answering her and didn't know if he could contain his need to burst out laughing.

Controlling himself he answered, "After having a baby, the bones in the pelvic area don't fully close for a few weeks. Several births can cause the pelvic bone to never fully close."

"Good God!" she answered. "What must a mother look like after four, five, six births?" "Thank you for calling me back," and with that, she hung up.

The doctor called his staff into the conference room shortly after his conversation with her and related the story to them at which point they all fell into fits of laughter. His only comment was, "I have never had a patient who took a mirror and searched her vaginal area for stitches after birthing a baby." It made the staff's day as it had been a hectic one at the office.

FOURTEEN

With two infants to care for, It was becoming very difficult living in a third floor apartment, running up and down stairs while the babies napped to do the wash in the basement, so the Trotsky's decided to search for another place to live.

Quite by accident and chance, Marie, while grocery shopping, bumped into an acquaintance, Sophia, whose relative owned a big house near a park. After exchanging pleasantries, Marie mentioned that the family needed to search for another place to live. Sophia told her she would call her brother to see if it was still for rent and took her phone number to let her know.

"It's Sophia," she said when Marie answered the phone. "My brother said the house is vacant and asked me to give you his phone number if you want to go see it."

They met at the house located at 22 Forest Ave. The house was red brick with lots of windows wherein light entered, with two bedrooms and bath upstairs and one bedroom off the main living room, a sitting room and kitchen where a door led to the downstairs basement. Hardwood floors were blanketed throughout the house.

There was a small one floor apartment behind the two story house where an elderly couple lived: a retired cop and his wife, Mr. and Mrs. Walsh.

"We'll never be able to afford this," Marie whispered to her husband. He agreed and when he asked the owner how much rent was, he was surprised to find out that it was only $70.00 a month which didn't include utilities, but they figured they'd scrimp on everything not necessary to be able to afford to live there, so they signed the lease and happily went back to the apartment to inform the landlord that they were moving.

It's not easy to rent a third floor apartment, so the landlords were not happy about the couple moving but recognized their determination and wished them well as they packed up their furnishings and moved to their new home.

The house seemed so spacious compared to the little apartment they rented. They were especially happy that the toddlers could have their own bedrooms.

Taking care of an infant and toddler became extremely wearing on Marie. She didn't weigh a hundred pounds and her anemic condition surfaced making it more difficult for her to keep her strength up.

She went into a depression and called her husband at work asking him to come home. When he arrived, he found her sitting on the floor crying; the children were in the cribs asleep.

"What is the matter with you?" he asked, which made her cry all the more.

"I don't know," she answered sobbing.

"Get ahold of yourself or I'll put you up on the hill. I need to go back to work," he said, and slammed the door as he left the house.

The hill was a state run mental institution for "Loonies".

And that was the beginning of the end of their marriage, but it would take several more years and many more tears before it totally broke down.

She experienced terror as she thought of ending up on the "hill," so she called her brother who was an assistant pastor in a nearby parish.

"Calm down. I can't understand you," he said. "What's wrong? Are the kids alright?"

"It's not the kids," she answered. "I called Steve to come home cause I can't stop crying and when he did, he got mad and said he'd put me in the nut house on the hill."

"I'm on my way," he said, and with that he hung up without waiting for an answer from his sister.

He called her name as he entered the house.

"I'm in here, in the living room," she answered.

As her brother paced back and forth across the living room floor, she related her account of what had happened.

"What's the phone number at his work?" he asked.

With his hands shaking while dialing, she started giving the numbers to him. He was connected to her husband and asked him to come home immediately.

It's not clear, at least from my point of view, how this phone call was received by Steve, but I conjure up one scared man who, when he hung up the phone, nervously hurried to his car and drove home to meet his angry brother-in-law.

Steve apprehensively opened the door and saw Danny sitting on the couch with his arms around his sister comforting her as she silently cried.

"Steve, I want you to know that if you try to put my sister on the hill, it will be over my dead body. I will fight you with every bit of energy I have. I have friends in high places including doctors and psychiatrists I can contact who will not allow you to do this. My sister needs help cause she's worn out taking care of the children. I suggest you call her doctor and get her an appointment pronto so she can get the help she needs and be assured that I will be monitoring this crisis daily."

Steve called their family doctor after his brother-in-law left and got an appointment that afternoon for his wife. By the time she arrived at her scheduled time, she was shaky and had red eyes from crying. She explained what had transpired between her and her husband to Dr. Richards and after examining her he said, "You are worn out from taking care of everyone but yourself. Can you get away for a few days alone to rest?"

"No, we don't have the money for me to stay anywhere," she commented.

"Well, then, I'm gonna give you a prescription for tranquilizers to help calm you down. What about getting help at home with the children? Can someone, a relative, come and help?"

"No," she answered softly. "There's no one."

"I want to see you in a week to make sure the drugs are working for you, so we'll make an appointment for a week from today."

Before taking her home, her husband stopped at the drug store to drop off the script. When he left to go back for it, she called her brother and informed him of her visit to the doctor.

"I knew it was that," he said. "Two babies in fifteen months with a home and husband to care for is difficult, wore you out. I'll call Ma and see if she can take care of them occasionally - give you a break. And Sis, don't worry about ending up on the hill cause I'll be watching out for you."

By the time she hung up talking to her brother, Steve pulled up in the driveway. She looked out the window and as she watched him exit the car, she became aware that her feelings for him had been waning for some time, but was never as aware of it as the present time when he had been so cruel to her.

He came in and handed her the envelope containing the pills, pecked her on the cheek and left to go back to work. She searched the pill bottle to find the name of the tranquilizers her doctor had prescribed and found the name at the top - Milltown. It was a couple days before she felt relief and during that time, she was scared to show depressive signs to her husband for fear he would find way to follow through and put her on the hill.

The tranquilizers made her sleepy but not confused and she was able to go about her daily duties with rest periods at the same time her little ones napped.

When she returned the next week, Dr. Richards felt satisfied that she was coming around with the help of the medication and told her that she could cut the pill in half the following week. During their conversation, she asked him, "Did you give my husband mean pills cause he's been unkind with his mouth for the last few months?"

"You know that he's been on blood pressure medication for a while and there are side effects to all meds but the one I was concerned about was that he wouldn't be able to sexually perform, and he would never tell me. Men don't admit to that, but you would know, so I would expect you to tell me. Is that the problem?"

"God, no that man is a virile as the day we married. That's another problem. I'm worn out at night and he wants his sex. Like you said, too many demands on me."

Their religious beliefs didn't allow them to practice artificial birth control, so they used rhythm method or he "pulled out". Her monthlies were never on time; always late which made her frightened that she could become pregnant again. With the situation of their dissatisfaction in their marriage, Marie couldn't imagine another child being brought into the world.

Although she never considered that he would be unfaithful to her as a result of her tiredness, there was a time when she picked him up after work and while waiting with the children in the car outside of his workplace, she opened the glove compartment of the car and noticed a package of condoms, some of which were missing.

The fear she felt caused her to cry softly so as the children could not observe it. When he came out of the building and opened the car door, he asked, "What's wrong?"

"What are these? We don't use them. Why are they in the car? Have you been cheating on me?"

"Those? The guys and I blew them up and filled them with water and let them go over the balcony outside the building," he answered. Whether the explanation was true or not she accepted it as gospel and dropped it only to have it surface many years later.

Steve worked a lot of overtime to make ends meet and at one point when her daughter was an infant, Marie took a job as a legal secretary. Her mother sat the children, but the position didn't last long as she began to experience stomach irritation and was diagnosed with gastritis which Dr. Richards believed was the result of the stress of her wanting to be home to raise her children.

It wasn't very often that she went against her husband's wishes, but this was one of the times she insisted on giving up the job and staying home stating, "I'll get a nighttime job, but I will raise the kids."

That wasn't necessary. They decided to tighten the belt financially and make $13.00 a week do for groceries which included her daughter's Similac, their cigarettes, and maybe a quart of Ballantine beer now and again.

She took her children with her, one sitting on her hip and the other by the patty, to the supermarket each week and made sure she didn't spend more than the allotted amount. After placing her daughter in the child seat of the grocery cart she would always say, "Be good and mommy will buy you a box of Animal Crackers when we're done shopping, but be naughty - no Animal Crackers." Promises of Animal Crackers kept the little ones quiet while she maneuvered around and through the grocery aisles, but when it came to moving toward the checkout lane each week, her daughter, who couldn't pronounce it clearly, would ask, "An-mal Crackers, Mommy?" There wasn't a time when they didn't get their five cent box of crackers even though there were other times when some lavish items had to be taken off the conveyor belt because there wasn't enough money to pay for them.

The problems they had when she was struggling with depression disappeared after she took the tranquilizers and Steve's temperament was better as long as he got sex almost every other night, which seemed excessive to her, but then she had no way to judge what was normal for a married couple. Having had no experience about the sexual appetite of men, Marie couldn't figure out why if Steve didn't get his due, he took it out on the children, knowing she would respond to his sexual advances to keep peace.

There was always a few dollars left on the kitchen counter following a Sunday dinner which was left by either her brother or mother and while she was embarrassed taking it, she was grateful to have the help.

Her children were beautiful, happy little ones, although she started to notice that Steve was more caring to the daughter than to their son, having pet names for her and demeaning ones for him. As years passed, this would cause heated discussions between the couple.

FIFTEEN

Derek started kindergarten on a very hot day in September, the month he turned five. Mother and grandmother were ready on his first day of school to take him to the parish parochial school where when he said goodbye, he started to cry and turned to reach his little hand out to his mother, who hesitantly handed him over to the kindergarten teacher.

The "mothers" then proceeded to skamper around the side of the building into the back where the kindergarten room was. Peeking through the window, Marie saw her son off to the side crying and her heart broke at the sight.

"I'm goin' in to get him," Marie said to her mother.

"No, give it time and just watch," she answered. "You'll see that he'll settle down and join in with the other children playing."

They stayed at the window peeking until she saw that her mother's advice was right, for while cupping her hands to the window and squinting to see between the blinds, she noticed that he started playing with a toy car, running it back and forth across the table top where he was given a seat.

She couldn't wait for the kinder class to end which was only in the morning, so she could get her son and just like when he was born wanted to make sure he was still all together.

Marie was early to pick him up and was waiting in the hallway when the door opened and he appeared fifth in the line holding a drawing he had colored for her. When he saw her and his little sister, he broke into a big smile and ran to his mother who kissed him, took his hand and led him from the school to the car and took him home.

On the morning of the third day, Derek came down with a fever that topped out at 102 degrees, so Marie kept him home from school and treated him with baby aspirin and cool baths. Within twenty-four hours, and just when she had her son's illness under control, her daughter came down with the same sickness and was treated as was her brother with aspirin and cooling down baths.

While in kindergarten, Derek caught and brought home to his sister similar bugs constantly with high fevers for both which meant a trip to the doctor and a shot of antibiotics. So when it continued, Dr. DeMarco suggested the children be seen by a nose throat surgeon believing their tonsils were diseased and needed to be removed.

After Dr. Bogosian examined the children, he suggested the tonsils be removed and said, "We should do both at the same time and get it over with."

Marie didn't look forward to both of them going to the hospital and in surgery at the same time, but agreed. The following week they were admitted to the same hospital they were born in for their tonsillectomy.

"The doctor said I could stay the night and sleep in a chair," Marie told the assisting nurse on the pediatric ward.

"Yes, they'll be in the same room after surgery and we'll get a rocking chair for you to sit in, but we don't provide a bed."

"I probably won't sleep anyway, so it doesn't matter what kind of chair you provide," she answered.

Her son was taken to the OR first and as he was wheeled away, she cried softly so he couldn't see her. "Please, Lord, take care of my little guy and bring him through with no complications," she prayed.

Her daughter was only three and a half and was not aware of what was going on while sitting on her mother's lap in a surgical toddler's gown, wide eyed looking around the hospital room. She reached up her little hands, placed them around her mother's neck and started to cry.

"It's OK, honey, Mommie's here and I will take care of you," she said holding back the tears. She rocked her in the chair provided and held her tightly wondering if she made a mistake having them both done at the same time.

"Everything went well," the doctor said as he greeted her in the waiting room. "Your son will be right out and we're ready to take your daughter in."

The two gurneys on which lay her son and daughter passed each other in the hall. Her daughter was given a mild sedative like the one given to her brother to calm her fears and help with the crying. She kissed her daughter and slowly let her little hand slide out of hers as they walked down the corridor toward the OR.

Hurrying back to the room where the orderly was taking her son, she said another prayer this time for her daughter. Derek was groggy but knew his mother was in the room as he lifted his arms up to her and tried to say "Mommy" but couldn't because his throat was so sore. Marie took him up and into her arms. Sitting in the rocking chair, she rocked softly and started to sing, *"If you go out in the woods today . . . .",* her children's favorite song called *"The Teddy Bear's Picnic."* He fell asleep during the time she began and before she ended her song, so she laid him in the crib and quietly pulled the sides of the crib up.

It seemed like forever before she heard anything about her daughter. Her anxiety was beginning to quicken. She started pacing the room and then, she heard the gurney wheels squeaking down the hallway and ran to the doorway. Her daughter lay on the gurney, her eyes wild with fear and her nose packed with cotton. "We had a little difficulty removing her adenoids and I had to cut deep," the doctor said. "I had to pack her nose as she was bleeding quite heavily."

Marie cried. She cupped her daughter's little outstretched hand with her two hands and walked beside the gurney with her and into the room. "I'll lift her," she said to the orderly and as she did, the rocking chair was pulled up and she sat in it with her daughter and began to sing as she had for her son. *"For every bear that ever there was, will travel there for certain because, today's the day, the teddy bears have their picnic."*

"She's not going to be able to speak, but when they both wake up we'll start to give them popsicles, as many as they want," Dr. Bogosian said.

Steve had taken the morning off to be with his children and had to go back to work as soon as they came out of the operating room. There were no personal days with pay in the early 60s. Docking his paycheck meant that much less for the family's necessities.

Uncle Danny was in the hospital for sick calls and the giving of the last rights to the dying faithful. He stayed with his sister as long as he could before returning to the rectory.

Marie didn't use the rocking chair for sleeping because it didn't fit in between the two cribs where she needed to be vigilant in case her children cried out in need which they did numerous times throughout the night. The popsicle "wagon" which was down the hall at the nurses' station got plenty of action for the whines of Derek and Cheryl.

Because he would be making spiritual rounds the next day at the hospital, and because taking another day off for Steve meant his paycheck would be docked a second time, their uncle offered to help his sister take the children home from the hospital.

Release papers being signed by the doctor with instructions for home care were all in order when their uncle walked into the room. Together, brother and sister carrying brother and sister headed down the corridor toward the elevator.

"Wait a minute," Uncle Danny said.

"What?" questioned his sister.

"Well, I can't let anyone think they are my children, so I think we better take the freight elevator in the back of the building."

"You gotta be kidding," she replied.

"No! come on," and he turned around and headed toward the freight elevator with his nephew in his arms.

Being so tired, she didn't argue with him, got on the elevator aside him with her daughter in her arms, pushed the 1st floor button and descended down.

When the elevator door opened on the first floor, Danny stepped out and hurried ten feet ahead of her so as not to give the impression, should a parishioner be around, that these were his children. Danny proceeded to the parking lot where he parked his car, helped his sister and the little ones into his car and took them home.

SIXTEEN

Shortly after the children's operations an ad appeared in the local Sunday newspaper about new homes being built in a small town south of the city where the family lived.

"Look at this," Marie said to Steve. "It says that for a $350.00 down payment, we can buy a manufactured home in Nolen just twenty minutes from Suttonville, and the payments are only $95.00 a month. The house has three bedrooms, a bath, kitchen, dining room and living room for only $13,500.00."

"How are we gonna get the down payment?" he asked.

"I don't know but somehow we'll get it," she answered.

After Sunday dinner Marie told her mother about the new homes being built.

"I could let you have the down payment," her mother replied.

Overjoyed at the news, but also concerned about her mother's financial position, she asked her how she could afford to give the money.

"I have money saved for a rainy day and I've built it up enough to share some with you. You need your own home. Go look at the homesites and I'll stay with the kids."

There was only one home to view, the model, when they arrived and that was the expensive one - $16,000. The builder, Mr. Sidley, a large muscular blue eyed, gray haired man with a pot belly, dressed in construction clothes welcomed them into the builder's trailer.

He questioned them about finances after showing them an architectural drawing of four homes.

"It appears that based on your present income, you could only afford the home on a slab and even then it could be close as far as the bank financing the loan. Plus you will have to get your mother to sign a statement disclosing the fact that the down payment she is giving you is not a loan but is a gift or you won't get a mortgage.

"Steve, can you get your company to stretch the truth a bit about how much you make, add more to your base salary to be sure of qualifying for the loan officer?" Mr. Sidley asked.

"I don't know," he answered. "My brother-in-law is a partner in the company, but I'm sure it will have to go through the comptroller."

The company agreed to "fudge" his base salary. The application for the loan on the slab was applied for and approved.

Being a pre-fabricated house, it would be built in sections trucked in from the manufacturer forty miles away and would take approximately ninety days to set up.

The excitement the couple shared knowing they would move into their own home soon was a tremendous jolt for their marriage although there wasn't an immediate crisis at the time, so she picked her son up each day from kindergarten and drove out to watch the workmen fit each section into place on a slab foundation on a lot 75 x 120 feet.

The house at 15 Turkey Run Way was finally completed and in January of '61, they moved into it. There was no money for new furniture but that didn't bother them. The excitement of living in their own home was enough to forget about needing updated material things such as new furnishings.

The floors were tiled with linoleum squares throughout the home which made it cold on the feet without slippers or shoes. The frames around the windows were aluminum which caused them to build up frost similar to a refrigerator freezer. The inside window frames had to be fanned to remove the frost buildup in the winter. The only bathroom had no window and was very small; it permitted just one person at the undersized sink while another could squeeze into the shower in the tub. Behind the bathroom and petitioned by a wall was a small storage room which held the clothes dryer and some tools with the only entry being a door on the outside. The two-windowed master bedroom with ample closet could accommodate a king sized bed, dresser and chest of drawers.

One bedroom held a twin bed, dresser, and desk and the other bedroom, a smaller one could hold a twin bed and dresser.

At the far end of the hallway was the broom closet. The linen closet was situated at the other end. The windowless kitchen had a small work space, but had enough room for a fridge which was set in between the wall and cupboards. The stove and washer fit alongside the sink.

The living and dining area was L-shaped having no separation between them. There was a five by five foot, twelve inch square sectioned window in the living room.

Derek continued to go into the city to the same parochial school on a school bus that picked him up early in the morning and dropped him off late in the afternoon.

The neighbors, with young children, were in the same bracket as the Trotsky's in that nobody even tried to keep up with the Joneses because there was no extra money to do so. There were only two out of the forty-eight homes that were on a slab, the rest being either raised ranch or houses with all the rooms on the same floor.

Marie befriended a woman across the street whose name was Connie. Connie and her husband Bob moved in their home with two kids, who were born a year and a half apart, and had two more children, all living in a three bedroom home with no basement.

Thinking it was odd having so many children and they weren't even practicing Catholics, Marie asked her one day during the neighborhood coffee klatch, "You know what causes that don't you?" to which Connie replied, "Nothing we use works!"

As time passed, all the families settled into their day to day routine - shoveling in winter, mowing in summer and found time for a few trees to be planted and flower boxes to be filled with petunias and geraniums.

Cheryl turned five and started kindergarten and somehow Marie knew that this first day of school for her daughter would not be the same as for her son, for when she took her to kindergarten, and gave her a kiss goodbye, her daughter looked at her mother and said, "See you Mom" and turned to walk into the kinder classroom without looking back, much to her mother's surprise, but then no two siblings are alike in a family which would become factual years later to Marie.

With both of the children in school and having no one to take care of, Marie decided to look for a part time job; one that she could leave after her children left for school and return home before they came home.

She found a position working for an elderly eighty year old lawyer whose family felt it important that he remain active, so they insisted on keeping the rent up to date on an office in an insurance owned building. Mr. Clemons was a kind gentleman who had difficulty hearing. He was six feet tall, very slim but still wore a business suit and tie to work. He was driven to the office by a son and although he hardly ever got any phone calls or client visits he kept himself busy going through legal journals and law books.

He constantly repeated himself with stories of when he was a state's attorney much to Marie's chagrin. "Did I tell you about the time I had a criminal up for ...?" and on and on he'd go staring off into space never realizing that she wasn't listening.

"Yes, I remember that story," she replied. He just kept telling one or another story over and over again which caused her to quit the job after a nasty occasion when he became angry and said, "You're not listening."

Working for him should have been an experience in understanding the old and aging citizens, but she dismissed it until a much later time when it would surface again in her personal life.

SEVENTEEN

Back to the morning coffee parties with the "girls" in the neighborhood was pleasant enough for they all had the same problems in their marriages and the raising of their children, but as time passed, the coffee turned into alcohol in the afternoon before the husbands came home. Funny how it creeps up on one - alcohol that is. Before realizing it, one drink becomes two, becomes three, and on and on.

On a summer afternoon, with windows open and fresh air blowing through the curtains, Marie heard the wail of a woman which she recognized as coming from her friend Connie who lived across the street.

Before she could react, Connie's little six year old daughter pounded on the door crying, "Mrs. Trotsky, come quick! Mommie's hanging over the TV crying and I don't know what to do."

Running across the street with the little girl trailing aside her, she opened her friend's door and found her hanging over the television, head almost touching the floor, sobbing hysterically.

"Con, what's the matter?" she asked.

"You and all your Catholic shit - be good, don't lie, and on and on and on. You mean you don't know?"

"No, tell me."

"Bob's been screwing around on me with the secretary at work," she answered.

"No, not Bob. No, I can't believe it," she answered.

Marie could smell alcohol on her neighbor's breath and thought maybe she was in such a state of intoxication that she was having an illusion.

She sat her down and asked her, "Come on Con, I can't believe this. Are you sure?"

"Yes, when he called and told me he was working overtime last night, I got a sitter and drove to the plant to see if he was there. I asked the guard to call him to the front desk to which the guard replied, "Oh! He left at 4:30." But his car was there, so I waited in the parking lot off to the side and saw a car pull up to his driven by a blonde. He kissed her goodbye and got out. She drove away and while he was opening the car door and before he got in, I drove to within a few inches of him and flashed the lights."

"What the hell is going on here?" I asked him.

"It's not what you think," he replied.

"Yeah, and I've seen you kiss your sister like that, right? Who the hell is she?"

"The secretary in my department. We just went for a sandwich."

"Right, and is she married?"

"Yes, she wouldn't do anything immoral. She loves him," he answered.

"And if I were to call him and tell him all this, he would not believe me, huh?"

"Right!"

Now he was shivering from standing outside in the cold evening air. Connie, on the other hand didn't feel the cold - she was too hoppin' mad. Course maybe he didn't really feel it either cause the electric current of fear was racing through his body.

"What's her name?"

"Geez, Con, you're making a mountain out of a molehill."

"I said, what's her name, or do I have to get it from your boss tomorrow and while I'm at it were you supposed to be at work and did you verify that on your timecard?"

Well now she had him cause yes, he was supposed to be working and had a friend clock in for him when he was out.

"Her name is Cindy - Cindy Alberston," he replied.

"OK then find another place to stay tonight. I don't give a shit where and we'll talk about it tomorrow. But don't come home tonight."

She backed up the car and drove "Joey Chitwood" style out of the parking lot and headed home.

When she arrived home, she frantically searched for the phone book and looked up the number of the Albertson's. If she had to call every one of them searching for a Cindy, she would, but as luck would have it, at least for her, the first number she dialed proved to be the only one she had to dial.

"Hello!" she heard a voice say.

"Yeah is this the Albertson residence?"

"Yes, I'm Cindy, can I help you?"

"Well, actually I was looking for your husband. He left this number at my office and I haven't had time to return his call til now."

"Oh! Just a minute and I'll get him."

And Connie heard her say, "Phone for you, Chuck."

"Hello, Chuck speaking," he said.

"You don't know me, but I think your wife and my husband are having an affair. Could you meet with me tomorrow morning and discuss it?"

"No, I'll meet with you now wherever you say," he answered.

"You know that strip mall where Stan's Sporting Goods is?"

"Yep."

"Half an hour?"

"I'll be there. I'm driving a forest green Buick four door."

A bit shaky as she drove to the strip mall to meet Chuck, Connie pulled into the parking lot and noticed the green Buick parked in front of the sporting goods store. She got out and started walking toward the Buick. Before she took five steps, a man got out of the car and started walking toward her.

"Connie?" he said.

"Yes, Chuck?"

"Yes, there's a coffee shop at the end of the mall. Let's go in and get a cup?"

They sat in a booth facing each other not knowing who would begin. When the waitress came and took their order, they both felt as though what would come out of the conversation would "cut them to the quick" but someone had to start, so, Chuck began by saying, "I'm not surprised. I expected to find out about it but not this way, not by her lover's wife. She hasn't been coming home every night after work, claiming to be working overtime. I knew it! Knew deep inside she wasn't working, but what was I to do. We have kids. Tell me how you know."

Connie was trying to hold back tears as she related the suspicious she had and told him the account of her sitting in the parking lot outside the company where both of them worked.

"Well, that's it," Chuck said. "I'm not going to put up with an unfaithful wife and she can't deny it after you caught them, so I'm gonna go home and confront her with it and ask for a divorce."

"I don't see how I can divorce Bob," Connie said. "With four little kids and I don't work. I can't provide for them on my own, so I'm stuck. I don't think it's a good idea for us to meet again. It's too painful facing you knowing what I know and I'm sure you feel the same especially since there's nothing more to say."

"I agree," Chuck said. And with that he asked for the bill, paid it and walked out the door leaving Connie sitting in the booth with her feelings of sorrow to deal with alone.

When she arrived home, Bob was not there and she was grateful that he did not try to come home that night cause she didn't know what she would do if he did.

After relating the story to Marie in the morning, that afternoon Marie heard yelling coming from Connie and Bob's residence and noticed that Bob's car was parked in the driveway and Connie's father's car was parked behind it.

A fly on the wall would have witnessed Connie's father pacing back and forth across the living room, pointing his right index finger at a seated Bob while angrily saying, "I can take care of my daughter and these kids you know. She doesn't need your shit to survive and that's something I'm willing to do if she wants, but if not, if she decides to forgive you and try to make the marriage work and I find out you screwing around on her again, I'll tie your ass down. Take a carving knife, and cut your pecker off. "

After that, Marie noticed that her dear friend's drinking became compulsive and that she wasn't so far behind her in the "toddy" hour, but Marie passed it off as being a personal problem of which she had no reason to interfere and wouldn't become aware of this same habit sneaking up on her for a long time

EIGHTEEN

Marie's father, Mitch, had remarried, but drove the eighty miles from Pennsylvania twice a year to visit Marie and enjoy his grandchildren. Marie always felt she needed fortification when her father called to say he was coming; the Scotch bottle came out of the cupboard shortly after his arrival.

"Want a drink, Dad?" Marie asked.

"I'm allowed two a day, so yes, I'd like one," he answered.

Mitch always stopped at two, but for Marie one led to two, maybe three, probably four. Her father took notice and asked his sons about his daughter's drinking on a previous trip to which neither one of them had an answer. On this trip, Marie was loaded not just with alcohol, but loaded for bear and wanted answers from her father. When he came into the kitchen, she turned to look at him and said, "Where the hell were you when I needed you?"

Taking him completely off guard and not wanting to bring up her mother's participation in desiring the divorce, he hesitated trying to find the words he knew she needed to hear while her brothers, who were in the living room and overheard her, tried to shut her up.

"Take the children outdoors for a walk," Mitch said to his sons. "This has been coming for a long time. Your sister and I need to talk."

After she heard the door shut, she put her hands on her hips, looked at her father and said, "Well?"

"There are things you may or may not remember that happened between your mother and me when you were very little that led to the divorce." "I'm not going to criticize her for her part in it. She's been a good mother to you children and I respect her for that, but for her and I, we just couldn't stay together."

Before he could say another word, Marie, with tears streaming down her face, said, "But why didn't you love me?"

"Love you? Oh! My God, I always loved you. You were my baby." Tears were now streaming down his face also.

"Then put your arms around me and hold me, Daddy," she cried.

Mitch put his arms around his daughter and the two of them sobbed together. When he let her go, they both knew that the pain of loss they suffered was at that moment healed.

At that same moment of healing, her two brothers and two children were peeking through the large front window wondering when they could come back in the house and what they'd find when they did. When they entered, they witnessed a father and daughter who had found each other again and reconciled.

Marie would always be grateful for that day when she confronted her father, for two years later he died of a heart attack.

NINETEEN

Marie's relationship with her husband became slowly strained as his sexual appetite increased and hers was decreasing. Their love making was unexciting. His love making seemed robotic to her in that he was going through the act unemotionally and while she always reached orgasm, she needed him to show more affection toward her.

The children were entering early teenage years so they had to plan their sexual rendezvous around periods when the kids were either at a daytime function or long after they went to bed and were sleeping sound.

They had just finished having sex one night when she asked him to hold her to which he responded, "It's late and I have to go to work tomorrow. Go to sleep." And with that he turned over away from her and within a minute was snoring. His unemotional mood left her hurt, empty, and used. Too busy taking care of her family, she hadn't noticed how cold he had grown or was it that emotionally, he had always been indifferent and she just hadn't realized it.

The following week, she drove to the church where her brother was an assistant pastor. She pulled into the parking lot and past the three car garage noticing his car was gone. Feeling sorrowful and needing spiritual comfort, she parked the car and walked up the steps to the church. Finding the door open, she entered the vestibule and headed down the aisle to the front of the church. Choosing a pew near the altar, she knelt crossed herself, buried her face in her hands and while crying prayed, "Dear Lord I feel so empty and unloved. I need your help to understand what I have done wrong to make this man so unattached and non-expressive toward me."

She felt a hand on her shoulder, turned and looked up into the face of her brother.

"What's wrong?" he asked

She stood up, turned to him and with her arms around his neck she sobbed, it was difficult for her to speak while crying so hard, but she managed to say, "Danny, I don't know. I feel so unloved."

She couldn't tell him about her sexual incident with her husband. One just didn't discuss those things especially with a male family member.

"Marie, didn't you sense that Steve was not an emotional man when you met and married him? The family saw it but figured that you knew what you wanted, so we didn't bring it up."

"No, I was so young and naive that I only saw a quiet man who was so handsome and felt lucky that he could fall in love with me. You know I have never been what you could call sexy and now I find myself questioning what I did."

"Are you saying you want to end your marriage?"

"No! Maybe I can change him." *Famous last words…..*

Being so close to her, her brother didn't want to counsel her on her marital problems, so they sat together in the church while she calmed down.

After she had settled down, she turned to him and said, "I'm sorry for coming here and interrupting your day. I'll be OK now. I'm goin' home. The kids will be coming home from school soon and I need to be there for them."

"You can call me anytime you need," he said.

"I know. You've always been there for me and I appreciate it," she replied. "Don't worry 'bout me."

Tears were cascading down her cheeks as she drove out of the parking lot and headed home, for she realized that something was drastically wrong with her marriage but couldn't put her finger on exactly what it was.

Even though he recognized that their marriage was in trouble, Steve still had control over her expecting her to submit to sex every other night which she did, although hesitantly, so he couldn't complain. His sexual appetite being satisfied was enough for him to dismiss any problems they had, at least as far as he was concerned.

They started fighting. A lot. Oddly enough, it wasn't over money. That's what most couples fight about. No, she needed something he couldn't give; he didn't know how, but it would take many, many years before she became aware of it.

A creative endeavor with sewing helped the last time she felt down and although she wasn't a particularly good student in school, she decided to start reading novels which mentally threw her into a fantasy world although she became more addicted to novels of real life stories such as mysteries and medical miracles. Joining a book club, she read twenty-five novels and was able to drown out the noise of a blaring television that stayed on from the moment her husband came home from work until eleven when he went to bed.

Marie's mother, Marion, was sixty-four when she was introduced to a seventy year old gentleman widower named James O'Reilly. The Irish twinkle in his eyes and his gentle laugh was cause for the family to become very fond of him. They dated for two months before James asked Marion to marry him and in June of 1968, one year after the death of her ex-husband, Mitch, Marion and James married at St. Stephen's Catholic Church; the one Marion had attended for years.

Her son, Daniel, officiated at the ceremony; her eldest son, Mitch, Jr., gave her away; her daughter, Marie, was her maid of honor. A reception was held at James's large four bedroom house which he rented from his sister.

TWENTY

Nineteen sixty-eight was a year of changes for the Trotsky family for Marie, while reading the newspaper one Sunday, noticed an ad for part time secretaries at a nearby defense contract company that produced military as well as commercial simulators for training pilots. A neighbor was a sales rep for the company. Noticing him outside mowing his yard one day, she approached him.

"Hey, Jake, I read where the company you work for is looking for part time secretaries. Do you know anything about it?"

"No, but I can find out. Are you interested?"

"Yes, the kids are in school all day now and I'm bored at home all day. Need something to keep me out of trouble, so yes, if you can find out what it's all about, I'd appreciate your looking into it."

She didn't hear from him for a week and thought he'd forgotten until one evening he called. "Hey, Marie, I've got some news in regard to that job you mentioned last week. Sorry I didn't get back to you sooner but I was out of town on company business," Jake said after she answered his phone call.

"You need to call a number I'll give you and ask for Bill Walsh cause he knows all about the job and is doing the hiring."

"Thanks," she answered.

She hadn't worked in a long time and knew her shorthand and typing was rusty. Making that call she was shaky, but calmed down when a man answered the phone.

"Bill Walsh," he said.

"Yes, Mr. Walsh," she said. I'm calling about the ad in the paper for part time secretaries. My neighbor, Jake Greene, gave me your name. I'd like to know more about the job."

"Well, first of all, just call me Bill," he answered. "What we're looking for are secretaries who can fill in for one who is out either on vacation or sick leave until they return. There are no benefits because you are not considered a full time employee. You'll never know when you will be called but if you find that you cannot fill in, you

M.E. Pickard | 93

have the right to refuse. Does that sound like anything you'd be interested in?"

"Definitely," she answered.

"I'll need to interview you. Let's see. How about tomorrow morning at 9:00?"

"I'll be there," she said.

When he arrived home from work that evening, she told her husband of the interview. He had no opinion either way, but didn't try to dissuade her from the interview either. He thought some extra income would help.

She showed up early for her interview and waited for an employee to bring her to the second floor cubicle that Bill occupied. The receptionist at the company, Laurie, she recognized as a family acquaintance; her brother having gone to the local college with Marie's brother; her other brother having played basketball for the church where Marie attended and was a cheerleader in her teens.

Laurie and Marie talked about the "old days" for a few minutes before Sharon showed up to escort her to her interview.

Seated across the desk from Bill Walsh, she took note of the big smile on his face before noticing anything else. He was a little older than she by maybe a couple years, had brown hair and eyes, was short and somewhat overweight, but was well dressed and neat from the look of his very orderly desk.

"So you think you'd like to work for Sim-U-Flight Corp. on a part time basis?"

"Yes, the kids are getting older, are in school all day, I'm bored and thought a job would fill in the extra time in my day."

They talked about her employment background and the fact that she hadn't worked in a few years.

"Your defense industry background is helpful in employing you here," he said. However, I have to ask you to take a typing test. I see the anxious look on your face, but please don't worry cause I'm sure you'll pass it. Do you have time now to take the test?"

"Might as well," she answered. "I'd rather get it over with than come back another time after considering it for hours adding to my nervousness about it."

She was taken to HR to complete the typing test on an IBM Selectric typewriter and was allowed to practice before the actual timing of the test.

After a few minutes of rehearsing, she opened the door to the testing room and asked that the test be given. Nervous as she was, and making some mistakes, which were allowed, she moved along and when the time was up, was surprised that she had passed with a score as high as it turned out to be.

Returning to Bill's desk, he informed her that she was the first to answer the ad in the paper and was hired at the rate of $6.00 an hour. He indicated that he was given the go ahead to hire four secretaries for this "Kelly Girl" operation that he had drawn up and presented to management for approval which in the long run would save the company money in that they would not have to go outside the corporation to find fill-ins when permanent administrative secretaries were out.

So, in August of 1968, Marie started a new job with the Sim-U-Flight Corporation filling in for a clerical employee in the Engineering Dept. who was on vacation for two weeks.

The same year, the same month, and half a world away, a young Navy seaman was fighting in a "conflict" in a foreign land that didn't sit well with the citizens of the United States. A connection that never could have been possible had Marie not gone to work for this company would occur years later for these two individuals.

Her first day at work, she parked in the lot behind the building and entered it through the back entryway. Stopping at the guard's desk, she gave her name, was given a visitor badge, and waited for Bill Walsh to escort her to her first assignment.

There were two wings to the building that had two floors. The wings were connected to the large reception area where to the side of it, the medical office was located. The cafeteria was behind a limestone cement wall that had broken coquina shells and corals in it and was located at the rear of the receptionist's desk. One wing was committed strictly to Engineering and the other was for Administration, Marketing, HR, and Payroll. In the south end of the Engineering wing and attached to it was another elevated building which could house the finished product - the simulator - and was known as the high bay area which included manufacturing.

She was nervous on her first day as she was escorted to her temp position by Bill who introduced her to Pete Martin, a military contracts project manager on the second floor of the building. Co-workers of the department welcomed her with good-natured remarks about how appreciative they were to have her on board which helped her deal with the nervousness she was feeling.

Susan Forbes, his secretary who she was replacing, had left a neat desk with instructions to be used to help with the organization of each day she would be there.

Most of her first day was spent getting oriented to the departments she would have to interface with including the Xerox room, print room, as well as reading through the list of instructions of how to answer the phone and make travel arrangements for the engineers who traveled, mostly to Central Florida.

She felt so productive that evening when she arrived home after work. A feeling of independence overcame her when she received her first paycheck a week later and she couldn't wait to cash it.

Because her children were on the threshold of puberty, she decided that it was time to broach another subject, so corralled her husband one evening.

"I think it's time we discuss the birds and bees with the kids," she said. "You talk to Derek and I'll talk to Cheryl about sex."

"What the hell do I have to do that for?" he asked. "Jesus, I learned from the other guys when I was his age. No one talked to me. Certainly not my father."

"OK, then I will," she answered

She took her son aside one afternoon when his sister wasn't around and said, "Derek, we need to talk about sex. I realize that at thirteen, you're young, but your uncles discussed it with me at your age. I don't believe in sex before marriage, but if you decide to have sex at some point down the road, then I'm asking you to use a condom. Impregnating a girl is no laughing matter. When it's all over you will have eighteen years to pay for the mistake you make by not protecting her."

Embarrassed, he put his head down and said, "Jeez, Mom." That said, she went to her bedroom, took a package from her husband's nightstand and handed him a cellophane wrapped package that contained two condoms and left the room. Steve and Marie agreed that religion was not going to make them have a child when they didn't want and couldn't afford any more children.

A few days later, when Derek was away, she approached her daughter and told her she wanted to have a discussion with her about sex. They went into her daughter's bedroom and closed the door.

"It won't be long before you get your monthly period and I want to explain what that means."

"Mom, I already know," her daughter replied.

"Still, it's important to understand that when that happens, if you have sex, you could become pregnant."

"Yeah, but," she said.

Interrupting and insisting to continue, Marie said, "It isn't just a matter of pregnancy. There are diseases you could contact from sexual intercourse. All I'm saying is should you decide when you're older to have sex, please protect your body from becoming pregnant or getting a disease. Come to me and ask for help, OK?"

Desiring this discussion to end, Cheryl said, "OK" and quickly whizzed by her mother, out of the bedroom, down the hall and out the front door, but she would remember their talk years later at a time when she would silently thank her mother for it.

The second week into Marie's work assignment, she heard the click, click, click of high heel shoes approaching. The blonde woman who was wearing the shoes stopped at the desk next to where she was sitting and started talking to the secretary.

As the secretary started to introduce the blonde to Marie, they both recognized that they already knew each other. She was the girl who was dancing at Jake's that night so many years ago when both girls were in their late teens and before they married.

"What are you doin' here?" Jackie asked.

"You two know each other?" the secretary asked.

"Yes," We met a long time ago at a hangout place in the ward," Jackie answered.

"So, what are you doin' here?" she asked again.

Marie explained how she read in the newspaper an ad for temporary help, contacted Jake Williams and got a job.

"Do you play golf?" Jackie asked.

"Poorly," was the answer. "But I try."

"Think about joining the company golf league. We have a good time on Mondays after work at the state golf course."

Ever since the children were little, the Trotsky's camped with the Murphy's on the Delaware Water Gap fifty miles north of New York City. They tented at first, but when she worked for the lawyer, Marie saved her earnings to buy a used fold out camper which felt luxurious compared to a canvas tent which, when you touched the sides of it during a storm, caused the rain to come through.

Golfing in a league wasn't particularly something she wanted to do especially since her game wasn't anything she was proud of, so she thanked Jackie and said, "Yeah, I'll think about it. Thanks for asking."

She completed the first assignment and was asked to take on another the following week as that secretary was going on vacation.

"You did a great job," Bill told her when he asked her to accept another two week assignment.

"Sure, I'd like that," she answered.

The following week, she was introduced to another project manager, John Raskee, who appeared to be her age.

"Jeez," she said to herself. "He looks like Marino. Handsome devil."

He was tall, six foot, with light brown hair and hazel eyes. From what she could observe his weight was distributed evenly throughout his body. When he smiled, his expression was soft and gentle.

She had no problems on the assignment, picked up on company procedures without difficulty, and was starting to feel very relaxed. Starting to feel really good about herself, she realized that she hadn't felt that good in a long time.

The coffee cart made its rounds mid-morning and mid-afternoon each day, and she looked forward to getting John's coffee and klotching with him during the breaks.

They got along famously, laughing and telling stories of their pasts. There came a point when she wondered if he had more than an employee/boss interest in her but dismissed it as something she probably fantasized about from watching too many soap operas when the kids were small. Besides, her husband and her were getting along better, probably due to the fact that she was getting out and socializing with adults albeit in a workplace atmosphere.

Bill Walsh called her one day before the assignment was completed and asked her if she could come to see him when she could get away. At first she was concerned, but dismissed it and went to see him on break.

"Right now, you're the only employee in our temporary operation," Bill said. "I need to hire three more and wondered if you knew anyone who would be interested in working a non-permanent position?"

"Well, my sister-in-law, Jeanie, just finished business school and may be interested. She did work assembly line here at the company before going to school and I do know one thing about her and that is she's a hard worker. Do you want me to ask her?" she answered.

"Yes, and tell her to call me if she is interested."

"Jeez, Marie, I don't know if I could pass the typing test," Jeanie said on the phone after Marie asked her if she was interested.

"Oh, why not give it a try and call Bill. You'll like him. He's a regular likeable guy."

Jeanie made an appointment to be interviewed with Bill and showed up nervous and early for the meeting.

Introductions made, she opened the conversation with "Did my sister-in-law tell you that I have no experience and just finished business school?"

Knowing she was anxious, Bill put her at ease with his calm demeanor and told her that for the most part, she didn't have to worry about speed in typing, but because of the rules concerning affirmative action, he had to have her take a typing test.

"I passed?" she said excitedly to Bill after returning from the testing room.

"Barely," he answered. "But don't worry about it. These managers need someone to answer the phone, take messages more than understanding engineering jargon and trying to type it."

"Are you ready to accept an assignment for next week which will last a week while the secretary is on vacation?"

Hesitantly, she agreed to take on her first temporary assignment, went through processing at the guard station the following Monday morning and was escorted to an engineer manager nearby where Marie worked. The employees under Donald Ayers, the manager, made her feel welcome, showed her the desk she would sit at and started explaining how the four line push button phone worked. She felt her heart sink, put her head down and when she looked up, saw her sister, in-law standing across the desk and in front of her.

"I don't know if I can do this," she said.

"Sure you can," answered Marie. "And I'm here to help you get started. My boss told me to help you out on your first day seeing as how things are slow in his department."

"Thank God," she commented.

They sat side by side at the desk the entire day so that any questions Jeanie had could be answered.

At the end of the day, Don Ayers approached Jeanie and asked, "So what do you think?"

Afraid to answer him she smiled and looked at her sister-in-law who said, "She did fine, Don. What do you think?"

"No problems here. Be looking forward to seeing you tomorrow morning, Jeanie." The smile on her face was obvious. She was pleased that she had made it through the first day as a secretary cause she never expected to be hired with no past clerical employment history and typing skills with speed so below those of secretaries with extensive past histories.

Jeanie showed up early for work the next day and took her place at the desk. She had told her sister-in-law, "I may be calling you for help," which she did many times that day, but as time passed on through the week, Jeanie started to become accustomed to her work environment and did an excellent job.

And so it was that the two "sisters" started working at the same company, a working relationship that would last eight years.

TWENTY-ONE

Marie's husband had "pet" names for his children. His son - jerk, dummy; daughter-lovey, sweety.

"We named him Derek," Marie said one morning when Steve had just got through belittling his son. He continued using deprecating names to Derek which broke Marie's heart. She knew if she persisted in correcting him, he would only continue criticizing Derek, so she figured it better if she said nothing and decided to lift her son's morale by telling him over and over how great he was.

Derek was having trouble in school - coming home with headaches every day, so Marie made an appointment with the doctor to have him checked out.

After a thorough examination Dr. Roberts said, "Derek, will you wait in the reception area while I talk with your mother?"

"Get him out of that Catholic school," he told Derek's mother after Derek left. "Some kids just can't take the strictness of the nuns. I'm in the same parish as you and my children don't go to the school. Not that the education isn't excellent. It's the rigorous expectations the sisters put on the kids."

"You mean at the end of the school year?" she asked.

"No, I mean immediately, this Friday," he answered.

Marie called the principal, Mother Timothy, when she got home from the doctor's appointment.

"I'm taking the children out of school and putting them in public school nearby," she said.

"You're taking them away from God?" Mother Timothy asked indignantly.

"What, no! The doctor has a concern regarding Derek's emotional welfare and believes it's in his best interest what with the strict atmosphere of parochial education."

"And you with a brother who is a priest. Mother of God," she said. "Do you know what punishment that will be placed on you by God for doing this? I'll pray for you and your family."

"You are threatening me with damnation?" Marie asked. "Don't bother praying for me. I thought you'd be more understanding than this. They won't be back from this day on," and she hung up on Mother Timothy.

Derek started fifth grade middle school and for a while his disposition was positive which made his mother think that this was the answer to his emotional problems.

She received a call from the school psychologist shortly after enrolling her son in the school.

"Mrs. Trotsky, my name is John O'Brien and I'm the school psychologist at Derek's school." "I would like to have you come in so we could discuss your son."

"Why," she asked. "Something wrong?"

"No, at the present time, it's minor, but I feel we need to have a talk. I have already talked with him and found our discussion somewhat troubling. I'd prefer that he not know about this, so it would be better if we meet during school hours. Is 1:00 tomorrow OK? Would his father come with you?"

"You've got to be kidding," she answered. "He doesn't believe in psychology, but I'll ask him."

"We need to talk before the kids come home from the park," she said to Steve when he came through the door after work that evening.

"About what?" he asked.

"Derek," she answered and told him about the phone call from the school psychologist.

"No goddamn way am I going to any meeting with a shrink," he said, "You want to go, go ahead, but leave me out of this."

"With or without you, I'm goin," she said.

The Trotsky family shared an evening of silence making the kids wonder what went wrong, but afraid to ask, decided it better to say nothing. Besides, their parents probably had a fight before they came home which was becoming a common occurrence.

She was early for her appointment with John O'Brien. He welcomed her into his office, offered her a chair and started asking questions about her son.

"Have you noticed he is quiet a lot of the time at home or is it just at school?"

"He appears to be a happy kid although sometimes he shuts himself in his room, but I thought that normal for a kid his age," she answered.

"I'd like to come right to the point," he said. "May I?"

"By all means," she answered.

"Emotionally, I believe your son is suffering from deprivation of his self-esteem and after talking with you, I believe I've targeted the problem. Is he close to his father? By that I mean do they do things together?"

"They used to go fishing down at the pond nearby, but don't anymore," she answered.

"What about your daughter? Is she close relationship with her father?"

"Well, yes, I guess," she answered. But at that very minute, she remembered how much ridicule her son had taken from his father while her daughter had received very little or none at all.

With more discussion, she broke down crying and told Mr. O'Brien of the name calling Derek received from his father.

"How about you and your relationship with your husband? Is it affectionate and touching outside of the sexual act?"

She cried harder and as he handed her a tissue, he said, "I have a concern for both you and your son. If something isn't done and soon, there'll be problems down the road for him - possibly delinquency with drugs and/or alcohol and no interest in his studies."

"As for you, if something doesn't turn around, I'm afraid you could end up having an affair searching for the affection you don't receive from your husband."

"What?" she cried. "Never! I consider my marriage vows extremely sacred."

"Do you think I could come to the house and talk with your husband? Maybe, just a little understanding conversation with him about your son and possibly at the same time revitalize your marriage into a more loving, caring one."

"I doubt it," she answered. "But I'll ask him and let you know."

Before leaving his office, she calmed herself down, but on her way to the parking lot and before entering her car, she couldn't help thinking about what John O'Brien said about her having an affair. It made the hairs on her arms stand up.

She waited til Steve had read the paper after dinner to mention the meeting with the psychiatrist.

"I saw John O'Brien today and he asked if he could come to the house and have a meeting.

"Who?" he asked.

"You know, John O'Brien, the school psychiatrist," she answered. "He wants to come and have a talk with both of us about our son."

"I told you, I don't believe in that shit," he answered.

Realizing that this would take a lot more than asking, she cuddled up to him and started talking in sexual overtones which got his attention at once, ending in the bedroom having intercourse. When they finished and both lit a cigarette, she knew she had him at an advantage. She waited and finished their cigarettes before saying, "So what do ya think? Can I call John and have him come over tomorrow night when the kids are at the basketball game?"

"Oh! All right, but this is your idea, not mine and I still think it's a bunch of bullshit," he answered.

The next evening, John O'Brien arrived right on time and was shown into the living room to an easy chair. Introductions made, he said, "First of all Mr. Trotsky, I'm not here to criticize anyone, but just to help your son with his seemingly low self-esteem. His grades are in jeopardy because of his lack of interest in his studies. He seems to be off by himself most of the time. You have a great boy and one thing is evident, he thinks the world of you, loves you very much. All I'm suggesting is maybe a little more time together doing father and son activities and showing more affection. As far as I can ascertain, your daughter is not suffering from any lack of your attention and maybe that's why her grades are so good."

Steve was quiet and said very little, but his head was moving in an up and down position of agreement.

Realizing that further comments would be of no value, John O'Brien said, "Well, that's about all I have to say. Do you have anything you'd like to mention?"

"No!"

Marie knew it didn't go well, but then so did John O'Brien,

"Thanks for your time then, Mr. Trotsky. And if I can be of any further service to your family, please don't hesitate to call me."

Marie hadn't quite closed the door when she heard her husband say, "What a bunch of bullshit that guy is. Psychiatrist my ass. Doesn't know his ass from a hole in the ground. I told you I didn't want to have him here. Don't ever put me in that position again. You hear me?"

She tried, but felt the agony of defeat in her attempt to help her son. "I just thought . . . "

"Well, don't think again. I'm goin' to bed. You coming?"

"Two times in one day?" she thought. No way!

"No, I'm gonna read a while.

Reading became her escape.

Because there wasn't much conversation with her husband, working had also become an escape for her as she looked forward to communicating with adults who had the same interests as she.

TWENTY-TWO

She had a week off between assignments before being called back to work for a manager in manufacturing whose name was Paul Lombroso. Paul's technical expertise of production/ manufacturing was extraordinary, but he had another talent which, if it paid as much, he could have given up his day job. He was a wizard of comedy. Everything that came out of his mouth, if it didn't concern the mechanics of his job, was funny.

He stood five feet three and had Italian olive skin. His ancestors were definitely from Naples, of which he was proud. It was said that at one time he was in the Pennsylvania Mafia; although how he could have gotten out without landing at the bottom of the ocean "sleeping with the fishes" is beyond comprehension.

Anyway, other than the stature of his body, it was said, although not to his face, that his face looked like a barracuda - bulging eyes and prominent nose that stuck out almost parallel to his upper lip, with a receding dark black hairline, so Marie was a little concerned when she was asked to work for him for four weeks while his secretary was on medical leave.

"How ya doin'?" were the first words he said to her when introduced by her boss. He said these words Italian style like Howyadoin with no lapse in between each word.

He showed her to the desk where she would be sitting for the next month and after she sat down he said, "What's really important about this assignment is that you get me my Pepsi when the cart comes around in the morning and in the afternoon and get yourself a coffee too, on me. The coffee/Pepsi kitty can is in the middle drawer of the desk. Just let me know when it needs refilling."

"Also, there is a weekly periodical that comes every Friday addressed to me. Comes in a sealed brown paper envelope that has no return address on it. Don't open it cause the weekly edition of *Screw* magazine is enclosed in it. There's some porn in it which I would not want you to see but you might be interested in whose face is pictured in the toilet bowl in each edition. Usually it's a prominent statesman with caption that would knock your socks off."

And with that, he turned and walked in his office leaving her looking at him shocked, bowled over, and wordless.

"Jeez, I don't know about this," she thought. *"I mean I'm no prude, but this guy."*

One day traveled speedily into five and at the end of the week, she found him to be not only hilariously comical, but compassionate, for she overheard a conversation he had with someone who was in desperate need of financial help who he offered money to, no strings attached, payable whenever, if ever.

That Friday when the mail came, she noticed the brown paper envelope and didn't unwrap it, but handed it to him along with his other opened mail.

"Thanks for remembering," he said.

Returning to her desk, she heard him laughing hysterically and turned to see what was goin' on.

He raised his arm beckoning her in his office. She pushed her chair back and entered as he showed her a picture of the toilet bowl with Nixon's face in it, caption underneath.

They sat at his conference table - he drinking Pepsi, her drinking tea - and laughed at all the non-porn items printed in the magazine. It became a weekly morning break ritual until her assignment was completed and she knew she would miss this generous man whom she came to love and respect.

Before she left his employ, National Secretaries Week was being celebrated, so he took her to a restaurant called The Vault. He bought her lunch which consisted of a new drink for her - Vodka Gimlet - and quite a few of them. They ordered a sandwich and as they ate, he said to her, "Ya know, I fed enough of those Gimlets to you to try to get in your pants, but I don't dunk my pen in the company ink well," and with that he paid the check and got her back to work just before quitting time.

Her sister-in-law Jeanie had accepted a permanent job working for a manager in systems engineering. Although her clerical skills were not high speed, her work was very accurate and she gained the respect of all the engineers who worked in the department, plus her quick witted remarks could get a laugh or at least a smile out of the most poker faced individual. She had proven herself to be very accommodating and was a welcomed co-worker in that department.

There was a Carnival Inn located on the main drag, half a mile from the plant, where co-workers would go on a Friday night after work to "unwind." The lounge featured two-fers or two drinks for the price of one which made the bar all the more inviting to those who imbibed, so it became a ritual to "stop" after work on Fridays for happy hour.

Although invited to meet her, Steve, being a quiet man, particularly around groups of people he did not know, didn't want to join her but had no problem with her stopping, especially since she was with her brother's wife and she usually was home before the happy hour was over - six thirtyish. One night a week couldn't hurt and because the kids went to sports events, it gave him time to be alone at home after an intense day at work.

Finding it more and more desirous to be away from her husband, Marie joined the company bowling league. The league bowled on Wednesday after work at the ABC Alley on the north side of town. She was not the athletic type and was put into a team of high handicappers. Matter of fact, she had all she could do to pick up a ten pound bowling ball, let alone throw it down the lane. Her highest score during her bowling days was 130.

Realizing she didn't want to go home after work - there'd always be something he could bitch about - she joined the golf league that played on Monday evening after work which meant she had to get to the golf course by 4:30 to tee off. Same as bowling, she was no "Patty Palmer" and hit the ball so many times, she tired from swinging, but still, it got her out and communicating with friends of like mind.

TWENTY-THREE

Her friendship with Jackie blossomed as they found that they had so much in common - the number one being a deteriorating marriage with their husbands.

Jackie's husband, Al, liked to go to the local bars, drink boiler makers, bet on sports, and chase the ladies. He worked in construction, was a good looking guy - five-six, blonde haired with green eyes - but had no sense of responsibility for taking care of his family. They included a wife and four children, two boys and two girls, which left Jackie to support not only him and his drinking habits but the responsibility of putting food on the table. He rarely smiled, appearing to be angry most of the time, so when he left the house after the evening meal, Jackie was glad he was gone. Still, knowing he might come home drunk and angry and pick a fight with her left her in fear, especially for her children although he never touched them, but instead took his frustrations out on her.

The wash was not done according to his liking one time because the ironed shirt had wrinkles in it which angered him to the point of grabbing Jackie by the arm. "Don't you even know how to iron a shirt for Christ's sake?" he asked. He flung her across the bed and stormed out of the house.

Even though it was summertime, she claimed she was cold and wore a sweater to work the next day so no one could see the bruises on her arm.

Jackie knew when he had a new girlfriend because he didn't come home all night, instead staying at his girlfriend's house and leaving for work from there which was OK with her. She didn't have to put up with him. Of course in winter, there was no work, the ground being ice covered and frozen, so he drove to the local "Eagles Nest," a hangout for unemployed construction workers.

As her children grew, he stopped harassing her after his older son came in from baseball practice and found his mother on the floor, his father standing over her, fist clenched above his head and ready to strike her again.

"What the hell do you think you're doing to my mother, you drunken son of a bitch?" his son said. He grabbed his father, got him in a headlock, put him out the front door and locked it before attending to his mother and helping her up off the floor to the sofa.

His father started banging with his fists and kicking with his foot on the front door screaming, "Let me in and I'll show you."

"Mom," he asked, why do you put up with him?"

Before she could answer, the distant blaring of a siren could be heard getting closer and closer to their home. A neighbor had called the cops.

Although Al was sober enough to hear the siren, he wasn't sober enough to run faster than the sheriff's deputy who chased him through the yard and grabbed him as he was attempting to climb over the fence.

"Well, what have we got here?" the deputy asked as he pushed Al up against the fence and cuffed him.

"A wife beater, huh?" "Maybe a night in the county jail will cool you off - give you something to think about before trying it again. And with that, the deputy put him in the back of the squad car, locked him in and went up the steps to the house to get a statement from Jackie.

She was sitting on the sofa crying, her son sat aside her holding an ice bag to her bruised and swollen face.

"This has happened before hasn't it?" the deputy asked.

"Yes," she answered. "But I've been too ashamed to call for help cause I thought he'd stop eventually, but I never thought my son would get involved."

"You want to prefer charges?"

"Yes," she answered.

"Finally," her son said. "She's put up with this since we were little kids. I just can't watch my mother going through any more of his abuse."

"I'm taking him to be processed and he'll sober up, spend the night in the county jail. Probably get out after arraignment in the morning, but if you have any more trouble with him, call us, hear? No need to allow this to continue."

"Thank you officer," her son said. "I'll watch out for my mother."

"Night then," and the deputy walked out of the house, entered the car and drove off with Al tied up and swearing in the back seat.

TWENTY-FOUR

These marital discourses Jackie never shared with anyone until she and Marie became close friends. They shared stories of maltreatment from their husbands - Jackie's physical violence and Marie's emotional and verbal abuse.

Steve began to realize that he was losing control over Marie since she went back to work. She had always agreed with everything he said because she thought he was more intelligent than her; that she was lucky to have such a handsome, smart, reserved husband. He kept her in check when, during meaningless arguments, he belittled her, one time calling her a titless wonder. She ran down the hall into the bedroom, slammed the door, flung herself on the bed and cried. He had a smirk on his face. No apology was ever made.

Work affected Marie like a shot of Novocain in the mouth before drilling a cavity. It temporarily relieved the hurt she felt from her husband's cruel remarks. She was being noticed and appreciated not only for her exemplary performance at work, but for her outgoing personality.

The fighting became more frequent in the Trotsky household, so she started "stopping" more and more as time passed. She didn't want her children to have to listen to the hostility and figured it better that if she wasn't there, it wouldn't happen.

After school, her son stayed for sports activities, then went to his girlfriend's house and didn't get home til dusk, so he wasn't home, probably by choice, to have to listen to the bickering between his parents.

Her daughter caught the brunt of her father's resentment and complaining. She did not get involved in extracurricular activities after school but instead came home to help out with household chores before her mother got home after happy hour.

Marie's sister-in-law and she befriended two male co-workers who worked in Jeanie's department. The women enjoyed the camaraderie of the opposite sex. There were no innuendos of impropriety in their friendship by other employees as they knew that these "4," who also happened to be married, were just having fun. "Who's stopping?" became the end of the week question, which became the end of every other day question, which became the end of the day question. "Stopping" ended up at the corner watering hole, the Carnival Inn.

Marie knew her feelings for her husband were deteriorating but still felt guilty that somehow she was responsible. After all, as unemotional as he was, he didn't run around, came home from work and paid the bills, but something was missing and she just couldn't figure out to what degree she played a part in it, so she sought the guidance of a psychologist.

"From the information you gave my receptionist when you made the appointment, I understand you have need of advice concerning your marriage," Dr. Michaels said.

"Yes," she answered. "And I need to confront my feelings to see if I can save it."

She sat for fifty-five minutes telling him about how she met her husband and how the years had passed since then - fifteen in all, and, how on this very day, they should be celebrating their fifteenth wedding anniversary.

"I'm not in the mood to celebrate. Something's wrong and I just don't know how to fix it if I can and if it is fixable," she said. "He's gotten mean, pickin' fights, belittling me and my son."

"How's your sex life?" he asked.

"Well, if you consider having sex with a robot, not so good. I mean I never have a problem reaching climax, because I have always believed sex starts with the mind. There is no foreplay, just sex, in and out and roll over to go to sleep.

"What do you want me to tell you?" he asked.

"I don't know what to do," she answered.

After listening to Marie speak about her marriage, the doctor said, "I'll tell you what I'm hearing. For many years, you were a furnace of fire in your love for him, but now the fire is going out, leaving just a pilot light and if something isn't done about it, the pilot light will go out."

"Will he come in for counseling?" he asked.

"Are you kidding?" she answered. "He doesn't believe in counseling, telling your business to some schnook, quack, so no, he won't come."

"Then there's nothing I can offer further. I don't think you need to come back because I believe you'll find your own answers as to what to do."

And with that comment he stood up, excused her, and she left his office knowing that the bond of the union between Steve and her was devastatingly broken. Thirty-five years later, she would come to understand why.

TWENTY-FIVE

The worst possible state of their fading marriage was bound to happen eventually. Marie arrived home at 6:30 from happy hour one evening two weeks after her counseling meeting with Dr. Michaels. She didn't get five feet inside the front door when her husband said, "Well, here she is." Her son was fifteen at the time.

"Don't," she begged.

Ignoring her he said, "Here she is, Derek, your mother the whore. Did you know that your mother is a whore?"

Derek didn't answer his father. He followed his mother into the kitchen and held her in his arms as she cried.

"Don't cry, Mom," he said.

"Do you know what a whore is?" she asked her son.

"I do and my mother isn't one," he answered.

Although Marie had never been unfaithful to Steve, at that point the marriage was irrevocably shattered and even though she felt no vileness toward him, she knew she didn't love him anymore.

Feeling trapped, she also didn't care about anything except her children and found comfort in getting up and going to work each day. She tried to be civil but her heart wasn't in it; so the silence in the family circle became deafening.

She decided to sleep on the sofa from that point on which further aggravated her husband. One evening when the kids were out, as she was walking down the hall, he came up behind her and pushed her into the bedroom where she fell across the bed.

"You're gonna fuck," he said angrily as he started removing his pants.

Although he didn't hit her, she was fearful for her safety and acquiesced to his demand. Removing her clothes, he pumped and worked his swollen penis into her until he reached orgasm, never noticing that burning tears were sliding down the corner of her eyes and on to the pillow. While she never had a problem reaching orgasm, she didn't care to reach one this time and she didn't.

Saying nothing to her, he got up and went to the bathroom to clean up leaving her lying on the bed emotionally diminished and disgusted with him. Trying hard not to, she couldn't help the hatred that started rising within her like vomit coming from her stomach to her mouth.

Sitting on the side of the bed, she said to herself, *"One day, you'll be sorry you did this to me and the children."* At that moment, she started planning her divorce knowing that she had to wait until her daughter graduated high school before she could make her move.

Marie was too embarrassed to inform her family of the situation between her and her husband. She especially didn't want her mother and brother to know. She took solace in her friendship with Jackie. The two women shared with each other feelings that no one else could possibly understand unless they had walked down the same road.

Jackie quit her job at Sim-U-Flight and went to work for a hotel, The Hansen Inn, as their sales and services manager where because of her business sense and helpful attitude, she kept occupancy rates higher than her predecessor. She sought out traveling commercial and military businessmen from corporations all over the country who came to Suttonville, New York for conferences and meetings.

She stayed after her working hours were over and, although she didn't drink, she ended her day in the cocktail lounge buying drinks for the hotel guests, most of who were sales reps who met for a nip after a long day in negotiations with local companies.

After bowling and golf, Marie many times would stop at the Inn, have a drink and hang around a while because she didn't want to go home. Her desire to escape her husband's unfair criticism of her was becoming harder and harder to deal with plus, he was using vile language especially the F word around her and the children.

Listening to fuck this and fuck that was everyday language, particularly when she realized that it was used to upset her, trying to egg her into an argument. Then he could take advantage of her emotionally-fragile psyche and get her to cry, wherein he knew he had her under his control. She was already taking tranquilizers and didn't know how much more she could tolerate at the hands of her unloving husband.

Marie came to know a lot of the traveling businessmen, both military and civilian, who stayed at the Hansen Inn because they were involved in negotiations of contracts for simulators for all branches of the armed forces as well as the commercial airlines. Many were engineers working as civil servants who interfaced with the salesmen of Sim-U-Flight.

She knew all her company's "marketeers" who were stationed in-house as well as those who came into the plant from district offices across the U.S. for sales meetings and simulator acceptances.

Marie stopped at the inn one evening and while waiting for Jackie, she bumped into one of the salesmen, Tom, who started buying her drinks. She had a lot of booze that evening and the next thing she remembered was that she was in his room, on his bed, naked and he was trying to have intercourse with her. Before she revived herself, all she felt was a sweaty back, thought it disgusting, pushed him away, put on her clothes and ran out of the room crying. Not a word was spoken between them.

Even though her marriage was finished as far as she was concerned, the guilt she felt all that night lingered into the next morning. She couldn't bring herself to go to work knowing that Tom was in town for a conference and she would have to face him.

She figured she did a good job of not showing her guilt around her husband and children, but found it difficult to stop thinking about what she had allowed the night before when the phone rang. She answered it and heard the voice of one of her dear friends and co-worker who said, "Jackie called and told me what happened last night. Where are you? Why aren't you at work?"

"I can't," she cried. "I've done a terrible thing. I keep thinking the kids know it. I could care less about their father, but, my God, the kids."

"Get your ass in here," Karen said. "If you're not in in an hour and a half, I'm comin' over to get you. You understand?"

"Yes, but….."

"No buts about it, get in here and we'll talk about it."

She dried her tears, dressed and drove to the plant. As she was opening the door, she looked toward the lobby and saw Tom standing there with customers. She wanted to turn around and walk back out, but before she could, Karen walked up to her, took her arm, and guided her to a conference room nearby.

"You think you're the only one this has ever happened to?" Karen asked. "It's your first time, isn't it?"

"Yes," Marie answered.

"Get through the day and it'll be OK. Knowing that I knew, Tom stopped me and said he didn't know that you had never been unfaithful before and how sorry he is. He really feels bad, like he took advantage of you."

"He did take advantage of me buying me all those drinks."

"You didn't have to drink them," Karen said. "Look, I understand your marriage is in the toilet and you've had it rough. Do you know how many people turn to affairs at times like this?"

"What? You mean you?"

"Yes," Karen answered. "For two years now, I've been seeing someone who helps me get through a loveless marriage."

"I just can't," Marie answered. "Probably my Catholic upbringing and all the guilt the nuns shoved down my throat. Everything you did was wrong in parochial school, but more than that, I took my vows seriously when I said them."

"I can't speak to that cause I wasn't brought up Catholic, but I've heard others speak of 'Sister Mary Guilt' and I really feel sorry for you. Can you go to work now that we've talked?" Karen said.

"Yes, and thanks for being my friend and confidant. I appreciate it."

With the help of Karen, she decided it would be better for her if she tried to put the whole scene behind her, but even though she tried not to, she still felt pangs of remorse whenever she saw Tom which was maybe once a month.

Marie kept a low profile for a while after which she decided to meet Jackie in her office one evening after work. They were gonna go and check out a band at a nearby hotel, a competitor of the Hansen Inn that Jackie thought could be booked for a gig at the inn in the future. In order to view and hear the band, they chose to sit at a table near the bandstand.

After ordering a drink, Marie noticed that there were people on the floor who were having a really good time dancing to the tempo of the trio playing disco. Her eyes glanced at a man who could move to the rhythm especially well. He was five-eight, hundred forty-five pounds with brown hair that was cut crew and was wearing a maroon golf shirt, tan slacks and wing-tipped loafers on his feet.

A man she knew asked her to dance the bump which she willingly accepted. She had just sat down in her chair when the man in the maroon shirt approached her.

"Would you like to dance this one?" he asked.

"Sure," she answered.

As they started dancing he told her his name was Jeff Stetner and that he was from Jacksonville, Florida. Before they could say another word, the music had them moving to a beat that was too fast to converse, so they danced to the rhythm like they had danced together before. They stayed on the floor dancing until the trio took a break and when he escorted her back to the table, he pulled out an empty chair next to hers and started talking to her.

"I didn't ask your name," he said.

"Oh! It's Marie," she answered. "And this is Jackie."

Pleasantries exchanged, he turned his attention back to Marie.

"Well, Marie, you sure can dance. I've never danced with anyone who could follow me as well as you," he said.

He told her he was in the Navy, was a computer programmer who was in town on military business at the Sim-U-Flight Corp.

Hearing that, she almost choked on her drink, regained her composure and said, "I work there."

"Jackie, did you hear that?" Marie asked. "He's in town on business with Sim-U-Flight."

And Jackie's mind pinged - business!!!!!!!!!!!

"Where are you staying?" Jackie asked.

"Here," he answered.

She told him that she was sales coordinator for the Hansen Inn and she'd like to buy him and his shipmates a drink if they'd like to stop before returning to the base in Florida.

Jeff and Marie danced a few more times, but she noticed that when his buddies joined them at the table, Jeff was covetous of any one of them talking to her for any length of time and would interrupt the conversation.

When he went to the men's room, Marie whispered to Jackie, "We need to get out of here and go back to the inn. He's possessive, won't let the others talk to me. I don't like it."

"OK," Jackie answered. "We'll tell him that I have to get back and take care of some business I left."

They stood up as he was returning from the men's room.

"Where you going?" he asked.

"She needs to get back to the inn," Marie answered.

"Where is it located?" he asked.

"Due north right across the river," she answered. "You can see the sign from here." It was nice dancing with you. You sure can move to the music."

When Jeff went to pay his bar tab, Marie and Jackie hurried out of the lounge toward Jackie's car where they quickly opened the doors and sped away over the bridge and into the parking lot of the inn.

"Ya know," Jackie said when they entered the Patio Yard, "There's a good chance of getting some business with him."

"Yes, I can see that but not on my time," Marie answered.

They took a seat at a round table near the exit door to the Patio Room and began chatting.

A few minutes later, Jackie kicked Marie's ankle and nodded toward the door but before she could say anything, Jeff pulled out a chair next to her and sat down. His buddies headed toward the bar to order a drink before returning to the table, drink in hands, and sat down. He seemed to be obsessive about his shipmates having a direct conversation with Marie which aggravated her. Realizing this, he directed his attention to Jackie.

"So," he said. "This is a damn nice hotel. I can't believe the amenities it offers with three bars, pool, spa, and steam room. I need to talk to you about rates before I leave to go back to Jacksonville. We'd probably prefer to stay here on our next trip."

Speaking to his buddies he said, "What do you guys think about staying here next trip?"

To which they answered in unison, "Yeah!"

It was getting late. Marie looked at her watch and decided to go home, but when she stood up to leave, Jeff stood up beside her and asked her if he could drive her back to get her car.

Jackie was busy talking to one of the sailors about rates, so Marie, although slightly hesitant, accepted his offer and left with Jeff. When they parked alongside her car and she started to get out of his car, he asked her to stay and talk a minute. She shut the door, he lit her a cigarette, handed it to her and said, "I've never met anyone like you. I mean I've met lots of women before but you seem to have it all going for you: personality, looks, God can you dance, and you're so enjoyable to talk to."

She was taken aback for a second before answering him.

"I have no desire to get into a romantic relationship with anyone. I have a marriage going down the drain, but I also have two teenagers who need me to remain in it til they're out of school, so if that's what you're looking for, I'm not the one."

"No!" he exclaimed. "I didn't mean it that way. I understand because I don't have that good a marriage either and I have three teenage kids, so I can't dissolve my marriage either."

"So you want to have an affair?" she asked.

"It did enter my mind," he said. "But I know I'd never see you again if I expected an affair, so I'd be happy with a friendship. Can I call you when I come back? And will you have dinner with me?"

"I don't know," she replied. "Let's see when you come back, but I warn you, I'm not interested in an affair. If that's what you want, go find someone else, and don't for one minute that think I don't understand that you might consider me a challenge because I refused your advances."

"Got it all figured out, huh?" he asked.

"I was raised by two brothers who didn't hold back on their knowledge about what's on men's minds," she replied.

"OK, well, I consider myself warned and will respect that," he said. "So can I still call you when I return?"

"OK," she answered and opened the door to his car and left.

He sat there for a minute smiling, shaking his head and thought, "I think I just got told where the cat shit in the bucket. I gotta see this woman again."

After she got safely into her car and pulled out of the parking lot, he left his car and went into the hotel to his room for a good night's sleep. He had an early flight the next morning.

Jeff called her at work a couple of times after he got back to the base in Florida just to see if she was OK, but actually, he was worried that another man could slip in before he returned and win her over which was what he intended to do. They chatted but she didn't think much of it, believing she had set him straight on romance.

Marie befriended the company nurse, Gail Kennedy, who was a feisty Irish woman born in New England and had no problem showing it. Her mouth was quick on the uptake of snide remarks made to her by anyone including management, but most of those remarks were made in good humor just to get her goat. She was older by a couple years than Marie, was divorced and was pissed that her husband had left her for another "fat" woman he met while he was undergoing therapy in a mental institution for a nervous breakdown.

Her coal black hair hung down in pageboy along the sides of her face. She had a hard look about her even though she had lovely blue eyes. Although her body wouldn't be considered one that would be seen on fashion cover, she thought it good enough to be able to wear a bikini. But she was one hell of a nurse, and trained at a VA hospital in upstate New York which probably is where she learned to be so direct. If she liked you, she'd do anything for you. On the other hand, if she didn't, avoiding her was the only way to get along with her. She was nicknamed "Florence" as in "Nightingale."

Marie was in her medical one morning when a manufacturing employee came through the door, right arm bent with his index finger pointing at the ceiling.

"What the hell is the matter with you this time?" she asked.

The poor man put his head down.

"OK, let me see it," she said. "That's nothing. I'll put something on it, bandage it and off you go." Which she did and off he went.

"And don't be bothering me, coming in here over every little thing that you think needs tending," she yelled as he was walking away.

"Now where were we?" she asked Marie after he left.

"Florence, how could you treat him like that?"

"Him? He just wants to get into my pants and there's already one asshole in there," she said nonchalantly leaving Marie bent over in laughter.

Could be gossip, but it was said that when negotiations were being conducted, the night before, the salesmen took their customers out on the town for dinner and drinks. Drinking continued after dinner and most times into early morning causing ive hangovers for the customers the next morning before having to go into the conference room to discuss terms of a contract.

Huh!

It was also rumored that the salesmen had a signal with the bartender to cut themselves off vodka or gin in their drinks and substitute water with an olive so they wouldn't get drunk and would be clear of mind at the negotiating table.

There was always a line outside Florence's medical the next morning after a night on the town. She had a concoction she made which integrated Alka Seltzer and a couple drops of spirits of ammonia that was known to bring one out of a hangover. It worked because those clients who stood there and got their "morning after" straightened up and flew right. Right into the conference room for deliberations before melting down around 3 o'clock and starting all over again partying that evening.

TWENTY-SIX

Marie was about to leave for the golf course one Monday afternoon when her phone rang.

"Hey, what are you doin' after golf?" Jackie said.

"Think I'll go home," Marie answered. "Why?"

"What do you want to do that for? Come on down to the inn after. We're having a birthday party in the Cooped Up Lounge for one of the customers in town from Orlando. It'll be fun."

"I don't know. Steve's been pitching a fit every time I turn around. It'll just give him something to bitch about if I don't go right home, so I think I'll pass."

"Promise me you'll think about it. Goin' home ain't gonna make it better. He'll just pounce on you again, start yellin' and raising hell about anything he can drudge up."

She knew her best friend was right and answered, "OK, Why not? I might as well do something if I'm gonna get blamed for it anyway. See you later."

She wasn't in a partying mood when she arrived in the Cooped Up Lounge that evening but she put on a happy smile anyway and crossed the room to the elongated table where ten men were sitting with Jackie seated at the head. There was a big birthday cake in the middle of the table and the birthday boy was sitting on a chair behind it.

Marie ordered a scotch and water and tried to join in the festivities of the evening. Jackie noticed that her friend was exceptionally quiet and inattentive which was not like her.

Marie was ready to leave, but when the band struck up she noticed that the music was comparative to that of her favorite Latin orchestra, Sergio Mendes. She walked over and stood on a stair above the dance floor to listen to the music. Although she was stationary, her body started moving to the rhythm of the music, swaying her hips from side to side when she felt a tap on her shoulder.

"You like this music?" she heard a man's voice comment.

She turned around and looked into the bluest eyes she ever saw. He was six feet tall, red hair, light complexion with freckles on his face. She remembered being introduced to him at the party but didn't take too much notice as her mood was strained.

"Yes," I do, she answered. "It's my favorite kind of music."

"Do you dance to it?" he asked.

"Yes, my older brother taught me how," she answered.

"Shall we?" he inquired and led her to the dance floor.

When she put her arms around him, she felt his muscular shoulders and a feeling of his strength moved her. They danced an entire set before she looked at her watch and noticed it was getting late and she needed to go home.

"Please don't leave yet," he said.

"I have to," she remarked.

"At least let me walk you to your car. It's dark out there in the parking lot."

"I'll be OK," she said.

"I insist."

As they walked to the parking lot, he introduced himself, saying, "By the way, my name is Clark Ross, and I already know yours is Marie."

She was driving a light blue Ford two door. He asked her to unlock the passenger side so he could sit a minute and talk with her and although she was a little uncertain, her instinct told her she could trust him, so she unlocked the door.

Sensing her hesitation, he didn't sit on the passenger seat. He sat on the edge of the floor and left the door open while they talked about nothing in particular.

A half hour passed and although she found herself enjoying chatting with him, she insisted that she needed to leave, so he stood up, said goodnight, shut the door, and turned to walk through the parking lot into the motel.

"What a nice guy," she thought as she drove out of the parking lot onto the street and headed the seven miles toward home.

Steve was sleeping when she arrived home. She felt lucky that maybe she wouldn't have to put up with his verbal abuse this evening. Or maybe she would.

She didn't. He was fast asleep.

Marie was getting ready to go to the cafeteria at 11:30 for lunch the next day when the phone on her desk rang.

She was surprised to hear the nasal voice that she recognized as being the one that belonged to the man who walked her to her car the night before.

"It's Clark," he said. "Remember me from last night?"

"Yes," she answered.

"What are you doing for lunch today? Can I take you to lunch?"

"Oh! Well, I go to the cafeteria, but if you would like to come with me, I'll meet you at my desk. How did you get my number?"

"I asked around," he said. "Be right up."

He was an electrical engineer, a civil service employee who was town from Orlando on acceptance of a Navy flight simulator.

When they entered the cafeteria, she noticed that all eyes were on them and as she looked around for a table, she noted most of them were filled with company employees.

It made her uncomfortable that they were being stared at so she put her tray down, he followed suit, and they left the cafeteria.

"Does that mean I don't get to take you to lunch?" he asked.

"No, but I just don't like the way we were being gaped at."

"Is there a restaurant around here and can you take the time to go?"

"Yes," she answered. "Just across the river from here is a nice Italian restaurant."

"We can take my rental car," he said.

After they were seated at a table in the Italian restaurant, they ordered a drink and started talking about anything and everything including their life histories. He was married with three children, all of them under the age of ten years. He didn't reveal any problems he had with his marriage and even went as far as to tell her that there were none.

It was wonderful to be able to communicate with someone so interesting, and what a great listener he was.

Two drinks later with no food ordered yet, she told him about her disappearing marriage. She couldn't understand why she shared such a personal account except that he was so easy to talk to. He listened so intently that two hours later, she realized she had been away from the office that long and became concerned, so he paid the check and they headed back to the plant.

Because she was uneasy that she might be seen with him, she said, "Leave me off in the parking lot."

As she was getting out of the car he asked, "Can I take you to supper?"

"Oh, no, I don't think that would be a good idea," she answered.

Although she was worried, no one seem to notice that she had been away that long, so she thought it best not to bring it up by apologizing.

She finished the day's work and went home feeling lighter than when she arrived in the morning.

He was walking around the perimeter of the plant when she arrived for work the next day. She started to open the door when a man's hand grasped the door handle and opened the door for her. When she turned around to thank him, she saw that it was Clark. They exchanged pleasantries and went their separate ways - she to her desk and he to the high bay area where he was inspecting the flight simulator.

At 11:30 her desk phone rang. "How about lunch today?" Clark said, and she thought, *"Yeah, that would be nice,"* so she accepted.

"Shall we go to the same place?" he asked.

"Sure, why not, but I don't dare stay away from my job that long again," she answered.

They went back to the Italian restaurant, were seated and ordered a drink. This time their conversation included philosophy and religion and he stated that he was a member of a church in Orlando where the bible was read and the scriptures learned to be spoken from memory.

"I'm Catholic, know no verses from the bible but do believe that my heavenly Father loves me and takes care of me and those around me," she answered.

"Wouldn't you be better off if you read the bible and memorized some of the passages to help you in life?" he asked.

"I take it on faith," she said, "and I really don't want to discuss religion further. You have your way and I have mine."

"Oh, oh!" he thought. *"Now I've done it and made her angry which is something I didn't want to do."*

They ordered and he took her back to work worried that he wouldn't see her again.

"What about tonight - supper?" he asked.

Once again, she put him off and said, "No," so he didn't push it.

She lunched with him two more times before she agreed to have supper with him.

He was staying at the Hansen Inn. There was a small lounge located in the front of the motel off the lobby called the Front Door Lounge.

"I'll meet you in the Front Door Lounge at six," she said.

Not knowing what to expect of herself nor of him, she was very edgy and as she started up the outside steps toward the motel thought about turning around and going home.

"There you are," he said as he opened the door. "I've been waiting for you in the lobby. Come on and I'll buy you a drink before supper."

"Uh! OK," she answered.

They had two drinks, no wait, probably more like four and didn't go to dinner. Although she wasn't drunk, they ended up in his room located on the second floor in the front of the building facing the street.

Ah! Alcohol!

Anyway!

He helped her remove her clothes.

"You have a nice body," he said.

"No, my breasts are small," she said bashfully.

"No, they complement the petiteness of the rest of your body," he said.

They lay down with the sheet for covering. He was gentle as he entered her, and as he kissed her lips, they climaxed at the same time. When the clock on the courthouse across the river began to strike, she turned her head upward, looked out the window and saw that the dome where the clock was located read eight o'clock, but this time, she didn't worry about hurrying home and allowed him to hold her in his arms for a while.

"This feels so good," she said to him.

They fell asleep for a short time and when she awoke at nine she didn't disturb his sleep but got dressed and left the room.

On the drive home, Marie had no qualms but what she'd be put down again, but she thought, *"What can he say? He can't do any further damage than he's already done,"* and she didn't care.

Amazingly, he was already in bed, so she got her bedding from the linen closet; made up the sofa and went to sleep.

Clark remained in town for three weeks. He was running tests in preparation for the acceptance of the Navy simulator for which he was responsible. As much as possible, they saw each other, their trysts becoming more and more comfortable each time they met. They were lovers.

He was called back to Florida when some of the tests he was conducting were not up to par. He would return when the Sim-U-Flight engineers perfected the system, maybe a couple months later.

Their last night together, a Friday, was spent in his motel room making love and conversing about their lives and where they would go from here. She left his room early, and on her way home, decided that she couldn't do this anymore; the guilt was becoming overbearing for her, but she did not tell him.

When the phone rang at her home the next morning, she didn't answer it knowing the call was probably from him. The second time the phone rang, it rang twice, then a hang-up - her and Jackie's signal that one or the other needed help, so when it rang again, Marie picked it up and heard Jackie, say, "Answer the phone, will you?" Clark is at the airport waiting to board, trying to reach you."

"I know!" Marie cried. "I can't do this anymore. The guilt is devastating me. We're both married and committing adultery while our spouses know nothing, and even though my marriage is over, his isn't, so, no, I'm not gonna answer it."

"He'll just keep calling," Jackie said.

"Let him," she answered. "He'll be airborne soon and forget all about this. Gotta go, pal." and she hung up crying.

The following Saturday morning, Marie was in the kitchen cleaning up after breakfast when the wall phone in the kitchen rang.

"Hello," she answered.

"Can you talk?" Clark said.

"What are you doing calling me at home? Are you crazy?" she whispered.

"I had to talk to you and tell you that I know I love you," he said.

"Stop this," she said anxiously, hoping Steve, who was sitting on the sofa in the living room, wouldn't hear.

Thinking quick, she said, "Yeah, OK, Jackie, I'll be right over when I get through with the dishes," and she hung up.

Peeking around the corner of the kitchen into the living room, she saw that he was reading the morning paper and she was grateful that he hadn't taken notice of the phone call, but then he didn't take notice of anything she did lately anyway, which was a blessing this morning. Clark didn't call back.

Marie knew nothing about a direct line from the Sim-U-Flight plant to the federal training center in Florida. She had been working away at her desk on Monday morning when her phone rang at 11:25. She was ready to go to lunch, had just stepped away from her desk, but decided to turn around and answer it anyway.

"I love you," she heard Clark say. "Please don't hang up."

"Where are you?" she asked.

"At work," he answered.

"It costs too much to call long distance," she said.

"This is a dedicated line to the plant that I can use for business," he answered.

"Did you call from your house Saturday?" she asked.

"No, I used a pay phone at Sears," he answered. "I took Gina there to buy some paint. While she was selecting a color, I slipped away to call you."

"God in heaven, you called when your wife was with you?" she asked.

"She wasn't nearby and didn't know," he answered.

"We can't do this," she said. "It's wrong not so much for me because I'm just waiting for my daughter to graduate before I divorce, but your marriage is still intact and I'm not a home wrecker. The guilt is killing me."

"No, we'll find a way to make it work," he said, and she could tell he was softly weeping but she wouldn't let it deter her.

"Time will take care of this, you'll see, and it will become a pleasant memory for both of us," she said. "You won't be comin' back for a couple months and that should give us time to let this go and walk our separate ways."

"I'll never forget you and I'll never give up on us," he said. "I've pushed my return trip up a month which means I'll be coming in next month. We can discuss how we can be together then. Promise you'll wait til I come back, please?"

"I'm not gonna sit around waiting for you when there is twelve hundred miles between us and our relationship is so unsecured. Let's give it time and see what happens," she answered.

"Okay, but I won't change my mind about you," Clark said.

In the early 70s, disco became the "in" dance. As mentioned before, the Hansen Inn had three bars: the one in front of the property, the one in the center and the Patio Yard located in the back of the building. The Patio Yard had a large circular area that contained a bar, a stage for bands, a large dance floor, and an indoor pool with a spa located behind a flagstone wall.

These were also the days of hot pants and sizzle dresses that came just below the bootie, with matching panties, and boots that came up to the knees. Because she was so petite, weighed only a hundred eight pounds, Marie could wear them all and did. She could dance all the latest dances: the bump, hustle, boog-a-loo, and because she could dance, her popularity increased tenfold with guys who would cut in on her dancing partner so they could dance with the best.

She bleached her hair blonde and had her tresses professionally set every Saturday in a French twist. Her fingernails were glossed as well as her toenails. Although she didn't flaunt it, she finally felt some sense of attractiveness that had been denied her for years by the one she had loved.

It was just before Halloween when Clark returned. He had called Marie before to let her know what day and hour he would be arriving and asked her to meet him at the hotel. She was excited to see him again, so she was early arriving at the inn and decided to stop for a drink. She fidgeted searching for her wallet to pay for the drink when she felt a hand on the back of the bar stool and the stool was turned around to face him.

Upon seeing Clark, she threw her arms around his neck and hugged him with such intensity that she almost fell off the stool, but he caught her in his arms and helped her sit back down.

"Hi, my love," he said.

"Hi, yourself," she answered. "Can I buy you a drink?"

"I never had a lady buy me a drink before," he said. "It's always been the other way around, so I'm surprised."

They had a couple drinks before retiring to his room. The intercourse was especially intense. She let out a scream as they both drove their bodies into the passion that led them to a full blown orgasm without foreplay. When it was over they lay in each other's arms a couple of minutes before lighting a cigarette.

"I guess we should go eat," he said.

"Let's order in and make love again," she replied.

"Whatever the lady wants, she gets," he answered. He went to the phone, called the hotel restaurant and ordered for both of them.

She went home early that Friday evening. The guilt of committing adultery was becoming unbearable for her to deal with. She didn't sleep well and on Saturday morning, the kids were gone to a sports event, she knew what she had to do.

TWENTY-SEVEN

Steve was finishing mowing the lawn. He entered the back door and saw her sitting in the rocking chair crying.

"What's wrong?" he asked.

"I have something to tell you," she answered. "I've met someone else and I'm so sorry. I never wanted this to happen, never thought it would."

"Does he live here?" he asked. "Do I know him?"

"No, he lives in Florida; comes to town on business."

"How far has this gone?" he asked.

"You know me better than that," she lied.

And with that said, he walked out the door, got into his car and drove away.

When he came back, the kids were home searching in their parent's faces for what had gone wrong. It was too quiet, but they couldn't detect anything concrete except that something was amiss.

"I'm going to see Mother," Marie said.

No one said anything.

"She drove the two miles to her mother's house, went right to the phone and called Clark at the hotel.

When he answered, she said, "I've told him," and she cried.

"Where are you?" he asked.

"At my mother's," she answered.

"Calm down. Let me think. The Carnival Inn is across the bridge from where your mother lives. Meet me there in half an hour."

"I can't," she cried. "I'm too shaken."

"Either you meet me or I'm coming to your mother's and get you," he said.

"God, no you can't do that. Mother doesn't know anything about us. I'll meet you there."

It took her ten minutes to get across the bridge. She didn't want to go into the lobby, so she paced in front of the motel til he arrived.

When he drove up, he rolled the window down and said, "Get in."

She got in, put her face in her hands and cried.

He tried to take her in his arms to soothe her, but she resisted pushing him away.

"I guess I'm a slut just like he's been calling me all along," she cried.

"I never wanted to tell you this because I thought it better to stay out of it, but it's broken my heart knowing the abuse you have taken from him for so long that you're beginning to believe all the terrible names he's called you."

"What a time to have to tell you this," Clark continued. "I've been called back to Florida again because for a second time, the simulator isn't ready for testing and acceptance. I leave tomorrow afternoon," he said wearily. "And I honestly don't know when I'll be back, but I intend to help you through this even if it is from a distance," he added.

"Oh, God!" she exclaimed. "Everything is falling apart for us. Is it punishment for breaking a commandment?"

"No," he said. "God doesn't punish. We do it to ourselves with guilt." "It's something over which we have no control, at least at present. Will you come to the airport and see me off?"

"Yeah, I think Jackie will bring me up," she answered.

The next day, they kissed goodbye before he got on the plane and as he walked away from her he said, "Keep your head up. I'll be back. I love you."

He boarded the plane with a tear in his eyes knowing that he had to leave her in such a fragile emotional state of mind, so as the plane ascended into the sky, he said a silent prayer, *"Dear God protect and comfort her during this time of disturbance in her life,"* knowing that was all he could do for now.

Divorce was a subject they had discussed in the past few years, but Marie's husband didn't believe it could ever happen. At one time during a divorce discussion he had told her, "You want a divorce, I'll head out of here to a state where you'll never find me."

"What about the kids?" she asked.

"Let your mother or brother take care of their them. What do I care," he answered.

In view of the fact that she confessed her unfaithfulness to him, he acquiesced, and moved into an apartment.

Marie called Frank Murphy, her attorney, one she had worked for when her daughter was a year old, and set up an appointment with him.

"I need you to represent me in a divorce action against my husband," she said.

"What happened? Is there someone else?" Frank asked.

"No," she half lied. "The marriage hasn't been good for a few years now and I don't intend to stay in it any longer, especially since the kids are in their late teens." She told him about the verbal abuse she had suffered from her husband for years.

"In view of the fact that he had been verbally cruel to you and your son, I can go for irreconcilable differences, but it's thin ice we could be skating on. Some judges won't grant it, others will, but I'll start the paperwork. Is he agreeable to the divorce?"

"Yes," she answered. "He said to contact you and we will agree to everything we own together being split in half, including the equity of the sale of the house and any assets we may have. I don't want alimony, just support until the kids are eighteen."

"Are all the credit cards in both your names?" Frank asked.

"Yes," she answered.

"You need to get a credit card in your name only and cut up the ones in both names, and if you have a problem getting one, I'll help you," he added.

She left his office and went directly to the bank where they had their checking and savings and requested a credit card.

"Have you ever had a card in your name only?" the bank manager asked.

"No," she answered.

"I'm sorry," he added. "I can't issue one to you because I don't have a credit rating for you alone. It's all in your husband's name with you as a second signer."

"Great," she thought and turned to walk away.

"Wait a minute," she exclaimed. "I had one in my name at Williams Dress shop but haven't used it in a while. Does that count?"

"Yes, it does," he answered. "I'll check it out and get back to you."

Luckily, she was issued a credit card a week later in her name, the balance of which could not exceed $200.00.

Frank sent the documents for filing to Steve for signature which Steve returned promptly. A court date was set. Jackie offered to be a witness to the cruelty she witnessed by Marie's word of mouth.

The day of the divorce hearing, Marie was anxious. She hadn't told her kids about it because she didn't want to upset them. She knew she'd have to tell them but decided that after the decree was granted would be a better time. The hearing was set for 11:00. Jackie and Marie met in Frank's office to review the testimony that would be given.

Frank greeted them and invited them into his office. "I'm not going to represent you in court," Frank said.

"Why?" Marie questioned. "Is something wrong?"

"In a manner of speaking, yes," he answered. "My partner will represent you because your case is being heard by my brother-in-law, Judge Tom Smart, in his chambers and if word ever got out that you once worked for me, the proceedings could be considered a conflict of interest and could be, if he wanted it to be, questioned by your husband.

Her nerves were frayed when she entered the judge's chambers and took her seat in front of him. Frank's partner, Don Milligan, started the questioning and when he asked her to tell his honor what Steve had said to their son when he was fourteen, she hesitated. Encouraged by her lawyer, she put her head down in shame and repeated the account of her son being told by his father that she, Derek's mother, was a whore. His honor looked up from his desk with an expression of disbelief. Other testimony was given including Jackie's in regards to noticing that her friend had been on tranquilizers ever since she had known her.

Testimony given, his honor raised his gavel and said, "Divorce decree granted." Don Milligan escorted Marie to the entry where his honor stood holding the door open. As she approached him, the judge put his right hand on her shoulder and said, "I hope you'll find happiness now."

As they descended the courthouse steps, Jackie asked, "How do you feel being a single woman again?" to which Marie answered, "I want my mother."

She went to a pay phone and called her mother. When Marion answered the phone and heard her daughter's voice, she asked, "Is it over?"

"Yes, Mom," Marie answered. "Can I come get you?"

"I'll be ready and waiting for you," her mother said.

When she picked Marion up, she had tears in her eyes while backing out of the driveway.

"Where shall we go," Marie asked, not waiting for an answer.

"I know, the Vault," she added.

The Vault, the same restaurant Paul Lombroso had taken her to on Secretary Day. The walls were curved from ceiling to floor. At the entryway was a huge iron gate the hostess opened to let you in which caused a patron to feel like they had stepped into a vault.

It was after one o'clock when they were seated at a small table with wall separating the main dining room from the smaller one, so there were only a couple late lunchers seated away from them.

"Are you OK?" her mother asked.

"I never wanted this to happen," Marie answered wiping away her tears. "Did you feel this way when you divorced Dad?"

"Yes, I did," Marion answered. "Nineteen years is a long time to be married and there is a feeling of loss no matter what happened to cause the breakup, but I know you believe you did the right thing, so dry your tears and accept that fact so you can move on with your life."

"Have you told your children?" Marion asked.

"No, not yet. I'll tell them tonight," she answered.

They had intended to order lunch, but neither one of them felt hungry, so they had a couple of drinks and decided to leave.

After she dropped her mother off, she drove the two miles down the road toward her house dreading the thought that she would soon be telling her children that their parents were no longer married.

She waited until after they'd eaten before asking them to join her in the living room before leaving for the school dance.

There was no way to soften the blow, so she said, "Your father and I are divorced as of this morning," and waited for their reaction and was surprised when there wasn't any.

Her son spoke first, saying, "Well it's not like we didn't know this was coming. Does Dad know?"

"I don't know," she answered.

They lowered their heads. She cried and went to them, saying, "I'm so sorry," and realizing that at that moment enough was said, she walked into her bedroom, closed the door and sat on the end of her bed sobbing.

She heard the front door close and knew they had left for the school dance and was grateful that they had a place to go to help them forget.

TWENTY-EIGHT

Somehow, Steve found out who Marie had been seeing or as he liked to put it, screwing, and shortly thereafter, someone started making phone calls to Clark's house but only when that someone knew Clark would not be home, either traveling or at work.

"Hello! Is this Gina?" the voice asked.

"Yes, and who is this?" she asked.

"You don't know me but did you know that your husband has been having an affair with a woman in in Suttonville whose name is Marie?"

"You must have the wrong number," she answered. "Clark would never do that."

"I know for a fact that he is. He calls her from his office every day. Wasn't he out of town on the 10th?"

"Well, yes on business in Suttonville," she answered.

"He might have been on business but he was also screwing around on you in room 207 at the Hansen Inn. Isn't that where he stays?"

"Yes, who are you?"

"Who I am isn't necessary for you to know," the voice answered. "I can give you dates and times they've talked on her home phone and places they go when he is in town. I'll call again; keep you up to date."

And the connection went dead leaving her sitting and wondering if what the caller said could be true. She didn't panic and decided to keep it to herself for the time being putting the conversation on the back burner, believing that it was a hoax, because she didn't want to confront her husband without proof.

She also didn't even want to consider it, so she didn't want to answer the phone again if the voice, which she couldn't discern as either male or female, tried to connect with her again. Caller ID wasn't available which made her realize that not answering the phone at all wasn't an option.

Although fretful, she remained silent.

When next he called Marie, Clark said, "I told Gina about us."
"Why?" she asked.
"Because I can't live this lie any more either. It's tearing me up."
"Oh no, what did she say?"
"She blew up, headed for the door, and took a walk down the road."
"Go and get her, bring her back. Tell her you're sorry. I never meant for this to happen."
"I'll call you tomorrow," he said.

She didn't get a call from him the following morning at 11:30, thought nothing of it, probably a meeting he had to attend, but when she didn't hear all week, she began to wonder what went wrong.

She got his work number from a directory that was at her disposal and when she dialed his number, he answered and said he would call her back on an outside line.

"I did as you said and went out looking for her but couldn't find her, so I waited up for her to come home. She showed up at 2:00 in the morning and she was loaded. Wouldn't tell me where she'd been but said some guy picked her up and took her to a bar where she offloaded on him about what had happened before he drove her home," he said.

"Relieved that she was alright, but strained, I went in to soak in a hot tub of water and she pushed open the door, leaned down, put her right hand in the water, grabbed me by the testicles with her long fingernails and dug into me causing me to scream out, the pain was so bad."

"How does that feel you son of a bitch?" she said to me. "I married you and not a Latin man because they all have mistresses and I didn't want a marriage like that. I figured you would not be unfaithful to me. What have you done to us? Oh, I get it. Is she pregnant?"

"No, she isn't," I answered. "I just love her."

"That hurts even more. I guess I could almost survive this if you got her pregnant, but love her?"

"So the person who called me and told me of your so called love affair was right." It was more of a statement than a question.

"What call?" he asked.

She told him about the first call and two more after that she had received. He was at a loss to connect who would do such a thing.

"You need to know that she called in the cavalry," Clark continued. "Her old Aunt Flora flew in from Brazil to "straighten me out." Aunt Flora paced the floor with finger pointed at me while giving me a heavy dose of "shame on you."

"Then to top that off, she called our pastor who called me in for a little conversation about committing adultery and how Jesus would never forgive me if I don't beg His forgiveness and protect my marriage by never having anything to do with you again - no correspondence, no phone calls."

"And when that was all said and done," Clark continued, "she called my boss and told him about the affair and the phone calls she received from who knows who. My boss told her that it was a conflict of interest having an affair with a company employee the government does business with and he would find out who the caller was and where the call was coming from. If federal lines were used to make the call, it was an offense involving harassment."

"He called me in his office and told me I was off the acceptance team and would never travel to Suttonville, New York, again."

"Oh my God," Marie said. "Who would be so cruel as to call her?"

"I've been told that initially it was thought it might be you but that theory was dropped. So it appears to be someone who wants to break us up, someone you know," Clark said. "The lines to your house were tapped and after recognizing that it wasn't you, the tapping took a turn to another possible caller. Who, I wasn't told."

"What a mess we've gotten ourselves into," Marie said. "And to think I tried to prevent this from happening from the beginning. I should have listened to my instinctual warning."

"So it's over?" she cried.

"I didn't want it to be because I still love you, but, and there has to be a but, I adhered to Gina's request to preserve my marriage for my family's sake," he answered.

"Take care of your family," she said crying and hung up the phone.

She felt a knot in the pit of her stomach and held back the tears long enough to rush to the ladies room, enter a stall and flush the toilet to camouflage the sound of her crying. When she composed herself, she left the ladies room, made up an excuse to her boss for leaving, and went home to call Jackie.

The best friends met in Jackie's office that afternoon. Jackie closed the door when Marie entered.

"Oh! God," Jackie said. "You look terrible. What happened?"

She told her friend almost verbatim the conversation she had with Clark that morning. She couldn't hold back the tears and let them flow like water off a waterfall.

"How could I have gotten myself in this in the first place?" Marie said. "I mean it's not like I didn't know it probably would end up like this; was even sure it could. Still, I'm heartbroken."

Jackie was "seeing" an engineer who worked in the same government office complex where Clark worked, but never kidded herself that it could go anywhere. Her lover was married with a teenage daughter and he too came in town on acceptances for an Army helicopter simulator.

Silent for a minute and allowing her friend to vent her pain, Jackie put herself in Marie's shoes and didn't like the outcome of what her affair could come to. Although to her, it was comfortable having a long distance affair, there was always the fact that she could get too involved with the outcome like her friend, but unlike her friend, she and Berry never promised each other a future and kept the relationship undemanding.

The two "sisters" went into the Front Door Lounge where they ordered a glass of wine and sat for a while before Marie decided to go home and try to adjust to never seeing Clark again.

Broken hearted and not understanding that events in life happen for a reason, she couldn't know that in time, her search for love would be realized. Plus, she had teenage kids and couldn't let them see her misery over what they probably hoped would happen. Kids wanting their parents, no matter what, to stay together.

Marie and Steve's divorce had been finalized a few months before the breakup with Clark. At the time Steve moved out, she had told him to take anything he needed besides his clothes: bedding, dishes, a chair and handed him one-half of the savings account that was in both their names.

She didn't ask for alimony, just child support for a year until her daughter graduated at which time she and Jackie had plans to move to Florida.

Steve had hope that in time Marie would take him back, so he came and went on the weekends and took his children out. In the meantime, he started a relationship with a married woman he worked with at the Sexton Engineering Co. who was crazy about him and wanted to leave her husband for him. He promised her nothing and encouraged her to stay in her marriage and forget about a future with him which she reluctantly did.

TWENTY-NINE

Jackie started hostessing cocktail parties in the Patio Yard, some of which were formal, especially before the holidays when the group of traveling businessmen would begin to slack off for the season. She wanted to be sure she got their business the following year and she knew that throwing a party would almost guarantee their return to the hotel. Hoping it would get her mind off her friend's loss, she always invited Marie to join in the soirees when she held them.

There were five of them, divorcees that is, who palled around with each other. It was a time of bra burning, a feeling in the air of female freedom from the abusiveness of husbands who exerted control over them by various means, especially financially. These women worked and although their salaries were not as high as their male counterparts, they were able to survive on what they did bring home after taxes.

The patio parties were one place the girls flocked to particularly because the drinks were free and they got to meet men to talk and dance with. The women knew these men were married but didn't care, because they came and went according to their traveling needs and both male and female found companionship in each other.

Problems only surfaced if the camaraderie went beyond friendship and into an affair, which did happen to more than one of the women. Carmella was one who fell in love with a good looking airman from Texas named Chad Wilkins, who told her his wife had died recently of cancer leaving him with two little girls. He promised her that they would have a life together when things at home settled down and his daughter's grief over the loss of their mother faded.

Carmella and Chad traveled to nearby attractions when he was in town for extended periods of time, but she missed him terribly when he went back to Texas.

"What a great couple those two make," Marie stated to Jackie.

"If she moves out of town, we sure will miss her," Jackie answered.

"Well, seeing as how we intend to leave the area anyway and head to Florida, we'll not be that far from her which means we probably could make a trip to Texas now and again."

Chad had given Carmella his phone number and although she had never called him before, she was feeling lonely one evening, so she decided to call him.

"Hello," a woman's voice answered the call in Texas.

"Is this the Wilkins' residence?" Carmella asked quizzing.

"Yes, it is," the voice replied.

"Is Chad there?"

"Who's calling?"

"My name is Carmella, his girlfriend calling from New York. Who am I speaking to?"

"His wife," was the answer.

"He told me his wife is dead."

"Nooooo, I'm very much alive," she answered.

Both women were in shock, crying at the same time. Neither one of them could speak.

The wife got her composure first and started asking questions.

"What did he tell you? That I died? Having an affair is one thing, but claiming I was dead is another. My God, how do I live with him after this and with two little girls and another on the way?"

"What, another on the way? I am so sorry to cause you pain. I'll never bother you again," Carmella replied. Then she hung up.

Carmella's phone rang but she didn't answer it believing it was probably the wife calling, and she had no intention of listening to her crying because she was in shock and crying herself.

But why did he give her his phone number she asked herself.

She didn't go to work the next day faking sickness. Her nerves were shot and she knew she had to compose herself before facing the workplace, her girlfriends and co-workers.

She did call her best friend and while talking to her, Carmella cried throughout their conversation. Even though her friend tried to console her, her efforts proved fruitless, but she knew Carmella's strength would carry her into acceptance and she would go on with her life.

When she returned to work, her phone rang.

"It's me, Chad," he said.

"Leave me alone," she answered. "What a piece of work you are. I never want to hear from you again. How could you lie about your wife?"

"Let me explain, please. I love you!"

"Tell your wife that and leave me alone," Carmella answered.

After a few tries, he gave up and stopped calling her. He never returned to Sim-U-Flight and she never heard from him again.

Could it be another wife called her husband's boss, turned her husband in, and caused a "never return" to Suttonville again?

Other military and civil servant program managers traveled to Sim-U-Flight during the "quiet" period in Marie's life. She had no compulsion to have a tryst with another probable lover and that's when Major Don Ellis entered her life. He had flown many missions as an Army helicopter pilot in Vietnam. He was a strappin, handsome, six foot, brown haired, blue eyed, olive skinned, charismatic, cool customer who decided he wanted to bed her the moment he laid eyes on her. And so, like he was trained, he waited for the opportune time to make his move.

That time came at one of the soirees hosted by Jackie to which he was invited. This party was a special one in that it was semi-formal, so the divorcees got together and decided to wear long dresses. Marie's was Kelly green with a small cutout in the middle of the bodice in which some cleavage could be seen. She had her blonde hair fashioned in a French twist, her makeup applied perfectly. She was a knockout turning the heads of all the guys who attended which caused Major Don to move in sooner than he had anticipated.

He approached her as she was standing near the bar nursing a scotch and water.

"Hi, my name is Don Ellis, and from what I'm observing, you're the belle of the ball tonight," he said.

"Thanks," she replied. "But do you say that to all the girls you approach?"

"Only the beautiful ones," he answered.

"Well, at least your honest," she laughed.

"I'd buy you a drink, but you already have one, and seeing as how they are on the house anyway, maybe you would let me buy you one another time?" he questioned.

"Maybe," she said. "But not tonight."

"OK, then how about dinner tomorrow night?"

"There's a going away cocktail party for one of the secretaries who is leaving and moving to Florida," she said. "It's gonna be in the Patio Yard, but it's not private so I suppose you'd be welcome. Beside the marketeers will be there and will be happy to buy you a drink or two, so why don't you show up around 5?"

"That I'll do," he said. And he moved on to circulate among the other partiers.

Her friend, Jackie, came up behind her and whispered, "Sooo, what's goin one with the hunk?"

"He asked me out for dinner," Marie answered.

"Well all the women have their eyes on him, so if you think it's worth it, awareness of that fact should be noted."

"Nah," she answered. "I told you enough is enough in the romance department. He's harmless, and if he so desires, let him chase someone else."

The Patio Yard was filled to capacity the next evening. Drinks were flowing, friends were laughing and dancing and sure enough Don showed up at 5 sharp.

Heading toward Marie, he smiled and said, "How about dinner after?"

Standing next to Don, one of the marketeers, Frank Smith, overheard Don's request and remarked, "We're springing for a goodbye dinner for Veronica tonight here in the restaurant and, of course, you're invited. OK?"

Am I ever gonna get this woman alone, thought Don. He agreed to attend the dinner, but only if he could be seated with Marie.

After being seated and ordering a Martini, they talked about his military career. He commented on the fact that his helicopter had seen a lot of fired upon damage; that he'd seen a lot of wounded and dead soldiers, some of which he flew into the jungle and carried out under fire while piloting his copter. He showed her a card he carried that depicted a cross-bones and skeleton logo with a "EXECUTIONS FOR HIRE" on the front of it which gave Marie a chilled feeling.

They danced for a while, had a couple more drinks and she ended up accompanying him to his room. They removed each other's clothes and as he laid her down on the bed, she became fearful, for as he started caressing her, he became rough holding her wrists too tightly down on the pillow. There was no foreplay. He appeared to be in an attack mode and it scared her. She knew she had to get out of there and, panicky, started thinking of how when she turned her head and saw the message light flashing on the phone on the nightstand.

"Your message light is on," she said.

"Forget it," he answered.

"It could be important."

"What? Oh! Shit! Right. The baby was sick when I left the base. Wait a minute while I call and check on her."

"*Baby?*" Marie thought. *What a son of a bitch. I'm out of here.*

"I need to go to the bathroom," she said. While he dialed with his back turned away from her, she quietly picked up her clothes and tiptoed into the bathroom, hurriedly put her clothes on, opened the door, and as she slipped out into the hall, she heard him say, "Yes, Tylenol, call the doctor then call me back. I love you too."

After hanging up the phone he waited for her to come out of the bathroom, then noticed that the door was partially open, so he called her name. When she didn't respond, he walked to the bathroom and pushed the door open to find no one there. He was naked so he didn't go to the door leading to the hall but even if he had, he wouldn't have seen her anyway as she was running two stairs at a time down the stairwell, through the lobby and out the front door.

Even though it was late, she drove to Jackie's house, saw the lights on and tapped on the door window.

"I'm a shaken mess," she said when Jackie answered the door.

"What happened?" Jackie asked.

She told her what happened and added, "God, I had to think fast. I don't know what would have happened if I had said, 'Forget this!' to him, and I know nothing about rough sex, but there is no doubt in my mind that if it had continued, there definitely could have been some violence to it. I never want to even see that maniac again."

Think she learned?

THIRTY

Things were quiet for a time. Marie was content to go to work, golf, and stop for a nip after work with her friends before going home to her teenage kids.

And who should appear shortly thereafter but Jacksonville Jeffery, in for what he thought would be the final acceptance on a Navy simulator for which he was a computer programmer.

This time he and his shipmates stayed at the Hansen Inn as he was looking forward to bumping into Marie in the lounge, but decided instead to look her up in the plant even though he didn't need to report until the following day.

Dressed in his khaki uniform he approached her while she was sitting at her desk typing.

"Hi!" was all he could say. He was nervous and decided the best way to broach a conversation was to say as little as possible hoping she would give him a comeback for an opening dialog between them. Plus, it was possible that in the time since he had last seen her, she was seeing someone else.

"Oh! Hey," she answered back. "How ya doin'?"

"Good. I thought I'd stop by and say hello."

"Glad you did," she answered.

"Uh, do you think you will be stopping to see Jackie after work?" hoping the answer would not be, "No, I've got a date."

To his delight, she said, "Sure. Are you going to be there?"

"I'm staying there," he answered. "I stopped in the plant to let them know I arrived and would be reporting tomorrow morning for the setting up of acceptance testing," he lied.

"Well then I'll look forward to seeing you later," she said.

"OK, later," he answered and as he walked away, he felt like jumping up and clicking his heels together. Couldn't, so he put a big smile on his face and left the building.

"Guess who's here?" she asked after he left and she called Jackie.

"I know," Jackie said. "He stopped in here right after he checked in. Wanted to know anything about you I could tell him. I think he was fishing for info on whether you were seeing someone or not. I didn't tell him anything. Not even that you were divorced. Gotta go. See you later."

He was nervously waiting for her in the Cooped Up lounge when she arrived. She'd had stopped in her friend's office beforehand searching for information about what he said to her.

He had positioned himself facing the doorway to the lounge and sprang off the barstool to greet her when she entered the room giving her a hug and a kiss on the side of her cheek. Their conversation was casual for the first few minutes. He couldn't wait to let her know that he would be in town for an extended stay.

"I'm here for at least a month," he said while searching her eyes for an expression of any kind. He needed to know if it would please or displease her. To his delight, she smiled and said, "Geez, that great."

A need of this narrator to express Marie's personality, if the reader hasn't already gotten a clue, is that she loves everyone and until she is used or abused, doesn't look for the negative in people she befriends and even when it becomes visible either by omission or deed, she has a hard time believing it.

And so another relationship started for Marie with a sailor named Jeffery.

She told him that she had gotten a divorce since last seeing him; that she had met and lost someone she'd fallen in love with, and even though it didn't work out because he had small children, she was fragile emotionally and did not want another involvement.

"So can you and I be friends?" she asked.

"Absolutely," he replied, although he wanted more than that. Still, he decided to let the friendship take its course to wherever it was meant to go and was delighted just to be in her presence.

Although he wanted her sexually, he didn't want to scare her away, so they met often after work and sometimes for lunch enjoying each other's company.

Halfway through his stay, he had a three day weekend and asked her to go on a weekend trip.

"We'll get two rooms if you like," he said gingerly. "Or we could make the trip in one day and return."

His sensitivity and kindness toward her was starting to mellow her broken heart, but she held firm and told him she needed to return home the same day, not wanting to leave her children overnight.

"Oh, hey, I understand," he said disappointed.

Fall was returning to the northeast on the day they traveled the interstate in late September. Red, orange, yellow and henna colored leaves lined the highway making the view of the mountains breathtakingly beautiful.

During their stroll through a museum, he gently took her hand and she did not resist. He directed her to a nearby wooden bench and when they sat down he said, "Do you know I'm falling in love with you?"

Saying nothing, she turned her head away from him not wanting him to see tears welling up in her eyes.

When he turned her face to his, he kissed away the falling tears and said, "My God, the pain you must be going through. I had no idea you were so hurt and I'm sorry for what he did to you, but if you'll let me, I'd like to help you through it."

He took a tissue from his jacket and wiped away the tears that kept coming, that he couldn't stop any other way, and taking her in his arms held her tightly until the sobbing stopped.

Faced with his tenderness, at this point, her resistance was down. She believed that he was sincere when he told her of his love, but she didn't think about loving him in return. She felt depleted emotionally and knew she needed someone to care about her, needed his affection, so she slowly put her arms around him in an embrace that ended with a kiss; one that although not sexual, was pleasurably exciting.

When they returned to the Hansen Inn, he asked her if she wanted to come up to his room; she declined.

"I think you should know that I've been there, done that before and it led to emotional suicide, so no thanks."

"It's alright," he said. "But I need to get you home."

When he dropped her off in her driveway, her son was looking out the window.

"So how was your trip?" Derek asked smiling.

"It was a nice getaway."

"So when do we meet him, Mom?" Derek asked.

"Oh, I don't know if it's that important. He's only here for a little while."

Because she was still upset about losing Clark, she wanted to close the discussion. She changed the subject, asking her son about school.

The following Monday, Jeff came to see her asking her to go to lunch with him. They ate in the cafeteria; fellow employees catching glimpses of them at a table in the corner that none of them dared to sit at knowing they were invading the couple's privacy - while at the same time making snide comments about the affair which, although they didn't know it, hadn't been consummated yet.

Not wanting to push her, Jeff asked, "What's on for tonight?"

"I'll pop in the lounge for a happy hour drink with you after work," she said.

He still had somewhat of a problem with jealousy and didn't want her to get there ahead of him as he had to work later than quitting time.

"Tell you what," he said. "Why not go home and I'll pick you up at your house. We can stop at another place for a drink, maybe have some dinner. What do you think?"

She didn't want him to meet her kids and wanted to drive her own car. She made another suggestion, "No, I'll go home first then meet you in the lounge. Call me when you're ready to leave the plant."

Although disappointed, knowing that if he didn't agree, he'd lose out, he settled for her offer.

Realizing that she was starting to have feelings for him, she cautioned herself about those feelings not wanting to go through the pain of loss again.

Jeff hurriedly completed his assessment of the day's labor and quickly left the plant for the motel where after showering, he called her saying he was in his room and would be in the lounge in a few minutes.

Over the next few days their relationship remained platonic. If they continued to see each other, making love was bound to happen, but Jeff had a very personal reason not to rush into sexual rendezvous and was trying to decide how to tell her about it while waiting for her in the lounge.

It took a lot of thinking and courage but he managed to confront his problem, so he asked her to sit at a table in the back of the room.

"I haven't pushed you for sex, but it isn't just because I am afraid you'll run," he whispered. "There is another, more personal reason I've backed away." Squirming in his seat, his eyes wide open and full of apprehension, he said, "Uh! It's hard for me to express this to you. I'm just as proud as the next man when it comes to my manhood, but I need to tell you that my penis is very small, even with erection."

There, he thought, it's out.

Her eyebrows arched as she tried to comprehend what he had just revealed to her. She didn't want to further embarrass him by a shocked expression, so she put a blank look on her face.

"Do you think that matters to me?" she asked. "You have children, so it couldn't be that bad."

"I have to work harder than the next man to satisfy a woman and am exhausted after climax. I just wanted you to know, for if and when the moment in time comes for us to make love, you won't be disappointed."

"Intercourse doesn't start with the sexual organs," she replied. "It starts in the brain. I can count on one hand the number of times I have not climaxed, so don't worry about it. Why do men have to prove their masculinity by their sexual prowess anyway? Women give sex for affection. Men give attention for sex which makes both of them content.

Jeff's expression was ecstatic. He knew at that moment that it didn't make any difference to her. He also knew that he loved her and didn't want to let her go.

Acceptance testing of the simulator wasn't going well. Jeff knew he probably would be called back to Jacksonville soon. There were too many glitches that Sim-U-Flight needed to work out before testing could continue. He knew he'd come back eventually when the problems were worked out but also knew he'd be leaving soon… leaving her behind.

The call to return came the following week. They met for drinks and dinner and enjoyed the evening. He told her after they ate.

"I've been called back. The testing isn't going well," he said.

"Oh! No," she replied. "I knew it had to come to an end, but I thought we'd have more time before that happened. When do you have to go back?"

"In two days," he replied sadly.

They went to his room after dinner and some dancing in the Patio Yard Lounge.

He was extremely anxious about his ability to perform, fearful that he may not be able to satisfy her. That anxiety faded once they disrobed and he slowly moved her toward the bed while at the same time he covered her with hungry kisses about her lips and throat.

She responded to his lovemaking, energetically feeling the moisture. With his hardness he entered her and although she was aware that he did have to work at it, they climaxed together keeping their bodies intact for a few seconds after their sexual conclusion.

Neither one of them mentioned his concerns; there was no reason to and his satisfaction at being able to reach that completion for himself as well as her felt blissful to him.

In their nakedness, they rolled over on the bed and held each other's hand for a while before she said, "It's getting late, and I need to go home."

"I need to tell you something," he said.

"Don't," she responded. "I know what you're going to say, but it will only make it harder for us when we have to say goodbye."

"No," he said. "I have to tell you that I love you and that I will find a way for us to be together. Do you think this was just a one night stand? That I go to bed with every woman I meet? I've got you so under my skin that I can't let you go now, so be patient with me. Let me work some things out."

"You know that as soon as my daughter graduates, we're leaving for Florida," she commented.

"Don't you see? That makes it even better. Just give me time," Jeff said.

She hadn't yet told him she loved him as she was afraid of the word. It was cause for pain, so she couldn't believe he didn't ask her for her love, but she came to realize he believed she did love him and knew that it would take time for her to trust herself to say it.

He walked her to her car, opened the door, and held her tightly before giving her a goodnight kiss.

As she drove away he watched, realizing that his eyes were moist, but couldn't remember crying.

They saw each other the next day and night before his scheduled departure. When she left him that evening he asked her not to accompany him to the airport the following morning.

"It's easier to say goodbye here in my room," he said.

She agreed. After a romantic evening, he walked her to her car once more and watched her drive away. This time, they both tried to cover up the tears they found difficult to hide.

On his return flight to Jacksonville, his mind was fixed on thinking about her and how he wanted to be with her for the rest of their lives.

He was able to get a military long distance line now and again to call her. A call one morning in November resulted in someone else answering her work phone.

"Is Marie there?" he asked.

"No, she's out sick; has something to do with her lungs, but I'm not sure what. Can I take a message?"

"No," he replied and hung up.

"What's wrong?" he asked concerned when she answered her home phone.

"Oh! I have pleurisy and have to give my body freedom from all activity for the a week," she said. "There is no medicine, but rest, so here I am on the couch watching the idiot box. I'll be OK, so don't worry about me."

"Now, see, if I were there, I could baby you - take care of you," he said.

"My son is running errands for me, so don't worry," she answered.

She didn't want him to know that she was worried because she had no sick time and would be docked for lost time and had only fifty dollars in her wallet.

They talked for a while. He could tell she was getting tired and didn't dare stay on the line too long.

"Ah, love you," he said with his Texas drawl she loved to tease him about.

"I love you too," she said surprising herself, wondering where that comment came from.

"I knew it, I knew it," he replied laughing.

"Oh, that just came out. I guess I mean it," she said.

Her bed rest albeit on the sofa, was just what the doctor ordered, and although she was cautioned not to, she went back to work before a week was up. Jeff wrote her love letters often and she replied with affection as she was still too afraid of expressing love. As far as she was concerned, men leave; pure and simple, hence the hesitation in expressing her love for him.

A month later, he was able to get a line and called to tell her he would be back at the end of that week.

"I pushed Sim-U-Flight for this return," he said excitedly.

"I tried to find any information about the readiness from the program engineer, but got nowhere," she said. "So, I'm so happy to know I'll be seeing you that soon."

When his plane landed at the airport, he thought of calling her, but seeing as how it was early afternoon, he preferred to surprise her with a visit to the plant.

Hurrying down the aisle of the engineering wing, he stopped at her work station to find it empty. Searching the vast area, he noted her standing at a technical writer's desk talking with him. Jealousy started to climb into his thoughts, but he knew he had no right to question her, so he went and sat on her secretary chair and waited.

She entered her work area and saw him sitting on her chair, but knew she couldn't jump for joy upon seeing him - couldn't put her arms around his neck and kiss him - so she calmly walked up to him and put out her hand to shake his at which point they both laughed. They kidded no one because practically everyone knew that they were romantically involved.

Her boss, noticing the scene being played out outside his office, stood in his office doorway, said hello to Jeff and then to Marie, said, "Did you finish the specifications paperwork I gave you this morning?"

"Yes," she answered. "It's on your desk, your IN basket."

"Well, then, why don't you go on and get out of here early."

"Really?" she asked.

"Yeah," he said smiling.

Overjoyed, she tidied up her desk and Jeff and she left the building and headed for the motel.

He hadn't checked in, so while doing so, she went to Jackie's office to chat with her best friend.

"Do you know what you're doing?" Jackie asked.

"Whatdaya mean?"

"He's married. You've been down this road before. I'm just afraid you're gonna get hurt again."

"Nah!" Marie answered. "Like I said before, this can't go anywhere. Long distance love affairs peter out, pardon the expression."

She didn't know the news he brought with him at the time of her discussion with Jackie and would find herself in an uncomfortable position when she did.

"I've a asked Julie for a divorce," he said when they were seated at the bar having a cocktail.

"Oh! No," she replied. "I've been through this before and lost. Why did you do that?"

"Because I love you and want you to be my wife," he answered.

"What did Julie say?" she asked.

"She asked me if there was someone else," he said. "And I told her no, that we haven't been getting along for some time now and I think we should part."

"Did you tell your girls?"

"No, I'll leave that for later, although I think they know something is wrong. I've been sleeping on the sofa since asking her," he stated.

"Are you sure you want this?" she asked.

"I know I love you and want to spend the rest of my life with you," he answered.

"Did you assume I wanted the same?" she asked.

"Was that presumptuous of me?"

"Probably not, but I didn't expect this, so I don't know how to react. I mean although I knew it wasn't a one night stand, I didn't think it could possibly go anywhere what with you being married. I think it's time you met my kids, but I don't want them to know anything about what you have told me; not yet, " she said.

"Why not come get me this Saturday, meet the kids and we'll go for a ride somewhere after."

She told her son and daughter that she was seeing someone and asked if they wanted to meet him to which they both answered, yes, so on Saturday morning, Jeff came to the house and met Derek and Cheryl. After introductions were made, Derek said he had a baseball game to play and left the house.

Jeff was sitting at the kitchen counter having a cup of coffee when Steve appeared at the front door, rang the bell and stepped into the living room which made Marie extremely unsettled not knowing how he would react to another man in the house he shared at one time with her. He hadn't called to say he was coming and arrived unexpected. Upon hearing her father's voice, Cheryl ran down the hallway to greet him. Jeff, not wanting an embarrassing situation to escalate, got off the bar stool and place his coffee cup in the sink but didn't turn his head either right or left for recognition, but he wanted to make sure that Steve realized there was a man in the house.

Upon seeing Jeff in the kitchen, Steve angrily flew out the front door with his daughter following him. They got in his car. He backed out of the driveway leaving rubber on it and drove away.

Fifteen minutes later, Cheryl, crying, rushed through the front door and ran down the hall into her bedroom slamming the door behind her.

Marie ran to the door and said, "Let me in, honey. What happened?" to which Cheryl said, "Go away and leave me alone. You don't know what he said about you."

At that point, Jeff, after asking Marie's permission, knocked on Cheryl's bedroom door and said, "Cheryl, can I come in?"

Sniffling, she answered, "Yes."

He spent a couple minutes with her before returning to the kitchen shaking his head. "She can't tell you what he said," he remarked.

"It's that bad?" she questioned.

"Yes," he answered. "And I think I'd better go so you two can try and sort it out, repair the damage he's done. I'll call you later."

When Jeff left the house, Cheryl came out of her bedroom, threw her arms around her mother and said, "Daddy asked me if you let me watch while Jeff is fucking you. Said you were nothing but a no good alcoholic whore and unfit mother, a real piece of shit."

"Oh, God, honey, I'm so sorry," Marie cried as she held her daughter close to her.

Marie recognized that he had called her filthy names for years which the children had to have heard, but she didn't think he would go this far to get her with their child. His cruelty was beyond her grasp, having never known anyone could be so vicious, but that's what got her a divorce. The judge didn't like the fact that Steve had made similar comments to her son when he was a teenager which caused him to grant her petition for a divorce.

She worked hard to let her daughter know that she loved her and started to spend limited time with Jeff which he understood completely. He was into his second week of assessing the simulator and knew that the company building it probably wasn't ready for acceptance again which meant he would return to Florida only to come back yet another time.

THIRTY-ONE

Steve didn't return the following Saturday and did not send his support payment to Marie, but he hadn't supported the children for the last two months which caused Marie to have to pay only the bills that were necessary: food, electric, gas, phone, and fuel for the car. Her take home check amounted to $116.00 per week.

He had in the past told his kids that she was using his support check to buy drinks for her boyfriends which she denied and allowed the kids to view her checkbook to see where the money was going. Her mother and brother, Danny, made two mortgage payments amounting to $96.00 each to help her from losing the house.

It was getting close to the third month of nonpayment of the mortgage when she called her lawyer for help.

"Frank," she said. "I don't know what to do. He hasn't paid support in almost three months."

"Why didn't you call me?" We need to take him to court for non-support."

"Oh, Frank, I don't want to do that: the kids having to find out. It would devastate them."

"It would devastate them more if you have your house foreclosed on," he said. Knowing that she had planned to move, he asked, "When is your target date for moving to Florida?"

"June," she answered.

"That's two months away, he said. I'll call the bank and ask them to put a hold on the mortgage payments in view of the fact that you're moving to Florida and they will get their money out of the equity. In the meantime, I'm starting proceedings to force your ex to pay back support. It means going back to court and you'll have to appear."

The morning of the court hearing, Marie found herself extremely anxious, especially in view of the fact that she would have to face her ex-husband in the courtroom. She had no qualms about trying to get the owed monies, but she did have a problem trying to act civil around him after he had put his daughter through a traumatic experience when last he came to see her.

The hearing was set for 10 a.m. When the clock approached 10:15, Frank asked Marie if she knew where he may be.

"What time is it?" she asked.

"Ten fifteen," he answered.

She look at her lawyer and said, "Somewhere near D.C."

"You think he skipped?" he asked.

"Yes."

"Well now, his honor doesn't take lightly someone not showing for a hearing, taking his time, so I believe there will be a warrant out for his arrest."

"Oh, no," she said. "The kids!"

And sure enough the documentation was signed and a warrant issued for Steve's arrest.

Promising to call her the next day, Frank left the courthouse. She sat on the bench outside the courtroom shaking and at the same time not wanting anyone to see her upset and emotionally charged.

When Frank called the next day, he had some somber news for her. "The bank will either give you one month to catch up on the payments or sell the house and pay out of the equity, or they will start foreclosure on the property. What you need to do is get Steve to sign a one-time power of attorney for sale of the house."

"How can I do that when I don't know where he is?"

"Is there anyone who would know?"

"Possibly, my mother-in-law," she replied.

"Time is of the essence. I cannot stress that any harder than that. You need to get movin' or you'll lose the house. Try to find him and get back to me. Also, if Steve finds out that there could be a sheriff's sale of the property at the courthouse, he could contact a friend or relative to bid on it. Do you understand the importance of keeping a low profile about getting his power of attorney?"

"Yes," she cried.

And he hung up.

She prayed, knowing that only God could help her now, so she put her trust in God's hands and dialed her mother-in-law.

Choosing her words carefully, she said, "Mom, the house is going into foreclosure and I have to find Steve. He should receive his share of the equity in it. It's foolish to throw it all away."

"I don't know where he is," her mother-in-law stated somewhat indignantly.

"I understand, but if he should contact you please tell him to call me. With his signature on the listing, I'll put the house on the market, and he'll receive his equity."

"OK," she said and she hung up.

Knowing that she broached the subject with care, and that Steve's mother probably had a way to reach him, Marie prayed and waited.

The next day, he called. "What's this about selling the house?" "I happened to call mother and she said you called."

She had to weigh her words carefully so as not to make him angry, and said, "Don't you agree that you should get your share?"

"Well, why isn't the mortgage payment up to date?"

"You haven't paid support. I couldn't keep up with it, so it's going into foreclosure if I don't sell it."

"Didn't your mother and brother help you?"

Answering a question with a question, she said, "Why do you think it's their responsibility?"

Not answering that question, he said, "What do I need to do?"

Starting to breathe easier, she answered, "I need a one-time power of attorney from you to sell. You need to send it to Frank."

"And how do you get that? I'm not going to tell you where I am."

Silence.

He then added, "Put Derek on the phone and get out of the way of overhearing our conversation. I mean it cause if you search and find, you'll never sell that house and never move to Florida."

"OK," she said. "I'll go outside."

She called to her son and after giving the phone to him, she stepped outside the back door. Steve gave his son his address and told him to keep it on him at all times as he didn't want her to know where he was.

Little did he know that she didn't care to know where he was; only wanted to sell the house and get a new life going in Florida.

Steve called Frank, the attorney, to inquire how he wanted the power of attorney to be received.

"You need to send it to me," Frank answered.

"You also need to pay back support out of the equity you get on the sale, so I'm putting that in the contract."

"OK," Steve answered. "I'll see that it gets to you as soon as possible."

And he hung up.

Frank called Marie when he received the package containing the power of attorney.

"Call a real estate agent and sign a contract for a listing for sale of the property. I received the power of attorney and he signed to pay back support. I don't know how you found him but thank God you did cause you were on the brink of losing everything."

"It didn't take me long to figure that calling his mother would do the trick and even though she denied knowing where he was, mothers always know," she answered.

Marie called a former high school classmate, Virginia, who was selling real estate at the time and had the house listed within two days. It was purchased for $13,500 and she listed it for $27,500 which Steve never thought she would get.

There was a contract on the house within a week. Overjoyed, she knew that she would be leaving Suttonville, New York, after the closing; delighted that she could start a new life in Florida; ecstatic that the new life she looked forward to would bring her the contentment she had searched for a long time.

Around this same time, Jackie had put her house on the market after a judge had awarded her full equity in it in her divorce decree. In view of the fact that her ex hadn't supported his family for years and Jackie was their sole support which she could prove, Frank had requested and gotten full equity in the divorce proceedings.

The "sisters" would start a new life in Florida together and join another girlfriend there who had relocated two years earlier, the same friend who had been deceived by Chad Wilkins, the flyboy from Texas.

THIRTY-TWO

Marie hadn't heard from Jeff and knew that upon his return to Jacksonville, he couldn't or didn't start divorce proceedings, but strangely enough, his return to Suttonville occurred the last week of Marie's employment at Sim-U-Flight.

Because she had to have security clearances arranged on her desk at the time of their arrival, Laurie, the receptionist received advance information of traveling clients. Noticing Jeff's clearance badge, she called Marie to notify her of his impending arrival the day before he appeared.

Marie called Jackie. "He's coming back," she said distressed.

"Let me look," Jackie answered. "I don't think he's staying here cause I usually get advanced notice and I didn't get one on him."

"Doesn't matter," Marie answered. "He probably won't come near me anyway."

"How upset are you?"

"Ya know, I don't need this right now. Why couldn't the acceptance wait til next week when I'd be gone? I'll deal with it. What else can I do?" she questioned." Marie had given her notice and was ready for the closing that Friday. A going away party had been set up at the Cooped Up Lounge for both Marie and Jackie, but Friday morning Frank, her attorney, called her at work. "We can't close," he said sadly.

"Why?" she cried trying to steady herself.

"While searching for title, the buyer's attorney found a problem. Recently out of law school and just passing the bar, he's a new addition to the firm where his father is a partner. He's trying to have his father take notice, make a name for himself. He's requesting title insurance which will cost you $200. I need your OK."

"OK, how much does this delay cost me in time because this is my last day at work, last paycheck? I need that money," she asked.

"Three days," Frank answered.

"But that's next week," she exclaimed and started crying. "What will I do with no job and no money?" she sobbed.

"Hang in there," Frank said. "I' m in touch with an insurance agent right now. I'll call you back."

And he hung up.

The weekend would go by very slowly for Marie, for the dilemma of not knowing whether, and if so, when she would be closing had her tied in knots, so Jackie and she went for a ride on Sunday afternoon.

She couldn't figure out why Jeff had not even tried to contact her just to say hello. She was disheartened and was quiet during most of the ride until they passed what they recognized was a rental car on Main St.

"That's Jeff in the car," Jackie said.

"What?' Marie asked.

"Jeff and someone driving just passed us," she answered.

"Turn around and follow them," Marie said.

But before Jackie could find a place to turn her car around, she noticed that the rental car with Jeff and another man in it was behind her, so she kept going and turned off to the right when she noticed the rental turning into the driveway of a second rate motel that was sometimes used by traveling clients when their stay was extended for long periods of time. The reason being that it was less expensive to lodge there than in a first class motel such as the Hansen Inn.

"He's staying at the Colony," Jackie commented.

"Why?" Marie said. "Because of me?"

"I don't think so," she said. "It's just cheaper to stay there."

He hadn't stopped at the Hansen Inn, not even for happy hour when others traveling with him had, but there was a reason why that Marie would find out about in the future.

The girls stopped at the Front Door lounge for a glass of wine. While Jackie went to her office to check her mail, Marie walked back to the Patio Yard just for old memories sake. She sure had enough of them, but one was particularly funny and happened on a Sunday afternoon in January; a time of year when northeasterners didn't venture out of their homes except to the local corner bar to watch football, shoot the breeze and drink.

Staying at the inn were two air force enlisted men in town for another acceptance. The Patio Lounge had a steam room; the men and women's separated but sitting side by side of each other.

Jimmy was a brown eyed, brown haired, heavily built, muscular man, who stood six feet tall, had a crew cut and could drink anyone under the table. His sidekick, Fred, was thin, although muscular, six-two, but with grey hair and big blue eyes.

Although married, they both had girlfriends they "saw" when they were in town, but for some reason the girlfriends were off doing something else, so they decided to spend the afternoon swimming and going into the sauna.

On winter Sunday afternoons the divorcees could be found spending time in the Patio Yard gossiping, swimming, using the Jacuzzi and sauna, so it wasn't surprising that the gang was all there enjoying a couple of beers with the flyboys when the guys suggested they all get into the women's sauna (swim suits on, of course). Florence Nightingale, the company nurse, had had a snootful of scotch and took it with her into the sauna. She tipped her glass over onto the coals from time to time causing them to steam.

There was a small six inch by six inch window in the door of the sauna where one could see in or out. With all the laughter and joke telling going on inside the sauna, no one noticed that the door handle was moving. Turning toward the door which was locked from the inside, Marie noticed an older woman trying to peak through the window on tippy toes.

Jumping up off the bench, she exclaimed, "Oh! Shit! There's an old woman trying to get into the sauna. Be quiet! I'll see if I can deter her into the Jacuzzi."

Opening the door and leaving just a small space to squeeze through, Marie stepped out of the sauna and found herself almost nose to nose with the woman.

"It's not working," Marie said.

"It was before," the woman said while trying to glance around Marie into the sauna.

By this time, Fred had placed his towel over the inside window so that nothing could be seen, but Florence could be heard laughing.

"I know. I just tried it and the coals won't heat up," Marie said. "Why not try the Jacuzzi for now. I'm sure they'll have the sauna fixed soon."

The woman walked away in a huff and headed to the Jacuzzi while Marie stood against the door of the sauna trying not to laugh.

As soon as the woman disappeared behind the flagstone wall in front of the Jacuzzi, Marie opened the door of the sauna and said,

"She's gone. Get the hell out of there." The flyboys ran to the men's locker, and Marie and Florence ran to the women's.

Because they didn't want her to get in trouble with the owner of the inn, they decided not to tell Jackie. During the time they were cavorting around, she remained in her office going over her recent mail at which point her boss came by and they were brainstorming ideas to bring in more business. They saw her again when they dressed and headed to the bar where she joined them.

THIRTY-THREE

"So, Ma, are we moving, or not," her son, Derek asked when she came home from her outing with Jackie.

Not wanting her children to worry, she commented, "Yes, Frank is working on getting title insurance. He'll call tomorrow. We'll close." But she wasn't sure if the statement was true.

A week before, she held a garage sale and let the kids handle the transactions and reap the monies received from it. There was an above ground pool in the back yard that looked like it was ready to fall down which was held up on the rim by electrical tape. Figuring they needed to let off some steam, she told them to let the water out, take an axe and demolish it which they did; the remains were set out to the curb for pickup.

Monday morning, Frank called to let her know that he had been successful in obtaining the title insurance and the closing would be in his office the following Wednesday afternoon at one o'clock.

"What are your plans for leaving town?" he asked. "Are you leaving right after closing?"

"Do you think the new owner will allow me to stay in the house a couple days as I had to cancel the movers and need to reschedule?" she asked.

"I'll call their attorney and get back," he said and hung up.

"Good news," Frank said on his return call. "The new owners said you could stay for upwards of a week if need be, and they don't want you to pay them for it."

"That's generous of them," she said. "But, I want to get on the road as soon as possible. Carmela has my apartment in Florida picked out. I'll spend a night with mother after the movers pick up the furniture and leave the next morning."

That taken care of, she wondered what she would do about the little dog, a long haired black Dachshund with brown paws Steve had gotten for Cheryl at the Human Society. Concerned about hiding him from the manager in the motel when stopping for a night, she called the vet and asked his advice.

She didn't dislike the dog. They had had other dogs before, but she swore Steve found the most difficult one he could just to be mean cause "Barnacle" was the most obstinate animal she had ever known. He found a way to pounce on the back door with his paws until it opened so he could get out and chase the kids to school.

Strutting down the middle of the road, cars would beep, horns would honk, and drivers would swear at him to get out of the way, but he wouldn't budge until he saw the driveway leading to the high school. Then he'd cross the road, head up the driveway and stop at the front door, wherein some smartass kid would open it and invite him in, laughing hysterically as Barnacle marched down the hallways looking for Derek or Cheryl.

"Will either Derek or Cheryl Trotsky please come to the principal's office to take Barnacle home," came over the loudspeaker to which the whole school went into laughter, teachers included. Barnacle had broken out again. You have to wonder if he knew what he was doing, helping one or both of the kids get out of school.

It was decided by the vet that doggie tranquilizers would be necessary to quiet him on the twelve hundred mile journey south. Two nights would have to be spent in a motel, so Marie began to put together a plan to sneak him in the room without the manager knowing.

After the movers left, they stood in the living room looking around the house they had shared as a family for fifteen years. No one spoke. It was goodbye to a past life and hello to a future one and although the kids were not as happy to leave as she, they came to understand it was the best decision.

After requesting the power of attorney, Derek had been in touch with his father by phone and asked him if he could come live with him. Because there was no further threat of jail, Steve told his son where he lived and, even though he had a girlfriend, he agreed to take his son in to live with him. He had received his share of equity in the house minus back child support. Steve resided in Boynton Beach, Florida, where he worked for a defense contractor.

Marie closed the door to the home and drove to her mother's house two miles away. She knew the hardest part of leaving was saying goodbye to her mother, but her mother encouraged her to move and get started in a new life.

They spent the evening hours talking excitedly about what life would be like in Orlando, Florida.

"Yeah, Disney World," her daughter said.

"That's for little kids," her son commented.

"We're all little kids when we go to a theme park," her mother joined in.

It was difficult to sleep that night. Her mother noticed that the light was on then off again, so the next time it went on, she when to the room her daughter slept in and lightly knocked on the door.

"Come in," Marie said.

"What's wrong?" Marion asked.

"I can't sleep," she answered.

Realizing that she might be getting "cold" feet, Marion said, "You've made this decision to go and I think it is a good one. I've always believed that you are a strong woman, capable of doing anything you set your mind to. Don't worry cause I know it'll be all right."

"Oh! God Mom what would I do without you? That's the hardest part, leaving you. Even though I know there'll be the three of us girlfriends helping each other, you've always been my rock, my comfort through tough times."

"There's the phone, and I'll come down and see you, so get some sleep. You start a long and wondrous journey tomorrow morning, a new beginning. Know that I will be with you, even though I'm not physically there, I'll be there for you in spirit," Marion added. "I want you to call me each night you're on the road so I won't worry about you and the kids," Marion added. "Tell the long distance operator that you want to speak to Marie Trotsky, person to person, and when I tell the operator that Marie isn't here, I'll know you're safe and in a motel."

The next morning, they got up early and said their goodbyes. The last picture Marie had in her mind was that of her mother standing on the front porch, waving her hand as she backed out of the driveway onto the rural road and headed toward I-81 S.

THIRTY-FOUR

Crossing into Pennsylvania, the threesome started to have a feeling of adventure, not knowing what lay ahead, but Marie was confident that all would be well and prayed for guidance from Above as she sped down the interstate in her old car, two teenagers and an awful rotten doggie.

She knew that because her children didn't have their driver's licenses she would have to do all the driving, so she decided that, if needed, three nights in a motel might be necessary even though she had concerns about sneaking Barnacle into any one or all of them. Still, she had the doggie tranquilizers and would use them in order to keep him quiet.

She had notified her ex sister-in-law, who lived in Maryland, of her relocation to Florida and received a phone call from her inviting Marie to stop for an overnight on the trip south. Marie and her sister-in-law, Lorraine, had a good relationship that didn't expire as a result of divorce from Lorraine's brother, Steve.

Upon arrival at Lorraine's and after the girls caught up, Lorraine invited the family out to dinner to a restaurant that had a revolving dining room located on the top floor of a condominium. The women drank a lot of red wine before ordering as well as after which got them home quite late. When Marie woke the next morning, she had a doozie of a hangover which she knew would make it difficult to continue driving, and although she was invited to spend another overnight while her sister-in-law was at work, she declined and decided to move on down the road, but later than she anticipated.

Marie's head felt like there was cotton in it as they pulled out onto I-95 late the next morning and she felt as though her teeth itched, but she didn't want to complain to her children.

Late that afternoon, her hangover improved some, but she decided to pull off near Rocky Mount, N. Carolina, and headed to a motel she spotted advertised on a sign along the highway.

"Now," she said as she turned around and looked at her daughter, "I think you should stay here with him, Cheryl, and keep him quiet, like down on the floor, if possible, while Derek and I go into the motel and sign in."

"OK, Mom." Cheryl replied timidly. Cheryl had a tough time controlling Barnacle on the journey and, in order to keep him contained, she wore a windbreaker so he wouldn't claw her while raising all kinds of hell in the back seat.

After parking the car around to the side of the motel and out of view of the front desk, Derek and Marie entered the office.

"We need a room for the night," Marie said, fingers crossed behind her back.

"How many?" the manager asked.

"Three of us. Me, my son , and daughter," she answered.

Holding her breath for a question she didn't want to have to lie about, she smiled and said, "How much?"

"$50," he answered.

She gave him a credit card, he gave her a key, and mother and son skedaddled out of the office to the waiting car where Cheryl was having a hard time wrestling with Barnacle, trying to hold him down so he couldn't put his face against the window to be seen by employees of the motel.

After registering, mother and son jumped in the car. Marie hurriedly drove out of the main parking lot and around to the back of the property where their room was located. Reaching the room, Marie parked the car and looked around, searching for anyone who might witness a dog being offloaded out of the car and carried into a room. Seeing no one, she rushed to the door, opened it with the key, looked around again and then motioned Cheryl to hurry toward the room with Barnacle who was wrapped in Cheryl's windbreaker papoose style.

They were hungry and decided to find a restaurant nearby, but before they left, Marie knew she had to get the tranquilizer into Barnacle, so Derek and Cheryl held Barnacle down while Marie tried to put a tranquilizer pill in his mouth to which he growled.

"Derek, put your thumb and forefinger on the side of his snoot and force his mouth open," Marie said, during which time, Barnacle was squiggling and growling and trying to break loose of the grip on him.

"Are you kidding?" Derek said. "That damn dog will bite me for sure if I try."

"He's your dog, Cheryl, so why don't you try to open his mouth while Mom and I get the pill down him."

"Oh! Shit," Cheryl replied, handing Barnacle over to her brother. "Hold him tight."

Suddenly, they all broke out laughing hysterically in unison. Derek lost his hold on Barnacle and Barnacle ran into the bathroom, backed up against the toilet and the tub and growled at them even louder.

"Shit," said Marie. "Someone's gonna hear him, report us and we'll get thrown out of the motel. I know what. Derek, grab your sister's windbreaker and throw it over his head while Cheryl and I squeeze across the toilet and into the tub and grab him at his backside."

"Jeez, Mom," Derek complained. But he got that look from his mother that said without words, NOW, so he headed toward the bathroom, windbreaker held with both hands with his mother and sister following behind him. Two steps into the bathroom, Derek threw the jacket over Barnacle's head and tightened it so the animal could not bite him. He pulled Barnacle away from the tub enough for his mother and sister to throw a bath towel over the backside of Barnacle to control his thrashing about.

The threesome finally got control of him by wrapping him up to his neck in the towel before Derek released the windbreaker. Derek was able to clamp his hand around Barnacle's mouth before opening it, as his mother had asked before, at which point Marie, who had already readied the pill plunger the vet gave her, stuck the plunger in the side of his mouth, plunged, then closed his mouth, held it shut and aged his throat until she was sure he swallowed it.

When they let him go, Barnacle ran into the motel room. Marie called to him with the promise of a "cookie" which he wasn't having any part of, so she laid two cookies on the floor and waited.

It didn't take long. It appeared that the tranquilizer was working, for Barnacle wasn't his frisky self. The family thought it better to wait a little while longer before leaving to go eat. Barnacle sat on the rug stretched out and went to sleep within minutes.

Fearing he'd wake up and raise hell ripping bedding and knocking over furniture, Marie decided on dining at a very nearby fast food restaurant where they ate hurriedly and returned to the motel room.

"Well, the drapes are still hanging," Marie commented. "Let's see if he did any damage. We may have to leave in the middle of the night."

When she opened the door, a docile Barnacle greeted them walking very slowly sideways. It was apparent that the pill worked; his eyes were glassy and, even though she felt sorry for him, she was glad she tranquilized him so he would quiet down and they could go out to eat.

Before the family retired for the night and as promised to her mother, Marie dialed the long distance operator, asked for herself and heard her mother tell the operator that "she" wasn't home to which Marie said, "I'll call back," which reassured Marion that Marie and the grandchildren were safe.

Barnacle slept on the bed in between Cheryl and Marie that night. They took turns putting their hands on his back to let him know that he was loved.

Next morning, Barnacle was back to his normal self. Very early, Marie snuck him out to relieve himself in the open field next to the motel before walking to the manager's office to return the key and check out.

Cheryl and Derek stayed in the room with Barnacle until their mother returned. The car was loaded and they did another "sneak out" only in reverse.

Back on the interstate, the weather was getting hotter as they headed toward S. Carolina.

Even though she knew that she couldn't ask her kids to help with the driving, Marie didn't want to stop again before reaching their destination of Orlando, Florida, so she only pulled over for pit stops and to order fast food to be eaten on the road. They crossed the South Carolina border late in the afternoon and pushed on into Georgia where they had to detour because of road construction.

When she reached the Georgia-Florida border, she had to cross the St. Johns River into Jacksonville. She didn't want her children to know that she had a high bridge phobia. Before she knew it, she entered the ramp leading to the bridge over the river. The bridge elevated two miles feet above the water. It was then that she started to feel her heart race, sweat forming on her forehead, and a shakiness about her hands. And she prayed for relaxation to make it over the suspended bridge.

"Hey, look at the tankers below," Cheryl said. "They're as small as ants looking at them from up here."

This caused Marie to grip the steering wheel tighter. She was afraid to look to her left or to her right and began to feel her lower jaw shake. She didn't speak.

Her son, noticing his mother's discomfort, said, "Shut up, Cheryl."

"Why?" she asked.

"Just shut up." He again stated. "And keep Barnacle quiet."

As she drove over the apex of the bridge and descended down toward the ramp, Marie started to feel the anxiety in her body subside, but was visibly shaken.

"Welcome to Florida, the Sunshine State," the sign read as they crossed into the outskirts of Jacksonville. Marie pulled over and parked the car trying to compose her trembling.

She looked ahead and noticed another bridge and knew she couldn't go through the fear again, but before she said a word, her son, who noticed the bridge also, said to his mother, "I'll drive over this one, Mother," to which she said, "OK."

They changed positions: son - driving, mother - a passenger. Marie sighed a sigh of relief as Derek pulled out into traffic and headed down the road. They needn't have worried because the large expansive silver bridge was not located on the path that would take them toward Central Florida, so Marie, fearing that they could be stopped for some infraction by a police officer, told her son to pull over so she could resume driving.

Cheryl didn't understand what all the fuss was about questioned, "What's the matter with Mom?"

"Some people have a problem with heights, makes them extremely nervous," Derek said.

"Really?" Cheryl asked. "Why?"

Knowing he couldn't help her understand, he said, "Oh, forget it." And it wasn't brought up again, at least not then.

The sun had set as they exited I-4 and took the off ramp toward downtown Orlando and on to SR 50. Looking for the Lakewood Ave. exit that would bring them out to Carmella's residence, they were tired. They knew that the apartment manager probably would not be in his office but didn't care if they slept on Carm's floor, but once they arrived at her apartment, climbed the stairs and knocked on her door, no one answered which caused Marie to sit down and cry. Her son sat beside her, put his arm around his mother and said, "Don't worry Mom, we'll find a motel."

"It's dark and we don't know where to look," she answered. But no sooner had she gotten the words out of her mouth when Carmella drove up in front of the building, honked the horn, got out and ran up the stairs to hug her friend.

"Your apartment is ready to move into, but not until tomorrow, so you guys can flop on my sofa and floor for the night," she said.

"Thank you," Marie answered. "Anything would do right now, I'm so tired…even a kitchen counter."

They all laughed and entered Carmella's residence and flopped on the floor, couch and chairs in the living room.

Although the unwinding of the trip was difficult, Marie finally fell asleep and only awoke when her friend shook her shoulder to tell her she was leaving for work.

"What time does the office open?" Marie asked.

"Nine and the manager is ready for you, so all you have to do is fill out paperwork and you're all set. I'll call you when I get home from work."

After they were shown to their second floor one-bedroom apartment by the manager that morning, they started to offload the belongings they were able to pack before leaving Suttonville. They consisted of clothes, air mattresses, some pots and pans, a stereo player with choice records, sheets, pillows and blankets, a set of golf clubs, toiletries, meds and other necessary items they brought on the journey.

When Marie contracted with the moving company, it was cheaper to have the furniture moved when the movers had a full load, so the expected time of arrival was two weeks after the furniture was picked up in Suttonville. Having been campers, it was not difficult for the family to "camp" in their new apartment.

The first order of business was to go grocery shopping and fill the cupboards and fridge with food. Because Steve was driving up from south Florida to pick up Derek, they didn't need as much food. She knew Steve would not offer to buy dinner that night, so a pizza was included in the shopping.

Steve arrived on Friday night and had to sleep on the floor in the living room with his son. It appeared as though his anger had not abated very much since the divorce for he farted, belched and said fuck in every other sentence all the time he was in their presence, which he knew would exasperate Marie, but she wasn't going to play into it. He was there only for an overnight and she knew she'd be free of his inconsideration and rudeness in the morning.

   Saying goodbye to her son was the hardest thing she had to do early that morning. "I love you, son," she said to Derek as she stood on tippy toes to kiss him, to which he made no reply, and after Steve pulled out of the parking lot she backed up onto the sidewalk, waved goodbye, and cried.

THIRTY-FIVE

Derek hadn't told her, not in so many words, that he didn't want to leave Suttonville, N.Y., the reason being that he was in love with a girl named Candy who he met in high school and had been "going" with for two years, so Marie thought that his indifference to her that morning was caused by his anger over the divorce. He was almost nineteen; Marie wanted a life of her own and she was determined to realize it.

When asked, Cheryl didn't care about graduating from Suttonville High and told her mother that she would just as soon complete her senior year in Orlando, especially since Marie had told her that they couldn't keep the house in Suttonville and would have to sell it and move to an apartment.

Marie kept in touch with her friend, Jackie, calling her a couple times a week until she received word that Jackie's house was sold; she would be closing and arriving in a week.

"I've got your apartment picked out for you," Marie said while talking long distance. "You have a two bedroom in the front portion of the property where kids under eighteen are allowed. "Cheryl and I are in the back, adults only part of the property. The manager accepted her as an adult because she'll be eighteen in a couple of months. I can't wait to see you."

"How's the job situation down there?" Jackie asked.

"I haven't started looking yet. I was waiting for you to arrive."

"Have you looked in the paper?"

"No, not yet," Marie replied.

When they decided to sell their homes and relocate to Florida, neither Marie nor Jackie took notice that the unemployment rate was close of 13%, so they had no qualms about the move and finding a job upon arriving at their new place of residence. They were full of confidence that they would.

Because she decided to wait for her friend to arrive, Marie spent her time getting to know the locations of her new surroundings. She sat by the pool and read while Cheryl enjoyed her own search of the area they would now call home. Marie did start checking the paper for employment opportunities and noticed the ads were sparse even in the Sunday paper, but brushed her concern off in the belief that she and Jackie would find work.

During the wait, she made the call she knew she'd make before arriving in Florida. Nervously, she dialed the number and when the secretary answered she asked for him. "May I tell him who's calling?" the secretary asked.

"Yes, tell him Stella is calling," Marie answered. Stella was her code name; Clyde, his. They were names they used whenever someone other than themselves answered the phone.

"Stella?" he asked breathlessly when he pick up the phone.

"Yep," Marie replied.

"You got here safe and sound. I've been praying for you for months," he said. "Are you OK? When can I see you? Where are you living?"

"In an apartment complex on Lakewood Ave.," she answered.

"That's just outside the Center," he said.

"I don't want you to come to the apartment," she said. "I don't want to upset my daughter, so we'll have to meet when she's not home."

"Yes, I mean I can take time off whenever. You name it," Clark answered.

They agreed to meet at a nearby national restaurant for lunch the following day. He was at the bar drinking a Martini when she entered and almost tripped over a waitress stand trying to get to her. He had tears in his eyes as he put his arms around her and picked her up holding her tightly to his chest.

"God you look so good," he said. "You'll never know how much I've missed you."

"Put me down," Marie replied. "People are staring."

"Who cares. Let them."

He kissed her on the cheek and lead her to a barstool next to his. When she was seated, he ordered her a Martini while keeping his eyes on her face.

"Tell me all about the trip down," he said.

Giving him up to the minute details of her journey to Florida, she noticed that he wasn't wearing his wedding ring.

When she finished talking, she asked, "Where is it?" while pointing to his ring finger. "Did something happen to your marriage?"

"No, I'm still married to Gina, but she insisted I give her my ring for the time being and until she feels comfortable asking me to wear it again," he answered.

"And I show up!" Marie commented. "Look I didn't come here to cause you trouble. Neither one of us needs that in our lives again. I'd just as soon never see you than to see another hurt, but I wondered if we couldn't be friends and put behind us the sorrows we both caused. And while we're discussing it, please don't tell Gina that I'm living here now."

"Yes, to question one and no to question two," he replied. "I want to see you from time to time. And Gina will not find out."

Uh Huh!!!!

They spent two hours together at the restaurant before she said she needed to leave.

"Give me your number so I can call you," he said.

She gave it to him and as he walked her out of the restaurant, he took her hand. Upon arriving at her car, he attempted to kiss her goodbye.

"Remember what happened the last time we did this?" she asked. "Too many people got hurt, so please don't."

Clark backed off. Marie got into her car and drove out of the parking lot and headed home.

A week later, Jackie arrived at the apartment complex and drove directly to Marie's apartment.

"God, it's so good to see you," Marie said. "And how was the trip down? Any difficulties?"

"Not when you consider that I traveled with teenage daughters, a dog and a cat," Jackie answered.

"Let's get you settled in your new home and then we'll have a good gab session," Marie said.

They entered the prearranged apartment and after their daughters left to seek out the area, Jackie looked at Marie and said, "We're not gonna make it," and with that statement, she slid down the wall in the living room, sat on her butt and cried.

"Hey, pal, where'd that come from? Of course we're gonna make it. We've come too far to give up now. You're just tired. You'll be more positive after a good night's sleep."

"But what if we don't?" Jackie asked.

"Look, if we don't find a clerical job, we'll have to search for anything else we can get. Shit, we can wait tables, clean offices. Even though we don't have experience in the working world, we have it in being housekeepers. And don't forget, we didn't come down here with no shekels to fall back on. We're not broke, so let's lighten up and take the girls out to eat when they come back. But most of all, we need to keep our spirits up for their sake. If they were to observe a negative attitude in either of us, it would make them insecure about the move, and let's face it, I don't think any of them wanted to relocate to Florida."

Marie told Jackie about contacting Clark.

"Are you crazy?" Jackie asked. "You're not gonna start that again are you? I guess I knew you'd call him, but I worry that you'll get hurt again."

"We talked about it," Marie said. "The ground rules are made by me and he agreed to abide by them. I didn't ask him for anything other than friendship and I'm confident that I can keep my emotions in check especially because I know he's not going to leave Gina."

They went to a restaurant in a strip mall down the street from their apartments, ate, laughed at the craziness of the journey to Florida from their hometown with its many unexpected experiences, and allowed themselves the luxury of ordering an expensive dessert simply because they could afford it.

Clark called Marie the next day and asked her out to lunch. She figured that she had made herself clear about a platonic relationship, so she accepted his invitation and met him at an Italian restaurant near her apartment.

"I've missed you," he said.

"Don't you understand that our love affair ended before I moved here?" she asked.

"I had hopes that we could rekindle it," he answered.

"In what way?" she asked. "Sneaking around to meet each other for lunch to have a tryst in out of the way motels?"

Clark just looked at her and said, "Any way I can see you."

"No," she said. "I'm here to begin anew and it doesn't include you again, not while you're married, and I don't want you to make it worse for your family by being deceitful to them. I'll always be grateful that you came into my life and helped me with your support to get out of a disastrous marriage, and maybe that was the reason we met. "

Clark had already had one Martini and was more than half way through the second when he pushed his glass across the bar to signal the bartender for a third.

When he looked at Marie, his eyes were bloodshot and glassy. She asked him, "How many of those have you had?"

"The next one coming up will be my fourth," he answered.

"How long have you been drinking this heavy?" she asked.

"Since our affair ended," he answered.

"Does Gina know?"

"You mean about you being here?" he asked.

"No, that you've been hittin' the sauce like this," she answered.

"She mentioned it; said she was worried about it, but I just shrugged it off," he said.

"Are you still taking your blood pressure pills?" she asked.

"Sometimes," he answered.

"Sometimes isn't good enough, Clark," she said. "Your face looks like a candle all lit up. Please don't order another," she begged.

"I won't," he said.

"Are you going back to work like that?" she asked.

"Think I shouldn't?" he answered the question with a question.

"Do you like your job?"

"It pays the bills," he answered.

"Please go home. Don't jeopardize your job."

"Can you drive?" she asked. Another question, she thought.

"Yep," he answered. He never said "Yep," always said "Yes."

Knowing that it was useless to try to reason with him any further, she said goodbye, got off the barstool and tried to leave. He lightly grabbed her arm and she pulled away, turned and left.

My God, she thought *as she walked to her car in the parking lot, the sacrifice he made for me is turning on him and now he has to live with that choice.*

The ultimate sacrifice was imminent.

The need to get the girls enrolled in the nearby high school the following week delayed their search for employment, but after the school year started, they knew it was time to seriously look for a job, so together Marie and Jackie started going through the want ads in the local newspaper. There weren't too many for secretaries or administrative assistants, not even in the Sunday edition, so the few that they found they started calling.

Universal Dynamique, a French corporation that had defense contracts with the U.S. government, had a small satellite office twelve miles from the apartment complex. Marie noticed that they had an ad for a secretary, so she dialed the phone number, talked to human resources, and made an appointment for an interview with Mr. Gordon Blanky for the next morning at ten.

"Good Lord," Jackie yelled after she noticed a particular ad.

"What?" asked Marie.

"There's an ad in the paper for a sales coordinator at a hotel near downtown Orlando. Could I be so lucky to have a chance at it?"

"Don't know," Marie answered. "But God knows you're qualified, so pick up the phone and make that call for an interview."

Jackie looked at Marie with an uneasy stare.

"Now," commanded Marie.

After Jackie hung up from talking to the manager of the Armada Inn which was located just outside of the Naval Training Center, she remarked, "Did you hear that? I got an interview tomorrow afternoon at one with a Mr. James."

The next morning Marie drove to Universal Dynamique and was escorted to the office of Mr. Blanky - a grey-eyed, bald-headed late fifties year old man who stood at about five eight and who was the contracts manager for the company. After being introduced to him, she searched his face for traces of personality and noticed a slight smirk that he held on his right side. He kept it plastered on his face through the whole interview which consisted of many questions about Marie's background in working for a company that received defense contracts from the U.S.

Satisfied that she had the experience necessary, especially since she took shorthand which he liked to use and was an excellent typist, he told her she would be hearing from human resources within a couple of days.

She thanked him and was escorted back to the entrance of the building, turned in her security badge and drove home to tell Jackie of her interview.

"So, do you think you got the job?" Jackie asked. "And what was he like? I mean did you like him or was he an old buzzard?"

"Hard to tell," Marie answered. She told her friend of the smirk and added, "He has a habit of putting his index finger to his front teeth while listening, but, well, I don't know. Probably nothing to get bent out of shape about."

"Good luck on your interview this aft," Marie said. "I'll be pulling for you and waiting to hear good news about it when you return."

The hotel property located outside the base and just north of downtown Orlando had sixty-five rooms, a small banquet/meeting room, and a bar with dining space in it that was open for lunch only, although the bar served alcoholic beverages til closing at 1 a.m.

Upon meeting Jackie, Mr. James, a very tall, mid-fortish, well-groomed man who had hazel eyes and light brown hair, was impressed with her self-confidence. They discussed her experience in selling guest rooms as well as the banquet and meeting rooms and conventions at the Hansen Inn. When she brought up the fact that clients who traveled to the inn in Suttonville, N.Y., were from the central Florida area and worked at the Center, his interest peaked.

"Do you think you could attract clients who come from Suttonville to stay at the Armada Inn?" he asked.

"I have many ideas of how to do that - one of them being to contact them by mail and phone to let them know I have relocated and where I'd be working," she answered. "It would also be a good idea, with your permission, of course, to offer a free cocktail with the mailout to get them to stop by."

The interview continued for another half hour with discussions of suggestions for bringing business to the Armada Inn. It was obvious to Jackie that Mr. James' ownership of this property made him king of it, and she knew he would have to be treated like one early on; that is if she got the job, but that didn't bother her. She knew how to put on the charm and was confident she could handle him. Even though his name was Mr. Fred James, she also knew that she could never call him by his first name.

"I'll call you in a couple of days," Mr. Fred James said as he walked her to the entrance door to the inn.

When she arrived home, Marie was waiting for her call. They decided to go sit by the pool to discuss the job interview.

"So, whatdaya think?" Marie asked.

"I don't know," Jackie answered. "He seemed nice, but for sure he has an ego that needs to be pampered, but I can play that part."

THIRTY-SIX

Marie was the first to get the call. Human Resources at Universal Dynamique called the morning of the next day to offer her the job with Mr. Blanky, but the starting salary was low, so she refused.

"Mom, are you crazy?" Cheryl said. "Is another employer pounding on the door to get you to come work for them?"

"I know what I'm doing," replied Marie. "You wait and see. I'll get a call back cause I don't think he interviewed anyone but me, and I'd really like to know why. I mean, he's a manager. How come he didn't interview from within the company for a secretary to receive a grade up?"

Her answer to that question would be solved shortly.

That afternoon, Human Resources called Marie again and upped the starting salary to where she felt she could accept it and did.

After setting up an appointment for her physical the following day, Marie jogged over to Jackie's apartment to tell her the good news. The door to Jackie's apartment was ajar and when Marie knocked and peeked in, she saw that her best friend was on the phone. Waving Marie to come in, Jackie pointed to the phone with her index finger then made a thumbs up.

All smiles, Marie heard Jackie say, "Yes, I can start next week. I'm looking forward to working for and with you Mr. James," and hung up.

Marie walked across the living room floor and hugged her friend saying, "Did I just hear you say you got the job?"

"Yep, and you, why are you all smiles?" Jackie asked. "You too?" She added.

"We're goin' to work," Marie said.

The girlfriends started their new jobs in their new urban city the following Monday.

Mr. Blanky introduced Marie to his staff as well as introductions to his boss, Jim Lloyd, and his secretary, Fran Collier. Fran was a tall, slim woman forty-five years of age who had blue-grey eyes and wore her long gray-blonde hair pulled back in a bun. She had a southern accent having been born in Arkansas. Marie noticed that Fran's demeanor was one of warmth for she took Marie's hand and held it lightly while smiling at her at the introduction and Marie knew she had a friend immediately.

The day consisted mostly of getting the "feel" of the department. Her desk was in a cubicle that she had to share with two other contracts employees and separated from Gordon Blanky's office by a hallway.

On her second day at work, promptly at 8:30 Gordon Blanky buzzed her and asked her to come into his office with her shorthand notebook to take dictation, which made her slightly anxious because she hadn't taken shorthand in a while and was afraid she may have gotten rusty and would not be fast enough. Her concerns were needless because Gordon took his time to think through his dictation thoroughly and paused between each sentence which gave her time to catch up taking it down if she was falling behind.

Marie knew from previous work environments that the "Mahogany Row" CEOs could care less about a lowly secretary - sometimes speaking, sometimes not - so down through her employment history, she formed friendly relationships with her co-workers, the telephone operators, janitors and cafeteria staff.

She always got to work before starting time and stopped to spend a minute or two with the operators before going to her desk. One day, while having a conversation with Millie, an operator, Millie asked her, "So, how you getting' along with old Gordy?"

"Good, I guess," Marie replied.

"Well that's good to hear cause he can't keep a secretary for more than a couple weeks; he's such a pain in the ass what with his sneaking around and looking over his employee's backs to the point of their irritation. I'm sure that if any one of them could find another job, they would be gone."

"Is that why the company went outside to hire?" Marie asked.

"Yes, even those secretaries who could use the money of moving to a higher grade wouldn't work for him."

"Thanks, I guess," Marie said.

"Hey, doesn't your mother live up north?" Millie asked.

"Yes, but I don't talk to her much cause of long distance rates, but I still miss her," Marie answered.

"You come in early in the mornings and I'll give you a Watts line so you can talk to her," Millie said.

"You would do that for me?" Marie asked.

"Sure, you treat us good and we appreciate it; not like some of the snobs who work here, so yeah, when I get a line, I'll see if you're alone, I mean without that old buzzard around, and give it to you."

"Again, thanks," Marie said.

"I've got one now, so go and call your Mom," Millie said.

No one was in the cubicle so Marie dialed her mother and had a ten minute conversation with her before Gordon Blanky peaked his head in the door and said, "Good morning. Bring your shorthand notebook and come into my office." Marie hung up on her mother but had informed her early in their conversation that should anyone come near, she would.

After having worked for him for a month, Marie understood just what the operators were talking about. He was always snooping around driving his male workers nuts with cut downs about their performance even though their work was high quality. He seemed to get a charge out of annoying them, but for some reason, which would become apparent soon, he didn't cause much friction with Marie.

"We couldn't tell you," Fran Collier said one day in the break room while she and Marie smoked a cigarette and drank coffee. "We didn't know you then, but you seem to be able to keep him content, so we're grateful for that."

"What happened to the others?" Marie asked.

"He picked and picked so much that they all quit and nobody wanted to work for him because of it."

"Then why isn't he picking that much on me?" Marie asked.

"Because he was told by my boss, 'One more secretary leaves because of you and you're fired,' and he knows Mr. Lloyd means it. The old buzzard is a whiz when it comes to contract negotiations, probably more learned than Mr. Lloyd, but his conduct leaves a lot to be desired."

"So knowing what I've just told you, keep it tucked away because you've got an ace you're holding should he start his shit with you."

"Thanks Fran," Marie said.

"Oh, and by the way, Pam Foster, who you met on your first day, and I are gonna stop at the golf course lounge after work. Would you like to join us? TGIF, you know."

"Pam Foster drinks?" Marie said. "I thought she was a goody-goody, wouldn't touch the stuff. Don't swear, bet she's never been laid either."

"Boy are you off base," Fran answered. "I guess you don't know her at all, so why not come and get to know the real Pam?"

"OK," Marie answered.

The women met at the golf course lounge and after talking for a while, Marie realized she had formed the wrong impression of Pam.

Pam was a tall, long brown haired, skinny, twenty-eight year old with green eyes who was from the farm country of Kansas. She had a captivating smile and a voice that expressed true sincerity when she spoke. After a couple of beers, she and Marie knew that they were forming a friendship that would last a long time, but at the time of this narrative it would last a lifetime; the two of them getting each other through the tough times that lay ahead for both of them.

The subject of the "old buzzard" came up in their conversation and Pam reiterated what Fran had already told Marie.

After enjoying another beer, the party broke up. The girls walked to the parking lot and drove home.

THIRTY-SEVEN

Marie was sitting alone by the pool the next morning which was a Saturday when her daughter, Cheryl, opened up the bedroom window and yelled excitedly, "Hey, Mom, somebody's on the phone wanting to talk to you."

"Who?" Marie asked.

"Jeff," answered Cheryl.

And Marie's heart flipped.

Marie ran up the stairs to her apartment, opened the door and saw Cheryl standing in the living room holding the phone out for her mother to accept.

"Hello," Marie said timidly.

"Can I see you?" Jeff said.

"Why?" she asked.

"Because I still love you," he answered. "I just want to see you."

"Where are you?"

"On the base at the training center," he answered.

"Yes," she said knowing she couldn't help feelings about him.

After telling him where she lived, she and Cheryl sat and waited for him to arrive.

"Mom, why do you think he called," Cheryl asked.

"I don't know what he wants," her mother answered.

"Do you care?" Cheryl asked.

"Of course I do. I just don't want to get hurt again."

They heard a car pull up in the parking lot below; heard the car door slam and listened as footsteps could be heard running up the stairs leading to their apartment.

He knocked heavily, and when Marie opened the door, he stood there with a bottle of wine in his right hand. He was dressed in civies.

Putting the bottle down on the floor after being invited in, he looked at Marie, took her in his arms and kissed her before turning to Cheryl and hugging her.

"How did you know we were here?" Marie asked.

"I had a sense of you when you passed through Jacksonville," he answered.

"I mean where in Orlando we lived?" she asked.

"I called information and got your number," he said.

Although her divorce decree permitted Marie to use her maiden name, she had chosen not to until both of her children were eighteen. She didn't want them embarrassed if she needed to sign a document for them.

Cheryl, feeling the need to see her mother and Jeff have time alone, left the apartment and went to the pool for a swim.

"How long have you been in town?" she asked.

"Two days. Two days of horrible anxiety of wanting to call you and being afraid."

"Of what?" she asked.

"That you wouldn't see me," he answered.

"I can't go through this again, especially because I thought I was over you," Marie said. "I don't know what you want."

"I just want to be with you," he said.

"How can that be possible?" she asked. "Are you still married?"

"Yes, but with you here now I can be reassigned TDY to the base here from Jacksonville until my retirement in a few months."

"I don't understand," Marie said.

"I'm going for a divorce," he said. "All I have to do is start the paperwork."

"I don't believe you," she said.

"You will when I return in two weeks with my belongings."

Then she believed him.

Jeff was staying at a motel not far from Marie's house. They decided to go to his room after dinner to "talk" but what they both had in mind was to engage in the sexual pleasure they could give to one another and that they knew they could experience once again.

When Jeff closed and locked the door to Room 144, he turned to Marie and took her in his arms, caressing her with kisses about her face and neck. They removed each other's clothes and climbed into the bed. They needed no foreplay. Only seconds passed before they burst into an explosive organism that left them happily depleted of energy. They smoked a cigarette before Marie left for home.

Cheryl told Jackie's daughters of Jeff's return and although Jackie was seriously concerned for her best friend's welfare, she didn't overly reveal that concern when she saw Marie the next day.

"Well, again, do you know what you're doing?" Jackie asked.

"Probably not," Marie said.

"OK, then."

Jeff left to go back to Jacksonville the next day with a promise that he would be calling Marie as often as possible before returning in two weeks.

Marie went to work in high spirits grinning most of the day before Mr. Blanky noticed that she seemed to be glowing. Even made a couple mistakes on her transcription, so he called her into his office and said, "Is it a man?"

"What?" she answered. "How did you know?"

"You're walking around in a cloud. Gotta be something like love," he said.

"Yes," and she told her of her sailor, but left out the part that he was married and getting a divorce.

Mr. Blanky had another concern that she would marry and be leaving and he'd have to find another secretary. Things were going pretty well for him and Marie, and he didn't want to lose her, but lately he started getting quick with criticizing her over little things he thought she was doing wrong.

He started coming to work earlier in the morning and one day caught her on the phone.

"Who you talking to?" he asked.

She was fearful, not wanting him to know she had a line to talk to her mother, so she lied and said, "a friend."

"Well, get your notebook and come in my office immediately," he said gruffly.

Anxiously, she grabbed her notebook and stepped into his office and sat across the desk from him.

During his dictation, he had a government contracts manual in his lap and couldn't find what he was searching for in it, so he slammed it shut and threw it across the desk and over Marie's head where it hit the wall and fell to the floor.

Angrily, Marie put her notebook in her right hand and heaved it over Mr. Blanky's head where it hit the wall and fell to the floor.

"Oh, shit," thought Marie. "Now I've lost my job."

So, Marie got out of her chair, went behind Mr. Blankey's chair and started to pick up her shorthand notebook saying nothing to him. She turned and started out of his office, but before reaching the door, he said, "Where are you going?"

"To clean out my desk," she answered. "I figure I'm fired."

"Oh no, young lady," he said. "You and I are gonna get along just fine."

"You balledheaded old bastard," she remarked. "You were just waiting for me to counterattack. Let's be clear. You've got a tiger by the tail now."

"And one more thing," she said. "I've been talking to my mother when you've been coming in early sneaking around the department to see what you can catch your employees doin'. Did you know how afraid they are of you? And none of them have the balls to confront you for fear of losing their jobs."

Mr. Blankey just smiled.

As the day progressed, Gordon Blanky felt secure that he would have no problems with Marie; he respected her for standing up to him.

The next morning Marie was talking on the phone with her mother when Mr. Blanky stuck his head in the doorway and asked, "Who are you talking to?"

"My mother," answered Marie with as stern a voice as she could muster.

"Oh well, when you're through talking, bring your notebook and come in for dictation," he said.

"When I'm through," she answered.

"How come you get a line to talk to your mother when those operators make me wait an hour for one to call corporate?" Mr. Blanky asked when Marie sat down in his office.

"If you treated them better, you'd be surprised how fast they could connect you, but you're so damn grumpy, that's the only way they can tell you to go to hell without saying it," she answered.

He smiled and asked her to go to lunch at a nearby steakhouse to which she accepted although she was shocked at the invitation.

She knew there had to be a special reason for his generous offer and found it out when they were seated at a table near the fireplace.

"May I order for both of us?" he asked.

"Sure," was her answer.

He ordered a bottle of German white wine and filet mignon with baked potato and salad for both of them, and she started wondering if he was going to hit on her; the thought was repulsive.

While they were enjoying a glass of the wine, he said, "I guess you're wondering who Greta is; she calls often."

"It's really none of my business," Marie answered. "But yes, I have wondered."

"She's a woman I met when traveling to South Florida on company business."

"You're having an affair?" she asked.

"We started out as friends before it became sexual," he answered.

"I'm surprised you're telling me,"

"It's called trust," he answered. "And I do trust you."

"Why?" she asked.

"You got spunk; you're up front and I don't think you would betray a confidence."

"Your secret's safe with me," she answered.

They discussed the lady he was seeing during lunch, and she started to feel a good relationship between the two of them.

When they returned to the plant, her co-workers were curious about what happened at the luncheon and why he had asked her out at all, but she passed their probing off by changing the subject after giving them an acceptable reason of an apology for his anger when he threw the contracts manual.

THIRTY-EIGHT

The following week, their friend, "Florence Nightingale," was flying in town to spend a few days with Marie and Jackie. They arrived at the airport early to pick her up and saw on the Departure/Arrival board that the plane was delayed an hour, so they decided to go to the Johnny Unitas Bar at a hotel across from the airport for a drink.

Sitting two bar stools away from them at the bar was a middle-aged man who had a dark complexion with thick, wavy, black hair and brown eyes, who could pass for Sonny Bono. He wore a wide lapelled white suit, was shirtless and had a large, long, thick, gold chain that held a sizeable medallion on it where it lay on his very hairy chest. Although he was sitting, it could be determined he was short in stature and appeared to be trying to listen to Marie and Jackie's conversation, but he was too far away to hear any of it, or he would have heard them having a discussion about their past days in a small town called Suttonville, New York.

While chitchatting, Jackie looked at Marie and said, I don't think we have been that promiscuous, do you?"

"Nah!" answered Marie.

Silence.

Marie looked at Jackie and said, "How many have you counted?"

"Seven. You?"

"About as many," answered Marie.

"Did you count the guy you met at the convention in Atlanta during the ice storm?" Marie asked.

"Forgot about him," Jackie said.

"And we have the brass ovaries to condemn men for playing around?"

White suit decided to make his move after hearing the last four words of their conversation and edged his way toward them, slipped onto a stool next to Marie and started a conversation.

"You girls come here often?" he asked.

"No, we're picking up a friend at the airport," answered Marie. And she turned to finish her conversation with Jackie.

"You girls from around here?" white suit asked.

"Yes, we live here now," Marie answered and turned once more to converse with her friend.

"Where you from originally?" he asked.

It was becoming a bit tiresome; his interrupting her conversation with her friend, so she looked him straight in the face and said, "What's it to ya?"

To which he had a shocked look on his face and said, "Oh! I get it," and pointing to Jackie with index finger then back to Marie, continued, "You two. I'd have never believed it."

"Believed what?" asked Marie.

"Ya know, lovers."

Marie, looked back at white suit shocked and started laughing hysterically which caused Jackie to ask, "What's going on?"

"He thinks we're lesbians," Marie answered laughing.

"I don't think that's one bit funny," Jackie said, which made Marie laugh all the harder.

"You mean you're not lesbians?" white suit asked Marie.

"No, Jesus, where the hell you from?" Marie asked

"LA," he answered. "We got a lot of gays out there."

Marie excused herself to go to the ladies room and when she returned, Jackie was sitting by herself.

"Where's Sonny White Suit?" Marie asked.

"That jerk asked me for your phone number. Said he'd like to call you when he comes back to town and I told him to get lost, and he did, but not before he said, "Does that mean you won't give her number to me?"

Realizing an hour had passed, they paid the tab and headed back to the airport to meet Florence. When she got off the plane, the women hugged each other. Florence had a specific reason for traveling to Orlando and wanted to share it with her friends.

"We'll get your baggage and go to my place," Marie said.

"I'm not staying with either one of you," Florence remarked.

"You're not going to a hotel!" Marie said.

"No, that's one of the reasons I made the trip. I've been seeing Stan Franklin. He's gonna pick me up at Marie's and then we're going to a hotel. Stan and Me."

"What?"

"His divorce will be final in a couple months, and then we're getting married," Florence stated.

"Well, I'll be damned," Jackie said. "And when did this happen?"

"He was coming and going to the plant for military helicopter acceptances and, well, it just happened," Florence said.

"Why didn't he pick you up at the airport?" Marie asked.

"I told him I wanted to tell you two, so we decided that he'd meet me at your place," she replied.

"Sure, OK," Marie replied. "He's a great guy."

That being said, they sped away to Marie's to meet up with Stan.

When they arrived, Stan was waiting for them in his car and got out to greet the girls.

"Hey," he said kinda sheepishly.

"You got time for a drink?" Marie asked after greeting him with a hug.

"Sure," he answered.

They climbed the stairs to Marie's place, she opened the door, invited them in and went to the kitchen to prepare a snack and drinks.

They had only one before wanting to leave, and Marie and Jackie could understand why.

"Keep in touch while you're here, Florence," Marie said.

They waved goodbye, pulled out of the parking lot and on to the highway.

Stan wanted Florence to become accustomed to the locale that would become her new home after they married. They did a lot of day trips while she was in the Central Florida area, so she wasn't able to connect with Marie and Jackie again although she kept in touch by calling them once or twice before leaving town, including a call from the airport to say goodbye before flying back to Suttonville.

During her first call, Marie shared with Florence the fact that Jeff had returned into her life, was divorcing and they were to be married soon.

"I hope you know what you're doing," Florence said.

"Look who's talking," Marie replied.

"Yeah, but he's hurt you before and I'm a little leery about him hurting you again, so be as sure as you can that he means it this time, OK?"

"I'm sure it will be all right," Marie said. "He's bringing his clothes and personal things with him. I'll keep you informed."

THIRTY-NINE

The following week upon arriving home from work, she saw Jeff's green Plymouth sedan parked in the lot and parked next to it. She looked around for him and saw him standing at the top of the stairs grinning.

"Hey there gorgeous," he yelled.

"You didn't tell me you were coming today," she said as she climbed the stairs.

Then she noticed two suitcases, two boxes, and his golf clubs on the landing.

"Does this mean what I think?" she asked.

"Yes," he answered. "She's agreed to a divorce and the TDY paperwork is being channeled to relocate me to the base here until I retire in six months."

Marie let out a yelp and threw her arms around him after which she opened the door and they entered the apartment.

"Welcome," she said.

While she was pouring them a drink, he moved his belongings into the apartment.

"We need to find a two bedroom while I'm here," he said. So, they went to the manager and was shown a spacious two bedroom place located in the far back of the complex which they agreed upon to rent.

"I'll sleep on the sofa tonight," he said, "and we'll start moving everything tomorrow morning like the important furniture: the bedroom, living room and television set."

She was overjoyed as she cooked dinner for him and her daughter, Cheryl, who was almost as happy as her mother.

"Do your kids know about the divorce?" Marie asked.

"No, I'm gonna tell them when I go back to finish some work I need to do and pick up my orders," he answered.

Jeff had a week of leave and they took advantage of every second of it going out for happy hours nearby, but mostly reveling in the fact that they were now together and would be married soon.

"When do you want to set a date for the wedding?" he asked.

"You're not even divorced yet, so let's wait til that happens before deciding," she answered.

"OK, but I do want you to do one thing soon," he said.

"What's that?" she asked.

"I leave tomorrow, so go and purchase a better mattress than the one on the bed and buy a wedding dress," he answered.

"OK," she said.

Totally moved into the new apartment, Jeff was anxious to get back to Jacksonville to complete his official procedure for relocation to Orlando.

They kissed goodbye the next morning in the apartment because he didn't want to have to drive away and see the tears in her eyes that he knew would occur.

As he rolled down the window, he yelled "I'll call you when everything is completed and I'm returning for good. And remember, Ah love you!"

He backed out of the parking lot and drove out of the complex heading for the interstate.

She went to the mall, started searching for a long gown the next afternoon and found a plain, eggshell colored one that was priced right and looked lovely on her. Her daughter agreed to stand up for her mother for the wedding, so they found a blue dress for her also. Happily, they left the department store and headed to a nearby restaurant to celebrate.

Marie had asked Jackie to accompany her to the furniture store so the next evening after work, she waited for her to come to the apartment. Jeff hadn't left her any money to pay for a new mattress, but she believed he would when he returned.

Just about the time that Marie wondered where Jackie was, the doorbell rang. Marie opened the door and Jackie stepped into her apartment.

"We'd better get goin'" Marie said as she picked up her purse.

"I have something to tell you," Jackie commented with a long face.

"What's that?" Marie asked.

"Jeff called me today," she answered.

"Oh, about what? The wedding?" Marie asked.

"No, please Marie sit down," Jackie begged.

"What's the matter?" Marie said.

"He's not coming back," Jackie said.

"What? Is this a joke?" Marie asked.

"No, God this is so hard. He's in the base hospital in the psychiatric ward. He had a nervous breakdown when he went back to Jacksonville."

"Well, I'd better get up there and see him," Marie answered. "Is he OK?"

"Not from what I can tell he isn't," Jackie said.

"Marie, listen to me," Jackie continued. "He's never coming back. He said he and Julie are talking reconciliation. I'm so sorry. He also asked me to tell you not to come to Jacksonville," she added.

Sitting down on the sofa, Marie started crying while staring straight ahead and wasn't able to grasp any further communication for a few seconds.

When she was able to assimilate what Jackie told her, she looked at her best friend and said, "How could I be so stupid to have believed him again? I don't understand why he contacted me if he wasn't sincere. I need you to do something for me."

"Anything," Jackie said with tears in her eyes.

"Will you call Julie? I need to know if this is true," she asked.

"Do you have the number?"

Marie found the number and while Jackie was dialing, Marie got on the extension phone preparing to listen.

When a female sounding voice answered the phone, Jackie asked, "Is this Julie Stetner?"

"Yes it is, and who's this?" Julie asked.

"You don't know me, and please forgive me for intruding. I am a friend of Marie and got a call from your husband, Jeff, today telling me that he was in the hospital, and that he would not be returning to Orlando to marry Marie. The reason for this call is that Marie is in shock and doesn't quite know what to believe, so would you be willing to shed some light on it?"

"It's true," Julie answered. "When he returned from Orlando, he started to tell our daughters that we were divorcing and that there was someone else he had fallen in love with that he was going to marry.

Our daughters became extremely upset, crying and begging him not to."

"He couldn't bear their reaction. He started crying and begging their forgiveness to which they replied, 'Never'. At that point I entered the room as the girls were running from it and I found him on the floor curled up a fetal position, sobbing, 'What have I done.'

"I couldn't get him to focus on what I was trying to say to him and called the paramedics who took him to the base hospital where he was admitted to the psychiatric ward.

"I've just come back from seeing him. We had an appointment today with his psychiatrist, who had him calmed down with the help of drugs. He is expected to stay in the hospital for a week, after which we anticipate his medical discharge from the Navy."

"Will you allow me one more question?" Jackie asked.

"Yes," Julie answered civilly.

"Do you two expect to reconcile?"

"Not as far as I'm concerned, at least not immediately," Julie answered.

"Thank you for your graciousness in talking to me," Jackie said. "You won't be contacted again."

The conversation ended, the line went dead, but it wasn't over.

Although it had started sneaking up on her while working for Sim-U-Flight, sneaking at a pace she hadn't really taken notice of, alcohol was becoming more of a habit in Marie's life, but now she was beginning to self-medicate more often to deaden the emotional pain she was suffering with the loss of Jeff, and so she spent the weekend drinking and crying much to the chagrin of Cheryl.

FORTY

When she went to work the following Monday, Mr. Blanky stuck his head in the cubicle to greet her. She turned toward him with tears in her eyes, then turned around and sat in her chair.

"What?" Mr. Blanky asked. "Oh, the sailor?" And he stepped into her workspace and whispered, "Come into my office and bring your notebook and shut the door."

When she shut his door, he asked very frankly, "Did he dump you?"

She couldn't answer him, just kept crying.

"I have my answer," he said. "Get your purse and come with me. We're goin' for a ride."

She did as he asked. They went to the parking lot where his Jeep was parked and after he opened the passenger side door for her and helped her into it, he walked to the driver's side, got into the Jeep, started it and drove away.

He was quiet and drove her through the countryside pointing out the landscaping and what used to be there before the central Florida area starting building up.

She stared ahead.

He pulled into the same steakhouse he had taken her to for lunch. They went into the restaurant, up to the bar and ordered a glass of white wine.

"One only," he said, "and then we'll go back."

As they sat at the bar, he looked at her and asked, "Do you have any of his belongings?"

"Yes," she replied. "I have clothes, military papers, and golf clubs, and I don't know what to do with them."

"Don't do anything right now," he said. "I'll go out to shipping and get the cardboard boxes you'll need to pack them and then I'll take care of sending them back to him for you."

"Why would you do this for me?" she asked.

"Because I don't think you should have anything more to do with him should he come sniffing around again, so the sooner the better we get this done."

They left the bar and went back to the plant but before she got out of the car, he said, "Now, you can choose to go home or stay a couple of hours and if you stay, I won't ask anything of you, but if you go, you'll be running away from a painful situation that could cause you to run from more of them the rest of your life, and let's face it, we all have situations that are hurtful throughout life, so it's up to you to make that decision."

"I'll stay," she answered.

It was going on one o'clock when she walked into her cubicle. She sat down and tried to focus on filing.

At two o'clock, he buzzed her on the intercom and said, "You've been back an hour. Do you want to go home?" to which she replied, "No."

At three o'clock, he again buzzed her and repeated, "You've been at work two hours. Do you want to go home?" to which she answered, "No."

At three-thirty, he once again buzzed her and said "Get out of here and go home, but drive carefully. Ya made it." She could hear the smile in his voice.

She went home and poured herself a vodka, rocks, and sat down trying to figure out how she was gonna pay the rent on the new two bedroom apartment alone and how she was gonna to tell her almost eighteen year old daughter that she had lost again.

At eight o'clock, Mr. Blanky called to ask her if she was OK.

She had a buzz on but wasn't too inebriated and thanked him for his concern, telling him she would be at work in the morning.

When she told Cheryl, her daughter just stood in the kitchen looking at her. Then Cheryl turned around, opened the door and left the apartment not saying a word which made Marie feel all the worse - a reaction, any reaction would have been better than nothing at all, but she couldn't blame her because she didn't feel like much of an example for Cheryl.

Having befriended a male co-worker shortly after her employment at Universal Dynamique, Marie asked him if he could help her move. She was able to convince the apartment manager to let her out of the two bedroom lease and back into another one bedroom, so over the next weekend, she moved into a first floor apartment in the same complex.

A month after moving into the apartment, Marie was home alone one evening when the phone rang. When she picked it up, she heard his voice say, "How are you?" and chills went up her spine.

"What do you want, Jeff," she asked.

"I need to get my belongings and wondered if you were gonna be home Friday night. Julie and I will be passing through Orlando on our way to the Keys," he added.

"You can't come here," she said. "I'll call Jackie and see if see will be home. You can pick them up at her apartment. Call me back in ten and I'll let you know."

"OK," he answered. "How's Cheryl?"

She didn't answer him. She hung up on him.

Although she didn't want to see him, but mostly because she didn't want her friend to suffer any more emotional pain from him, Jackie agreed to allow Jeff to come to her place to pick up his belongings that Friday night. After he left she headed to Marie's to tell her what happened.

"Jesus, can you believe he was asking all about you while his wife was waiting in the car?" Jackie said to Marie. "Talk about balls."

"He told me once when I asked him if he and Julie would get back together that as far as he was concerned, no, because she would never let him live the affair down and would cause him misery for the rest of his life," Marie said.

"They went to the corner bar, ordered a drink and Marie, holding up her glass, said, "Here's to misery."

But it still wasn't over.

The next week, Marie took the wedding gown back to the department store where she bought it and asked for credit on her account.

"Didn't I wait on you when you bought this beautiful gown?" the saleslady asked.

"Probably," Marie answered.

"Did you not get married?"

"He died," Marie said.

"Oh, no, I'm so sorry," the sales lady said. "I'll get you a receipt."

Marie took the receipt, put it in her wallet and left the store.

Cheryl graduated high school in the spring and made application to the local state college, was accepted and looked forward to attending classes in the fall. She and her mother didn't talk much about the heartbreak of the loss of Jeff. Cheryl had witnessed another one between her mother and Clark and although she had a right to her opinion, she kept it to herself.

Shortly thereafter, Jackie met a guy at a nearby upscale lounge across from the motel where she worked and was seeing a lot of him. It was obvious to Marie after having met Leon Morton that he was very controlling of her friend, Jackie to the point of going to the hair salon with her on Saturdays and waiting while she had her hair styled. What was especially disconcerting to Marie was the fact that Leon was determined to take up all of Jackie's time and didn't want her to spend any of it with Marie.

Two times the friends had planned to meet at noon at the motel for lunch, but shortly before noon, Jackie bowed out calling her friend and saying that Leon had called and was picking her up instead. After the second time, Marie didn't try again. She felt that Jackie had a right to happiness and was glad she met someone, but could see emotional risk in the relationship because of Leon's controlling and manipulative ways.

Marie was starting to feel somewhat better about her loss of Jeff. She formed a bond with Pam Foster, her co-worker. She wanted to use a week's vacation to fly to her home town to see her mother and someone had to fill in for her while she was gone.

"You're not gonna' leave me with that old bastard," Pam said of Mr. Blanky.

"It's only for a week. Surely you can take it for that long," Marie answered.

"Not for a damn minute do I want to work for him," Pam answered.

"Well, I'm going to see Mother and you're IT," Marie said laughing.

"Ohhhhhhhhh!" was all Pam could utter.

During that seven day period, Pam called Marie every day begging her to come back early.

"Tell him off. Tell him to go to hell," Marie said. "He loves it."

"I can't do that. Just get your ass back here as soon as possible cause he's driving me crazy - pick, pick, picky," Pam said.

While Marie was visiting her mother, Jackie married Leon and moved to Charleston, S. C. where Leon got a job working for the government. Marie didn't hear from her pal for quite a while, but their friendship would never be broken. The desire and need would arise for the "sisters" to reunite again.

Universal Dynamique, a satellite of the corporate headquarters, found it economically necessary to conduct business in the State of Florida because the company could pay cheaper wages, but the time came when a decision was made to close the plant giving the employees a week' notice, so many of them who had worked for a company in Southwest Orlando found re-employment with Hamilton International, Inc.

At the time they were laid off, government defense contracts at Hamilton had slowed to a crawl, forcing layoffs, but business was picking up at a fast pace, so the company recalled their former employees, many of which had gone to work for Universal at a much lower salary.

Mr. Blanky, some of the contracts employees, and Fran Collier were recalled which made them extremely joyful. A layoff party was held at the local watering hole and although Marie was worried about finding a job, she was happy that her friends had.

Pam Foster found a job in the sales office of a company who contracted with the Navy for twenty-five technicians and two word processors on the base at the Naval Training Center.

FORTY-ONE

Marie found it difficult to find another job and had very little money to fall back on. In a conversation with her mother, and because her daughter had graduated, it was decided that Marie would return to Suttonville, N.Y., especially because there was a temporary job being held for her at General Power, the company she worked for early in her marriage to Steve.

Her daughter started college that Fall and, with the financial help of her father, moved into an efficiency apartment. Cheryl got a job part time working in a department store to supplement her income.

After putting her furniture in storage, Marie put her car on the auto train and headed north to begin the word processing job. She arrived at Marion's home at the end of September and was welcomed by Marion and her husband, James O'Reilly, with open arms.

"I never thought I'd return to live here," Marie said shamefully to her mother.

"Oh, honey, we're so glad to have you back," Marion said as she put her arm around her daughter.

James stood aside his wife and agreed, saying, "We never wanted you to leave in the first place."

Marie knew she only had a couple days before she needed to report for her temporary assignment. She called some friends, but there was no brass band welcoming her back like the going away party held before she left.

Her sister-in-law, Jeanie, called and invited her to meet at the Bird Cage Lounge that Friday night so having nothing else to do, she drove to the lounge and spotting Jeanie went over to greet her.

Jeanie was talking with some employees who worked at Sim-U-Flight - some Marie knew and some she did not - but one she remembered clearly, a guy who worked in Engineering when she was employed there.

"Marie, you remember Bob Vistula, don't you?" Jeanie said.

"Yes, how you doin' Bob?" Marie asked.

"Good," Bob answered. "Thought you moved to Florida."

"I did," she answered, and told him about the Universal closing, the scarcity of jobs in that region, and that she returned to accept a part time possession at General Power, working on a proposal for a contract with the U.S. government that, if awarded, would mean she would be around for a while.

He told her that his wife asked for a divorce, left their house and took his four kids with her.

"I'm waiting for the divorce to be finalized," he added.

"I'm sorry," she said. "How you handling it?"

"Even though I see them on weekends, I miss the kids," he answered. "I can't believe she just up and left like that," and he snapped his fingers.

Marie knew that Bob had a reputation for cheating on his wife and figured she probably got fed up, got a good job and left him, but seeing that he was disheartened, she decided to keep her opinion to herself and remarked, "It happens."

He bought her a drink before asking her to dance.

She wondered how uncomfortable that could be because Bob was six feet tall. He had salt and pepper hair and green eyes. He carried his weight of one sixty evenly throughout his body, and although he wasn't muscular, he was fit, dressed well in sports attire and had a pleasurable personality.

They danced a couple more times before he asked her to go home with him.

After she agreed and on the drive in his car to his house, she looked at him and said, "You know what we are?"

"No, what?" he asked.

"Two emotionally lost souls, hanging on either side of a log that is plummeting down a swollen river," she answered.

"That bad!" he exclaimed.

"I think so," she answered.

Marie knew that when she accepted his offer, sex would be involved and didn't care, but then she didn't care about a lot of things lately.

Probably a one night stand, she thought.

The sex was OK, but the thing about it was that she didn't feel any emotions during it. "No I love you" by either one of them. Some holding, then sleeping and getting up and going to her mother's house or to work.

One night turned into many nights of staying with him for overnights at which point Marie's mother, Marion, became distraught about her daughter's life style and mentioned to her son, Daniel.

"I don't like that she stays with him overnight," Marion said on a visit with her son.

"Mom," he answered. "If you throw her out now, she won't care. There's been too much loss in her life. She's depressed and has hit bottom. All we can do now is support her and pray for her."

Marion decided not to mention her disappointment to her daughter. She prayed to God to intervene and help Marie - her prayer would be answered.

Adding to Marie's despair occurred when the temporary position was concluded, the proposal was finished and delivered, and the contract was awarded to another company outside of Orlando, Florida - Hamilton International, Inc.

"Talk about the wrong place at the wrong time," she said to Bob when she was informed and would have no job.

Bob sat in his Lazy-Boy and stared ahead.

"What?" she asked.

"I don't know how to tell you this," he said.

"Tell me what?" she asked again.

"I've met someone," he said sheepishly.

"What? Who?" she asked.

"You remember Sally James? Works in Mahogany row?" he asked.

"Yes," she said.

"Her", he said.

"Is it serious?" she asked.

"Yes," he answered.

"Well, we both knew this wouldn't last," she said.

"Is that all you have to say?" he asked.

"Bob, we have had one of the most honest relationships I've ever known," she answered. "Never promised anything and that's what made it so. I only have a few things here. I'll gather them up and leave."

"Just like that!" he exclaimed.

"Yes," she answered. "But thanks for being there for me."

And so she gathered her possessions and headed toward the door. He followed her and when she opened the door to leave, said, "I'm so sorry."

"It's OK," and stepping on tippy toes kissed him on the cheek and walked out.

There were no tears as she drove to her mother's house, but when she pulled up in the driveway, she sat in her car for a minute wondering, where do I go from here, a thought that would cross her mind many times in her future.

When she entered the house with her small overnight bag, her mother knew it was over and was grateful that her prayers had been answered.

FORTY-TWO

Her brother, Daniel, called two days later and said he was coming to see her. She loved Daniel so much, especially since he was a priest and never admonished her about her relationship with Bob.

Daniel said he'd be in around happy hour time and take her out, so she decided to eat a piece of chicken her mother had made the day before. After eating half of it, she felt something scratching in her throat and sensed that she may have swallowed a chicken bone. She tried to chase it with a swallow of beer and piece of bread, but it didn't budge. She could breathe and speak, so she called the doctor she went to when she lived in Suttonville.

After telling the nurse what had happened, Dr. Richards picked up the phone and asked, "Marie repeat to me what you told my nurse."

He listened intently before speaking. "I want you to go to the hospital immediately and don't drive," he said.

"No one's here to drive me," she said. ""And I don't have any insurance."

Paying no attention to the insurance statement, he said, "Then call a cab."

"OK," she mumbled.

I don't have the money for a cab, she thought, so she hurried to her car and drove herself to the hospital.

By this time, her throat was so sore it felt like strep throat. She parked in the lot and entered the ER, hoarsely explained her symptoms, and was given a hospital gown. Shown to a curtained section with a gurney in it, she was told to get undressed, put on the gown, sit on the gurney and a doctor would be in shortly.

"I don't have insurance," she said to no one in particular.

An intern came in and told her he'd have to x-ray. Upon reading the x-ray, the doctor saw that the chicken bone was lodged sideways halfway down her throat.

"We have called a thoracic surgeon who should be here shortly," the doctor said. "In the meantime, I'm giving you a Valium to help calm you down." He opened the curtain and left.

The surgeon, an India sounding last name, showed up and asked her questions.

"I know you can breathe and speak, so what we're going to do is give you relaxants in the hopes that the bone will move down into your digestive system and out of your body when you have a bowel movement."

"I don't have insurance," Marie said fuzzily.

Dr. India made no comment and left.

More Valium caused her to feel like she was intoxicated, a happy feeling.

Dr. India returned late that evening to check on her progress of the "passing the bone," but the bone had moved into another position that alarmed him, so it was decided that the Valium was not working and she would have to be taken to the OR to remove it.

Dr. India tried to explain what he needed to do, but in her drugged-like state of mind, she only caught pieces of his explanation.

A bright overhead light and many white masked faces is all she remembered seeing once in the OR before she succumbed to the anesthetic administered to her. Blurry awareness came to her as she began to recover in the OR, but she could move only the index finger of her right hand. The rest of her body was paralyzed. Her eyes were wild and the next voice she heard was, "Knock her out, she's coming to," and she passed out.

When she awoke in a room, she felt tipsy. Her surgeon was standing there; her voice was hoarse, so he told her not to speak while he explained what he did to remove the chicken bone.

"I used a surgical instrument that has a magnified light on it with pinchers much like tongs, to go down your throat and retrieve the bone," Dr. India said.

"But, I was also prepared to go in surgically, cutting into your throat, if need be, to remove it. I didn't have to do that. Do you want to see the bone? We saved it in a prescription bottle."

"NO!" Marie answered.

"Doctor?" she asked. "I don't have insurance and I don't have a job."

"Let's not worry about that right now," Dr. India said.

"Oh! One more thing," Dr. India said. "There were five other doctors in the OR watching the retrieval procedure. We don't get chicken bone swallowers that often and they wanted to witness the viewing of your procedure.

Before her release from the hospital the next morning, Marie was informed that her hospital bill would be submitted to a charitable organization that paid hospital bills for patients who were indigent, but first she had to apply for welfare benefits. The doctor's bill of $900 could be paid in monthly payments when she found employment.

Marie went to the county office where she applied for welfare benefits which were refused because she lived with her mother. When she got home, her mother was waiting for her on the porch and went to greet her as she got out of her car.

"What an experience!" she declared. "Talk about humbling. Mother, there were bums sitting on either side of me while I was waiting to be called to be interviewed. Smell! Did they ever stink? And after all that waiting, I still didn't qualify for welfare. I guess I'd have to be falling down in the gutter and homeless to get them."

"Things will turn around," Marion said.

This would be the turning point in Marie's life - she'd hit the bottom of the barrel!!

The following week, Marie's beautician, Donna, called her.

"Hey," Donna said. "Don't you have a daughter living in Orlando?"

"Yeah! Why?" Marie asked.

"Well, you know Mary Stewart, don't you? Used to live in your old neighborhood?"

"Yeah," and again "Why?"

"We decided to drive her station wagon to Orlando and go to Disney stopping only for pit stops and fast food. Do you think we could crash at your daughter's place?"

"I'll ask her and call you back."

Marie got a message to her daughter through her daughter's employer to call and when Cheryl did, Marie told her of the girls plan to drive down and ask if they could stay with her being that they had no money for a hotel.

"Yes," Cheryl answered. "I want to see you, Mom, and how have you been?"

"We'll talk when I get there, probably late Saturday. See you then."

The three of them started out at sunrise on Friday morning taking turns with driving and drove all day and night, arriving at Cheryl's on Saturday.

Cheryl was pacing on the landing of her second floor efficiency when they pulled up in the parking lot.

Cheryl ran down the stairs to greet her mother. They embraced, hugging one another tightly.

Introductions were made, the car was offloaded and the women sat in the living room gabbing about the trip down.

"We brought sleeping bags and setting them on the floor will be fine," Donna said to Cheryl. "We only got away for three days, so we'll go to Disney tomorrow. Most of our time will be spent touristing the area, so you won't see that much of us and we'll try to stay out of your way."

"Are you going to Disney with them?" Cheryl asked.

"No," Marie answered. "One of the reasons I made this trip is to tell you that there is no work in Suttonville. You remember Betty Jones? Used to live in Suttonville and worked at Sim-U-Flight?"

"Yes, Why?" Cheryl asked.

"Well, she's living in Texas now and says there's lots of work there. "Sim-U-Flight has a satellite office there and Betty is sure she can help me get a job. I can't stay at Gram's forever, so it looks like I'm gonna have to accept Betty's offer and move to Texas, so I've come to see you before I leave."

"Oh, I thought you might come back here," Cheryl said.

"I'm guessing there's no work here either," Marie answered. "You know Jackie left the Armada but I don't know if Mr. James replaced her or not."

"Call him, Mom. Maybe he would hire you."

"Oh, I don't know about that," Marie said.

"Please?"

"I think this is a shot in the dark, but OK. Where's the pay phone located?"

In the parking lot of Cheryl's apartment, they found the pay phone, looked up the number of the Armada Inn and Marie dialed.

When Mr. James was connected by the front desk operator who told him who was calling, he said, "How are you, Marie?"

"Oh, fine," she answered.

"What have you been doing with yourself?"

""I lost my job and had to return to my hometown in New York, but now I've come to visit with my daughter before going to Texas."

"What's in Texas?" he asked.

"I have a friend who lives there who believes I can find employment. She has invited me to stay with her until I do."

"You know, I didn't replace Jackie when she married and left town. So I believe that you two being friends and probably think similarly, maybe you'd be interested in being her replacement."

"I don't know what to say," Marie commented.

"Why don't you come and we can talk about it," he said.

Meanwhile, Cheryl, listening to the one-sided conversation was getting excited over the possibility that her mother may return to the area.

"OK, how's one o'clock today?" Marie asked.

"See you then."

"Mom," Cheryl said. "He actually may hire you?"

"I don't know. We'll see. I'll try."

Inwardly, Marie, was amazed that she made the phone call because she didn't expect he'd even remember her, but serendipity was about to step in again and she'd find that losses become gains.

Cheryl drove Marie to the Armada Inn and parked in the parking lot on the side of the property. Mr. James was talking to an employee at the front desk when Marie walked through the door.

"Be with you in a minute," Mr. James said.

Marie noticed diners having lunch in the dining room and a couple were eating at the bar adjacent to it.

"OK, Marie. Let's go to my office and talk," he said when he finished his conversation with the head maid.

"Opening the door to his office, which was an altered guest room, he offered Marie a chair.

"I never expected to be interviewed, so I didn't bring my resume," Marie said.

"That's OK seeing as how I have known you since Jackie started working here and trust that you can make some good decisions about how to promote the property. Your people skills are right up there with Jackie. We need that type of personality to bring in business."

"She shared a lot of her ideas with me both here and at the property in our home town," Marie said. "So I'd sure like to give it a try; plus my daughter is in her sophomore year in college and we both would like to share a home again. However, I do have to go back north to get my car, pack it, and put it on the auto train. Will that be a problem?"

"No, how much time do you need?"

Marie hesitated fearing that if she took too much time, she'd lose the opportunity to come back.

Mr. James, taking notice of her hesitation, said, "How is two weeks? Will that give you enough time to get back here?"

"More than enough," Marie said joyfully.

"Then it's settled. I'll see you on May 14th." "Oh! And by the way, at least for the time being, take a room in the back part of the motel until you find an apartment."

"Thank you," she and added, and as she opened the door to leave, looking at Mr. James she said, "You won't be sorry."

Crossing the parking lot, walking toward her daughter's car, Marie was jubilant.

"You got the job, Mother?" Cheryl asked.

"Yep," Marie answered. "He's giving me two weeks to get to Suttonville and get my car, even offered me a room at the inn when I return until I can find an apartment for you and me."

"Let's find a pay phone and call Gram," Marie said.

Her mother answered the phone on the second ring and accepted the reverse charges from the operator.

After Marie told her about finding employment, Marion said cautiously, "Marie, Bob Vistula called here last night. He was looking for you. Said he was in Orlando on company business and I told him you were also there visiting your daughter. He asked me to tell you where to find him if you called. Do you want the number?"

Marie was surprised and answered, "Where is he, Mom?"

"Wait, I have the number on a pad. "Here it is. He's at 407 555-1234 in room 217."

"That's the number of the inn I'm going to work for," Marie said.

"I didn't know whether to tell you or not, but you know, I don't have the right to keep this from you even though I think it not a good idea that you contact him."

"Oh, Ma," he's no problem. I'm coming home to pick up my car and clothes and coming back here, so don't worry."

Cheryl heard the conversation. When her mother hung up she said, "Not again, Ma." "You're not going back with him, are you?"

"No, I'm coming back here."

When the inn operator put her call through to room 217, Bob answered. Recognizing her voice, he said, "Where are you? Never mind that, can I see you?"

"Yes," Marie answered.

"Let me take you to dinner," he asked.

"I have no car, so Cheryl will bring me to the inn and pick me up after dinner," was her answer.

When she knocked on his door, he opened it, gave her a hug and invited her in.

As she stepped in the room, she said, "This is where I came in or is it out?"

They laughed, but he knew what her next question would be.

"So, what happened to Sally and you?"

"We didn't make it," he answered. "She broke it off."

"I'm sorry," she said.

"I never should have let you go," Bob said. "Fly back to Suttonville with me. I'll pay for your flight. We can start over."

"Now this IS where I came in months ago, and the answer is no," she remarked. "I'm going back to get my car and returning here."

She wondered if her answer would mean that he wouldn't take her to dinner and she'd have to wait for Cheryl a couple of hours, but he took her to a little restaurant nearby where they talked, and he knew her mind was made up.

Saying their goodbyes in the lounge at the inn, she went to the parking lot where her daughter was waiting, got into Cheryl's car and waved goodbye.

FORTY-THREE

Marie flew home, spent time with her mother and step-father and headed out of Suttonville, New York, once again.

Driving the five hours to Virginia to catch the auto train, she reminisced about the trip she took, although only fifteen months ago, that seemed like years ago with her children. She felt jovial about her return to Florida and believed that she would never leave again.

She drove straight to the inn upon her arrival in Florida. Mr. James wasn't there, but she was expected. A key was waiting for her.

She opened the door to her room and starting offloading her belongings. Tomorrow would be a day for looking over the property, but for now, all she wanted to do was have dinner with her daughter who showed up after class late in the afternoon.

They talked excitedly about her return and how they would share a place together, and although Cheryl was working part time and attending classes at the university, Marie had no intention of asking her to pay board.

The next morning, Marie had a meeting with Mr. James who introduced her to his son, who although quiet seemed nice enough. The bookkeeper, however, seemed distant during their intro.

"She just met me," Marie thought. *"Wonder what her problem is."*

Marie would discover that the bookkeeper disliked Jackie and thought this would be another Yankee she wouldn't like either.

Marie was expected to hob knob with chamber of commerce executives as well as the training center officer's activities that the inn was involved in and she delighted in it.

Her biggest problem was that the occupancy of the conference room for meetings and weddings could only handle a small group, so selling a large one would be difficult. She did continue with promotional activities Jackie had started, but bringing in new business would be a challenge that she thought would be next to impossible.

In the meantime, she was still staying in the room Mr. James had provided for her while saving for the deposit and first and last month's rent for an apartment near the college her daughter attended.

If she had customers staying at the inn, she always stopped in the bar to buy a round of drinks before retiring to her room. When asked where she was living, she always answered, "nearby" never wanting anyone to know that she was living in one of the rooms and which one.

She was in her room one such evening after buying a round for a bunch of soldiers who were staying at the Armada when the phone rang.

"Marie, it's Jessie at the front desk."

"Yes, Jessie," Marie said.

"You know those guys you were buying drinks for tonight?"

"Yes, what's the matter?"

"Well, they're out poolside raising hell, drinking beer. When they were cut off from the bar, they went out and bought their own and we're getting calls from guests staying at the inn complaining. What should I do?"

"Let me think a minute,"

"Marie?"

"Yes, I'm thinking," Marie said. "Mr. James and his son are gone for the evening?"

"Yes," Should I call them?"

"No, but one thing for sure. If I go out there, they know me and they'll throw me in the pool, so I'm not going out. I'll call you right back."

After she hung up, Marie got an idea and dialed.

"Hello, is this the police dept.?" she asked.

"Yes, is there a problem?" the desk officer asked.

"My name is Mrs. Zubinski and I live across the street from the Armada Inn and there's a lot of hell raising goin' on. We can't sleep. Could you quiet them down?"

"Yes, ma'm. We'll have an officer go check it out. Do you want to be called back?"

"No, just get them to tone it down please. Thank you."

And Mrs. Zubinski hung up.

Mrs. Zubinski, aka Marie, snuck out of her room across the driveway and crouched low against a wall to the side of the pool and waited.

Shortly after, a squad car without lights and siren screaming came into the parking lot, parked and two officers got out and headed toward the pool.

"You guys having a good time?" they asked no one in particular.

"Yes, jeez officers, are we making that much noise?" one of them asked.

"Well, we had a call from a guest complaining about it," the officer stated. "You guys think you might have had enough to drink?"

"Yeah, sure, was the answer. We'll call it a night. Sorry."

"OK then, goodnight gentlemen," the officer said.

And the seven soldiers got out of the pool, dried off and retired to their respective rooms.

"Whew," Marie said to herself as she snuck back to her room.

Two evenings later, again after stopping in the bar to buy drinks, Marie got another call.

"Marie, it's Florence, you know, as in Nightingale," she heard.

"Hey, Florence, howya doin?" Marie asked.

"Are you sitting down?"

"Why, should I?" Marie asked.

"Yes."

"OK, I'm sitting down. Now what?"

"Jeff killed himself last week."

"What?" a shocked Marie asked.

"I'm sorry Marie. I thought someone you knew should tell you."

"How?" Marie asked.

"All I know is that he, well you knew he got a medical discharge, didn't you?" Florence asked.

"No," Marie answered.

"He went to work for a competitor of Sim-U-Flight based somewhere in Vermont and was due to fly from his home in Alabama to Vermont and never arrived. The awful part is that his daughters found his body when they arrived home from school. He'd shot himself in the head," Florence said.

"Marie, are you there?"

"Yes," Marie said crying. "Why?"

"I understand he'd been depressed but nobody expected this," Florence added.

"I gotta go, gotta process this," Marie said, and hung up.

She sat on the edge of her bed crying. The only thing she could do was offer up a prayer for Jeff.

And now it was really over.

Marie didn't know what to do. She needed to talk to someone. Jackie wasn't around, so she called Clark at work. Marie told Clark at a previous luncheon date weeks before that she was going to marry Jeff.

After telling him what happened, he suggested meeting at their favorite Italian restaurant outside the Center.

He was sitting at the bar enjoying a Martini when she arrived. Tilting his head in a sideways position, he looked at Marie and said, "I'm so sorry."

"I know," she said with tears in her eyes. "I just don't understand why he did it."

"Didn't you tell me that he knew if he and Julie reconciled, she'd never let him live it down?"

"Yeah, Oh! no," you don't think things got that bad, do you?"

"It hasn't been easy around my house since you and I," and his voice trailed off. "And I know it's just because of the kids that we stayed together."

"God what a mess," Marie said, adding, "Did you ever do it again? I mean have another affair after you and I?"

"One time," he answered. "I was on a trip to DC when I met a woman who looked a lot like you. We met in the bar, talked, went to dinner, and, well, you know the rest."

"Did you continue seeing her?"

"No, I couldn't. It was just a one night stand that I wished I hadn't gotten involved in, but thank God, nothing ever came of it and I've been a good boy ever since. That is unless…"

"Don't start with me," she laughed.

"Well, now, see, I've got you laughing," he said.

Marie took notice that his capacity for alcohol was elevated from the last time she saw him. His eyes were bloodshot and glassy, so she considered that he probably had more than one Martini before she had arrived but didn't mention it.

She had a Martini before her Ravioli and when she finished both, she got up to leave.

Clark swayed while getting off the barstool. "Do you have to go already?" he asked.

"Back to work," she answered. "Clark, please be careful with the sauce. I'm worried about you. Are you still taking your blood pressure meds?"

"Sometimes - now and then," he answered.

"I don't want to read your obituary in the paper so will you please get back on them and take care of yourself?"

"Yep," he smiled with a shit-faced grin.

A word to the wise would not be sufficient!

As she turned to walk toward the door, he said, "Marie, I still love you." Then he sat back down on the stool and ordered another Martini.

Conditions at the Armada Inn were becoming somewhat strained. Mr. James was upset that more business was not occurring at the inn after hiring Marie even though he knew the property had limits as far as the number of guests that could be served.

He became really upset when Marie, thinking it was just good business sense, sold a block of rooms at a reduced price to a teacher's union conference who was in town for three days.

"Who gave you the right to sell at a reduction?" Mr. James demanded after calling her into his office when he found out about the sale.

"I thought of the occupancy rate; that selling that many rooms would bring in the revenue you wanted," she answered.

"I don't want rooms sold that way," he said angrily.

She didn't realize until that moment that he considered the property his kingdom and that everyone else was literally under him. She also knew she was in trouble.

She had moved out of the room at the inn the week before into a two bedroom she could afford near her daughter's college and was getting settled feathering her nest.

The day after admonishing her, Mr. James called her into his office. "Marie, I don't think this is working out too well, so I'm going to have to dismiss you. Clean out your office and leave the premises by the end of the day. I think you'd be better suited working in an industrial atmosphere versus hotel promotion and sales. I'll give you two weeks' severance pay. That should help you financially until you find another job."

With that, he waved her off with his right hand, picked up a paper on his desk and started to read it.

There was no way Marie was gonna let him know that she was devastated over being fired, so she hurriedly cleaned out her desk, left the key on it, opened the door and quickly fast-stepped to her car. She threw her belongings into the trunk, got in her car, backed up, left the parking lot and headed to the apartment she had so recently rented for her and Cheryl.

She didn't know how to tell Cheryl. She felt like a loser, but at this fork in the road of her life, she couldn't possibly know that the best was yet to come.

FORTY-FOUR

Cheryl was in class when Marie arrived home. Some of her belongings had not been put away, so she started unpacking them and haphazardly placed them in places she knew they didn't belong, but she didn't care.

She sat down on the sofa and started crying when the phone rang.

"Hey, what are you doin' home?" Pam Foster asked. "I tried to reach you at your office and was told you no longer worked there. What happened?"

After telling Pam what had happened with Mr. James, Pam said, "Oh, I always thought he was an asshole anyway. Are you going to be home for a while?"

"Yes, why?" Marie asked.

"I'll call you right back," Pam said.

Five minutes later, the phone rang.

"What are you doin' for lunch tomorrow?" Pam asked.

"Nothing," Marie said.

"Well, be at Dagwoods' at noon cause I think I may have found another job for you," Pam said.

"With who?" she asked.

"Just show up," was Pam's answer.

"Marie drove the two miles to Dagwoods, a restaurant and bar that was frequented by middle class workers.

Walking through the door, she spied Pam sitting at a table with a man. He appeared to be short, had a hook nose and green eyes, was partially bald, and beside his chair stood a cane. He was about the same age as Marie - forty-two. His name was Ben Kildare.

When she was invited to sit down, he asked her if she wanted a drink. When Marie looked at Pam for counsel, Pam shook her head up and down, so Marie ordered Scotch and water.

They ordered sandwiches for lunch and when they all finished, Ben started the conversation asking Marie about her background in working for defense contractors which she found easy to discuss with him.

"Have you ever worked with the military?" he asked.

"Yes, when they came and went at Sim-U-Flight," she answered.

A little more than directly, she thought, and a smile appeared on her face.

"Did they use offensive language?" he asked.

"Yes, but it was never directed at me," she answered.

"Do you go to happy hour often?" he asked.

"Used to go three or four times a week, and my job at the inn had me in the bar after I closed my office a lot buying a round for military and civil service guests who stayed there."

"What I have in mind for you is a clerical position working for the Navy at the Service Instruction Command at the Naval Training Center. You would be interfacing with twenty naval technical writers, but this is not a civil service job. We, at Owen Ocean Systems Inc., are a contractor on the base who supply the Navy with machinists, technicians, and word processors. We have thirty employees in all and I am the supervisor."

"You mean just like that?" Marie asked. "I mean, hired?"

"Yes," Ben answered.

"You haven't given me a typing test," she said.

"Oh, that! I'll take Pam's word for it."

"When do you want me to start?" Marie asked.

"How's Monday?" he answered.

"Where do I go ?"

"You'll need to go to the front gate where I'll be waiting for you," he answered.

"We need to get you a badge and a car sticker, so I have to take you to Pass and ID where the Navy will take a photo of you and issue the sticker."

"OK, thank you," Marie said.

"You girls stay and have another on me," Ben said. "The bill is paid." He grabbed his cane, used it to get up from the chair, straightened himself upright and limped toward the door and out of the restaurant, turning back once to say, "Welcome Aboard."

"Sooooo, whatdaya think?" Pam said.

"I don't know what to think," Marie answered. "Just like that, he hired me."

"I already told him of your clerical skills not to mention being the only one who could get along with Blanky, so all he wanted to know is if you could get along with sailors."

"Jeez, I could have told him that."

Cheryl was home when she arrived from her interview. She told her daughter how happy she was; how seemingly nicer than Mr. James, Ben Kildare appeared to be, then breathed a sigh of relief and thanked God for another "miracle."

Ben Kildare's office was in a trailer in a field behind the command. After meeting Marie at the front gate the following Monday morning, Ben escorted Marie to the office and had her sign the necessary papers that would make her an employee of Owen Ocean Systems, Inc. He drove her down to the building to introduce her to her co-workers.

Sue (Susie) Gelb was hired a month before Marie. She was a petite girl, five foot tall, twenty-five years old, who had natural, wavy shoulder length light brown hair, green eyes and an infectious smile.

She offered her hand to Marie when introduced, asking her if she could get her coffee.

"I don't drink it," Marie answered. "Caffeine and I don't mix; makes me too nervous."

The sailors who passed her in the hallway had an inquisitive look on their faces, but said nothing until she was introduced to the ones she would be working with, and they were not overly enthusiastic about meeting her.

Knowing it would take time for them to accept her, Ben, decided to keep Marie in the trailer office with him for a while until they became accustomed to her presence and allowed her into their group.

There were no toilet facilities in the trailer, so when she needed a bathroom break, Marie would walk the short distance from the office to the command building which necessitated her going through two buildings separated by a portico. After a couple of weeks, she noticed that some of the sailors started to warm up to her being there and began to greet her, although timidly.

Although she didn't know where Susie disappeared to at lunch and after work, happy hour meetings with Pam at Dagwoods livened her up, and she started to feel at ease with her life which seemed to be going in the right direction.

Marie's experience with Jeff left her with a non-desirous feeling for attraction to another military man, so she accepted that the sailors' coolness toward her, thought it was probably a good thing and decided to keep her involvement totally on a clerical level.

One morning, Susie, who had been teaching Marie how to use a new software program - a word processor - asked her if she wanted to go to the Chief's Club for lunch with some of the sailors.

"We can go there?" Marie asked.

"Sure," Susie answered. "They allow women in and I'm sure you'll enjoy it."

"Yeah, but…"

"What?"

"You know the sailors don't especially like me," Marie said.

"Nah, that's all in your mind," Susie said. "Come on, it'll be fun."

"OK," Marie said.

They drove to the club in Susie's broken down '66 Chevy. When they arrived, ten of the tech writers were seated at a long table in the dining room.

Sitting down, Marie looked around at the faces of the ten and was surprised that they were smiling. They all had a drink in their hand, either beer or a mixed drink, and one sailor, Bobby Jenkins, lifted his vodka/7 Up and said, "Here's to you, Marie. We're glad you're here. Welcome aboard," to which Marie, who had ordered and received a shot, raised her glass and said, "Thanks for your welcome. I appreciate it. Oh! Ain't nobody get'in in my pants."

The sailor's expression was first of shock and then they started laughing hysterically. Marie was accepted into the pack.

Upon hearing the story at the Chief's Club, Ben decided it was time to relocate Marie into the command building.

The "luncheons" with the sailors at the club continued, but Marie was concerned that Ben would not approve, so she went to his office and asked, "Is it alright for Susie and I to be going to the club for lunch, albeit liquid, every day?"

"We work for the Navy, for those sailors, and if they want you girls to go to the club with them, and you wanna go, it's OK with me," Ben answered.

It became a habit to not only go to the club at lunchtime, but they started going after work at 3:30. This caused Marie to start wondering if alcohol wasn't becoming too much a part of her everyday life and even though she enjoyed the companionship of her new found buddies, the excessiveness of her drinking worried her.

Between meeting Pam at Dagwoods or stopping at the club, she wasn't home after work as often as she should be - wasn't there for Cheryl, who although she was in college, needed her mother's attention, but at the time, Marie was not aware of that need and would not deliberately do anything to hurt Cheryl. Mother and daughter did golf on the weekend, but Marie's unconscious inattentiveness would come back to haunt her in years to come.

She knew she had to do something about her drinking, so she decided to sign up for an evening class at the local community college two nights a week.

"At least that will keep me out of the bars twice during the week and on weekends, I'll be studying," she thought.

She decided to start with algebra and although math had always been difficult for her, she stuck to working at it passing with a B.

Knowing that Marie was a golfer, one of the sailors came into the word processing room the following week and said, "Hey, Marie, don't you play golf?

"Yes, why?" she asked.

"One of the officers whose son searches for lost golf balls is selling them for twenty-five cents a piece in the office behind ours. I thought you might be interested."

Marie had a problem with officers and although they didn't ignore her, she still felt uncomfortable around them, so she asked Susie to go with her to buy the golf balls.

Susie opened the door leading to the officer's office and hit the back of his chair with the door. A sailor sitting at a desk next to the door that exited to a hallway looked up at Marie. Their eyes locked and she was mesmerized. His hair was brown and wavy; his smile was full and showed two front teeth that were slightly separated; his eyes were greenish gray with eyebrows that were full. Because he was seated, she couldn't tell how tall he was, but likened him to be around five eight. It was winter, so he wore his dark uniform.

"Yes, can I help you?" the officer said.

"Golf balls," Marie managed to say.

"You wanna buy some? They're twenty-five cents each."

"OK," Marie said. "I'll take four."

She handed him a dollar, stepped back and Susie closed the door.

"Hey!" Susie said. "You look like you've been struck with lightning.

"What's that sitting by the outer door?" Marie asked.

"That's a Scott Nicholson," Susie said. "That also happens to be married."

"Forget it," Marie said.

Ah Huh!

A couple times a year, usually in summer and around Christmas, Marie and Clark met for lunch at their favorite Italian restaurant. Clark's continued need for alcohol and returning to work after drinking began to worry her, but she decided that badgering him about it would prove to be useless, so she didn't mention it whenever they met. Every time they parted, Clark would add, "I still love you."

The car Marie drove to Orlando was still running, albeit rusting out especially on the floorboards on the driver's side. There was a large hole through which when driving through puddles, water splashed through leaving water stains on her slacks.

The first time she drove Ben to the bank and other errands, he took note of the holes and offered to have two of his technicians fix them.

Tony Martini and Randy Jones were not busy interfacing with the sailors one day, so Ben asked them to take Marie's car and go to her apartment to see what could be done about the holes in the floorboards.

When they returned before quitting time, the floorboards were fixed.

"What's that you fitted in there?" Marie asked.

"It's a metal realtor's sign we "borrowed," then rubber malleted it to fit into your floor so you won't get splashed on anymore.

"Where'd you get it?" Marie asked.

"A sign in the front of somebody's yard. They won't miss it."

"What if I get caught with it?"

"Nah, we placed the printed side face down. Don't worry about it."

FORTY-FIVE

The pain woke her up in the middle of the night. It was excruciating and even though it was centered around the waist in her back, she was afraid she was having a heart attack, so after pacing the floor for two hours, she called to Cheryl who was sleeping.

"I think you better take me to the hospital," Marie said.

"Why, what's happened?"

"I have a lot of pain, mostly in my back, and I'm worried that it might be a heart attack.

Cheryl drove her mother to the hospital located two miles away let her out in front of the ER, parked her car and hurried into the emergency room.

After explaining her symptoms to the resident in charge, the doctor told her he thought she might have gall stones but would need to do some blood work, an x-ray, and thoroughly examine her.

The tests came back positive for gallbladder disease - the x-ray showing at least seventeen stones that could be seen as tiny round rings.

"Those are the ones we can see," the doctor said.

"What does that mean?" Marie asked.

"There are more that we can't see," he answered. I'm going to give you pain medication and suggest you contact a general surgeon as soon as possible.

"I can't possibly be having gall bladder problems. I thought you had to be fat, fair and forty, and I only qualify for the forty."

"Still, the x-rays are proof. Do you need the name of a surgeon? I can recommend three who have privileges in this hospital."

"Yes," she said.

She was given the names, left the hospital and returned home.

The next day, she didn't have any pain and went to work. She told "her" sailors and co-workers of her distressful night, showed the names of the surgeons to them, one of which her boss had known, Dr. Ross, so she decided to make an appointment with him.

"After examining Marie, Dr. Ross said, "There's a good possibility you won't have another attack, but if you do, it could be worse. My suggestion would be to have it removed as soon as possible while it's inactive."

"I'll get back to you," she said.

"Don't wait too long. I don't want to have to do emergency surgery while you're under attack. It'll take a lot longer to recuperate."

Marie went back to work and discussed it with her friends, one of whom was an overweight senior chief whose wife, he told Marie, had to have surgery during a gallbladder attack.

"You don't want to wait," he said. "It took my wife a long time to bounce back after her operation. She told me to tell you she'd be happy to talk to you about it, if you want."

"No," Marie said.

She was guarded about talking to the wives of the sailors for fear of them having suspicions about her and their husbands, and God knows she had had enough of that with Jeff and with Clark, even though he was not military.

She called Dr. Ross' office and made the appointment for pre-surgery, after which it was determined that she would have the operation the following week.

Marie called Marion, her mother, and told her of the intended surgical procedure.

"I'm comin' down," Marion said.

"Thanks, Mom, I needed to hear that."

Florence Nightingale, aka Gail Kennedy, had by this time, married and divorced Stan Franklin and was living and working in the area, so when she found out about the surgery, she insisted on walking Marie into the OR on the morning of the procedure.

The evening before surgery, Marie's brother, Daniel, called from upstate New York to give her words of comfort.

"Where are you right now," Daniel asked.

"In the living room with Cheryl and Ma," she answered.

"Do you have a phone in the bedroom?"

"Yes, why?"

"Go into the bedroom and pick up the extension."

"OK."

Picking up the extension, she said, "Now what?"

"When was the last time you had confession?"

"What? Long distance? Jeez, I don't know ten years, maybe."

"Yes, special case," her brother said.

"Bless me Father (she almost said Daniel) for I have sinned…" and allowed herself to confess her sexual indiscretions to her brother who knew of them anyhow.

After he gave absolution, Daniel said, "Good luck, Marie. I love you," and he hung up.

Marie, her mother and daughter, were preparing to leave the apartment, heading for the hospital, when the phone rang.

"I'd better get it," Marie said.

"Hello,"

"Is this Marie Maxwell," a voice asked. (Marie had renewed her maiden name after Cheryl turned eighteen.)

"Yes,"

"This is the Bakersfield Funeral Home. Have you thought about purchasing a funeral package?"

Without waiting for an answer, he continued, "We would like to set up an appointment for a counselor to talk to you about pre-need."

"What? You've got to be kidding me," Marie answered. "I'm on my way to the hospital for surgery."

"Sorry," and he hung up.

Talk about timing.

She told her mother and daughter about the call while driving to the hospital.

"It's a good thing I have a sense of humor," Marie said.

They all laughed.

Arriving at the hospital, Marie was given a sedative and pain killer even though she was not in pain, and strangely enough, she slept well.

"Up and at 'em," she heard the next morning when Gail showed up at five o'clock, waking Marie up. Gail had a package in her hand, set it on the night stand to steady it and pulled out of the bag a bottle of Clan MacGregor scotch.

"Jeez Florence," Marie said. "They won't let me have that here."

"Just leave it there and let's find out," Florence said.

Marie was prepped with an IV, placed on the gurney and wheeled out of the room with Florence walking beside her, in full nurses uniform. Cheryl and Cheryl's grandmother following her down the hall. At the OR entrance, they were told to go to the waiting room. They kissed Marie goodbye.

Dr. Ross stood by her gurney before she entered the OR and told her the anesthesiologist would arrive shortly to discuss any qualms she had about her surgery.

When he arrived, she told him what had happened with the chicken bone.

"You awoke before they expected you to," the doctor said.

"When one has surgery, it's necessary to paralyze the body, so the patient can't move during the procedure," he added. "When you heard the nurse say, 'Knock her out', it was because they realized you were waking from the anesthesia sooner than expected. When you did wake up, there was no impact. You were able to move your limbs and your body; correct?"

"Yes."

"Please trust me. I will get you through this. Now take a deep breath please."

And the last thing she remembered was the clock on the wall that registered 7:45.

Her mother was sitting in a chair beside the hospital bed knitting when Marie started "coming to."

"When are they coming to take me?" she asked Marion.

"They already did."

"What time is it?"

"Nine thirty."

"I've come and gone already?"

"Yes."

She wasn't aware when her surgeon stopped by to check her out on the first day, but on the second, he arrived around lunchtime. He saw the bottle of scotch setting on the stand beside her bed and remarked, "A bottle of scotch?"

"Yes, my friend brought it to me to take home after I'm discharged," Marie said apprehensively.

"You can have a wee nip now if you wish," Dr. Ross said.

"Now?"

"Yes, I'll have an aid at the nurse's station bring you some ice and fill your water pitcher. I'll stop back to see how you're doing after rounds." He left her room.

After an aid brought ice and water, she placed a handful of the ice in a paper cup, poured herself a short one, added water, sat back and sipped her drink.

She felt the buzz immediately and it warmed the cockles of her heart.

Dr. Ross returned an hour later and told her that she was doing so well, that she could probably be released earlier than expected.

"I thought the surgery would take longer," she said.

"Because you are not obese, not overweight in any sense of the word, there was very little fat to cut through to get to the gallbladder which made the time spent on the operating table that much less and hastened your procedure. And oh, by the way, I have the stones in a prescription bottle. Would you like to see them?"

"Yes. How many are there?"

"Twenty-eight."

She accepted the bottle, opened it, and took a stone out the size of a pea. It disintegrated between her thumb and forefinger, flaking like tiny granules of sand into her lap.

The sailors came every day of the five days she was in the hospital, usually after 3:30 when they would have been at the club.

Her room was filled with both military and civilian friends who partook of her bottle of scotch and had their happy hour in her room. Some snuck in beer while others brought their own paper cups. In a two-bed space, the room was filled with well-wishers for Marie. There came a point when the floor nurse, who came in twice on one of the visits to tell them to keep it down, had to order the visitors to leave because they were disturbing other patients on the ward not to mention the poor woman sharing the room in the bed near the window.

FORTY-SIX

One night a week after work, the girls went to a bar where ladies drank free called "The What If" lounge that was located in a local nationwide motel. Drinks flowed and delicious hors d'oeuvres were served without charge to women - men had to pay for their drinks. Marie and her friends took advantage of the Tuesday nights although they knew it was offered to bring in traveling executives who would frequent it hoping to "get lucky" while in town.

Marie and Pam were sampling the hors d'oeuvres one Tuesday when a tall, grey-haired middle aged man came up to Marie and asked her if he could get her a drink. He was dressed in sports clothes; a white golf shirt with collar and brown Hager slacks. He wore leather loafers that appeared to be new.

Laughingly she answered, "I guess you don't mean buy me one since they're free to women."

"No, I'd buy you one if that would get me an introduction," he answered.

The girls decided that if asked, they would fake a first and last name, so Marie came up with, "My name is Pearl."

"Well, Pearl, it's nice to meet you," he said. "My name is Clyde. May I hold your plate and escort you to a booth?"

Marie looked at Pam and Pam said, "Sure, we'll be happy to sit with you."

"You girls inseparable?" he asked.

"You can't be too careful nowadays," Marie answered.

Seated in a booth, the three talked about their jobs and where they all came from.

"So, what do you do, Clyde?" asked Pam.

"I own a vendor machine supply business," he replied. "You know, candy, cigarettes and necessities found in a machine in the men's room."

"Like Condoms?" Marie asked.

"Yes," he said smiling.

He noticed that Marie was starting to rise from the booth.

"Do you think you might have dinner with me tomorrow?" he asked.

"No," she answered.

"Look," he said. "You can drive your own car and I'll meet you at a restaurant, any one you want."

"There's a very trendy French restaurant two blocks from here," she said.

"Fine. What time?"

"Six o'clock?" she asked.

"I'll see you then," he replied.

The next day at work, "her" sailors overheard her talking about the meeting with Clyde the night before and being protective of her had to know every detail of where and what time, which she gladly shared with them.

"You know," one of the said. "Be careful cause most of these guys just want to get in your pants."

"Jeez, I wasn't born yesterday," Marie answered. "I'm just having dinner with him."

She left work, did some shopping and drove to the Adour French Restaurant.

Entering the foyer of the restaurant she was met by the maitre d' who wore a tuxedo, white silk shirt with cummerbund and greeted her, "Welcome to The Adour."

"I'm here to meet someone," she said.

"The name please?"

"Clyde, ah, oh shit, I didn't get his last name," she said embarrassed at her declaration.

"Will it be just you and Mr. Clyde, Madam?" he asked stone faced.

"Yes," she answered. She wanted to back up through the door and go home.

"I'll wait a couple more minutes," she said. "He may have gotten delayed at the bank."

What bank, she thought to herself, but it sounded good.

Within seconds, the phone rang, the maitre d' answered it and asked if she was "Miss Pearl" to which she didn't immediately reply because she forgot which false name she used when she met Clyde.

"Miss Pearl?" he asked again.

"What, oh, yeah" and she walked to the phone and answered it hoping he called to cancel.

"It's Clyde, Pearl," he said. "Where's the restaurant? I'll call a cab and get there."

"A cab? No, it's two blocks south of the inn. Look, I'll come get you. Just wait under the portico."

When she hung up, she looked at the maitre d' handed him the phone, and thought, *He thinks I'm a call girl.*

She picked Clyde up, drove him the two blocks to the restaurant and after they were seated, he insisted on ordering for her which was okay with her since the menu was in French and had no bill of fare on it.

They talked while drinking white wine. Shortly after dining, he asked her, "Would you consider visiting me in Washington?"

"No," she answered.

"Not even if I buy tickets?"

"No, I hate DC. Too crowded."

"Not DC, state of," he said, "I'm in the Central Florida area to pick up my new vessel, a Hatteras, and sail it back to Washington by way of the Panama Canal and up the western coast of the U.S."

"No, I don't think so."

"Can I have your phone number and call you to see if you'll change your mind?"

"You can have my work number, and by the way, my name isn't Pearl, it's Marie."

She felt at ease releasing the information.

He laughed and told her he thought he knew why and couldn't blame her.

Even though it was early and he invited her up for a drink, she declined and drove home.

The next morning at work, one of the sailors asked her how the evening went. After she told him about the invitation to go to Washington and the fact that Clyde was picking up his new Hatteras, the sailor damn near fell over.

"Do you know what a Hatteras is?" he asked.

"A boat?"

"Come with me," and he guided her to his desk to show her a picture of the Hatteras.

"It's a fuckin' yacht," he cried. "The guy's got money and you're not goin' to take him up on his offer?"

"You're the one who told me to be careful."

"Yeah but this guy's got to be on the up and up. I'm talking, M-O-N-E-Y!"

"I don't know him and I ain't goin'."

Clyde called her the next morning and once again asked her to come to Washington. She declined and that was the last she heard from him.

FORTY-SEVEN

The sailors at the Command often sponsored picnics in a park across the street to which the employees of Owen Ocean Systems were always invited. On this particular Friday picnic, Marie and Susie were told that they could go, so they left the building at 11:30 and crossed the street to the park where the sailors were cooking hot dogs. Beer and wine flowed.

Marie walked into the park a few feet behind Susie. As she stepped onto the concrete floor where the beer was being poured, one of the sailors stepped in front of her.

Whereas the other sailors had changed to civies, he was in uniform and appeared to be slightly inebriated, his hat cocked on the side of his head, his eyes somewhat glassy.

"Hi," he said a little slurry. "I'm Scott Nicholson."

Oh my God, it's him, Marie thought.

Not knowing what to say, Marie uttered a "hello."

"How are you?" he said.

"Fine," was the answer.

Awkwardly he tried to talk about nothing in particular.

"Hey, Marie," yelled Tom Johnston, a Navy Chief. Tom was in his truck in the driveway parallel to the park. Four Navy Chiefs were in the back of the pickup.

"Come on, we're going for a beer run," he said.

Marie looked at Tom then at Scott and didn't know what to do and for a moment, there was silence between them.

"I'm coming," she shouted and started to walk away.

"Lunch," Scott said.

"What?" she asked.

"Lunch tomorrow. Will you have lunch with me tomorrow?"

"Yes," she answered cheerfully and hurried to the truck where Susie sat in the front seat.

"Move over Susie and let Marie in," Tom said.

"What was that about?" Susie asked Marie.

"Not now," Marie answered as she turned to look back toward the beer keg area and noticed that Scott was walking away toward the Command building.

Tom drove to the PX to purchase a few gallons of red and white wine. Because they were not military or dependents of, Susie and Marie were not allowed in the commissary, so they waited outside for Tom and his buddies.

"Soooo," Susie said.

"He asked me out for lunch tomorrow," Marie answered.

"He did? And what did you say?"

"Yes, but he'd been drinking, so I don't think he'll even remember."

"Remember what I told you about him being married?"

"Oh! This won't go anywhere."

Famous last words!

"Look at you. You're as giddy as a teenager."

Tom and the chiefs came out with the wine, they all piled into his truck and headed back to the park for an afternoon of drinking and picnicking.

That evening, Marie sat listening to music on her tape recorder and thought about Scott's invitation to lunch. She had to admit that she was excited about going. She had some concern about his marital status, but figured she could handle it as she'd been down that road before and didn't actually believe he wanted anything more than friendship.

Ah! Huh!

Marie went to work the next morning in anticipation of seeing Scott again and enjoying lunch with him, but wasn't sure he would remember or show up.

Susie was getting excited for her and as they waited for the morning to pass, 11:25, 11:30, and no Scott.

"See, I told you he wouldn't show up," Marie said. She was talking to Susie with her back to the door in the word processor room.

"Who won't show up?" he said.

When she turned around, Scott was leaning against the doorjamb. Embarrassed, she answered, "You."

"I didn't forget. You ready?"

"Yes. Let me grab my purse."

Scott and Marie exited the side door of the building where his white pickup was parked in a reserved spot. He opened the passenger side of the truck and helped her in.

Backing out of the space he asked, "Where would you like to go?"

"Dagwoods is just outside the base. We go there often."

"Dagwoods it is then." He headed toward the front entrance and passed the guard station and headed toward Dagwoods.

They didn't say much on the way to the restaurant. She didn't know what to say which, for her, was something that very seldom happened. Excited as she was, she didn't want him to know, for she didn't know what he was thinking about her.

When they got to the restaurant, they decided to sit at a table. He ordered drinks for them and after looking over the menu, he told her that he wasn't hungry. She ordered a sandwich. They had another round of vodka and tonic and began to open up to each other, more like she to him.

Talking about her previous life (living in upstate NY) and comparing it to her present gave her unintended pleasure as Scott listened intently.

He told her he had been in the Navy for almost twenty-one years and was soon to retire. His tours of duty included Vietnam, but he didn't speculate on it. He said he was married and didn't speculate on that either, so she didn't ask him for more information about it.

They had two drinks each before she decided she needed to get back, so he paid the check and they returned to the Command.

Susie was waiting when she returned and was full of questions about the luncheon.

"So, how'd it go?" she asked impatiently.

"Good," Marie answered.

"Oh, come on. What happened?"

"Nothing. We had lunch and talked a little that's all."

"Did he ask you to go out again?"

"No."

"Huh! I wonder what's goin' on in his mind."

"I told you before, Susie, friendship."

"Right. You don't believe that any more than I do."

Scott didn't work in the same part of the Command as Marie, so she didn't see that much of him - maybe a passing in the hall now and then, but they said "hi" to each other and went their own ways.

Outside the back gate, but a part of the base, was a golf course that had a pro shop and bar housed in a small building. Senior Chief Bobby Jenkins, who had taken a shine to Marie, asked her and Susie if they wanted to go to the 19th Hole bar in the clubhouse one afternoon after work. A bunch of the sailors were going for a beer, so they accepted and drove their own cars.

Upon entering the bar of the clubhouse, Marie noticed that the sailors were seated in chairs that were located around a table that had a padded vinyl booth backed against the wall, so she went over and sat down on the booth side.

There were pitchers of beer at the table which kept everyone's glass filled as soon as the glass became three-fourths empty. The sailors insisted that the girls couldn't pay for their drinks even though Susie ordered Tequila shooters before downing a beer.

The door to the clubhouse opened, Marie looked up, and Scott entered and headed toward the table at which point, Susie, kicked Marie under the table. Marie wasn't aware that she'd been set up - that Scott had asked Bobby Jenkins to "get" Marie over to the 19th Hole.

Scott sat down next to Marie.

"What are you doin' here?" she asked Scott.

"What, I don't have a right to be here?"

"Oh, no, I just didn't expect you."

"Bobby asked me to stop after work, so here I am. I hope you're not disappointed."

"No," quite the contrary. I'm glad you did."

Another beer and Marie started to feel slightly under the influence. By this time, Scott had placed his left arm over the top of the booth behind Marie.

Placing her arm around his shoulder, she said, "Do you mind if I do this?"

Placing his hand above her right knee, he said, "Not if you don't mind if I do this."

The sailors were getting the message of their body language.

They remained in that position until Scott realized how much time had passed and said he needed to leave, much to Marie's disappointment, but she was delighted he showed up and happy to have been able to touch him.

After he left, Bobby said, "Something goin' on here?"

"No," Marie answered. "We're just friends."

"Yeah, well, I ain't never seen friends touch each other like you two just did."

"Bobby, that's all there is. And probably I had a little too much to drink."

FORTY-EIGHT

Marie's evening classes continued two times a week and she was happy that her marks in algebra were so high. Still, she had put her nose to the grindstone and vowed to "get through" the class she knew would be the hardest for her. That's why she chose it first believing that if she passed, the other courses would be a breeze.

She got home from a Thursday night class one evening, put on her headset to listen to the stereo when the phone rang.

"Hello," she said.

"Marie?"

"Yes, who's this?"

"It's Scott Nicholson."

"Oh! How ya doin'?"

"Good. I'm at the bowling alley. I guess I thought you'd be here."

"No, I just got in from class. I'm not a good bowler. Matter of fact, I'm a terrible bowler."

"Ah, ah. Do you want to meet me at the club for a drink?"

"I don't know if I could get in through the back gate. I think it's closed."

"Oh, OK."

"But if you want, you could come over to my place. I don't have anything to drink, but you're welcome to stop by."

"I'll stop for a six pack and be there in a little bit."

She opened the door when he knocked and welcomed him into her apartment. He was dressed in civies. He handed her the six pack. She got two glasses and opened the cans of beer, pouring one for her and one for him. They sat on the couch and drank their beer and talked of their individual hopes of the future. She told him that she and her brother were looking into buying a place together when he retired from the priesthood, and he counting the days of the short time he had left in the Navy.

He went to the fridge and got two more beers after they had finished their first one. When he returned, he sat close to her on the sofa, no space in between the sides of their legs. When they finished the second beer, Scott put his arms around her and kissed her gently on the lips. She opened her mouth and met his tongue and the hug became robust. The electricity she felt in his embrace vibrated through her entire being and she knew she would surrender to his sexual touching of her breasts. Together, they rolled off the sofa and onto the floor where they removed their clothes. He entered her and she spasmed into an orgasm that sent her passion to a space somewhere within her mind that she had never known before and she cried out in ecstasy. They found themselves spent and soaking in sweat.

They lay on their backs on the rug. Scott said, "That was pure pleasure."

"Whistles and bells," she said.

It was getting late and they both realized they had to work the next day. Scott got up, put on his clothes, took her in his arms and held her before going to use the bathroom. When he came out, she was dressed. He asked her to open her hand and when she did, he placed a two inch wooden doll in her hand that she had in her bathroom that said, "Love."

"Yes, I do," Scott said and he walked to the door, opened it, and left.

She was flighty the next day at work, and although there wasn't that much work to be done on the word processor, she made mistakes which was noticed by Susie.

"OK, what's goin' on," Susie asked.

"Nothing."

"You're not here. Where are you? That last document you typed had four typographical errors in it. Johnny brought it back to me and asked what was wrong with you."

"I made that many on a one page document?"

"Yeah. What's up?"

She looked at Susie and said, "PC paid me a visit last night."

"PC?"

"You know. Prince Charming."

"O my God, you mean Nicholson called you?"

"Yes, and came over too, and don't use his name cause I don't want the other sailors to know, so we'll call him PC."

"They're bound to find out sooner or later if this keeps up."

"Later is better."

"Speaking about this keeping up, where is it going?"

"I don't know. Maybe just a one night stand."

"Like I said, I hope you know what you're doing. You're gonna get hurt."

"I can handle it. I don't expect anything from him. He's married and I don't expect him to do anything about it, plus I wouldn't even ask him to. Ya know, after what I've been through with men, there are times when I think it better to see a married man. I can't ask for and he can't give, so it's safe, at least for me and hopefully the wife doesn't find out. There's no commitment. I can't be told when and where I can and cannot go which leaves me able to be autonomous, and I like that."

Susie and Marie went to lunch off base that day. When they got back to the command, there was a vase with a dozen yellow long-stemmed roses sitting on Marie's desk. The card read, ""Love, PC."

Bobby Jenkins leaned his head in the door and said, "Who's PC?"

"Prince Charming," Marie answered.

"And who's PC?" he asked again.

"Someone I met recently at the What If Lounge."

"By the looks of those roses, it appears as though IF happened," he laughingly said. "Wouldn't you like to know?" she said.

"When do we get to meet him?" Bobby asked.

"Eventually," she answered.

Looking over Bobby's shoulder was Scott, who said, "Who's PC, Marie?"

"Wouldn't you all like to know," she answered blushing.

Bobby thought he detected a twinkle in Scott's eyes; looked at Marie and saw a glimmer, wondered about it, but put it to rest because Marie had told the sailors that none of them was gonna get in her pants.

Scott started calling Marie on her office phone. Sometimes Susie answered and knowing who it was, just rolled her eyes and handed the phone to Marie without a word. "Lunch?" he asked the next day.

"OK, where?" Marie answered.

"Meet me outside the side door," he said. "Eleven-thirty."

Searching over her shoulder in case anyone would observe, Marie left the processor room at 11:25 and hurried toward the side entrance where Scott waited outside the door. They got into his truck and went out the back gate heading toward Dagwoods. When he parked in the lot, he turned to Marie and took her into his arms and kissed her. She submitted to the attraction that led her to him that day months ago when she went to buy twenty-five cent golf balls. They went into the restaurant, sat at the bar and ordered a scotch/rocks.

"I think I was seen by one of the sailors," she said.

"So?" he asked.

"I don't want to get you or me into trouble."

"Don't worry about it. There'll be no trouble."

"I wanna see you again," he added.

"Isn't that kinda difficult? I mean you being married and all?"

"I'll find a way. I meant it when I handed you that wooden doll - love. You never knew it but when you used to come into the command from the trailer on your way to the ladies room, it was always at the same time. I timed it. I could have set my watch to it. Ten thirty every morning. I made sure I was standing in the hallway outside my office five minutes before that so I could see you. You never looked right or left."

"I didn't know you were there and you're right. I didn't look around. I was timid about getting to know the sailors. I had a difficult relationship with one that hurt me before, after I moved here. It caused me to steer clear of anyone connected with the Navy, but I must confess, I noticed you when I went to buy the golf balls."

"So you play golf?"

"Poorly. Do you?"

He didn't dare tell her he had a four handicap. She'd never go play with him if she knew.

"Now and again," he said.

"There's a command tournament coming up in a couple weeks. Susie and I are gonna run beer. Are you playing in it?" she asked.

"Yes. You mean Silly Susie?"

"What, Susie, you know who works with me."

"Yes, Silly or drifty the guys call her."

They laughed both knowing that sometimes Susie did act like an unmanned boat drifting in water. It was time to go back to work.

When they arrived at the Command, they kissed goodbye. She got out and went in the back entrance. Bobby was standing in the hallway waiting for her. He followed her to her workspace with two other sailors following.

"Sooooo," Bobby said. "What's this about not wanting anything to do with sailors."

"Yeah," said another. "What's Nicholson got that we haven't?"

Marie raised her arms, stuck out the index finger on her right and left hands, and spaced them eight inches apart. The sailors didn't say anything, turned and left the room.

"So it's out," Scott said. "So what? And by the way, it came back to me how you made a distance between your index fingers on what I had that my shipmates didn't. Why did you do that? I mean it's kinda obscene."

"I could have done this," and she took the thumb and index finger on her right hand and made a space of two inches.

"Besides, they all left and nobody has asked me why you since," she said.

FORTY-NINE

They started spending more time together during the day at lunch as well as after work. Instead of going to the club, they went to Dagwoods where they sat with Pam and a few of the employees who worked for Owen Ocean Systems.

Marie couldn't understand how Scott could take the chance of staying away from his residence every evening and into the wee hours of the morning but figured it wasn't any of her concern, so she didn't pursue asking him.

She was surprised when one night he said, "We're going to be together."

"And how do you think that will happen?"

"I intend to tell Bernice."

"And then what?"

"We'll be together. You know I love you and intend to marry you when I'm free."

"Don't you love your wife?"

"Love had nothing to do with it. I had to marry her, she was pregnant."

"I don't believe in HAD TO. Why didn't you protect yourself and her?"

"The passion of the moment, I guess. Since our son was born, I've stayed in the Navy deploying to parts of the world where a family could not be taken - an island off the coast of Italy was one and Vietnam was another, although I believed that we were right to go to Nam. I even volunteered to go."

"Why?"

"Bernice had been married two other times before I married her and always to military men who divorced her. She had a son with her first husband and a daughter with her second."

"And a son with her third - you."

"Yes."

"I swore this wouldn't happen to me again."

"It won't. Trust me to handle my telling her."

"What does she do?"

"She makes more money than I do working for a law firm researching medical information that helps the lawyers win lawsuits for class actions."

"A position like that could get you alimony," she said laughing.

"I wouldn't ask for it. I just want to be free."

Scott knew that there was a good chance that Marie would find someone else if he didn't move fast, knew that he could lose her forever. Although he was living a lifestyle of material comfort - he owned a fishing boat, lived in a large house in a suburban classy neighborhood, drove a new pickup, and had money to spend - he wasn't happy married to Bernice.

"A sailor enlists at an early age, goes to boot camp, goes to school, then out to sea so he has no time for dating," Scott said.

"Women are allowed to come to the clubs on base and that's usually where they search for a prospective husband. Maybe they spend a couple months together after they marry before he deploys to God knows where. He leaves and she's happy with the benefits she receives as a military dependent."

"When he returns home from so many deployments and before retiring, the sailor and wife are thrown together every day and find that they have nothing in common - nothing they worked for jointly as civilian couples do, which causes the man to have an affair and/or seek a divorce."

"So that's what happened with Jacksonville Jeff," Marie thought.

Scott and Marie made love often when they were together. Their desire to please each other was as strong as the first time when they slipped to the floor of her apartment. Marie could orgasm two and three times as he unselfishly held his own release back so she could thrill and cry out each time, and although he was no egotist, Scott was proud that he could satisfy her.

"I told her," Scott said to Marie a week later.

"And what did she say?"

"She wasn't happy, but she didn't cry or carry on. All she said was, "Three divorces in a lifetime. Three times and I'm out.""

"That has to be so hard on her. I love you so much Scott, but I'm not sure this is what I want to contend with, not even for a short time."

"It'll work out. I promise, Marie."

A month went by, but Scott didn't make an attempt to see a lawyer to start divorce proceedings and when questioned, he wasn't very convincing about why. The pot boiled over one afternoon when Scott and Marie went to Dagwoods for a beer. Scott noticed a shipmate when he parked in the lot, got out and started talking to him. Marie noticed a package on the floor of the passenger side. She picked it up, opened it and discovered a pair of size eight bedroom slippers. She knew they couldn't be for her, she wore a six.

Scott opened the passenger side door and put his hand out to help Marie exit his car, but Marie held up a slipper and asked, "Who is this for?" at which point his face fell. "It's her birthday," he said sheepishly.

"You know what? Take me home immediately. You're divorcing but giving her presents? Something isn't right here."

He tried and tried to convince her that he had progressed toward getting his divorce but to no avail. She wasn't having any of it.

"I said H-O-M-E," she spelled.

Scott walked around to the driver's side, got in the car, backed out of the lot and drove her home where, when he pulled into a parking spot, she got out of the car, slammed the door and walked up the stairs into her apartment banging her front door shut.

She poured a drink, sat on the sofa and although she was hurt, she didn't cry. She was too mad.

"What the hell is the matter with me?" she said. "Am I that needy that I let myself get involved with a married man again? Am I that naïve that I believed him?"

These questions she would find the answers to at a later time in her life.

She called Pam seeking the sisterly comfort that only another woman could give and offloaded her pain to her friend. Pam wanted Marie to meet her at Dagwoods but Marie declined.

"I've got some thinking to do," Marie said.

Marie thought about what her next move would be all night long and made up her mind that it was time for a showdown no matter what the consequences.

She arrived at work the following day and waited until ten o'clock to place the call. She searched for an empty office where she could close the door for complete privacy telling the chief who was nearby that she had to make a personal call to her bank.

"Hello, I'd like to speak to Bernice Nicholson," she said to the receptionist who answered.

"Just a moment and I'll connect you," the operator said.

Marie's nerves were raw, running through her body like electricity through a plugged in wire.

"This is Bernice."

"Bernice, you don't know me, and I'm sorry to disturb you. My name is Marie Maxwell. "I've been seeing your husband, Scott, for a few months. My reason for calling you is to ask if you two are getting a divorce."

There, she said it.

Silence. Deafening silence. Marie had her answer.

"Really," Bernice said. "And when was he gonna tell me?"

"I'm sorry Bernice. You won't hear from me again and neither will he."

"Wait! Will you meet me? Anywhere - anywhere at all."

"I don't think that is a good idea."

"Please. There is a cocktail lounge on 50 call The Cock 'N Tale Lounge that has a fireplace in it where we can sit in comfortable chairs and talk. I can be there at noon. Please meet me, OK?"

"There's been enough people hurt. It wasn't my intent to hurt you."

"I understand that. I'd like to talk to you."

Hesitantly, Marie said she'd be there. Both women needed to size up each other looking for the attraction Scott found in each of them.

Scott didn't come near Marie's workplace that morning. He didn't try to call her and she was glad that he stayed away.

Susie, aware that Marie was especially irritable, didn't ask any questions of her either, figuring it better to wait until Marie was ready to release what was bothering her.

Marie left the building at 11:30 desiring to get at the lounge ahead of Bernice, but Bernice had the same idea and showed up early also. They had given a description to each other of what they looked like, so when Marie parked her car and headed toward the steps of the building, she noticed a woman sitting on the bench aside the entryway of the bar.

How do you greet someone whose been told of her unfaithful husband and you're the one he is unfaithful with, Marie thought.

"Marie," she said.
"Yes, Bernice?"
"Yes."

Bernice turned and opened the door to the bar holding it for Marie to enter. She appeared to be a lot older than Scott by at least ten years, was noticeably overweight almost to the point of obese, had mousy brown short hair and grey eyes, and was dressed in a Grey wide lapel business suit that was too tight for her bulging upper body.

They were seated at a table in the lounge, ordered a drink and sat for a few seconds before Bernice spoke.

"How long did you say this has been goin' on?"

"Six months now."

"Did you know he was married?"

"Ya know, this wasn't such a good idea after all. I didn't come to get the third degree. I feel bad enough as it is."

And with that declaration, Marie stood up and started to leave.

"Wait," Bernice said. "I just wanted to talk to you."

"Why?"

"Well, I guess I wanted to see what he found so appealing in someone else, and now I know, but I must say I'd expect him to pick someone more buxom than you, someone who has more meat on the bones."

Marie wanted to tell Bernice that she didn't expect to find him married to a hefty beanie beefy, but decided to keep her mouth shut and try to get through the encounter.

"Did Scott tell you that this has happened before? That there was another woman named Gloria that he was gonna leave me for? She was married to a shipmate of his and Gloria was a friend of mine. They lived next door to us in Groton. In the end, Gloria reneged on him and went back to her husband."

"Yes, he did tell me," Marie said, and even though she could have, Marie didn't want to add anything about herself and the broken promises she had suffered through. There'd be no sympathy there, more than likely delight.

"I need to go back to work now," Marie said. "I'm sorry you've been hurt. I have no intention of seeing him again."

"Please don't tell Scott we had this meeting," Bernice asked. "I want to be the one to break it to him."

"Do as you please. I'm done with it," Marie answered and headed for the door.

Uh huh!

FIFTY

Marie didn't go back to work, but instead went home to lick her wounds with a scotch/rocks. She didn't know if she was more hurt or more angry with Scott, but there was someone she felt she could trust, someone who had eyes for her since she started working at the command, so she called Bobby Jenkins.

"I heard you got some shit goin' on," Bobby said when he pick up the phone.

"What are you doin?" she asked.

"What do you need?"

"A friend, and Bobby, that's all I need right now."

"Got any beer or vodka?"

"No, just scotch."

"I'll pick up a six pack and be right over," Bobby said.

"Don't tell anyone where you're going," she said.

"My lips are sealed. See you soon."

While she waited for Bobby to show up, she thought about how much she liked him, not enough for a sexual encounter, but more like a younger brother, dear friend. She also knew he had a serious drinking problem and that, more than anything, would keep her from any feelings she may entertain for him.

She remembered the night when the gang stayed at the club longer than usual and she was afraid to drive.

"Don't worry about driving," Bobby said. "I'll follow you out the back gate to your apartment and if you seem to be driving zig zag, I beep, you can park your car and I'll drive you home.

The next morning Marie, at the departmental POD (Plan of the Day) assembly which Susie and Marie were invited to attend, said to Bobby, "Gee, I must not have been too smashed cause you didn't beep at me."

"What?" Bobby said.

"You know, beep at me to pull over and you would drive me home," Marie answered.

"I don't remember that at all. Did I follow you out the gate?" he questioned.

She vowed never to get in a car with Bobby after that.

At a Christmas party the chiefs held in the conference room at the command, Marie picked Bobby's name out of a hat for gift giving. She went to Spencer's where joke gifts as well as naughty gifts could be purchased and found a seat belt for a bar stool which Marie immediately bought for him which he found to be side-splitting and so did his shipmates.

Anyway, half an hour later Bobby showed up, put the six pack on the counter and after removing a can from the pack, asked, "What the hell's goin' on?"

She told him of her meeting with Bernice to which he replied, "Jesus lady, if you were a man, you'd have two brass ones."

"I've been down this road before and I think what made me mad was the fact that I allowed myself to get caught up in the passion I felt being with Scott. I let myself fall when I should have never gotten involved in the first place. He was the one who started with this "you and me shit." I didn't expect it."

"Well, he's only got a few weeks left before retirement. Can you keep away from him til then?"

"I have to Bobby. Oh, shit, what about my job? The captain finds out about this and I could be fired. He'll ask Ben to can me before he'll administer any reprimand to Scott, and I don't want Scott reprimanded. I pray all I get is a slap on the wrist for being so damn stupid."

"Uh, don't look out the window, but a certain sailor is sitting on the wall that faces this apartment and it ain't Popeye the sailor man with a can of Spinach in his hand."

"Oh, God Bobby. Now what do I do?"

"Well, I'm gonna finish my beer and go to my car and not look right or left, up or down, get in it and drive away."

"Is he a violent man?"

"I don't think so, but you never know what he could be thinking. He knows my car and knows I'm in here."

"Good, let him sweat it out. You think he hasn't left my bed and gone home to hers, screwing both of us?"

"Not on my watch," Bobby said. "I'm outta here."

And he left.

She listened at the door, but didn't hear any commotion, no yelling, so she assumed Scott had left before Bobby.

Five minutes later, there was a knock on her door. She had no peephole in the door and didn't ask who was there, but instead opened it to find Scott standing there looking forlorn and exhausted.

She started to shut the door in his face. He put his foot in the way to stop it.

"Please let me in," he said.

"What do want? A little hey hey?"

"You know better than that," he said.

"No, I don't. Was that all it was? A little poon tang, something different than you were getting at home?"

"At first, yes. Jeez lady, all the sailors thought you were hot stuff."

"So you wanted to be the first to make a run on me, especially since you knew I'd told them none of them would get in my pants."

"No, that's not the way it is," he said.

"And when were you gonna tell me about not asking for a divorce?"

"When I got home last night, Bernice asked me to go to dinner. After we were seated, she told me that you called her, that she met you. I can't blame you, but you need to know that I will get a divorce. We discussed it after she told me about your meeting. She asked me if I loved you and I told her 'yes' to which she got mad as hell, threw her fork across the room and left the restaurant."

"You can forget it," Marie answered.

Then another knock at the door.

"Shit, who the hell is it this time?" Marie stated.

Marie opened the door to find Bernice standing there, hands on hips, and before she could close the door, Bernice stepped in and started yelling.

"You son of a bitch," Bernice said. "I didn't believe you meant it when you told me that you loved her. I thought you just wanted to play dip the wiener now and again with the slut."

"Hey, now wait a minute," Marie said. "You need to leave now and don't come back here again or I'll call the police and get a restraining order on you. And while we're at it, take your husband with you. And another thing, I didn't have a gun to his head demanding that he leave you. This was what he wanted."

"You can have him," Bernice said. "But it's gonna cost him dearly because before I'm through with him, he'll be lucky to own a pair of skivvies."

And Bernice went out the door, stomped down the stairs to her car and drove out of the parking lot.

Scott stood in the living room with his hands at his sides, his head hanging down. When he picked his head up, tears were streaming down his face, he collapsed on the sofa, put his head in his hands, shook his head back and forth.

"I'm sorry," was all he could manage to say.

"I think you need to think this over. I mean divorcing Bernice. I think she'd take you back." Marie said.

"There's no going back. I've come this far and intend to prove to you that I mean it," he said.

"Come back when you can show me a divorce decree. We can talk about it then. In the meantime, we've all been through a dreadful emotional upset. You know, I could lose my job over this. Fraternizing with a military man, especially when the company I work for has a contract with the Navy."

"You won't lose your job," Scott said. "I'll go to the captain and make sure that our affair doesn't affect your job."

He got up to leave and put his arms out to her. She backed away from him. He walked toward the door, opened it and left saying, "I still love you."

FIFTY-ONE

He wasn't at his desk the next morning when she went to work. Bobby came into the word processing room and told her why.

"He went to the captain and told him about you two," Bobby said. "He asked me to tell you that everything will be alright, that you won't lose your job. He's been transferred to another command on the base to finish out his enlistment until he retires. The captain thought it was the best way to work things out for all concerned. Oh, yeah, he's moved into the chief's barracks while waiting for his divorce to finalize, and no matter what happens with you and him, he intends to go through with it."

Marie was flabbergasted and when Bobby finished, she cried softly and left the building to head for the Owen Ocean sales office where Pam was located. When she got there, Pam asked her boss for a couple hours' time off and they left and headed to Dagwoods. They sat at the bar and Marie relived every detail of what had happened between Scott, Bernice and herself.

"God, now what?' Pam asked.

"I don't know," Marie answered. "I know I love him, but I just thought I couldn't take any more emotional suicide over this. I don't even know where he is right now."

"Well, I'd guess he means it, if he's moved out of his house and into the barracks."

"Ya know, I didn't believe him before, so many lies, but now I do. I just don't know what I want to do about it," Marie said.

"Well, think fast cause he just walked in the door and is hiding behind the post in the entryway."

As Marie turned toward the door, Scott stepped out from behind the post and stood there and Marie waved to him. He started walking toward her.

"This is where I exit," Pam said. And she got off the bar stool and left.

Marie's right hand motioned to the bar stool Pam had just left and Scott sat down.

"Did Bobby give you my message?" he asked.

"Yes."

"I told you this would happen. I got a lawyer who is going over the papers and will get back to me this week. Bernice is asking for everything - house, truck, and she sold my boat out from under me already."

"How could she do that?"

"She forged my name on the bill of sale."

"Oh, God, not for me. You're gonna lose everything."

"It's worth it, but I think she meant it when she said I'd be lucky to walk away with my skivvies. I'm not totally broke yet, so let me buy you a drink, OK?"

They sat for an hour drinking scotch/rocks and tried not to talk too much about the future cause they really didn't know what it would bring. He placed his hand on her knee and she placed her arm around him.

He paid the tab and took her hand guiding her off the stool toward the door. His truck was parked in the lot. They got in and headed toward the base and parked in the lot outside the barracks where he now lived.

"I want to show you where I live. Want you to prove that I've started legal proceedings toward my divorce," he said as they entered the barracks.

When he got to the room assigned to him, he opened the door with the key he had been given from base housing. Marie walked in and looked around. His bed was the size of a hospital bed. There was no television in the room. There was a set of drawers aside the bed and a small closet where he hung his clothes. He had to share a bathroom with shower located down the hall with other sailors who lived there.

His retirement was coming up in six weeks, after which he could no longer live in the barracks. He needed to find a job, but was not allowed to start his search for one until a month before his departure from the Navy.

The news he got from his lawyer about the divorce proceedings was not good.

"I went to court this morning. When the judge read the decree he said he could not grant it because I was giving everything I owned to

Bernice. We needed to negotiate another contract that would make it fairer to me, so I have to go through negotiations once more before it can be granted. I don't like it either, the waiting to be free, but I have no say in the matter and was willing to give her all I have to be free of her which includes my entire retainer until my son turns eighteen. His eighteenth birthday is a year away which isn't that bad. At that time, I will get my full retainer, will not have to give her any of it because she makes more money than I."

"Do you think I fell in love with you because you are loaded with money?" Marie asked.

"No, I know that, but when I come to you, I'll probably be owning only a pair of skivvies.

"I have eleven hundred dollars in the bank that will help us somewhat. I mean we won't be broke," Marie said.

"It'll be tight for a while, but we'll make it through," Scott added.

Believing that he was intent on his divorce, Marie fell back into his arms. They decided to christen the narrow bed in his room so they enveloped in each other's arms, ending with an electrifying climax for both of them.

Although he didn't move his belongings into her apartment, Scott and Marie spent their evenings there where he spent the night before arising early in the morning and returning to the barracks to shower and dress prior to heading to work at his newly appointed command on the base.

FIFTY-TWO

Christmas was a week away. Marie's mother, Marion, now widowed, decided to spend the holidays with her daughter. Marion and Danny, Marie's brother, booked a flight to Orlando on Christmas day two hours after Danny's last , but a snow storm whirled through upstate New York causing their flight to be cancelled. Marion flew in the next day and they celebrated Christmas a day late.

Marion had not met Scott previous to her visit, but immediately appreciated his quiet demeanor and politeness in showing her respect. She also didn't know that he was in the process of divorcing which would have made her upset that he and her daughter were co-habiting before he was single. The couple usually left work at the end of the day and went to Marie's apartment to have a happy hour with Marion before leave-taking later in the evening to go to the barracks for the night.

Realizing that they wanted to be together, Marion told Marie that as far as she was concerned, they should stay home and sleep in Marie's bed.

"I can't do that out of respect for your mother," Scott said when Marie told him, so they continued to go to the barracks to sleep which became cumbersome with both of them sleeping in a hospital wide bed, not to mention that if she needed to go to the bathroom while staying with him, he had to escort her down the hall and wait outside so another sailor would not enter while she was in there.

One evening after having too many beers, Marie needed to go really bad, so she put on one of Scott's khaki uniform shirts which covered her from the neck down to her thighs, put on her socks, and he walked her down the hall to the "head" (sailor talk for the urinal).

She was just beginning to pee when Scott said, "Stop" and she heard footsteps entering the head. Not knowing what to do, she froze but couldn't stop the stream from flowing into the toilet. She looked down and saw two little feet walk by encased in fluffy bugs bunny bedroom slippers and knew it was a child. She heard Scott laughing as he talked to a man outside the door of the head.

She finished and yelled, "Can I come out?" to which Scott, who couldn't keep from laughing, yelled back, "Yes, it's only a little guy."

"I don't think that's one bit funny," she exclaimed as she entered the doorway.

"I couldn't stop him," Scott said. "He just took off and headed to the urinal while his father and I stood outside, and after I told his father that you were in there, we found it to be very funny cause neither one of us wanted to come in and tell you."

"This shacking up in the barracks has to stop," Marie said. "And I think I know how to put an end to it." She placed the long distance call to her brother, Danny, the next day. "I need your help. Mother has been here a month now and doesn't want to return home. I have no problem with her staying, but it's ruining my private life with Scott and I don't know how to handle it."

"I'll catch a plane in a couple of days and come down to talk with her," Danny said. "And if she's adamant about living there, I'll help her find her own place."

"God, Dan, I don't want her to think don't I love her and want her to live here, just not with me."

"No, you have a right to your own life. She'll see that and will be happy in her own apartment. I'll call you back when I have flight reservations. In the meantime, tell her I'm coming, but not why, and don't worry about it."

Danny arrived the next afternoon, rented a car and drove to his sister's apartment where his mother waited anxiously to see him. They talked for a while before he asked her when she was planning to return home.

"I'm not coming back," she said. "You and your brother can sell my furniture and send my clothes to me. There is nothing there I want except my personal belongings."

"Where do you intend to live?" he asked.

"Oh, I like it here with Marie."

"Mother, you know how you like to get out each day, go to and do some shopping. Living here doesn't allow you to do any of those activities."

"Did Marie say I couldn't live with her?"

"No, I just thought you'd be better off living nearby in an area where you could be independent, that's all."

Marion became very quiet.

"Where's the paper?" Danny asked. "Let's look for a furnished apartment for you."

She was still silent.

"Here's one in nearby Winterton," Danny said. "Why not take a drive and look at it? And, it's a couple miles from here, so you'll be close to Marie."

Hesitantly, she followed her son down the stairs into his car and Danny drove to the apartment complex to look at the one advertised in the paper.

The building was an old, well maintained three floor stuccoed structure with sixteen units in it that had housed winter visitors in past years before it was turned into rentals for senior citizens. Marion fell in love with the location for she could walk to stores, a pharmacy, and best of all, a Catholic church located two blocks from the apartment building. She would find a doctor a block away in the coming months and knew the Florida weather to be advantageous to living a longer, fuller life compared to the sloppy, cold, cloudy weather that existed in the northeast.

The apartment Marion was shown was an efficiency one-room with attached bathroom and small kitchen located on the first floor. Thrilled at the amenities she could enjoy in her seventy-five years of age, she signed a lease. Danny and she went to the local K-Mart to purchase small appliances and bedding after which they went to lunch before returning to Marie's apartment to tell her that she was moving.

"I didn't think you'd find anything that fast," Marie said to Danny out of hearing distance from her mother.

"She was upset at first, but when she saw the unit, she lit up and there was no problem with her accepting the move," he said.

"Thank you, Danny," Marie said. Scott was with them at the time and reiterated the fact that they would watch over Marion. Cheryl, who lived nearby, would be in attendance for her grandmother also.

Time for Scott's job search was nearing which meant he would have to leave the barracks. His divorce negotiations were not going well. It seemed that giving all he had was not enough for Bernice and she needed to see him squirm.

FIFTY-THREE

General Technical Services, Inc. (GTS) had a contract with AUTEC (Atlantic Underwater Testing and Evaluation Center) Deep Water Weapons Range on Andros Island in the Bahamas to supply administrative and technical support. The range ran parallel to the east coast of the islands and operated a Naval base on North Andros.

Scott was informed of an opening on the island as torpedo post-run shop manager where he would oversee the maintenance and testing of Navy torpedoes. The salary was excellent, so he applied for the job, was granted an interview, and drove to West Palm Beach where the company's main office was located to be interviewed. After the interview, he was flown on the company plane, a forty seater, to the island to view the shop and talk with the employees he would be overseeing.

Upon his return from the island, he was offered the position and was to start working as soon as he retired from the Navy which was a week away. Although he wanted to be married to Marie before leaving, it didn't seem as though that would happen. He had to leave without her.

"Maybe it's a good thing," Marie said to him when he returned. "It'll give us time to be apart and sure that this is what we want."

"Are you saying that you are rethinking us?" Scott asked.

"No, I love you, need you, want to be with you, but it's been so hectic. I believe the break from each other will be good for both of us," she said. "I'll still be here waiting for you to come back for me."

His retirement party was held in the club with his shipmates surrounding him. He wanted and had Marie at it which usually isn't protocol, but his insistence of her presence was honored and she attended as he was presented his shadowbox by his buddy, Tom Johnston, who would one day make another presentation of a different kind to Marie.

Although he would return in two weeks, Scott departed two days later for "paradise" leaving a tearful Marie standing in her doorway as he didn't want her to accompany him to the airport for his flight to West Palm. He knew they would both find the experience to be too painful when they kissed goodbye.

Marie went to work the next day but was quiet, which was unusual for her as she always had a big smile and happy hello when approached, so she stayed in the word processor room and kept to herself wondering what would be forthcoming and if she and Scott even had a future together after all they'd been through.

Will he forget about me when he gets there, she wondered.

With no divorce decree in sight, she thought it possible they would never find each other united as one in marriage.

Marie went to work each day and because it was a long distance call from Andros and had to be placed hours in advance of connection, she sent Scott letters confirming her love to him. She and the gang from Owen Ocean Systems "stopped" at Dagwoods after work as usual, but she was not as jovial as she had been in the past. They cracked jokes and talked about working for the Navy but were careful not to offend as they all knew Marie would probably someday be the wife of a Navy retiree.

She drank too much on one of the stops and decided she shouldn't drive. She called Cheryl and asked her to come pick her up, a phone call that she would regret later in her life. Although Cheryl did come for her mother, not a word was spoken by either one of them on the drive home.

Marie arrived home one evening after happy hour to the phone ringing. When she answered it, Scott was on the other end.

"Hi," he said.

"Oh, God, where are you?" she asked.

"On the island."

"I hear the static."

"I called to tell you I'll be coming home in two days."

"What? Did you get my letters?"

"Yes."

"But you didn't write back."

He didn't answer, but told her that he loved her and would be seeing her soon.

Marie cried saying, "I never knew how painful this absence was gonna be. I'm so sad and lonely missing you."

"It's the same for me, but it's almost over. I can't stay on the phone for long. It costs an arm and although the company will take it out of my pay, I haven't yet received my first paycheck. Hang in there, honey. I'll see you soon. Know that I love you."

And he hung up.

Marie stood in the living room and started to feel that her life was turning around, and she knew that the one she had waited for, her PC, would return.

Bouncy and busy the next day at work, the sailors knew something was up and started asking her if she'd heard from Scott. She decided not to tell them that he was coming back, surprise them, so she stifled her joyfulness and only told Pam.

Scott flew in the afternoon of the second day, a Friday after the phone call, and went right to the command to see her. When he walked into the room, she looked up from her computer, jumped up and flew into his arms. Seeing that they needed to be alone for a few minutes, the staff, the sailors, left the room until such time as they thought they could reenter and shake hands and talk with him.

When they returned, Scott and Marie were nowhere to be found. They had slipped through the side door Scott had introduced her to months before when he took her out to lunch the first time.

"How long are you here for?" Marie said.

"Sh," Scott said. "I have good news."

"What?"

"I'll tell you when we get to the apartment."

He pulled up in the parking lot, they got out and ran up the stairs. Marie fumbled searching for the key and when she finally found it in her purse, she shakenly tried to open the door with it, but couldn't as Scott grabbed her, turned her to him and held her in an embrace that sucked the air out of her lungs.

They stood on the landing for a couple minutes holding each other and with tears in their eyes, Scott took her key and opened the door.

When they entered the apartment, he took a document out of his pocket, held it up and said, "I am divorced. We can get married."

Marie collapsed on the sofa, read the document and noted that he was indeed free. She couldn't speak for a few minutes staring at him in disbelief.

"I only have a few days before I have to return to the island. When would you like to marry?" he asked

"When do you have to go back?" she asked.

"Tuesday morning, so we don't have much time."

"I never thought this day would come, so I've made no plans for it. Let's go see Pam and ask her if she is busy on Monday."

They drove to Pam's office. Pam knew that Scott was coming home so when they walked through the door, she was not surprised.

"What are you doing Monday at noon?" Marie asked.

"Why? You guys want to go to lunch?" Pam asked.

"No, we want to get married and seeing as how you are a Notary, we want you to perform the ceremony," Scott said.

"What? Son of a, I'll be damned. I don't know what to say," Pam answered.

"But you can't tell anyone 'til after we're married," Marie said.

"Where?" Pam asked.

"Noon at my apartment," Marie said.

"OK, In the meantime, I'll search for vows you two can say."

"Make them simple and short," Marie said. "We don't have much time as he has to leave to go back to the island early the next morning."

"OK, I'll put something together and call you tomorrow. Jeez already," Pam said smiling.

Scott asked her what kind of a wedding band she wanted. They went to the mall and she chose a wide gold band with a diamond in the middle. Scott's wasn't as wide, but was a plain gold one wider than what most men prefer. Marie insisted on paying the price of $75 for it.

"I'll go back on Tuesday morning. I still have one more move paid for by the Navy, but I think it best if we store your furniture. One perk of being a manager is that they give me a three bedroom furnished trailer to live in. I have to pay the electric and phone. I get free meals but only have to pay a pittance for yours, so we should be able to save some money while living there."

They spent the weekend talking about the life they would share on an island in the Bahamas, a new start for both of them away from the negative atmosphere that surrounded them since they met.

Marie decided that she wasn't going to buy a new dress for the wedding. She had a yellow v-neck silk one that she loved, and Scott would wear the lime green polyester suit he bought shortly after he met Marie.

Needing a best man, Scott approached his friend, Tom Johnston late Friday afternoon at the club.

"I need you to wear a suit and come to Marie's house on Monday at noon," he said.

"Are we going to a funeral or a wedding?" Tom asked.

"A wedding - mine and Marie's," Scott answered.

"What? So you're really gonna do it?"

"Yes, Tom, I love her. Will you do it?"

"Sure."

"One thing. You can't tell anyone where you're going til after we're married."

"OK."

They spent a lot of time with Cheryl over that weekend, who, when asked, refused to stand up for her mother. She didn't think it was a good idea for them to marry with all the uncertainty they had been through and felt that the marriage wouldn't last, so she couldn't be a part of something she didn't believe was right.

Although it hurt Marie to have her daughter refuse, she was determined to marry Scott and throw the dice letting them fall where they may. Even the best of intentions in a relationship sometimes don't work out.

Scott was up earlier than usual on Monday morning, his usual waking time being around 4:30. Marie woke up when Scott put his arm around her shoulder, slid it under the sheet and gently cupped her right breast in his hand. She stirred, turned over and put her arms around him.

"Think we should wait til we're man and wife?" she asked.

"It never stopped us before," he answered.

So, on the morning of their wedding day, they took joy in their sexual intercourse arriving, as always, in a unison orgasm that they knew they would share for the rest of their lives.

Even though there would be only four people at their wedding, the waiting for Tom and Pam to arrive was nerve-racking, so they had a glass of red wine. Scott had bought a yellow long stemmed rose for Marie to hold while repeating the vows which they ended up writing themselves. They consisted of three lines in which they promised love, patience, encouragement, and support in the finding and development of each other's goals and respect for the decisions the vows will cause them to make.

Tom was on time, but Pam called to say she was running late, so they all had another glass of wine.

When Pam arrived half an hour later, she was a nervous wreck, asked for a drink, so they all had another glass of wine.

At last the time came when the vows would be exchanged. The vows were said in minutes. Pam pronounced them man and wife then signed the marriage certificate which sealed the union of Scott and Marie Nicholson.

"I'd better call the command and tell the guys at Owen Ocean Systems that Marie Nicholson won't be back to work til tomorrow morning," Pam said with a twinkle in her eye.

After hanging up the phone, Pam laughingly commented that she talked to one of the technicians who said, "You mean Marie Maxwell, don't you?"

To which Pam replied, "No, I mean Marie Nicholson. I married Scott and Marie a short time ago."

Tom wanted to get out of the monkey suit he wore, so he had a drink before wishing them well and left to go back to the command.

Pam had to get back to work, so before Tom left, she proposed a toast to the new bride and groom.

The apartment was quiet as they stood there holding each other and Marie started to cry.

"What's the matter?" Scott asked.

"After all we've been through, it's just a release of emotion," she said. "I'd better call my mother and Danny."

Marion wished them both well and appeared to be genuinely happy for the couple.

When Marie told Danny, he became angry with Marie asking what about their mother.

"Cheryl is here. She'll be sure her Gram will be OK. I don't expect we'll be living on the island that long, just long enough to save some money."

Danny hung up on his sister leaving a dead line on the phone in her hand. She was shocked, never expecting him to be disappointed that she married Scott.

Having very little time before leaving, Scott had to take Marie to the base Pass and ID to get her a military identification card. After completing the paperwork, Marie received her ID and privilege card which assured her benefits which included the exchange, commissary, and medical insurance.

They went to a nearby steakhouse for dinner that evening. Marie ordered surf and turf, but before she could finish it, she got sick to her stomach and had to be taken to the apartment leaving her dinner half eaten.

After she took Pepto, her digestive track calmed down. They went to bed early as Scott needed to arise at 2:30 to leave for W. Palm to catch his plane back to Andros.

He was dressed and kissed her forehead as she lay in the bed the next morning.

"Don't get up," he said. "I'll be in touch by phone in a couple days. You know that in a week, I've made arrangements for you to fly over and scout the island to see what you'll want to bring with you when you move. In the meantime, know how much I love you; you are my life."

And he quietly walked out the bedroom door through the living room and opened the door leading to the porch, closed it and left leaving Marie misty eyed.

FIFTY-FOUR

Word that Marie and Scott married passed around the command swiftly, so when she entered the building the next morning, her coworkers and the Navy chiefs she worked with were on hand to congratulate her.

"Gee, we didn't think you guys were that serious," one of the sailors said.

"We're happy for you two. He's a great guy," another said.

But one of the chiefs, an egotistical womanizing chief made a different comment about the marriage.

"I can't believe you married Scott. He's the biggest run-around in the command and had more girlfriends than anyone I know, and I've known him ten years."

And he turned and walked away leaving Marie standing in the hallway in tears.

"Don't pay any attention to him," Bobby Jenkins said after being told. "He's got a lot of nerve when he can't wait to travel so he can hook up with some babe in another city far away from his wife. He's got one in California he sees when he has to go out there."

"I knew he had a girlfriend out there," Marie said. "She used to call and I answered the phone, but I would never tell anyone about her cause I felt like I was one of the guys."

"He's jealous, pure and simple," Bobby said. "Remember when you said, 'Not one of you is gonna get in my pants?' when we first met you?"

"Yes, why?" she asked.

"Well, he was goin' around soundin' off about how he'd challenge your statement."

"He never came near me, never tried to get me to hop in the rack, as you guys always say."

"No, he got involved with someone here on base and forgot about it."

"I'd have told him where the cat shit in the bucket had he tried."

But Marie still felt bad, bad enough to wonder if she had made a mistake.

The vibes between Marie and Scott were connecting exceedingly well that evening when she got home after work. She sat down with a glass of wine and started crying when the phone rang.

"Hello," she said.

"Hi, honey," Scott said.

He noticed that she was not composed.

"What's the matter?"

"One of the chiefs made a sarcastic remark about us getting married, said you were a womanizer."

And she broke down in tears.

"Who?" he asked.

"Alan," she answered.

"I told you about her. Other than that, there has been no one until you."

"Did we make a mistake?"

"God, no. Don't cry. You know how much I love you, and you'll be coming here in a week. Hang in there. I told you months ago that we'd be together and I meant it. I've got to go. I've used up my long distance time. I love you."

She hung up the phone wondering about their decision to marry, went to bed and cried herself to sleep.

Upon waking the next day, Marie decided to let fate take a hand and went to work avoiding those she thought might give her a ration about marrying Scott. She and Susie went to lunch at Dagwoods returning to the command at one o'clock.

Henry, one of the technicians who worked for Owen Ocean Systems, came into her work area and said, "Your husband called. Said he was coming in to OIA at 5 on Flight 52 of the Silver Eagle Air and wants you to pick him up."

"No, I was supposed to go over to Andros next week," she exclaimed.

"Well, that's all I know. Asked me to give you the message."

"Is this a joke?" she said. "Is there such an airline as Silver Eagle. I've never heard of them."

"Let's look it up in the yellow pages," Henry said.

"Sure enough, it's listed and an 800 number listed with it," he said.

Marie called the 800 number and asked if there was a flight 52. The reservationist said, "Yes, arriving OIA at 5 P.M."

"Where does it originate?" Marie asked.

"In the Bahamas," was the answer.

Marie was ecstatic that he was coming, probably to get her. Her joy bustled around her as she walked down the hall to tell Bobby.

"See, I told you," he said. "It looks like we'll be losing one of the best sand crab civilians we've ever had working here, but I'm happy for you and Scott."

Elated and singing on her drive to the airport, Marie arrived in plenty of time before Scott's arrival at 5 o'clock. She stood outside the gate of Silver Eagle Airways and watched as each passenger exited the plane, a small commuter plane. When she saw him step out of the doorway, he was looking around. She was jumping up and down while holding on to the chain link fence that separated them.

Then he spotted Marie and hurried toward the opening in the fence, dropped his bag and threw his arms around her, picking her up in the air while twirling her around.

"How, what ...." she was trying to ask him.

"I'll tell you on the way home," he answered.

When they got to the apartment, she poured a glass of wine for each of them and asked, "Now tell me how you were able to come back so soon."

"I had to find a reason to return so soon after leaving and although the company I work for knew you were coming over in a week, I couldn't find a good reason to come back. I talked to one of technicians, a former sailor who has been on the island a long time, and he advised me, although it wasn't the kindest of reasons, to request funeral leave."

"What?" Marie said flabbergasted.

"It was the only way to get back to get you. God, I didn't know what to think after talking with you last night. You were so upset."

"Whose funeral did you tell them you had to return for?"

"My mother's."

"Oh my God, no. And how do you expect to return if she does die while we're there? She's in her late sixties."

Before he could answer her, the phone rang. Marie answered it.

"This is the Floral Leaf Flower Shop. I have an arrangement for the Nicholson residence, but I don't have an address. Would you be kind enough to tell me where to deliver the arrangement?"

Holding the phone away from her ear, Marie was taken aback and stood there with a fazed look. Scott took the phone out of her hand, asked who was calling.

Repeating the message and after finishing, Scott directed the delivery be made at the apartment.

Even though it wasn't cold, it was after all August, Marie felt a chill up her spine and for a second time in two days wondered if she made a mistake.

They didn't talk about it after that, not even when the floral arrangement was delivered. It included a greenery of ferns, white roses, and yellow chrysanthemums with a card that said, "So sorry for your loss" and was signed by his employer.

"The company plane leaves on Friday morning. I've made arrangements for us to be on it," Scott said.

Marie was staring at the arrangement and made no comment.

"Did you hear me?"

"What? Oh, yes."

"In the meantime, I think we'd better call a moving and storage company to pick up the furniture and take with us only what we need. I know you want your personal items, certainly your clothes, so we can start packing now."

"Yeah, OK."

The moving storage company could pick up the furniture no sooner than Friday morning, so Marie asked Cheryl if she could be there when the movers came and oversee the pickup.

"Well, Mother, I guess you know what you're doing, moving to the Bahamas, and I'll be glad to help as best I can, so don't worry about the furniture. I'll be here. Just go and enjoy the beginning of a new life on Paradise Island with PC," she said sarcastically.

With some doubt lingering which Marie didn't show outwardly, she vowed she would do her best to make a go of her marriage to Scott which is something she never would have been able to do if she didn't love him so much.

They started packing her car the day before their flight. Marie was coming down the stairs with Scott behind her holding suitcases when she stopped and saw Clark riding a bicycle through the parking lot. She still occasionally had lunch with him, maybe twice a year, but hadn't seen him in a few months.

Clark stopped the bike and said, "I heard you got married. Congratulations."

"This is my husband, Scott Nicholson," Marie said. "We're moving to the Bahamas where Scott has taken a job."

"I wish you luck in your new life," Clark said. And he peddled away, out of the lot and down the street. Marie thought she saw a tear fall down his cheek but said nothing about it to her husband."

"Who's that?" Scott asked.

"An engineer who used to come into the company I worked for in Suttonville, New York, on simulator acceptances.

"Seems like a nice guy," Scott said. And if he had any inkling of the relationship between Clark and Marie in the past, he didn't show it.

Marie kissed her daughter goodbye on Thursday afternoon before leaving for South Florida to catch the plane the next day to the island.

"Don't worry about anything, Mom. I'll take care of the movers."

FIFTY-FIVE

Marie and Scott boarded the propeller airplane, took their seats, fastened their seat belts and waited for the plane to taxi down the runway into the air.

Scott took Marie's hand and said, "At last we're together as man and wife and heading to a new life. I must tell you it's an island, not totally paradise, but I think you will like the U.S. citizens who work with me."

The flight took an hour, during which when gazing out of the window, Marie saw the turquoise and blue colored ocean down below that surrounded tiny islands covered with white sand and palm trees, and she thought she surely was being taken to paradise. But when the plane landed and they exited it, Marie stepped into a humidity that was worse than Central Florida's. Wanting to make a good impression on his co-workers, she had chosen to wear a cocoa brown sleeveless dress with a white linen collar and white inch-sized polka dots on it, panty hose, and heels on her feet.

They were met by Jack Singer who had brought his car to the island when he signed up to live and work there three years before, but whose wife remained in Jacksonville which was just fine with him. Introductions made, Jack placed the luggage in the back of his Jeep and they headed down a dirt road toward the trailer Scott had been given to live in.

Jack pulled up outside their new home and opened the door while Scott insisted on carrying his bride across the threshold and into the living room. He set her down and started talking about how much room they have - three bedrooms so they could invite friends from the states to come visit and stay, and even a washer/dryer located alongside of the air conditioner which had been turned on to cool the trailer before their arrival.

Scott stopped short while excitedly mentioning all the plusses and said, "Oh, my God, look at Marie's legs."

Marie looked down and saw hundreds of tiny brown insects on her stockings and knew from past dealings with them that they were fleas, dog fleas.

She screamed, jumping up and down brushing the fleas off, and ran out the door, down the steps and into the walkway with Scott following her and Jack following him.

"I can't live in there," she said crying.

"I know, I know, honey. I'll take care of it."

"Well, where do we live if not there? Are there any motels on this island?"

"No," Scott said sheepishly.

"Did you know about this when you came to get me?"

"No."

"Jump in the Jeep and we'll go to Housing," Jack interrupted.

"Get my bags out of that god damn flea trap or they'll infest in them too," Marie said.

While Marie and Scott climbed into the Jeep, Jack ran into the trailer and retrieved the luggage, threw it in the back of the Jeep and started for the Housing Dept.

Marie was sobbing, "Why I ever let you talk me into coming here is beyond me. This certainly ain't no paradise island, No motels. Shit!!!!!"

Poor Scott, who didn't know there were fleas in the trailer - they didn't bother him - tried to reassure his new bride with words of comfort while holding her in his arms as she cried.

Jack pulled up outside Housing, and he and Scott went in to talk with the department head, leaving Marie to scan the seemingly barren area she would be calling home for she didn't know how long.

"We have no other living arrangement but can put you up in the BOQ (officer's quarters) while we bomb the trailer to get rid of the fleas," the housing manager said. "That's the reason we don't allow animals on the island any more. Too much trouble with flea infestation. If they attacked your wife to that degree, we'll probably have to bomb three, four times before they're all gone. Sorry."

So, Scott, Jack and Marie lugged the baggage up the stairs to the second floor of the BOQ to a furnished room that had a double bed, bureau, small sofa, and little television and an attached bath.

"We'll go the PX and get a larger television," Scott said, and hoped to God they had one to sell being that the PX was housed in a small trailer and didn't stock a large assortment of anything electronic, but full stocked alcohol which employees filled their carts with.

"See, it's not so bad, honey," Scott said. "We can stay here until the fleas are gone, then we'll have a nice place to live."

Marie didn't answer and just looked dejected.

Jack in the meantime, thought it time for happy hour, so he asked, "Anyone for a drink?" to which Scott, after searching Marie's unreadable face, said, "Yeah, we do."

They left the room and headed toward the Officer's Club, a very small one that only served alcohol, no food. There was a bar and a few small tables and chairs. While in the Navy, Scott was enlisted and not allowed in the "O" club, but because he was a manager on Andros Island, he was acknowledged as though he was an officer.

Top shelf booze was two 'fers, the cost being two for $.45. Tanqueray gin, Chivas Regal scotch, Smirnoff vodka, Jack and Coke and expensive rum, which most people drank were among the favorites of the employees. There were three bars on the base: the O Club, for Navy officers, although there were only two of them; the Deep Six, which was frequented by hourly employees not allowed in the officer's club; and a pizza bar which served beer, wine and snacks for hours when the base cafeteria was closed. There were no restaurants inside the base, only a couple native eateries outside in the town of Nicholls that served conch cooked ten different ways.

The island itself was only a hundred four miles in length and forty miles wide with a population of less than five thousand.

When they entered the O club, they headed right to the bar and took a seat on a wooden stool.

"Nurse," Jack Singer yelled.

The lady bartender turned around from taking inventory behind the bar and said, "What'll ya have?"

"Vodka rocks," Jack said. Scott and Marie joined in asking for the same.

"This is Scott's wife, Marie," Jack said to the bartender.

"Hey, I'm Beverly," she said with her hand extended to shake adding, "welcome aboard."

She was older than Marie by a couple years, probably around forty seven, and Marie took to Beverly immediately shaking her hand. Beverly's smile was genuine and full, and although she was not a particularly good looking woman, her short blonde hair was not styled and she wore very little makeup, but she had a manner that Marie found inviting.

The threesome ended up staying longer than they intended, drinking a lot of booze, before realizing that it was too late to get to the cafeteria for supper, so they headed to the pizza bar to order a large one before retiring to their places of residence.

Non-management employees were not given a trailer of their own to live in nor could they bring family to the island. Jack lived in a three bedroom trailer that was shared by himself and two male employees and because all employee's meals were supplied by General Technical Services in the cafeteria, there was no need to have cooking appliances in the trailers.

Scott arose early the next morning to go to the shop leaving Marie sleeping, and as he kissed her before leaving, he thought about how many difficulties and delays she had gone through for the love of him which made him love her even more.

Marie awoke when the cleaning lady knocked on the door.

"Want d room cleaned?" she asked.

"No," Marie answered as she put on her robe and went to answer the door. Upon opening the door, Marie saw a large black native Bahamian woman standing there with a big smile on her face. Marie could see the gold fillings in her front teeth and wondered how she could afford to pay for them if her only job was cleaning.

"How often do you come?" Marie asked.

"Every day if you want, Mam."

"Oh, no, we don't change sheets that often at home, so you won't have to come every day."

"Is my job," the maid said.

Realizing that the woman was paid to clean every day, Marie told her it was okay and asked her name.

"Tilda," was the answer.

"Well, Tilda, I don't know how long we're gonna be here before we move into our trailer."

"Oh, you d one has fleas in your home."

"What? Does everyone know about it?"

"It a small island. Word goes 'round."

"You the wife of the new man; he "so good lookin' too."

"That'd be me. Now don't you go flirting with him Tilda. Good lookin' woman like you just might take him away from me."

Tilda laughed heartily and said, "I got me a big, good lookin' man at home, so no worries there."

I bet you do, thought Marie."

"I got other rooms to clean, so I best be moving on," Tilda said as she backed out of the doorway, turned, and walked down the hall.

Scott returned to the barracks at lunchtime to take Marie to the dining hall. While walking down the street, Marie noticed potholes in the street, some as big as two feet diameter and a foot deep.

"I didn't notice these last night," she said to Scott.

"You were pretty loaded when we left the bar. I kinda guided you home."

"I don't think I want to bring my car over here with these potholes. It's an old car and could never survive hitting one even once," Marie said.

When they stepped into the cafeteria, heads turned towards them making Marie feel self-conscious.

"Hey," Scott said to Marie, "I got the best lookin' woman on the island and they all know it."

He lead her toward the buffet where the food carts were loaded with salads, cold meats, hot meats, veggies, potatoes, desserts and beverages and she helped herself to a little bit of a lot of it.

They chose a table that was unoccupied and sat to eat their food when Scott's boss approached and asked if he could join them.

Scott stood up and said, "Sure. Have a chair. I would like to introduce you to my wife, Marie. Marie this is my supervisor, Ed Clancy."

"Welcome aboard," Ed said. "I'm sorry for your loss and so newly married too. When you get settled, my wife and I would like you over for a cocktail."

Marie put her head down and thanked him for his condolence after which Ed Clancy left.

They finished lunch. Scott walked her back to the barracks telling her he would be back at 3:30 and they could go to happy hour at the O club.

"I need to tell you how to get around the island, but I'll do that when I come back for you," he said.

"I have some notes to write and personal things to take care of which will take me a while, so after three is good for me," she replied.

Scott kissed her goodbye and headed back to the shop.

Marie passed the time writing notes to her family and friends, hanging clothes, and reading a book she brought with her.

They went back to the O Club when Scott returned and ordered a round of drinks from Beverly. Shortly after sitting down, Marie noticed that she was itching on her backside and started scratching herself.

Beverly noticed and asked her what was wrong.

"I don't know," Marie replied. "I've got an itch on my back below my waist that's driving me nuts."

"No-see-ums," Beverly said.

"No what?" Marie asked.

"No-see-ums," Beverly answered. "They'll bite the hell out of you. Go in the ladies room, drop your slacks and look in the mirror."

As Marie headed toward the ladies room, Scott put his head in his hands and sighed.

When Marie dropped her drawers, she saw that her backside was bright red and swollen almost like she'd been bit by mosquitos.

Returning, she asked Beverly, "What the hell are no-see-ums? You ought to see my ass. It's beet red. They went through my clothes?"

"That's why they call them that. You can't see them they're so small. Sometimes against a dark background, they appear like specks of white. They're indigenous to tropical climates like Andros and yes, they're so small they can pass through fabric."

"How do you deal with them?" Marie asked.

"You spray yourself all over with Cutters and that's the only way. You must have some sweet blood, honey, cause they don't bother everyone."

Marie looked at her husband with that same disgusted look he'd seen yesterday. She turned and said to Beverly, "I'll have a double."

Scott and Marie had two more drinks before walking to the dining hall for dinner. They filled their plates and Scott started talking about the island.

"There is a bus that runs every fifteen minutes around the base. It makes stops at all the bars as well as the beach which I'll take you to tomorrow," he said. "There is also some activities for dependents of managers who don't work such as drawing classes and pottery. There really isn't much to do here if you don't work, and I'm so sorry that we have to shack up at the BOQ, but for now that's the best we can do."

"Every month, there's an excursion to Nassau on the company plane, but we have to make reservations a week in advance cause everyone wants to get off the island and go to the big city."

"I was called today by the housing office and told the trailer was bombed. The way they can tell if they killed all the fleas is to lay a white towel on the floor and wait for the fleas to come to it, and they did; the fleas that is, so they have to bomb it again."

Marie didn't say anything, which is unusual for her, and that gave Scott a feeling of dread insofar as his wife's acceptance of her new surroundings, but he dismissed his unease knowing he was doing everything he could to make her comfortable.

On Saturday, Scott and Marie took the bus to the beach and soaked up the warm Bahamian sun. Although she was forty-four, she could still wear a bikini; cellulite could not be seen anywhere on her body. As they walked to the water, she could feel the warm, white sand between her toes and the water was as temperate as bath water. Strolling along the edge of the beach, hand in hand, she asked her husband, "What do people do here for excitement besides drink?"

"We can go to the cove up ahead and look for Charlie the shark. He hangs around there a lot. Oh, I forgot, there's a theatre that shows a movie every night."

Delightful, Marie thought facetiously, but didn't say a word.

They returned to the barracks, showered, dressed and headed to the O Club for a dinky. When they sat at the bar, Beverly asked Marie how the bites were.

"So far so good," she answered. "Scott bought some Cutter's and I practically took a bath in it."

"Attta a girl," Beverly said. "What'll ya have? Same?"

"Yes,"

And they made it an early night, heading back to the barracks to make love. On their way back, Marie screamed and pointed ahead of her.

"What the hell are they?' she said.

"Oh, them? They're land crabs."

"There must be hundreds of them. They're six inches diameter and how come they run sideways with their black tentacles up and eyes open looking at me?"

"I don't know. They're just part of the island," he answered and didn't dare tell her about the boa constrictor he saw curled up under the trailer.

As he started caressing his wife, Marie burst out laughing.

"Since when does our lovemaking become something to laugh at?" he asked irritably.

"I'm sorry, honey, but with everything that has happened since I got on the island, did you ever stop to think that maybe I wasn't meant to come here. I mean maybe it's the booze, or maybe I'm just coming down off the experiences I've had, but all of a sudden I just had to laugh. It has nothing to do with you."

Still irritated, Scott said, "Well, let's just turn over and go to sleep then."

Marie got up, went to the bathroom, closed the door, sat on the john and howled with laughter. Scott put the pillow over his head and said, *Women!!!!* to himself.

But her paradise island experience wasn't over yet.

FIFTY-SIX

Andros Island is hit by a hurricane on average every two and a half years.

Scott opened the door to their room in the barracks, stepped in and called to his wife.
"Honey? Honey?"
"What?"
"We have to pack our things and be on the ready to leave."
"Oh, we're goin' to the trailer? Well it's about time."
"No, not the trailer. God, I don't know how to say this but to just come right out and say it."
"There's a hurricane coming and all U.S. citizens have to leave the island. Private planes have been contracted in helping with the evacuation."
"What? It's beautiful outside, sun shining. Is this a joke?"
"No, we have to be at the ready to get out. Managers leave last, so I want you on one of the first planes to fly off the island."
"Wait a minute. Let me understand. A hurricane is coming? When?"
"It should approach Andros in two days and is considered dangerous: a category 5 which could destroy the island to the point of nothing being left."
Marie knew nothing about hurricanes being that she was from the northeast where they never were a hazard.
"Jesus X," she said. "I haven't been here two weeks; fleas, no-see-ums, giant crabs and now a hurricane. I'm not going without you."
"But, honey, I'll be one of the last to leave, and I'd feel better knowing you're safe in West Palm.
"No, I go with you," she said arms folded across her chest as she stomped her right foot.

"What are they going to do with us when we get to West Palm?" she asked.

"We're being put up in a Holiday Inn," he said. "Some employees are down at the airport waiting now for a flight out; some who have built homes here are staying and weathering the storm out in a cave nearby their residences. Those citizens are on their own and had to sign a statement that they would not sue the U.S. government should the island be devastated to the point of being wiped out including their lives."

"Do we pack a bag?" Marie asked.

"Only what we need. The rest I'll put up in the rafters."

"How much time do we have?" she asked.

"A day," he answered.

Scott left the barracks to go and secure what he could at the shop promising Marie he'd return as soon as possible leaving her to pack a bag of necessities for both of them.

As she packed, Tilda knocked at the door and when Marie opened it, Tilda asked her if she wanted the room cleaned.

"My God, Tilda, there's a hurricane coming. No need to clean. And what do you do when a storm comes? I mean how do the native Bahamians survive?"

"Oh, we open d back door and open d front door and let d water pass through." Tilda answered.

"Well, I'll say a prayer that God spares your home and loved ones and protects the island from the rampages of the storm."

"Tank you, Mam," and Tilda walked down the hall to the next room.

Scott came back for Marie later in the afternoon.

"We don't evacuate until tomorrow morning," he said. "In the meantime, most of the managers are going over to the O Club and down a few cause it don't look like anyone will sleep tonight, so come on honey. We've done all we can do here."

When they entered the O Club, other managers were at the bar putting 'em away. They had sent their wives out ahead of them on one of the private planes that were transporting employees and their families back to the mainland.

Beverly was still bartending and she poured Scott and Marie their usual and set it down in front of them.

"I've been asked to stay and tend the bar and go out tomorrow," she said. "But I don't know anyone going at the same time. I mean most of those managers and their wives snubbed me from day one," she said in a low voice so as not to be heard.

"You go with us," Marie said, and Scott agreed wholeheartedly.

There was a commotion and when they turned to check it out, they saw the Navy Base Captain enter with an oar in his right hand, wearing a life vest, which broke the anxiety that everyone at the bar was trying not to show.

"I'm ready," Captain James said. "Beverly, give me a double anything. It's gonna be a long night."

The more they all drank, the more they lightened up. None of them left until late into the evening and they all wondered what they'd come back to, if coming back would even be even be an option at all.

Marie and Scott didn't sleep well that night. Scott held her in his arms. Her fear of the unknown was becoming obvious to him, and although he wouldn't admit it to her, he was anxious about the future of not only living on the island, but how Marie would react to returning to it after the storm.

They both awoke before dawn the next morning and prepared to leave the building with what Marie could fit in one bag of luggage. Heading to the small airport, the island already looked deserted, for most of the company employees had vacated.

The terminal building was no bigger than two double-car garages. For it was expected to fill only the flight requirements of the company plane.

Scott and Marie checked in and were told to take a seat until their names were called for their flight. They waited two hours before being called to proceed to the tarmac, as a private plane had landed and was ready to board passengers. Somehow, Scott had been successful in getting Beverly on the same flight as he and Marie, so she waited with them, visibly shook up.

"Hurry up and get on the god damn plane," the pilot yelled out to the passengers who were walking toward the plane. "I can't shut it down cause I've had a problem with the prop battery. Come on, come on, hurry up."

At this point, Scott recognized the pilot, someone named Charlie, who had been fired from the company for drinking while piloting the company plane, but he didn't dare tell Marie or anyone else for that matter.

They boarded, all sixteen of them, took their seats and buckled up. Charlie closed the hatch, took his pilot seat, and started down the runway, finally lifting off into the sunny sky and heading toward the southeast coast of the United States.

He was probably half an hour airborne when turbulence hit the small craft and it dropped five hundred feet, leaving Marie's heart in her throat and she clutched her husband's hand and started tearing up.

"Is this the end of us?" she asked.

"No, honey," Scott said as calmly as he could. "He just hit a pocket of air," although he wondered if they'd survive it himself.

"Sorry about that Charlie said over the intercom. Just some turbulence, nothing to be afraid of. I'll get you to West Palm, and oh, by the way, there's a locker in the back of the plane filled with liquor. Open it up and help yourself."

Meanwhile, Beverly, who was sitting across the aisle from them, started crying uncontrollably, so Marie extended her hand out to her in an effort to help calm her down.

The booze locker was opened by one of the managers. He held up a bottle of scotch and a bottle of rye whiskey, found some glasses, and passed the booze and glasses around to the passengers, who each poured three fingers in their glasses and drank it down.

The plane landed in W. Palm. The sun was still out and the passengers were driven to the Holiday Inn to stay until it was safe enough to return to the island. Most of them huddled in the lounge drinking. Beverly was glued to Scott and Marie for a while before going to check out her room. She returned with two rolls of masking tape and four candles and stood by the table Marie and Scott were sitting at and started crying.

"What are you doing with that?" Marie asked.

"The front desk manager gave them to me asking that we go to our rooms, tape the windows, fill the bathtubs with water, and place the candles in a centrally located table ready to be lit so we could see our way around. I can't stand this any longer. My car is in the company parking lot. I'm goin' inland to Orlando. I tried to get through to my sister and all the lines are tied up. Thanks for everything, you two."

And with that, she turned and walked toward the lobby.

Marie looked at Scott and said, "I want to go to Orlando too. I need to be sure Cheryl and my mother are OK."

Marie's car was parked in the company lot also. Scott, seeing how frightened she was, agreed that they should get out of the way of the storm, go inland and check on the family.

Scott drove out of the parking lot and headed to I-95 N in an effort to evade what became hurricane David. It didn't take long to realize that citizens from south Florida were trying to escape the tempest because I-95 was a parking lot full of traffic heading north to dodge the storm. They found themselves in the middle of a convoy of cars, vans, eighteen wheelers, campers, trucks and even some cars pulling their boats to escape a storm with the magnitude of 150 mph winds.

"Oh, my God," Marie said. "The highway is packed with people trying to escape. Will we ever make it before the hurricane hits?"

"Honey, we'll make it. It's still sunny outside. There are no clouds, just slight winds. We'll get home."

He wasn't so sure himself.

Bumper to bumper traffic from West Palm to the turnoff leading to Kissimmee took eight hours when it would have taken four.

"There's a motel up ahead," Marie said. "Pull off, we'll get a room and I can call my daughter and mother."

"Sorry," the innkeeper said when they entered the motel lobby and tried to get a room. "There's not a room available from here to the Georgia border."

"But we were evacuated off Andros Island and have no place to go," Marie said.

"Sorry," was all the innkeeper could say.

They left the motel and decided to drive on into Orlando searching for a room, but when Scott tried to start the car, it wouldn't start.

Although rain was starting to fall, Scott opened the hood and tinkered around in the dark not being able to see a thing and gave up. He put the hood down and got into the car dripping wet.

"There's a pay phone out there," Marie said. "I'll call Pam. Maybe she'll come get us."

She put the quarter in the slot and got a busy signal, and tried, and tried, and tried unsuccessfully again and again until an operator finally answered.

"Don't hang up," Marie said into the mouthpiece.

"The lines are all tied up," the operator said.

Marie couldn't contain herself and started sobbing, "We've just been evacuated off Andros Island in the Bahamas, and we're stuck in Kissimmee with a car that won't start and all the motels are full. I need to get through to my girlfriend to come get us to spend the night. Please try to get through. I'm begging you."

"You poor thing," the operator said. "I understand that the island is wiped out from the storm. What's the number? I'll get you through. Stay on the line and don't hang up. Hold on."

Marie held on for what seemed like a lifetime before the operator came back on and said, "Are you there? I have your party on the line."

"Yes, I'm still here," Marie answered.

"Go ahead then and God bless," the operator said.

"Pam?" Marie said pleadingly.

"Yes. Where are you?"

"Outside a motel in Kissimmee and the car broke down and we can't get a room. Can you come get us?"

"I've been in bed with some bug, but I'm almost over it."

"We'll sleep in the car then. Don't worry."

"No, I'll come. Give me directions and I'll be there as soon as possible."

Marie gave Pam directions and went back to the car. She told Scott that Pam was coming and they waited.

An hour and a half later, Pam pulled into the parking lot, beeped the horn and Marie and Scott jumped into her car. Pam turned the car toward Orlando and hit the road.

Pam pulled into the driveway alongside her apartment, got out, ran up the stairs and opened the front door with Scott and Marie following her. The rain hadn't stopped.

"I need to call Cheryl and Mother," Marie said, and went to the phone to place the calls.

"Mother, where are you?" Cheryl asked when she answered the phone. "Are you all right?"

"We're at Pam's. Do you want to come down?"

"Yes, I'm scared. We've never been in a hurricane before. I'm leaving now. Did you call Gram?"

"I'm calling as soon as I hang up."

When Marie placed the call to Marion, Marion wasn't aware that a hurricane was approaching but told Marie not to worry, that she would be safe and wasn't afraid.

The foursome stayed up late watching the television for reports of the storm. It had reached West Palm, but there was no information about the damage. The forecaster stated that it appeared the hurricane would follow a path parallel to the coastline of Florida and move up the coast, leaving only wind and rain to the interior part of the state and the group breathed a sigh of relief.

When they did sleep, it was restless sleep. Finally, Scott decided to get up and wait for daybreak. The sun rose the next morning. The storm had taken the course predicted by the weatherman, but had done some damage to a little coastline city named Selena Beach, Florida (a city that would become an integral part of her life), although the winds had diminished considerably by the time it passed over the beach community. Deciding he had to do something about the car, Scott called Tom Johnston, and together they headed down to Kissimmee to see if they could fix it.

Scott and Tom were able to get the car back in running order and returned with the it in the afternoon. Scott called the hotel in West Palm trying to find out what damage had been done on the island and when he needed to return.

He reached his supervisor, Ed, in his room at the Holiday and after explaining what had happened, asked about damage.

"We don't know too much at the moment, but do know it wasn't as bad as predicted," Ed said. "When can you return?"

"Tomorrow around noon, I expect. It's all according to how bad the traffic is between here and West Palm and if those who headed north before the 'cane will be heading south soon after it."

"Well, try to get back ASAP," Ed remarked. "Managers will be the first to return to the island to assess the damage before we can let employees and dependents return. If there's no facilities for food and lodging, no one will be returning."

It was decided that Marie would stay with Pam until Scott called to let her know if it was safe to return to the island. Scott was worried about leaving her, knowing she'd had a terrible first impression of living on Andros and wondered if he could expect her to go back.

He left early the next morning, telling Marie that as soon as he sized up the situation, he'd call. They kissed goodbye and he hopped in the car and headed for the interstate. Because Marie's car was old and could possibly break down again, Scott drove it leaving Marie to rent a car and drive to West Palm when it was safe.

Waiting for it to ring, Marie hung around the phone in Pam's apartment after Pam left for work. She knew she probably wouldn't hear from Scott for a day or two but wanted to be there when he called. She didn't want to go back to the island, but her love for him was so strong, that she knew she would return anyway and put her negative feelings aside.

He called a day later. "Honey, it's amazing. Everything still stands, even the trailers. The only damage was blown down palm trees and loose electrical wires which have been repaired. You know the people who owned homes here? Not a one of them was touched although I understand they waited out the storm in a cave with a television watching the Giants/Redskins game and they saw the whole game. Of course they had cases of beer with them. They claimed that when the cane came to the island, all they heard was the sound of a train passing on either side of the cave."

"I'm not coming back to the trailer until I know those damn fleas are gone."

"I know, hon. We'll stay in the BOQ until you're satisfied that not a one still exists. Can you rent a car, drive down, stay in the hotel tomorrow?"

"Yes."

"OK, I'll reserve a seat on the morning flight the day after. I've gotta go. There's more general cleaning up to do. Remember, I love you."

And he hung up.

Pam came home and took Marie to meet the gang at happy hour that evening, an enjoyable get together for her.

Next morning, Pam drove Marie to a rental agency and before she left, Marie said, "Ya know, Pam, we'll have two bedrooms when we move to the trailer, so why don't you consider visiting us? I mean all you have to do is get yourself to West Palm and then fly on the company plane to the island."

"Uh, I don't think so," Pam said laughing.

"Chicken," Marie said and waved goodbye to her friend before walking to the office to rent a car. Minutes later, she pulled out of the agency in a compact car and turned into the interstate for the drive south.

FIFTY-SEVEN

Two days later, Marie was on the company plane heading across the Atlantic towards the Bahamas. When the plane landed, Scott was there to meet her and take her to the BOQ where they would stay until she was satisfied that the infestation of fleas in their home was exterminated.

After getting resettled in their room, they headed toward the club for a cocktail. Beverly, who was tending the bar and was glad to see them, started pouring their drinks.

"Isn't it amazing," she said. "The island still stands with very little damage," and she turned to tend bar at the other end.

When Beverly returned to refresh their drinks, she asked, "Did you guys hear about the young female employee that was picked up by the Bahamian police for possessing marijuana?"

"When?" Scott asked.

"Today. You know they frown on drugs on the island, but the worst part is, the one who turned her in was an ex-boyfriend who she had dumped two days before. I hear she's in the little jail outside the base. That jail ain't bigger than a two-car garage with a dirt floor and only has a three foot by six inch glassless window near the ceiling with bars on it. The police don't even feed their prisoners. Her family has to provide food for her. Word has it that the captain is trying to do all he can to bail her out, but negotiations for her release aren't going well which means she might have to go before a Bahamian court for trial and that could mean years in jail. Isn't that awful?"

A manager sitting at the end of the bar overheard the conversation and added, "I just heard that if the U.S. gets her off the island within twenty-four hours, they'll let her go on one condition. She is never to return to any island in the Bahamas again during her lifetime.

Another manager had entered the club and joined in the conversation saying, "I just heard that the company plane has left

West Palm to pick her up and fly her back stateside at which point, she will be fired. How's that for smoking a joint and breaking up a romance?"

A hush came over the bar, during which time it was evident the regulars were all thinking of what life could be in a Bahamian jail.

Marie stared ahead. Scott looked at Marie and recognized her repulsion at hearing the story, so he decided to change the subject, took her hand, and said, "I've got a surprise for you, a trip we'll take on the weekend."

"To where?" she asked.

"The north end of the island where there is a village of native Bahamians who still live in houses with palm thatched roofs."

"How we going to get there?"

"Jack offered to take us up in his jeep. It'll be a fun thing to do, explore the island and take in the lifestyle of the inhabitants."

On the journey to the north end of the island, Marie noticed how barren the land was. There was nothing but tall scrub grass and a dirt road leading to the village and although it was unbelievably hot, there was a breeze coming from the ocean that cooled her.

They stopped at the village and while Jack went to talk with the leader, Marie strolled with Scott to a hut where small, shoeless children were playing with their dog. Their clothes were shabby and either too small for some or too large for others which caused her to suppose that the clothes had been given to the children by a charitable organization such as the island church where the families worshiped.

Even though it was obvious that the family was very poor, the children were happy, laughing, running and throwing a stick for their dog to chase and return with, which gave Marie cause to think about the abundance the children in America had but were never satisfied with.

On their trip back to the base, the threesome came upon a motel, not far from the village, situated a few feet from the ocean, the view of which was breathtaking. The rooms were beautifully decorated in shades of lemon and mint green, and although there were no air conditioners, a ceiling fan kept the rooms breezy. No televisions were noticed, as well as no telephones, which caused Marie to wonder who stayed at this beautiful motel whose amenities included a swimming pool and circular bar.

They took a bar stool and ordered a drink from the bartender, who as far as they could see, was the only employee visible. Upon questioning him, Marie was told that members of the "Rat Pack," as well as other celebrities, came to the motel to escape the hectic pace of the life of being famous, hence the reason for the non-communication of phones and televisions.

Upon returning from their jaunt, Scott was approached by the housing manager who informed him that as far as he could determine, their trailer was flea free and they could move into it.

"I want to put a white towel down and observe myself," Marie said, so they went to the trailer, placed white bath towels on the rugs throughout the trailer, and shut the door to return in an hour.

One hour later and upon their return the towels had no specks of anything on them, let alone fleas, so they picked up their belongings and moved into their new home.

Things pretty much got back to normal after that, but Marie was dissatisfied with having nothing to do all day. Television reception came and went, with blackouts happening just at the point of a "who done it" movie to where reception went dead, and she never found out who done it. Scott suggested she take the bus to the beach, a five minute ride, and get some sun.

She placed her towel on a lounge chair and settled down to read a novel when Scott came running down the pathway yelling, "Honey, honey, get off the beach."

"What? Why?"

"There's a bunch of submariners coming ashore for some R and R who haven't seen a woman in months."

"What's that got to do with me?"

"They come right up the beach pathway and head to the beach bar and have to pass you on their way."

"But I'm older than they are. They'd have no interest in me."

"Age makes no difference when you haven't been with a woman that long. They're hungry and I don't mean for food. You don't look your age and certainly couldn't prove it by your body. Please don't make me have to get in a fight to protect you. Come on, let's go."

And he hurriedly helped her off the lounge, wrapped her towel around her shoulders and lead her to the bus stop to catch the next bus back to their home.

Kissing her goodbye as she boarded the bus, he said, "I'll be home soon."

"Shit," was all she could say as she took a seat in the front of the little bus that took her back to the trailer.

That evening, they went to the "O" club and drank too much. They didn't eat and by the time they left the bar, the dining hall was closed. While they were in the club, a downpour had filled the large potholes in the dirt roads with water. As they made their way back home, Marie, who was very drunk, slipped on the edge of a pothole and decided to sit down in it. She started splashing herself with dirty rain water and yelling "whee" as she flung the water up in the air, behind her shoulders and on her head as Scott watched in shock, and for a moment he didn't know what to do.

"Come on honey," he said as he helped her out of the large hole. "Let's get you home and in the shower."

"Nah," she replied. "I'll just sit here and bathe."

"Come on," he said gently. "I'll take you home."

She got out of the pothole and took his hand as he put his arm around her waist and helped her down the road and towards their trailer. He turned on the shower, undressed his wife, and gently placed her inside letting the water stream down her body as he washed her.

Next morning there was a meeting of managers and their bosses who were stationed at West Palm. The VP of the company who headed the meeting was in town to attend the conference.

The VP stood up and said, "Before I begin, does anyone know who the blonde lady was who was sitting in a pothole splashing herself with dirty rain water last night?"

No one said a word and no one looked at Scott, who wanted to vanish into thin air.

"Well, then, if no one knows who it was, I guess she was attended to and got to her place of residence, but it might be a consideration to suggest she take a couple days rest and relaxation stateside."

The meeting went on and was concluded within two hours. Scott hurried home to tell Marie, who was hung over, about the VP's introduction.

"Oh, my God," she said. "Did he know it was your wife?"

"No one said a word," he answered. "But I'm thinking it might be a good idea if you took the plane on Friday and went to see Cheryl, get away from here for a day or two."

"I just came back from the 'cane," she said.

"I know, honey, but I'm beginning to worry that this island may be too much for you. The stress of bugs, not to mention the hurricane, has taken a lot out of you."

FIFTY-EIGHT

The following Friday, she took the company plane to West Palm and drove her car from West Palm to Orlando to see her daughter and mother, promising to return on Tuesday. While she was gone, she began to realize that her husband was right and that she needed to get off the island and return to civilization, so she decided to broach the subject with Scott on Tuesday upon her return but decided to talk it over with Cheryl.

"Mother, I'd be glad if you came back and it seems to me that nothing good has happened to you since you went there, but it's up to you. Whatever I can do to help, let me know."

"I'm thinking of telling Scott it's time for me to leave. I'm planning on talking it over with him when I return."

He was waiting for her at the airport when she arrived back on Tuesday.

"You look refreshed," he said while searching for a reaction.

"I am," she answered.

"You wanna stop at the club before going home?" he asked.

"I don't think so."

As he was pouring her a drink when they arrived home, he asked, "Honey, what's wrong?"

"I think I need to get off the island. It's just not for me living here," she said. "I don't have the right to expect you to leave with me for this is a perfect job for you. My thought is that I'll return to Orlando, stay with Cheryl, and search for a job. When I find one and get a place to live, you could join me."

"Whoa, you don't go without me, no way," he said, and added, "Is it because you're not busy, are bored, or because you hate it here?"

"It isn't that I hate it here. I am bored. There's nothing for me to do, and I'm drinking too much."

"OK, well, I'll give my two-week notice tomorrow. I didn't marry you just to have you leave because of where we live. It doesn't mean that much to me."

"Yes, but we have very little money and no jobs stateside, so how are we to live until we find one?"

"Don't worry about it. We'll find jobs."

They went to bed early and made love for the first time in a while, leaving them both exhausted from their passionate release to each other. She slept well for the first time in a week.

"She doesn't like it here. There's nothing for her to do, and she's always been a very industrious woman who has worked all her life," Scott said to his boss, Ed, when he told him they were leaving.

"If that's all it is, I'm sure Esther can find a position for her here on the island. I haven't told you that we have been grooming you to take over my position in a few months, as I've been offered one with the company stateside."

"No, I didn't know that."

"Tell you what. Let me get with Esther. Why don't you and Marie come over for cocktails tonight after work, so we can talk about this. Say around five?"

"Okay."

"Now, how come all of a sudden, we've been invited to cocktails when that woman didn't have the time of day for me before? I mean none of the other managers wives have had us over since I arrived. Oh, sure, when I'd see them in the commissary, they'd bring it up, then nothing. Bullshit!"

"Can't we at least go and listen to what she has to say?"

"Ya know, I might just enjoy watching her squirm trying to get me to stay."

They arrived just before five. Esther fell all over Marie, complimenting her on what she was wearing and asking where she got her hair done, blah, blah, blah. This caused Marie to soak it up like a sponge, but not because she felt the compliment was genuine, but because she enjoyed watching the snob beg.

Ed made a drink for him and Scott before they retired to the porch to light up while Esther fixed Marie a drink.

"So," Esther said, "Ed tells me that you two want to leave the island."

"Yes," Marie answered.

"I'm sorry to hear that. Is it because you want to work?"

"Partly."

"Well, I might be able to help you with that. A position will be opening for you at the marina checking boat rentals in and out during the daytime hours while Scott is working. How does that sound?"

"Correct me if I'm wrong, but isn't that job already filled?"

"Oh, we can take care of that."

"Really. How?"

"The one who presently has that position, Laura, hasn't been doing that good a job. It's been coming for a while and we've decided to let her go."

"Strange that should come up right at the time we intend to leave. I couldn't possibly deprive someone of their job, especially a single woman who needs the money."

Esther's demeanor changed noticeably. She called the men back into the living room and served some cheese and crackers before becoming subdued, Ed and Scott noticed how chilly the living room became. Scott finished his drink and suggested Marie and he leave saying, he had paperwork to do.

"What happened?" Scott asked Marie as they walked back to their trailer.

"That bitch. She wanted to fire someone who needs the job and give it to me. I've come across that kind of shit before, and I'll have nothing to do with it, but I must say I sure enjoyed watching her knock herself out trying."

"Oh, honey, Jeez, he's my boss."

"I told you I want to leave, and that's what I intend to do. I also told you that I don't expect you to come with me. You'll never make this kind of money back home."

"It's settled then. You really think I'd let you go without me? I'll tell Ed tomorrow."

"I never would have made it as a military wife."

"I wouldn't have stayed in had I married you first."

The next morning, Marie waited in the trailer for Scott to arrive after telling Ed he was leaving.

He came home mid-morning and found Marie in the kitchen.

"You're not going to believe this," Scott said.

"What?"

"I've been asked to interview for a job in West Palm as a technical writer."

"What?"

"We can leave on the outbound plane in two days, at which time I'll go for the interview. Then we'll head back to Orlando. If I don't accept the interview, we have to pay our own way back to the states."

"God, what a mess this has turned into. Okay, you must know what you're doing. Just please get me off this damn god-forsaken island. Thank God we didn't bring our furniture and car here."

They packed up what little they had the night before leaving and didn't go to the club for fear they'd slip and let someone know they had no intention of staying, not even in West Palm.

Marie wanted to do one thing before leaving, so she went to the BOQ and searched the floors until she found her cleaning a room on the top deck of the building.

"Hey, Tilda," Marie said.

"Oh, hello, Mam, I hear you leaving the island."

"Can't fart on this island without someone knowing it," Marie said laughing. "I wanted to come say goodbye to you."

"You been good to me, Mam," Tilda said. "Most of the people who stay here won't give me the time of day. I learn to live with it, but you cared about my safety during the hurricane. Thank you and you have a good life with that handsome devil you married."

They hugged and Marie turned and left the room, but knew she would never forget the spiritually beautiful black woman who taught her a little bit about the important things in life.

Boarding the plane together the next morning, Marie turned and looked at the sparse and barren land she lived on for such a short time, smiled, entered the plane, took her seat, fastened her seatbelt, took her husband's hand and smiled as fully as she did the first day she landed after her marriage to Scott when her heart was full of the adventure of living on paradise island.

The company plane took off with the sun shining in a sky of blue, banked and headed northwest toward the coast of Florida and home.

They checked into a room at the inn upon arriving at West Palm. Scott let the human resources department know that he had arrived and would be in for his interview in the morning.

Needless to say, Marie was happy to be back in the U.S. and headed to central Florida the next day. She called Cheryl and told her of their arrival. She asked if she could talk to the manager of the apartment complex where Cheryl lived to rent them a one bedroom apartment that she would take care of the lease upon arrival the next day. Cheryl phoned back to tell her mother that everything was in order. She had secured a second floor one bedroom across the courtyard from where she and her boyfriend, Frank, lived.

When Scott arrived at the inn after his interview, he said to Marie, "They want me to start working for them as soon as we find a place to live. I told them that probably shouldn't take too long. Let's go home."

The couple hadn't unpacked that many items from their luggage, only sleepwear, so they were ready to leave the inn within minutes, which they did, and headed toward the interstate north to Orlando, Florida.

FIFTY-NINE

It was quite obvious to Scott that his wife was happier than he had seen her since their wedding. This made him feel confident that they would be able to make a life for themselves and find jobs in the Orlando area. They had a few hundred dollars saved which would tide them over until they secured employment.

Cheryl was waiting as they drove into the parking lot of the apartment complex.

"Mother," she cried, and ran to the car to greet Marie as she stepped out of the car.

"God, it's so good to be back," Marie said.

"It's so good to have you home," Cheryl said and turned to give Scott an embrace as well.

The apartment was small but they didn't have that much furniture anyway. They needed to call the storage facility to have their furniture delivered as soon as possible and were promised that it would be transported to the address Scott gave them within two days.

Next on the agenda-find jobs. Marie always believed that connecting with old friends produced results in the job market because most of the positions she found were because she asked friends if they knew anyone hiring. She remembered her friend, Fran Collier, who she worked with at Universal Dynamique, looked her up in the phone book and placed the call.

"Where on earth are you?" Fran asked.

"Here in Orlando," Marie answered.

"I heard you got married and moved to some island," Fran said.

"Yes, believe me it wasn't paradise island, so we came back. Fran, what I called you about is I'm searching for employment, letting everyone know in case they happen to know of an opening anywhere."

"Funny you should call. You know the company I was laid off from before going to Dynamique, Hamilton International, called me back and I've heard they are hiring secretaries. Let me contact HR and call you tomorrow, see if I can help. God knows anyone who can work for Gordon Blanky is top notch in my book. Oh, and by the way, they called him back too. I'll call you tomorrow afternoon. Good hearing from you."

While Marie was talking to Fran, Scott was searching through the want ads in the local newspaper which Cheryl had brought over.

"Says here that a company, jeez, just down the road, is looking for a trainee for maintenance and repair of building equipment," Scott said. "I think I'll call them and try to get an appointment for an interview."

After dialing the number of Maxim, Inc., he inquired about the ad in the paper and was connected to the manager of training who asked Scott to come in for an interview the next morning.

They worried about only having one car and needing to go in opposite directions to a job.

Scott's interview netted him a position starting the following week. It also netted him the use of a company van to travel around the state for repairs and new employee training of staple guns, saws, electric hammers and screw drivers. He could use it for transportation to and from the workplace.

Fran called Marie back telling her that she should come in and fill out an application.

Marie took a typing test, was granted an interview in Contracts working for the manager, and was offered the position the following day. All she needed to do was fill out the necessary paperwork, be fingerprinted, and submit to a security check as Hamilton International was a government contracts company.

The couples were grateful that they found employment so soon after leaving the island, especially because Scott's retirement from the Navy was still submitted to his ex-wife, Bernice, for child support until his son became eighteen.

The small apartment became annoying to Scott. He needed more room to putz around - a garage, yard to mow -so they started searching for a small home to buy knowing that they would soon have a higher income between their two jobs and his military retirement.

A month before the last retirement payment would be received by Bernice, Scott told Marie, "She'll be married to another military man before she receives it. She can't give up the security the military offers. I guarantee it."

And one week later, Marie, while reading the Sunday paper vital statistics, saw the marriage license for Bernice and a retired military man named, Stanley Knolls.

"I didn't believe you," she said to Scott. "I mean just go pick someone to marry, anyone just for the benefits? That's cold."

"Doesn't matter. That's the way she is," Scott said.

And Marie shook her head in wonderment.

Although in the divorce decree, Bernice agreed to give up Scott's retainer when their son became eighteen, she had a fit on the son's eighteenth birthday and called Scott.

"How could you take that money away from your son?" Bernice asked. "He needs it to go to college."

"I can't continue giving my entire retirement for four or five more years, and you agreed that it would end when he was eighteen, so it ends," he answered and hung up.

Scott and Marie found a new-two bedroom split-plan home in the center of a cul de sac on the southeast side of town that had a living room, dining area, kitchen and small television room off the kitchen. The home backed to a retention ditch owned by the county where they were told there would be no construction on the land. The two-car garage had the fittings for a washer/dryer and held the air conditioner and hot water heater.

Thrilled, they put down ten percent of the purchase price of $50,000.00 and applied for a VA loan which carried an interest rate of thirteen percent, but they knew they could re-finance in a year or two and didn't mind the rate as long as they could own their own home.

SIXTY

The day of closing, the furniture was delivered to 4718 Pepper Tree Lane. Because their furniture was old (it was brought to Florida when Marie relocated), the couple decided to go shopping for new, modern furnishings which included appliances, which put them in a considerable amount of debt. Still, their combined income allowed them to pay the debt off over time.

The next decision to be made was getting a puppy, and they decided to go to the Humane Society. On the day they were to go together, Scott had to go out of town to south Florida to teach a class, so Marie went alone.

"I guess we'll get a male doggie," she said.

"Yes and call him Chief," Scott answered.

So Marie went to the Humane Society and started her search for a puppy. She was shown into the room where puppies were kept after being weaned from their mothers.

"I'd like to see a male," Marie said to the vet tech.

"Over here we have a litter of them, both male and female," the tech said.

"Oh, look at him," Marie said. "He's jumping all over the cage trying to get some attention. Isn't he cute?"

"Yes," was the answer.

Then Marie noticed a pup quietly sitting in the back corner of the cage looking around and her heart flipped. The puppy was tan and white mixed in color. The puppy had short ears which were dark brown and flopped forward and her snoot looked as though it had been pressed into Oreo cookie crumbs

"What's the matter with that doggie?" Marie asked.

"Nothing," the tech said. "She's just quiet. She's the runt, the last one out and they usually have a quiet disposition."

"Oh, a female," Marie said. "Can I hold her?"

"Yes," and the tech went to get the puppy.

Marie knew the minute she held her that that was the doggie for her and Scott, but thought, wasn't she supposed to get a male?

In the meantime, a couple who had been standing next to Marie was eyeing the female commenting about how cute and well behaved she was, and just before they opened their mouths to claim her, Marie said, "I'll take the female."

"You have to wait three days before we can let her go," the tech said.

"Doesn't matter. I'll pay now and come get her as soon as I can take her home." She filled out the adoption papers and left the building wondering how she would tell Scott that she had found the puppy for them even though it wasn't a male.

Scott called that night asking if she was successful in finding a doggie.

"Would you believe Chiefess?" Marie asked.

"A female?"

"Yes, and wait til you see her," describing the color and disposition of the doggie.

In three days, they went to pick her up and bring her home, excited to be new parents. The puppy ran into the kitchen and piddled on the floor, so it was decided to purchase baby gates and keep her in the kitchen til she was paper trained.

What to name her? The couple sat at the kitchen bar having a drink trying to find just the right name for the cute little girl.

"I know," Marie said. "We'll name her Missy."

So Missy became the third member of the Nicholson family and would remain with them for many years to come.

Marie's brother, Danny, upon finding out that his sister owned a home, flew to Orlando to "inspect" it. He stayed in the guest bedroom and spent his time going to happy hours with Marie and Scott and taking his mother out to dinner.

Finances were becoming less taxing for the couple, so they decided to add a swimming pool to the property, although Marie didn't know how to swim and was somewhat afraid of deep water. Scott believed that adding a pool might help her get over her fear.

They knew when Scott accepted the job that he would have to travel four days a week, three weeks of the month, spending the fourth week teaching a class on the care and maintenance of the construction tools the company sold, so when he was out of town, Marie would meet the gang she had worked with on the base for happy hour.

SIXTY-ONE

    A year into her employment at Hamilton International, Marie started having low back pain which caused her to be unable to sit for long periods of time. When she got out of work, she would drive the half hour home in the anguish of having spent hours sitting at a desk unable to move about to relieve the ache in her back. This was wearing her down and contributing to some depression. Upon arriving home, she would fix herself a vodka/rocks with twist of lemon to ease her back pain which started a habit that continued nightly.

    After an examination by the company doctor and a workup of tests, it was determined Marie had an L-5 bulging disk, she could not sit for long periods of time, and she was put on temporary disability receiving sixty percent of her pay. Muscle relaxants and pain pills were prescribed to relieve her discomfort and, yes, she did sometimes mix them with the alcohol.

    Because she couldn't take on too much activity, even household chores, her depression became more prevalent. To complicate the situation even more, her menopausal years were upon her causing her to be irritable, with spells of highs and lows followed by tears over what was happening to her. The fact that Scott had to travel so much didn't help the circumstances, and their marriage started to suffer. Still, Scott professed his undying love for her, telling her that her condition would not last forever and he would always be there for her, to care for and comfort her.

    During one of Scott's at-home weeks at work, he took the Friday off and decided to spend the day with his wife but needed to go into the office to pick up his paycheck. He was driving around the back of the building when another car driven by a young female co-worker came around the corner in the opposite direction. She made a twisting, turning of the wheel of her car and smiled up at Scott. As she started to put her window down, she noticed that Marie was sitting in the passenger side of Scott's auto, put the window back up and hurriedly drove out of the parking lot. This caused Marie to quietly question what that was all about but she didn't say anything, instead filing it in the back of her mind for possible future use.

The future use came about very unexpectedly a few weeks later when Scott's boss threw an open house-warming party inviting all the employees and their significant others. The booze was flowing like water and the hors d'oeuvres were delicious. Scott ventured outside to light up and talk with one of his co-workers, Marie was at the appetizer table deciding which ones to place on her plate when the young woman who passed them in the parking lot came up to her and introduced herself.

"Hi, I'm Cathy Miller," she said. "You're Scott's wife, aren't you?"

"Yes," Marie answered.

They stood talking for a few minutes before Marie said she needed to refresh her drink and started to walk toward the bar. The company comptroller stopped Marie and asked, "Do you know Cathy? I mean are you friends?"

"No," Marie said. "I just met her. Why?"

"Well, it's really strange to me when a man's girlfriend and his wife get along so well, that's all." And with that statement said, he walked away leaving Marie speechless. She composed herself enough to saunter to the bar and order another drink - a double - and as she turned with her drink to walk away, she slipped on water that had spilt on the floor and fell.

Scott's boss ran to her aid and helped her up asking her if she was all right and did she need medical help. Marie was so embarrassed. Someone ran to tell Scott, and when he appeared, she quietly told him she wanted to leave.

On the drive home, she blasted him with accusations of being unfaithful to her, telling him what the accountant had said to her.

"She's just a co-worker," Scott said. "Honey, that's all she is. Sure we kid around sometimes during working hours at coffee break, but there's nothing going on between us, I swear."

"Bullshit," Marie answered. "And what was that all about the day we passed her in the parking lot? Good God, Scott, she's Cheryl's age. She told me during our brief conversation that she and Cheryl were born on the same day, same year."

"I know that," he said. "You think I'd fool around with someone eighteen years younger than me?"

"I don't know what to believe. I'm just so hurt and I don't think I can fully accept as true what you're saying."

Knowing he had to leave for south Florida the next day, Scott pleaded with her, trying to make her believe that he had always been faithful to her.

"The man who approached you at the bar has been trying to get in her pants since she went to work there, and he's trying anything he can to get her fired cause she hasn't accepted his advances toward her.

"And how the hell would you know this if she hadn't told you and why would she come to you? For counseling?"

"No, it was just in conversation once."

"Conversation is more like, 'how ya doin, good weekend, lousy weather' not confessing your love life to one who is just an acquaintance. Something's fishy here."

Upon their arrival at their house, they spent a very quiet evening watching television and only talking, not to each other, but to the doggie. Scott went to bed and Marie slept on the sofa.

The next morning she feigned being asleep when she heard him packing to leave for Miami and didn't get up until after he left.

She called Pam and told her of the previous day's drama.

"What do you want to do about it?" Pam asked.

"I don't know. I'm gonna do some thinking and decide. He's gone for four days which will give me some time."

It didn't take long for her to make her decision. She dialed the number and asked for Cathy Miller and was connected.

"Cathy," she said. "This is Marie Nicholson. We met at the housewarming party on Sunday."

"Oh, yeah, and how are you?"

"I've called to ask you a question I need an honest answer to."

"Sure."

"Are you having an affair with my husband?"

A moment of silence occurred before Cathy with quivering voice answered, "No, Marie. We're friends at work. That's all. Where did you ever get the idea that Scott and I were seeing each other?"

Feeling somewhat foolish for a second, Marie told Cathy of the conversation she had with the comptroller.

"He's been giving me a hard time since I started working there," Cathy said. "I have ignored his advances toward me, so now he's trying to get me into trouble or fired or both. Please believe me when I tell you there's nothing going on."

"Okay, I won't bother you anymore," Marie responded, and hung up.

She sat on the bed where she had made the call and, although she felt like a fool, she still wasn't sure she believed her.

She had to do something, so she called her mother who told her that Marie's brothers were both in New Jersey visiting their sister. Marie called, talked to her sister, Margaret, and asked if she could join them.

"Sure," Margaret said. "We'll have a family reunion. When will you arrive?'

"I'll get a flight and call you back," Marie said.

She called the airline and booked a flight that was leaving in two hours for Newark. Then she called one of her co-workers at Owen Ocean Systems, Tony Martini, and asked him if he would drive her to the airport to which he, without asking any questions, answered, "Sure." Calling a neighbor, she asked her if she could take care of Missy and was relieved when the neighbor agreed to.

Packing hurriedly, she was ready when Tony rang the doorbell. There was only one other need to take care of, so she left Scott a note telling him she was going away for a few days to "think things over," signed it and left.

The fifteen minute ride to the airport was quiet. Her friend, Tony, knew better than to interfere with what probably was a couple's temporary estrangement.

"Do you need someone to pick you up on your return?" Tony asked as he lifted the luggage out of trunk of his car?"

"No," she replied. "Not sure exactly when I'll return," and she kissed Tony on the cheek and walked away into the airport.

She boarded the direct flight to Newark, took her seat, fastened her seatbelt and ordered a drink as the plane took off and headed toward the northeast. Being too angry to cry, she wondered about her life with Scott and if they could get through this disturbing period in their marriage.

When the plane landed in Newark, she headed toward the down escalator to claim her luggage. Standing at the top of the escalator, she saw her brother, Danny, at the bottom of the escalator, down on one knee, with arms outstretched singing, *"Oh, no not in spring time, winter, summer or fall"* to which she joined in *"No, never will I leave you, at all."*

Of course in New York, Jersey, and big cities people don't notice crazies singing in airports, so folks hurrying to catch a plane just kept walking by, turning a head or two and smiling at the sight of two people singing to each other. If they ever knew they were brother and sister, they probably would have smiled brighter, although Margaret and the oldest brother embarrassed, were hiding behind a pillar and off to the side.

They retrieved Marie's luggage and headed to the parking lot to Margaret's car. Though it was cramped, Margaret had enough room for all of them to sleep for a couple nights. When they arrived at Margaret's apartment, she told them that she had a meeting to attend at the Grand Hotel. A suggestion was made that they wait for her in the lounge and have a drink before going to dinner.

With her two brothers, Marie entered the lounge and headed straight to the bar to order drinks. The brothers seated next to each other were talking man talk leaving Marie sitting on the other side with only her thoughts of anguish.

Marie was looking around the lounge at the décor when a voice said to her, "Do you come here often?"

She turned to the bar stool next to her, saw a fifty-ish age grey haired man dressed in a business suit, white oxford, button down shirt and tie and answered, "No, I'm from out of town."

"Can I buy you a drink?"

"No, I have one."

He told her he worked for Benson & Benson, a medical supply company whose corporate offices were located in Newark and that he was in town for a conference.

They carried on a conversation of various topics before he said, "I notice your husband joking around with the crowd. He's quite the comic."

"That isn't my husband. Those two are my brothers," Marie replied.

"I never saw brothers and sisters get along as well as you three do," he replied.

Then added, "Will you be here after my dinner meeting? I'd like to buy you a drink if you'll let me."

Marie didn't realize that Danny, who knew why she had traveled to see her siblings, was partially listening to her conversation with the medical salesman, interrupted and said, "Let's go, Marie. We have a table."

"Okay," and she jumped off the barstool and walked beside her brother toward the dining room leaving the salesman bemused.

"I know you're going through something with Scott," Danny said. "But that isn't the way to handle it and you don't know if anything happened anyway."

"You're right," Marie said. "But you know for a couple minutes, my ego inflated with the attention I was getting even though I know it was bullshit that he just wanted to get me to his room which I never would have gone anyway, but thanks Danny."

The reunion lasted two days before Marie's oldest brother needed to get back to Suttonville and to work, so, they loaded the trunk of Danny's car and headed north to their hometown. Marie had called her son earlier and asked if she could stay with him for a couple days.

"Yeah, Ma," Derek said. "Whatcha doin' in Jersey?"

She lied and told him a family reunion had been planned impromptu and having nothing better to do, she flew up to join her siblings.

During the three and a half hour drive, her reason for coming wasn't discussed. When they arrived in Suttonville, Marie was dropped off at her son's house. She took Derek out to dinner that evening and when they returned, the phone rang.

When Derek answered the phone, Marie heard him say, "Hey Scott, how are you? Yeah, she's right here. Just a moment. Ma, it's Scott." He handed his mother the phone.

"Hello," Marie said.

"When you comin' home?" Scott asked.

"I don't know," she answered.

"Can I pick you up when you do?"

"I'll let you know."

"Will you call me?"

"Yes."

"Honey, I---" and she didn't hear him say anything else. She'd hung up.

She missed him. Wanted to go home, so she called him two days later and told him what flight she'd be on the next day.

"I'll be there," he said. "I love you."

When she got off the plane, she spotted him standing in the concourse area, shifting from one foot to the other.

She walked up to him and he threw his arms around her, holding her close and didn't let her go for a minute.

"God, I missed you," he said.

She couldn't hold back any longer and said, "I missed you too."

"Please don't do that again. I didn't know where you were exactly except that you were with your family. I haven't done anything wrong, not with Cathy nor with any other woman."

They took the down escalator, picked up her luggage and drove out of the parking lot. She wanted to stop at Dagwoods. He thought it a good idea. When they arrived, the old gang was sitting at the bar, including Tony Martini, who acted as though he knew nothing about her escape north, and they had a couple drinks before going home.

They needed no foreplay when they got home, for the love making they gave to each other was spectacular with both of them climaxing at the same time.

Scott went to work the next day and Marie, who was still on disability, decided she needed to do something with her time besides being a homemaker, so she started searching for volunteer opportunities in the area. She came upon a group sponsored by the local community college who helped widows and divorcees with not only counseling, but also with classroom sessions to get them back into the workforce, especially if they had been out of it for a long time.

Marie was trained to counsel the divorcees, as she had been divorced and knew the feelings of loss that went along with the end of a marriage. She did one-on-one listening from the students assigned to her and gave them Briggs-Myers personality tests, helped them write their resume' and did mock interviews to prepare them to go out into the work world and find a job.

The pain in her back became less, but she still was advised not to go back to work where she had to be in a sitting position, that she probably would never be able to continue in a clerical job because of the aggravation it caused in her lower back.

Hamilton International sent her a notice that her disability would be discontinued. Scott and she discussed it and decided not to fight it and let it go. They could live on his salary as a middle class couple which they found acceptable.

SIXTY-TWO

Danny, Marie's brother, began to visit every chance he could get, flying in to stay with Marie, and stopping with her to meet the gang at Dagwoods especially when Scott was out of town. On one particular visit, he excused himself from the table they were sitting at. He didn't return for a long time, too long to have to use the men's room, so Marie got up from the table in search of her brother and found him talking on the pay phone that was located in the hallway between the men's and ladies' rooms. His back was to her as she entered the ladies room. She could not hear the conversation, but when she came out, he was still on the phone and she thought it strange that his call would take so long especially since he'd have to keep putting quarters in the slot, but she dismissed it as a problem possibly with the parish in which he was the pastor.

When Marie returned to the table, one of the gang commented, "He's been on the phone a long time, got a girlfriend in Orlando?" They all laughed and no one took the remark serious. Danny spent a few days with his sister before returning to New York and to his priestly duties.

A few weeks after his last visit, Marie got a call from the manager of the apartment building where her mother lived. "Please don't be alarmed. Your mother has been taken to the hospital. We couldn't wait for you to get here, so EVAC took her to be examined."

"What happened?" Marie asked frantically.

"They think she had a stroke," the manager said. "She must have been on the floor a long time before she was able to crawl to the door, open it and cry out. Someone heard her shouting in the next apartment and came to my office to get me."

"What hospital?" Marie asked anxiously.

"St. Johns," the manager replied. "Tell her we send our best with prayers and love."

Marie hung up the phone, grabbed her car keys and drove to the hospital where her mother was taken.

When she arrived, she found her mother in the ER on a gurney waiting for tests to be run. The left side of Marion's face was grotesque. It had the appearance of a Halloween mask in that it drooped, and her speech was slurred like a person who'd had too much to drink, but she recognized her daughter. Marie could just about make out what her mother was trying to say in words, not sentences.

She had called Cheryl, who when she entered the ER and saw her grandmother, turned away in fear crying. Mother and daughter sat in the ER after Marion was taken for tests and held each other's hands. The doctor appeared shortly after and informed them that he thought Marion would be okay in time and after rehabilitation, but that he was going to admit her and prescribe drugs that would help her.

Marie, seeing how upset her daughter became, told her she could leave and that she would keep her up to date on her grandmother's progress. When Marion was taken to a room, Marie went to her bedside, took her mother's hand, kissed her cheek and wept.

Marion raised her right hand and placed it on her daughter's shoulder trying to smile, but only her right side showed any indication of the appearance of a smile. Marie stayed until her mother fell asleep from the drugs given to relax her. She headed to the parking lot in a hurry to return home and call Danny and her older brother, Mitch.

"She was asleep when I left her," she said to Danny after telling him what happened. "Are you guys coming down?"

"Yes, as soon as I talk to Mitch," he answered. "I'll call you back."

"You know she loves all of us equally, but her boys, well, what can I say," Marie answered.

It took three days before Marie decided to call Danny after not hearing from him.

"Where the hell are you?" she asked. "I was able to bring her home to my house. She responded to the drug therapy quite well but is visibly depressed. She needs a shot in the arm, like you two getting your asses down here to see her. So when?"

I talked with Mitch today. I'm picking him up early in the morning, and we'll be on the road, probably take two days with one stop overnight."

"Can I tell her that for sure?" Marie said demandingly.

"Yes, see you soon."

And he hung up.

Marie entered her mother's bedroom. Seeing her mother laying in bed made her sad especially since Marion always had a smile on her face, but not on this day.

"Guess who's coming to town?" Marie said.

"Who?" Marion asked.

"Your boys."

And with that announcement, Marion's eyes lit up, she smiled and started to get out of bed.

"Hold on there, Mom. They won't get here for two days. They're leaving tomorrow and it's a long drive."

She helped her mother out of the bed and into a rocking chair, covered her with an afghan Marion had crocheted for her and sat on the bed conversing about the trip her brothers would be making the next day.

The sagging on the left side of Marion's face was less apparent. Her voice was stronger with completed sentences and it looked like she was on the mend.

The next day Marion wanted to get up and walk around, so Marie took her into the living room, put some old tunes on the stereo that her mother liked and danced with her. Marion asked for and got a glass of white wine which she enjoyed immensely before retiring to her bedroom for a nap.

The next day, Marion was visibly stronger and anxious about her boys coming for a visit. She tried to help Marie with household duties, but her daughter wouldn't let her. Marie suggested that Marion watch her favorite soaps to while the time away.

"They should arrive sometime later this evening," Marie said.

After dinner, Marion kept looking at the clock in the kitchen until Marie put the rocking chair on the patio, poured her mother and her a glass of wine and sat with her listening to old family stories. Every time she thought she heard the sound of a car, Marion would ask Marie to check it out until they heard the sound of her brother's car doors slam two times. Marie ran to the front door and saw her brothers coming up the driveway to the door.

"They're here," Marie said.

Marion hurried to the door to greet her sons, threw her arms around them and cried for happy. The boys entered Marie's house, helping their mother to her rocker, poured a drink and started asking about her and how she was feeling at the present time. Her left arm was bent and she held it against her waist.

That mother's happy, smiling eyes darted from one son to the other, her joy was visible at having them with her after having gone through such a difficult illness and although she wasn't without weakness, she was returning to her old self, especially with the help of being surrounded by her family.

Mitch had to return to Suttonville, and seeing that his mother was doing so well, he felt comfortable leaving two days later. However, Danny, decided to stick around to be sure that she would be okay.

Mitch made an airline reservation back to Suttonville and Danny and Marie drove him to the airport. After seeing their older brother off, Danny suggested they stop for lunch and drove into a seafood restaurant. Usually the siblings headed to the bar, but this time Danny followed the hostess to a table.

When the waitress came to ask if they wanted a drink, Danny ordered a vodka and Marie ordered a Gimlet. As the waitress started to walk away, Danny said, "Marie, I'm leaving the priesthood," to which Marie, with shocked expression on her face called to the waitress and said, "Make it a double," but before the waitress walked five more steps, he said, "I've met someone." Marie called out to the waitress one more time and said, "Bring one on the side too."

"What the hell are you saying?" she asked her brother. "And who's the someone? A woman who lives here?"

"No," Danny answered. "She is my part-time housekeeper. She has three children."

"What the he--? Who else knows about this? Your buddy Fr. Mulligan?"

"No one, but you," he answered.

"Well, but, don't you have to tell someone? I mean how do you get out?"

"You don't. You walk away."

"Jesus, Danny, I mean I'm no Polly Pure Heart, and I'm not gonna knock you, but where do you go from here?"

"I don't know."

"Tell me something about her."

"Like I said, she has kids which makes it difficult. She's had a similar situation as you and Steve in that she's been emotionally abused by her husband. I've been counseling her about her marriage."

"Aren't you supposed to counsel to stay together?"

"Yeah, just like I did you, remember?"

"Oh, God! Mother," Marie said. "This will throw her. I mean, 'My son the priest' and 'I want to be buried with the cloth he was anointed with at his ordination wrapped around my folded hands.'"

Danny just looked down.

Realizing her brother was bearing his heart out and was in emotional pain, she said, "Well, I'll do whatever I can to help you. Are you going to tell Mom?"

"Not immediately, not until Linda and I sort things out."

"So her name is Linda. It's obvious you love her or you wouldn't be doing this."

"It's so very lonely living in a rectory with no one around to talk to. I mean there's people around, but I can't talk about my feelings with my parishioners. It's the other way around. They come to me for advice."

"Does her ex-husband know?"

"No."

"How do you expect this to play out?" I mean there's a lot of variables with this move. Are you ready for the worst case scenario?"

"I think so. So many of my fellow priests pick up women when they are on vacation. They never wear the collar. I never wanted to do that. Some are alcoholics, drinking too much out of loneliness, and they can't even express their feelings to each other for fear of being found out and punished by the bishop."

"What kind of punishment are we talking here?"

"Being sent away to a monastery for what is called reflection, but it's really being sent away for some heavy psychotherapy and brainwashing to return back to another parish after having their hands slapped and told to behave."

"Jeez, I don't want to see you go through that bullshit."

The drinks were served. Marie put hers away within minutes and they ate their sandwiches in silence.

It was a quiet drive back to Marie's house where Danny found his mother waiting. She asked him to take her for a ride, and they left the house, leaving Marie stymied not knowing what to think of her brother's confession but she was sure that she would stand by him no matter what he did.

She was deep in thought when the phone rang. She picked it up and heard a voice, "Hello, you haven't met me. My name is Linda Houser. I'm a friend of Danny's. Is he there?"

"No, he just took mother for a drive," Marie said.

"I don't know if you were told anything about me, but----"

Marie interrupted, "He told me all about it."

"Oh!" Linda exclaimed.

"Don't worry, I can't judge him or you. I have no right."

"I'm catching a flight in later today. I wanted to surprise him so please don't tell him," Linda said.

"Whose gonna pick you up at the airport? I think you need to tell him, don't you?"

"I guess you're right. Tell him I'm coming in on DAL, and the flight number is 332 at 7:00, and thanks for being understanding."

"It's okay, and you can stay here if you like."

Danny came back with his mother who went into the bedroom for a nap. When Marie was sure she was asleep, she told her brother about the phone call from Linda. His eyes lit up. He told Marie he would pick Linda up and they would stay in a motel.

When Marie was introduced to Linda she took notice that Linda was a tall woman with short dark hair and Irish green eyes who was younger than her brother by fifteen years, but she had a big smile on her face when they met that intuitively felt genuine to Marie and she took to her immediately. Linda and Danny stayed in a motel for two nights before driving back to Suttonville. Danny came to see his mother before leaving, telling her he'd be in touch and would call her every day to check on her progress. A visit to Marion's doctor was positive in that he decided she could return to her apartment. He advised her to consider purchasing a Health Alert necklace she would wear should she have another spell which she promptly declared that she wasn't interested.

SIXTY-THREE

A few days later, Danny and Linda returned in separate cars with a U-Haul attached to the back of Linda's car which carried some of her belongings. They parked the U-Haul in Marie's driveway while searching for a place to live and found a trailer for sale that was affordable and moved into it within two days.

When Danny told his sister that they had just picked up and left, she exclaimed, "Just like that? Does the bishop know? Did you tell anyone?"

"No," was the answer.

"Well, what do you do now?"

"Find a job."

"How do you find a job when all you know is being a priest?"

"I don't know, but I'll find something."

Linda was a certified practical nurse and was able to find a position at a nursing home where she fit in beautifully. She had worked with the elderly for years and loved old people, loved to care for them, sing with them, dance with them and let them know that she respected their wisdom and loved them as her own family.

Danny found a job at the airport driving rental cars to the garage that were brought in after usage to be refurbished before being rented out again. One day he received a call from the president of the rental car company, a friend and former parishioner who offered him a position at the rental desk at a much higher salary than he was receiving as a driver.

"I've never forgotten how kind and non-judgmental you were to me when I had problems," the president of ABC Rentals said. "I won't judge you and want to help in any way I can. Do you hear me, Father?"

Danny was flabbergasted for he had forgotten the president after he moved away. "How did you find out I left the priesthood?" Danny asked.

"I have my ways," he answered. "Just let me know if you need anything, anything at all." And he hung up.

Marion knew that her son had left and was living in Florida, but was told that Danny was living with Marie and Scott. She started calling Marie's house early in the morning asking to speak to her son to which Marie would answer, "He's not here right now. I'll tell him to call you as soon as he returns." Then she would call her brother so he could call his mother, so she finally asked him, "When are you gonna tell Ma about Linda?"

"I shutter to even think about it," he said.

"Well, I can't keep lying. She's gonna find out soon anyway, so get a move on and tell her."

Between that and the diocesan bishop calling every couple days, Marie was starting to feel like she was running interference for the NY Giants, so she took matters into her own hands one morning after she'd had it.

Marie had forgotten what the proper title was when addressing a bishop and really didn't care anyway. When she answered the phone, he introduced himself and asked for her brother.

"He's not here," Marie said.

"Did you give him my messages?" his Excellency or Eminence or whatever he was supposed to be called said.

"He's getting your messages," Marie answered. "And to tell you the truth, I'd say he's choosing not to return them, so I'm asking you not to call this number again."

"Very well. I'll bother you no longer."

"Thank you," Marie said and she hung up.

Marie's mother had already called very early that morning, so she decided to pay her mother a little visit. Calling Marion, she said, "Are you gonna be home around eleven?"

"Yes, you comin' up?" Marion asked.

"Yep, see you soon."

Marie stopped along the way and bought a six pack of Bud. When she walked through her mother's door, Marion asked, "Am I gonna need that?"

"Maybe," Marie answered.

"What's going on?" Marion asked.

"Mom, if you were to find out that Danny was seeing a woman, what would you feel?" Marie asked directly.

"Does she live here?" Marion asked.

"What? No," Marie said, "Why do you ask that?"

"Well, he's been comin' down here a lot lately every chance he gets, so I guessed it's someone who lives here," Marion answered.

"You mean to tell me that you've known?"

"I'm not that old that I can't see what's goin' on with my kids," Marion said.

"So have you met her?" Marion asked.

"Yes."

"Do you like her?"

"Yes."

"Tell me about her."

"Oh, no you don't. You ask him."

"How can I ask him if he won't tell me."

"I can take care of that today."

"Okay, tell him to bring her around."

And they had a beer or two before Marie left to go home to call her brother.

He picked up the phone on the second ring,

"I told Ma about you and Linda," Marie said.

"What! Oh, Lord, is she mad?"

"No, she knew there was someone. She wants to meet her, so call her and go see her. The sooner the better, like today."

"I'll tell Linda."

"Oh, don't be a ninny. She ain't gonna give you a ration. She just wants to meet her. And let me know what happens. Oh, and by the way, I told the bishop to stop calling me. That you were getting his messages. That I'd say you chose not to return the call. Bye, now," leaving her brother standing holding the phone with a dumbstruck expression on his face.

Marion accepted Linda into her home with kindness and understanding and agreed with Marie that one couldn't help but see the goodness in Linda. She didn't interfere in their lives, deciding it better to mind her own business. Shortly after the introduction into the family, Danny and Linda were married at their trailer by a notary who worked at the rental agency. Marie and Scott witnessed the ceremony, and Marion sat in the rocking chair with the newest member of their family, Tiger, the cat, on her lap.

SIXTY-FOUR

Marie's daughter, Cheryl, graduated college with a degree in social psych and stayed with her mother and Scott for a time while searching for a job. The job market wasn't too good, so she accepted a temporary position as a receptionist at a building materials company.

Disgusted, after having spent four years in college and ending up in a receptionist position, Cheryl, after hearing that one of the salesmen was leaving, asked her boss if she could have the position.

"What?" he said. "A woman in the construction field? I don't think so. Do you know that you'd have to go to construction sites where the workers would cajole you with whistling and sexist remarks?"

"I can handle it. Just give me a month to prove that I can do it and if I don't, no hard feelings. I'll just sit at the front desk again."

"There are a few things we'll need to teach you about our products, like measuring for various items such as insulation," he answered. "Do you want to learn and if you don't pick it up quickly, there is no way I can send you out on the sites. I'll have to interview and hire someone else."

"Give me a chance to learn," she begged.

"Okay, then. We'll start tomorrow."

And learn she did. She was a fast learner but one of her greatest qualities was the ability to concentrate with patience, and so he hired her, the first woman construction salesperson in central Florida.

She continued living with her mother and Scott while saving money, and Scott was thankful for he felt that Cheryl kept her mother company while he was on the road.

Cheryl came to Scott one day and asked if he would co-sign for a new truck she wanted to buy.

"Sure," he answered. Scott had come to love Cheryl like a daughter and knew she would not stick him with the responsibility of having to make payments for her. Promising to return with the paperwork, Cheryl left the house and went to the bank which was around the corner. When she didn't return within an hour, Marie and Scott worried that she wasn't going to be approved for a loan even if Scott signed.

Two hours later, she drove up the driveway in her new truck, ran in the house and asked her mother and Scott to come and view it.

"Wait a minute," Scott said. "I didn't sign for you."

"No," Cheryl commented. "I figured that if I were going to be a salesperson, I needed to convince the loan officer to give me the loan without a co-signer. I had to wait as he was busy, but I was determined to wait all day if need be. It only turned out to be an hour's wait. He said he liked my spunk and gave me the loan."

There were many times when she approached a construction site when the workers whistled and made remarks about a woman selling building materials, but she ignored them and went to the trailer to approach the field manager about the products she was selling. She bought a leather jacket, western shirt, designer jeans, and cowgirl boots to wear when she traveled from site to site and pretty soon, as she got to know the "guys," the pestering stopped and she was considered one of them.

Cheryl decided it was time to move into her own place and found a one bedroom apartment near her place of employment. She saved enough money between her salary and commissions to purchase some nice furniture. It seemed as though she was on her way. She won a trip to Spain for outselling every other salesman in the company. When she returned from Spain, she put a down payment on a condo in an upscale section of the city which was also located near her job.

Then it happened. She called her mother and said she had met someone, a builder, and wanted her mother to meet him. There was a company holiday party that November that he was taking Cheryl to and could she bring him around before attending it.

"Sure," Marie said. "This must be serious if you want to introduce him to us."

Cheryl made no comment, only that they'd stop over on Saturday before going to the party.

He was a tall drink of water, six foot something, handsome, with dark hair, blue-green eyes, and was sporting a mustache. Polite was he after being introduced, saying, "yes, ma'am, and "no, ma'am" but there was something about him that Marie suspected wasn't quite kosher. She dismissed it as being too picky over her daughter's new boyfriend.

His name was Ronnie O'Reilly, Irish as patty's pig, and he swept Cheryl off her feet. Just before Christmas the next month, he called Marie and asked her if he could engage Cheryl on Christmas.

"You don't have to ask my permission. This is Cheryl's decision. If she wants to marry you, I will agree to the wedding," she answered.

"In my family, we ask for the hand in marriage of the mother," he said.

"How respectful," Marie said.

Cheryl's Christmas present was a full carat diamond engagement ring which made her deliriously happy, and although she wanted to wait a year before the wedding, Ronnie wanted to marry her as soon as possible.

The couple spent the holidays with both families, two dinners at both homes on the same day. Together at a luncheon, Cheryl asked her mother, "Do you think I should marry Ronnie?"

"Are you in doubt?" her mother asked. "Cause if you are, take all the time you need before marrying him."

"I'm not sure, maybe cold feet, but there are some things about him that make me wonder," she confessed.

"Well, in my opinion, I want to ask you if you intend to have children?"

"Why?"

"Cause, as far as I'm concerned, you already have one in him."

It didn't set well with Cheryl, and she never asked her mother for her opinion about Ronnie again.

The wedding was set for March of the following year. Cheryl asked her mother to go with her to pick out her wedding gown. She put on a particularly beautiful one, a white one with lace capped sleeves that covered her arms down to the top of her wrists ending in a V at the top of her middle finger. The neckline was low cut bordered with lace, the rest of which covered a silk long dress and Marie started crying at which point the saleslady said, "When a mother cries, that's the one for the bride," so Marie told her daughter that she would pay for her gown, and they trotted off to a restaurant to celebrate after making arrangement for fittings.

The wedding was held in a small century old chapel. Cheryl's father was there to give her away just four weeks shy of carotid surgery, but just before the ceremony, Scott became ill and had to be driven to the hospital.

"Mother, you don't have to be here for the wedding," Cheryl said. "You need to be with Scott."

When Scott heard Cheryl's remark, he said, "I'm okay. You need to be with your daughter. Go, Go, Go on." and he shushed his wife away to be with her daughter.

"Need to be, need to be," Marie kept saying to herself. *"Where the hell do I need to be?* Even though she was torn, she took her husband's advice and stayed at the wedding.

When the married couple left for their honeymoon, Marie's best friend and husband drove her to the hospital to see Scott. The Lincoln in front of them was carrying the bride and groom to the airport and the only reason Marie knew it was them was because a wedding veil was laying across the ledge of the back window of the car. There was something about the sight that caused Marie to feel sadness and she was afraid that sadness would follow her and her daughter for many years to come.

He was okay, Scott. Probably just a panic attack was diagnosed, and he was kept overnight before being released from the hospital. There are those who believed that he had a hard time being face to face with Marie's ex-husband knowing what he knew about the way Steve Trotsky had treated Marie while they were married.

The next day was Mother's Day. "Happy Mother's Day," Cheryl said affectionately when Marie picked up the receiver.

"Where are you?" Marie asked.

"We're aboard ship waiting to sail."

"How sweet of you to call me as you head out to your honeymoon."

And the next thing Marie heard was a curt voice in the background.

"Cheryl, hurry up and get off the phone. I have to call my mother too."

Marie knew whose voice that was.

"Gotta go, Mom, love you, bye."

And that was the beginning of years to come for Marie in getting to know the real Ronnie O'Reilly.

After returning from their honeymoon, Marie saw less and less of her daughter but considered that they were newlyweds, didn't make much of it until it became less often than she anticipated. Cheryl didn't come around and when she did, it was only at lunch time and then it was only if she was in the area. She began using her cell phone to contact her mother and when that became less often, she started getting in touch with Marie by e-mail and even that form of communicating with Marie started becoming a reduced amount of e-mails.

In the meantime, Marie and Scott began hitting the bottle more often, sometimes starting at noon on weekends. Marie was well into her menopausal years with symptoms of irritability and sweats especially during the night. Some of her opinions bordered paranoidal but what she didn't realize was that alcohol was only making matters worse. The marriage started to weaken to the point that Marie picked on Scott, accusing him of being unfaithful to her while traveling and insisted that he find another job so she could feel more secure about their marriage.

The way the separation from his job came about was a surprise to both of them. Scott and other managers had been using their company credit cards for personal use and while the company knew it, occasionally it was permitted especially to take the wives to dinner, but the misuse of the card was becoming unacceptable, so the company comptroller, who started all the gossip years before concerning Scott and Cathy Miller, turned him in to the president of the corporation when he noticed charges that were not in accordance with traveling expenses.

Marie had been shopping that day. She turned the corner onto the street where they lived and saw Scott sitting on the stoop leading to the front door with his elbows on his knees. When she noticed that the company car was not parked in the driveway, her heart did a double beat and she knew what had happened.

She got out of the car, he approached her and said, "I need to talk to you, but not outside," and took her by the arm and lead her into the house.

"What happened?" she asked.

"I got fired," he answered. "There's no other way to tell you but I had abused and overused the company credit card and was reported to the president of the company who called me in his office, admonished me and let me go. In order to pay back all the money I owe the company, I have agreed to sign over my stock sharing and pension accumulation, but worse than that, you have to sign that you will not try to collect any of it upon my death. If we do not sign, I will be taken to court and sued to get the monies back. I'm so sorry honey to involve you in this mess I created."

Marie took a deep breath, opened the cabinet door, poured herself a scotch, and sat down on the barstool at the kitchen counter. She didn't say a word for a couple minutes.

"Now what?" was all she could say.

"I'll get another job."

"Where? I mean will they give you a recommendation?"

"When I was called in the president's office, I told him that other managers were abusing their cards also, but when he asked for names, I wouldn't divulge them preferring that the company find out for themselves. They said they were gonna look into it and fire them also. But in the meantime, all they would disclose to a request from another employer is what they are required to do if called for a reference, that I worked there, dates of employment, and job description."

She didn't answer him and couldn't quite grasp her feelings about the situation only knowing that she felt shame and embarrassment for what he had done especially since she was aware of his spending company money and had warned him so many times to stop before he got caught.

She felt loss, not just because of her husband's abuse of company credit cards, but because she knew she was losing her daughter too. There was not as much communication between Marie and Cheryl and when Marie did try to call, Cheryl seemed preoccupied in trying to get her mother off the phone as quickly as possible. A repeat of Mother's Day happened more than once in their conversations, and Marie could hear Ronnie in the background saying, "Cheryl, get off the phone. I have to make a business call."

Just when Marie was beginning to feel like giving up, serendipity stepped in for the couple. Scott got a job working for a defense contractor at the Cape as a laborer and in order to make ends meet, he took advantage of the GI bill and went to night school. They had one car for a while before Scott went and bought a clunker that stood up long enough to get him to work and back.

SIXTY-FIVE

At the same time that Marie's life seemed to be falling into place, her sister, Margaret, after more than twenty years of living in a house of nuns, decided that life was not for her and with the help of psychotherapy, left the convent and took a civil service position at an Army base in south Jersey called Ft. Clark, assisting the chaplain in the religious education of the children of soldiers. She had two degrees, one in English and one in Religion and was paid well.

She found it difficult living in the secular world after having been separated from it for such a long time, and was not accustomed to what she called outrageous imbibing of alcohol that her superior enjoyed throughout the day. She decided to search for another position, one nearer to her family in Florida.

She found that position in religious education in a parish north of Orlando, whereby she would not receive a salary for the first six months although all living expenses would be taken care of by the parish pastor. After six months and if agreed to by she and Fr. Mahoney, she would receive a sizeable salary to set up and teach classes for the children. She was promised that she would have free will in the course planning and only needed to conference with him once a week.

After six months the agreement for her employment was recognized, and she felt as though she had finally found her calling. Fr. Mahoney received excellent comments from his parishioners about her ability to interest their children in the teachings of the church, so he gave her free reign, trusting her judgment and told her he would, if needed, be there to consult should she want his advice.

There was another reason for his confidence in her ability, and she found the reason why after working for him a year later. She was in her office one day when an employee approached her and asked to speak to her privately.

"Sure, come on in and sit down," she said.

"Can I close the door?" he asked.

"Yes, is something wrong?"

"Well, I really don't know who to talk to about a particular problem I'm having with Father Mahoney," he said.

"Oh, surely it can't be that bad. He's a good priest. What is it?"

"I'm tired of cleaning up after him in the early mornings," he said.

"What? He has a housekeeper," she said.

"That's not the kind of cleaning up I'm talking about," he said. "Cleaning up his puke, pouring coffee down his throat, and putting him in the shower to sober him up before he has to go to say Mass. It's disgusting and I can't take it anymore. How do you tell your priest that he needs help with alcohol abuse and still keep your job?"

"I'll talk to him," she answered.

BIG MISTAKE!!!!

"Thank you. I appreciate it," he said as he stood up and walked out the door.

She saw Fr. Mahoney in the hallway of the parish hall the following week.

"Do you have a minute?" she asked.

"Problem," he answered.

"I don't know. Could we step in your office?"

"Sure."

And she followed him down the hall to his office.

"Take a chair," he said as he closed the door. "Now what's this all about?"

She didn't want to expose the worker who came to her.

"It's come to my attention that, well, this is delicate, but that you might have a problem," she said.

"With what?" he asked.

"Alcohol," she answered.

"What? Where the hell did you get that idea from? And if it were true, what business is it of yours?"

She knew she overstepped and didn't know how to get out of it. Slightly shaking while sitting in a chair as he stood behind his desk looking down on her, she answered, "One of the workers came to me about it. Said he didn't want to be your caretaker after nightly binges of drinking."

"Really?" he asked. "Well the information you've been given is false. I have no problem with alcohol. A drink now and again at a social function is all I take. So who is this worker?"

She wouldn't say preferring to slither out of his office and go home as it was the end of the work day.

"You are excused," he said angrily.

She got up and hurried out of his office fast-stepping down the hall, out the door and to her car. She opened the door, slid in, turned the ignition, and sped out the parking lot toward her apartment.

She knew she'd done it and didn't know what to do next, so she called a friend, also an ex-nun, who told her that together, they should write a letter to Fr. Mahoney's superior complaining of his seemingly alcoholism which they did.

It didn't take long. Five days later, Fr. Mahoney called her into his office. He looked like a snake ready to strike. Hissing at her, he said, "I had a call from my superior who told me of you and your friend's letter. As much as I recognize the exceptional work you have been doing, I am at this moment firing you, for you have transgressed the amount of authority I gave to you after hiring you, preferring to take matters into your own hands after talking with a caretaker who has also been fired this morning. Clean out your personal belongings and vacate the building immediately. And, oh, by the way, don't bother to claim unemployment benefits cause I won't sign for you to get them."

She was silently weeping when she left his office and went to hers to pack her personal belongings in a box she found in the maintenance room. She believed she did the right thing in turning the priest in, but knew it would be hard to get another job in Religious Ed, for he would never give her a reference.

Saying nothing to the clerical staff, she stared straight ahead as she left the office, walked out the door, and headed toward her car. Opening the trunk, she put her things on the floor, and as she turned around to close it, she felt a trembling that caused her to shake uncontrollably, so she sat on the ledge of the open trunk and wept hysterically.

A passerby, a co-worker, stopped and asked, "Are you ill, sister?"

"No, no, I'm alright. Just some bad news. That's all."

Standing up, she closed the trunk lid, walked around to the driver's side of her car, got in and left.

She didn't want anyone in her family to know what had happened, so she confided to a friend who was involved in a movement within the church that was questionable, who helped her find a place to live. The rent was low and although it was an efficiency one-room apartment which included utilities, she snapped at the opportunity and moved in within days after her dismissal from her job. After she filed for it, Fr. Mahoney relented and signed the necessary claims for her to receive unemployment.

Realizing that she would have to eventually inform her family of what had happened, she went to her sister, Marie, and related how her dismissal had happened.

"I can't believe you did this," Marie said. "I mean did you really think that Fr. Mahoney would be canned? He's more important than you are and even if he does drink all night, if he can perform his priestly duties, the hierarchy doesn't give a shit."

"I don't care. I still think I did the right thing," Margaret said.

"Remember when you worked in the defense industry?" Marie asked. "You worked your way up to a department manager's secretary. Now, would you do the same thing if you found out he was drinking and go the plant manager to report him?"

"What? No," was the answer. "It's not the same thing."

"Why not?" Marie asked.

"A priest is supposed to set an example for his flock and he didn't."

"Jesus, Margaret, he's not perfect, he's human, capable of making the mistakes we all make. Only thing is because of your last comment, he has to hide his imperfections more than the rest of us or get down off the pedestal that we, as believers, have raised him up to, which is a mistake in the first place."

Margaret's bitterness was obvious to the point that Marie realized she needed to change the subject, so she asked her sister what her future plans were.

"I'll collect unemployment benefits for as long as I can and decide what to do next," Margaret answered.

"I'd ask you, but I suppose you wouldn't want a drink, even of wine," Marie asked. "I'm gonna have a scotch."

Looking at her sister, Margaret's eyes widened. She declined and left her sister's home.

SIXTY-SIX

Marie saw Danny and Linda often, but she noticed that Danny seemed to be in a fog most of the time when they were together. Once more, he took his sister into his confidence.

"I miss the priesthood," he exclaimed. "I've been looking into getting faculties in the Episcopal church, but I've been told I'm too old. They asked for and we went to a meeting so the church leaders could meet with Linda to see if she would be acceptable as a priest's wife, and I don't think she passed the test."

"Have you discussed this with her?"

"Yes, and she's going through enough realizing how much she misses her children. She's having headaches, and I think it's over the guilt of leaving them. You know we bought the house near you in the hopes that one of her kids would come and stay with us either in the summer or even live with us, but that hasn't happened."

"And you, you having some guilt too?"

"To a degree. I had a call from one of my parishioners recently stating that a group of them wrote the bishop citing that they don't care what I've done, they want me back."

"I didn't know you kept in touch with them," Marie said.

"I called a couple I used to play golf with," he said. "Ones that I was close with."

"It'll work out, Danny. Linda's a good person. Didn't you guys discuss this when you left to move here together?"

"We just never thought about it and expected her kids would want to see more of their mother if not me. It just hasn't happened."

Changing the subject, he asked, "How you doin', Marie? And Cheryl, how's she doin?"

"Something's wrong, Danny. She's not returning my phone calls, not stopping by anymore and I don't know why. We were so close, but since she married, I don't see her anymore. I know she has a husband to care for, but to hear from her once in a while would be appreciated."

"We haven't heard from her either. Why don't you ask her?"

"How can I when she doesn't return my phone calls? I saw her pulling out of the mall the other day, beeped my horn, waved, and she just kept right on going."

"Are you sure she saw you?"

"How could she not? I was pulling in and she was pulling out. We passed each other. I looked right in her face, she turned her head and drove away."

And if she didn't have enough stress in her life already, Marie received a call from her mother's doctor.

"Mrs. Nicholson," Dr. Whent said. "I think it's time for the family to discuss your mother's living alone. It's time to make other arrangements and I would like to discuss it with the family. Would you and your brother be available tomorrow afternoon for a conference?"

Although Marie knew this was coming, it seemed too soon and she didn't want to acknowledge it. She made an appointment with the doctor for the next afternoon at four o'clock. She contacted her brother, Danny. He was quiet for a few moments before telling Marie that he would attend.

"There is a home nearby where elderly who can no longer live alone go and share the home," the doctor said. "It's a step before a nursing home. Some residents have their own room and some share a room. I think it's time that your mother be taken to a living arrangement such as this for her own good. She's taken a few spills, ones that I'm sure she didn't tell you about because they caused no permanent damage, only bruising, but my concern is that she could take a fall that would immobilize her, leaving her either in bed or on the floor with no way to let anyone know for hours until she came up missing. I mentioned a call alarm button which she refuses to consider, so this is the only other way to protect her. I will call and get the necessary paperwork going when I hear from you. In the meantime, it might be a good idea to take your mother for a visit to see what the home looks like."

"This is so hard to accept, doctor," Marie said. Danny just nodded his head up and down.

"We'll get back to you," Danny finally said.

They decided to go to Danny's house to discuss the situation with Linda, especially since she worked in a nursing home and could shed some light on the options they were considering.

"She can't live alone any longer," Linda said. "What if she were to fall again and break a hip, laying on the floor in pain, possibly passing out? You know, Marie, you asked her to have a buddy system with the other old ladies checking on each other twice a day and she wouldn't do it. It seems to me that the only answer is to take her to a place where she will be cared for and watched in case she falls again."

They decided to take Marion to the share a home. Marie insisted on telling Marion where they were going and at first, Marion, said she didn't want to go, but with coaxing by her children, she agreed to go just to "check it out."

The attractive old house sat near a beautiful lake north of Orlando. It had a porch that surrounded the entire perimeter of the home with rocking chairs situated every few feet. They stepped into a vestibule that was wide, had hardwood floors and was decorated with pictures portraying painted flowers with frames that were faux gold. To the left was a large parlor with a fireplace and piano. There were two sofas where residents could meet for conversation. To the right was a dining room with a rectangular oak wood table that had eight chairs. Behind the dining room was the kitchen where three meals a day for the residents were prepared.

There were rooms upstairs for those who could climb and two rooms downstairs, one that was shared and the other that was a small room quartering a clothes closet, twin bed, dresser, rocking chair, and stand with television. The home manager mentioned the fact that because the small room was available, Marion could reside in it at the same rate as a shared resident.

"So whatdaya think?" Marie said to her mother.

"No!" was all Marion could manage to say.

"Mom, let's be realistic," Marie said. "We had a conference with your doctor who told us that you've been falling but not injuring yourself. What will happen when you fall, injure yourself, and nobody's there to help?"

Marion didn't answer.

"All we want to do is be completely secure in knowing that you are safe. You know we'll come see you and bring you to the house when you want. Please, mother, please consider moving into a safe and sound home."

"I'll think about it," Marion said defiantly. "I'd like to go home now."

Praying may have had something to do with it, for the next time Marie called her mother a few days later, Marion gave in and while she didn't want to, accepted the fact that she could no longer live alone and agreed to move into the shared living home.

"I'll want my own things," Marion said to Marie.

"I know, Mother," Marie said. "And you shall have them."

Because her apartment was furnished, there really wasn't much to move - a rocking chair, television, personal belongings, and clothes were about it.

Marion didn't want a phone in her room. There was one in the hallway outside her room, so knowing that the only ones who would call her was her family, she felt it was just an unnecessary extra expense.

Her family moved her into her new residence the following week leaving her feeling confident that she would enjoy a safer environment.

Marie received a call from the house manager the following week.

"Your mother doesn't come out of her room often and socialize with the others, doesn't play bingo or join in the sing-alongs that we have for our residents" she said.

"Mother isn't and never was a social butterfly," Marie answered.

"There's one other point I'd like to mention," the manager said. "She's not bathing as much as we think she should. I think she's afraid of getting into the bathtub and falling. We have staff that could help her, but she refuses."

"I'll come and check it out." Marie said.

The next Saturday morning, not knowing how her mother would respond to it, Marie drove to the home and introduced the idea that she would help her mother bathe.

"I don't need anyone to bathe me," Marion said.

"Mother, there is an odor about you. How often do you take a bath?"

"Often enough," Marion replied.

"Why not let me help you. I'll stay in the bathroom with you, help you in and out of the tub. Come on, honey, let's go to the bathroom and take a bath. You'll feel so much better."

"No, I don't want to," Marion exclaimed.

"Please, Mother!"

"Oh, alright," Marion said boldly.

Mother and daughter rounded up clean underwear, bathrobe, slippers, and headed toward the bathroom.

After they stepped into the bathroom, Marie closed the door and helped her mother disrobe. She viewed the petite body of an eighty-six year old woman whose flat breasts, which had never worn a bra, sagged almost to her waist and although her mother's body was old, her legs and thighs were smooth. The only fat on her body was her stomach, but then, Marion had always had a large one. As she started running the water for a bath, Marie kept her head down so her mother could not see the tears developing in her eyes but she swiftly stifled them. As the tub was filling, she tested it with her elbow much like she did when she bathed her babies many years before.

"Come on sweetie, let's get you in," Marie said.

She took her mother by her left arm and gently helped her into the tub, holding her tightly around her waist as Marion slowly slid into the water. She gently washed her mother's back, neck, legs, and feet before giving the washrag to Marion.

"Here, mother, you can wash your private parts," and she handed Marion the washrag.

After taking the washrag to her vaginal area, Marion looked up at her daughter and said, "I think I'm about done now,"

Marie helped her mother out of the tub, placed the toilet lid down, sat her on the toilet seat and started gently drying Marion at which time Marion started crying.

"Did I hurt you?" Marie asked.

"No," Marion answered. "But it's a sad state of affairs when your daughter has to give you a bath."

"Oh, mother," Marie was crying, "It's an honor to bathe you. How many shitty diapers did you change, how many baths did you give me when I was a baby?"

With tears in their eyes, mother and daughter clung to each other before they could compose themselves enough for Marie to help Marion put her clean clothes on and lead her down the hall and back to her room.

The Saturday ritual continued. Marie's mother still protested her daughter helping her bathe but always gave in and allowed it although neither one of them cried again while experiencing it. Marie never gave a thought to the fact that old women Marion's age were afraid to take a bath, afraid they would slip and fall in the tub and because there were no showers in their younger years, they had never gotten into the habit of taking one.

It was suggested at a meeting of family members at the home that it helps to interview a parent about their lives and past experiences, Marie took with her a small wallet-sized hand-held tape recorder on her next visit to see her mother.

"Let's go down by the lake and record your memories," Marie said.

"Who would care about me?" Marion asked.

"Your family, that's who," Marie answered.

She helped her mother through the grass that sloped down toward the lake where they found two lawn chairs and sat. Not really knowing how to conduct an interview, Marie started out asking her mother her birth date and who her parents were and who their parents were. They laughed as Marion recalled the experiences of her life especially when she had her children and her recollection of how she felt upon seeing each one of them for the first time after their births. An hour elapsed before they realized it, but Marie had her mother's voice on a recorder expressing what life meant to her now that she was an old woman.

"I'm gonna take this tape and type it up for the rest of the family and you can sent it to them for Christmas," Marie said.

"Go on," her mother replied.

"No, Mom, I believe they will enjoy it as much as we have enjoyed taping it."

Marie went home and transcribed the tape onto 5 x 7 pages. She bought quilted material and made a cover for the book. The front page had an oval cutout framed in lace where a baby picture of her mother was placed. She took the books to her mother to inscribe a message on the final page to each of her children and grandchildren and sent the books to them for Christmas that year.

The family was overjoyed reading about their mother's life, making statements such as, "I didn't know about that, did you?" or "She didn't tell me about that, did she tell you?"

That Christmas was a joyous one for the entire family for they knew more about the matriarch of the family than they ever could have known if she hadn't allowed Marie to interview her.

SIXTY-SEVEN

Two months later, Marie received a call from the shared home.

"Your mother fell outside the property while waiting for the church bus," the manager said. "We've discussed her situation and believe it's time for her to go to a nursing home."

And there it was, the words Marie and the family never wanted to hear: "nursing home."

Marie called her brother and, together with his wife, decided that the time had come.

It was also decided not to tell Marion on the day that Danny and Linda went to get her. Because she worked there, Linda was able to accommodate her mother-in-law's admission to the nursing home within one day after the call came. So that they could pack her belongings, Marie and Scott waited in Scott's truck outside the shared home while Danny and Linda went in to get Marion.

"Oh, God," Marie cried into her husband's shoulder, "I never thought this day would come. I hoped she'd go before it went this far."

When Marie looked up, Danny and Linda were coming down the front steps accompanying Marion toward their car.

Marie cried uncontrollably until Scott calmed her down saying, "Not now, mommy (that name was given to Marie when they got the dog), we have to go in and pack your mother's things and take them to the nursing home."

They entered the shared home and walked to Marion's room. Starting to pack, Marie couldn't stop crying. The same items brought into the home months before were being removed and taken to another, probably final, place.

Even though Marie didn't want to follow her brother and sister-in-law to the nursing home, she restrained herself and walked into the entrance searching for Linda, leaving Scott in the truck with Marion's meager belongings until Marion was situated in her room.

Linda came out from the administrator's office, took Marie by the hand and led her down the hall to room 123 where it seemed that Marion would spend the rest of her days on earth.

Marion looked at her daughter but didn't say anything. She was expressionless, and although Marie wanted to run to her mother, put her arms around her, and tell her she would take her home with her, she stayed in control knowing that Marion was in the best place possible for her.

Marie kissed her mother as Marion sat on her bed and told her she'd be back. She felt like she did when she left her children on their first day of school.

Danny, Linda, and Marie were asked to stop in the administrator's office before leaving. "We ask that you don't come back for at least five days," the admin said.

"But," Marie said.

"If she sees you before that time, she'll have a difficult time adjusting to new surroundings. It's for her own good, plus Linda will be looking in on her daily and reporting back to you. That should give you some comfort. Don't you agree? Oh, and while we're discussing it, your husband can bring her possessions to my office and I'll see that she gets them."

The family left and decided to go to Marie and Scott's home for a drink and to come down off the very emotional day they had just experienced.

"It's a beautiful facility," Marie said to Linda. "The entrance looks like the lobby of a high class hotel with Mahogany tables, Queen Anne chairs, thick carpet, and overstuffed sofas. And the floors shine. I didn't see a morsel on them as we passed down the hallway. The dining room is so pleasant decorated in colors of pink and light blue. The solarium is located in the sunniest spot of the building, and it's good to know that there is a beauty shop located on the first floor near Mom. Thank you Linda for seeing that she came here to live."

"For those who might decide to "take a walk," there is a security system that sets off an alarm if any of the doors on the floor are opened," Linda said. "No resident is allowed out of the building without either a healthcare worker or a family member, so she will be safe."

During this time, Marie had not thought about Cheryl, had not heard from her either, so she decided to call her daughter to let her know where her grandmother was living. She got her answering machine and telling Cheryl it was important, asked her to call her back. The call was returned two days later with no apologies for her tardiness. After informing her daughter of Marion's whereabouts, Cheryl begged off and said she would go see her grandmother soon.

Still not able to understand her daughter's coldness toward her, Marie sat down and tried to figure it out. True, her daughter's teenage years were not perfect after Marie divorced her father, but she was taken care of, had a roof over her head, food in her belly, and was not subjected to emotional or physical abuse, so what's the problem she asked herself. She knew they had had a close mother/daughter relationship and had no problem discussing topics such as sex and politics.

As time went by, the ugliness of it would come to light and linger for years.

Communication stopped between Marie and her daughter shortly after Marion entered the nursing home. Upon glancing at the sign-in roster at the nurses' station, it showed that Cheryl did find the time to visit her grandmother, but it appeared that she made sure she did it when she knew Marie would not be there.

Although her children took her out to lunch on the weekends and the family spent holidays at Marie's, Marion's health started to decline almost from the day she entered the nursing home, but her children knew she was safe which made them feel secure with that knowledge.

SIXTY-EIGHT

In the interim, Marie decided to go into business.

"Hot dogs, that's what I'll do," she said to Scott. "I'll buy a cart and sell them."

Never one to discourage his wife, Scott agreed that it probably would be a good idea, especially since it might help keep her mind off her mother and daughter.

They visited a commissary where Marie would buy the necessary food items to stock her cart, one she would hitch to the back of her car to take to a parking lot where people would want to purchase the famous New York Sabrett dogs for lunch. Next she had to find the right location to park her cart.

She found a location on SR 50 in Orlando, the main route from the space coast to the gulf. The buildings were empty, but the owner had no problem with her parking in his lot at lunchtime to sell not only hot dogs but kielbasa too.

Searching the local newspaper, she found a used cart, went to check it out and bought it. The cart was kept in the garage where each morning Scott would back the car to it and hitch it up to have it ready for Marie to drive it to her location.

The first day, business was good. Her commissary supplier directed her on firing up the hot dog cooker, cooking the dogs and kielbasa and using the bun warmer, after which, being sure she was able to take over, he left.

She wanted her mother to be the first one to purchase a dog from her and asked her brother, Danny, to bring Marion to the parking lot.

"What is she doing now?" Marion asked Danny as he drove her and his wife Linda to the site where the cart was parked.

"You'll see," Danny answered.

Danny's car pulled into the lot and as Marion was looking out the window, she saw her daughter standing aside the cart dressed with an apron and hat that had printing on them, "Kielbasa Kween & Hot Dog Kart".

Danny opened the car door to help his mother out. Marie set up a folding chair for her to sit upon and asked, "Hey lady do you want to buy a hot dog?"

"Yes," Marion answered.

"Where's your buck twenty-five?" Marie asked.

"I don't have any money on me," Marion said.

"Too bad. Maybe the gentleman who drove you here will buy you one."

Danny gave his sister the money for a drink, hot dog and chips. Marie pulled a folding table to her mother and set the food down for Marion to eat. Pictures were taken of the four of them.

There were times Clark and Marie called each other. When Clark called and she answered the phone, she heard, "Good morning, this is Clyde's Roofing calling to inquire if you need repairs on your roof," and if she were alone, she would laugh and tell Clyde, "No repairs today." They cared about how each other was getting along and two times a year would meet for lunch. At one of their semi-yearly luncheons, Marie told Clark that she was gonna sell hot dogs, so he and a co-worker showed up one day to buy one. She was happy to see Willy was with him. They talked until she became busy and the guys needed to get back to work.

Never considering that in Florida it was monsoon season, Marie started her hot dog business in August. One never knew exactly what time the rains would come but between three and five o'clock was a good guess. The first week, a doozy of a storm crept up on Marie before she could close down. The winds were howling, the rain pouring down and as she held on to her umbrella, she thought she would blow away, until a kind six foot two burly, bearded, truck driver wearing a cowboy hat, jeans and cow boots, pulled in and helped her close down. She thanked him for his help and soaking wet, she headed home.

Scott pulled up behind her when she was getting out of her car.

"I went to the lot and saw you were gone," he said. "Look at you. You're soaking wet. Are you sure you want to continue with this?"

"Yeah," she said. "I'm having too much fun."

"Well, you'd better let me teach you how to back up that cart. You don't know how and it could jack-knife without knowing. You could get yourself into a situation where you won't be able to pull out, have to back up and you'll be SOL."

"Okay, but not today, maybe tomorrow or the weekend," she answered.

She should have listened to him!!!!!!!

Marie soon learned that she needed to be at her location by eleven in the morning and out of it by two-thirty if she didn't want a repeat of the storm.

She was getting ready to close shop one day when a dark green truck pulled up. She turned and looked to see how many dogs she had left and said, "You're a little late, but I have a couple hot dogs left," and when she looked up, she was shocked.

She recognized the woman who got out of the truck who said, "Hi, Mom."

"Oh, wha......."

"Derek said you were selling hot dogs on 50. I just had to stop by and see for myself," Cheryl said.

Searching for words all Marie could say was, "You want a dog? On the house."

"Sure," Cheryl said.

She served her daughter a hot dog and as Cheryl ate it, they talked about nothing in particular. As she was leaving, Cheryl hugged her mother, climbed in the truck and promised she'd be in touch.

The following week, Marie decided she would locate her cart in the lot of a professional building. She got permission to park it and pulled in around eleven in the morning. After selling all the dogs and kielbasa in her cart, she cleaned and closed up the cart, started up the car and took notice that she couldn't pull forward because there were three four foot poles directly in front of the car.

"Shit," she said and put the car in reverse, but all it did was start to jackknife, so she pulled forward and tried again. The time she backed into a fence but didn't damage it.

She looked up at the all glass windowed building and saw silhouettes of bodies of people standing there looking out at her. Some were pointing, some were bent over in what she figured was laughter.

"God damn it," she yelled knowing she couldn't go anyplace because there was no room to either go forward or backward, so she did what any other woman would do, she sat there, put her head in her hands and cried.

There was a tap on the driver's side window and when she looked up with tears streaming down her face, she saw a young man in his forties who motioned for her to let the window down.

"I saw that you were having trouble," he said. "I'd like to help you, if you'll let me."

"Look what I've done," she answered. "Can't go forward nor backward. You think you could get me out of this pickle?"

"I have a boat on a trailer that I have to maneuver around all the time, so, yes, I think I can. Get out of the car and let me get you out of this space and onto the parking lot."

He jockeyed the car with cart attached until he had it in a position to pull forward and out of the lot, got out and said, "There you go."

Not knowing what else to say, she asked, "You want a hot dog, free of course?" To which he answered, "I don't eat them."

"Oh," Marie said.

"But," he added, "Can I buy you lunch sometime at a nearby restaurant?"

"Oh, no, but thanks just the same."

"Here's my card if you change your mind," he said and added, "I'd really like to see you again," and started to walk away.

"Wait a minute," Marie replied. "You see all those people in the windows of that office building? I guess they're all laughing at me."

"Not only that," he said, "but they were taking bets on whether you'd get out or not and that's when I thought enough was enough."

"You mean you work there?" she asked.

"Yes, I'm the CEO of the company who owns the building and I like your spunk."

"Call me if you'd like that lunch, okay?"

"Yeah, sure," she said knowing she would never call him and wondering why he would even be interested in her, he being younger than she.

He waved and walked toward the building. Marie got in the car and drove home. She told Scott what happened, not about the offer of lunch though.

He didn't say, I told you so, but asked her when she wanted to learn how to back the car up. Somehow the neighbors got wind of it and asked if they could bring their lawn chairs and watch as he instructed Marie backing up in the cul de sac, and, of course, they'd buy a dog or sausage from her while they watched.

    Marie's interest waned after the episode of the unbacked up cart, so she decided to sell it, much to Scott's relief, and didn't lose much of her investment in it - a thousand dollars or so.

SIXTY-NINE

Shortly thereafter, Danny came to his sister to tell her that he and Linda were divorcing.

"She wants to return to her hometown and be with her kids, and I want to try to be reinstated in the church, receive my faculties. I was defrocked, stripped of my priestly duties. It'll take a while, probably six months to a year, but I've befriended a priest who has offered to help me."

"Is this amicable, I mean between you and Lin?" Marie asked.

"Yes, the only complexity of it all is that she has to sign a document stating that she will not sue the church, will not cause any problems with my returning and will not mention our marriage in gossip. In other words, she'll keep quiet, which she has agreed to do. What I have to do is get written testimony from the bishop of the diocese in New York that I served under and one from the Florida diocese, that I am not an alcoholic, nor am I a pedophile and even then, this document must be offered to another bishop of a diocese outside of New York and Florida who will sponsor me before it is sent to Rome where it will be presented to a tribunal of ecclesiastical hierarchy for review prior to my faculties being reinstated. The paperwork is in motion and will be submitted as soon as the divorce is final."

"You mean that there's an agreement by all these church muck-e-mucks to go forward with this?"

"Yes."

"What about Linda?"

"She's leaving next week."

Marie called Linda and asked her to go to lunch.

"Are you okay with this?" she asked Linda after they were seated in a booth at a nearby restaurant.

"Yes, I've known for a long time that he missed ministry. He needs it and I need to deal with the guilt of having left my children. There is no animosity in this decision we've made. It's been coming.

We talked about it and we both feel better about making it. I will always love Danny, Marie. We just can't be married, but there are times I've wondered, would it have been alright had we had an affair that lasted for years like some of the priests we know have done with their "housekeepers" and kept quiet about it even though parishioners knew and didn't care?"

"And sometimes I wonder if I'll carry a big red A on my chest for the rest of my life because I fell in love with a priest?"

"Not in my book, you won't," Marie answered. "Is there anything I can do to help you make the move a little less painful?"

"Not really. We're lucky to have sold the house. Danny was given an upstairs apartment in the garage on the church grounds where he will live until he receives his faculties. The pastor is the one who is helping him become reinstated. I have a job waiting for me at the nursing home I left when we married and will stay with my friend, Lucy, until I get a place to live. I told Danny not to worry about sharing the equity of the house with me. It isn't that much anyway. I've always made it and with God's help, I will again.

"God, I'm gonna miss you, Lin," Marie said with tears in her eyes. "Will you keep in touch?"

"You know I will. We'd better say our goodbyes now before I fall apart."

"I'll get the check," Marie said

Linda stood up, hugged her sister-in-law and turned and walked out the restaurant door leaving Marie sitting in the booth dabbing her eyes with a tissue.

The following week, Marie received a call from her son, Derek.

"Mom," he said. "Cheryl's pregnant and wanted me to tell you."

Marie hadn't heard from Cheryl since the day Cheryl stopped at the hot dog stand.

"What?" Marie asked. "Why didn't she call me herself?"

"I don't know, Ma."

"I guess she doesn't want to talk to me," Marie said, her voice crackling. "But why?"

"Ma, I didn't ask her, just said I'd tell you and hung up."

"When is she due?"

"First of the year. It's a boy. Gotta go!"

Marie stared at the receiver of the phone in shock wondering why her daughter was acting so indifferent toward her. She couldn't figure it out but assured herself that she would get a call soon from Cheryl informing her that she was going to be grandmother.

Soon after Linda returned north, and shortly after Marie was told by her son that she was going to be a grandmother, Marion suffered another stroke and found it difficult to walk, so the staff advised that she use a walker which she promptly declined. A few weeks later, the head nurse, Jean, called Marie.

"Are you coming to see your mother today?" she asked.

"Do I need to?"

"At some time today, I would advise it," Jean answered.

"Tell me why?"

"We believe she suffered another stroke. She is having trouble talking."

"I'm on my way," Marie said.

When Marie arrived at the nursing home, she found her mother sitting in a wheelchair with the temple side of her head laying on the palm of her right hand that was resting on the arm of the chair.

"Hi, Mom," Marie said. She'd never seen her mother looking so bad, so old.

Marion barely whispered back, "Hi," She sounded like someone who had lost their voice with laryngitis.

"I love you, Mom," Marie said.

Again barely audible, Marion repeated, "I lov yo to."

Knowing her mother was disgusted sitting in the wheelchair, she found a nurse and expressed her wishes that her mother be taken to her room immediately.

"We thought the sunny room would do her good," the nurse said.

"I want her to be taken back to her room to her bed," Marie insisted.

"After the aide got Marion into her bed, Marie sat with her for a time before going to the head nurse, Jean, to asked what she thought.

"Don't putz around with me," Marie said. "I want the truth and I don't want to hear 'Wait for her doctor to tell you,' - tell me your opinion."

"Well, usually when this happens, it isn't very long before a patient passes. That's why I called you, but then one never knows. Although your mother is a teenie person who is strong willed, we can't say for sure. I knew you'd want to be informed when her condition worsened."

"For that, I am grateful," Marie said and walked down the hall to room 123 to sit with her mother.

As she lay in her bed, Marion's head was turned to the left. Her eyes were fixed staring at a corner of the ceiling. Her left arm was bent at her waist and lay across it with her hand curled up in a fist. She didn't speak nor did she move.

"Mother," Marie said. "If you can hear me, squeeze my finger," and Marie placed the index finger of her right hand into the cupped hole of her mother's left.

Marion squeezed her daughter's hand but kept her eyes transfixed at the corner of the ceiling. Marie sat with her for a while before deciding to go home and call her brother.

"Danny," she said after telling where she had just been, "How much longer?"

"I talked with her doctor minutes ago," Danny said. "He said she has no brain waves. Her meds have been pulled."

"What does that mean?" Marie asked.

"You will get a call from her doctor this evening, but essentially, she will die."

Even though she knew it would come to this at some point soon, Marie broke down sobbing.

"It's for the best," Danny said trying to calm his sister down. "She has no quality of life anymore."

After Marie hung up the phone, she put her headset on, sat in the rocker, turned on the stereo and played some classical music.

Early in the evening, Dr. Peters called Marie and explained what would happen.

"Your mother has no brain function. The recent stroke of a couple days ago caused her brain to just die. I was called by the head nurse in your mother's ward, and after examining her and discussing her deteriorated condition with your brother, and with his permission, I discontinued her meds. This happened to my father," Dr. Peters said. "His meds were pulled and he died the next day. I'm very sorry."

Marie slept fitfully that night. Scott tried to relax her with assurances of his love and support for her, and although she needed to feel his closeness, it wasn't helpful, so when he fell asleep, she quietly tiptoed out of their bed and went into the living room to sit in the dark and meditate.

The next day, she went to the nursing home. Finding her mother in the same condition as she was the day before, she once again placed her right index finger into her mother's left, cupped hand and said, "Mother, if you can hear me, squeeze my finger," to which Marion squeezed, but barely.

Marie remained in the room for an hour before leaving to go home for a break. She wanted desperately to have a conversation with Marion, but knew the impossibility of it, so she spoke words to her although she knew her mother could not answer.

"Mother," she said as she placed her hand over Marion's hand, "Cheryl's gonna' have a baby, a boy in the new year." There was no reaction. She tried to hold back the tears but she couldn't and ran into the hall, turned toward the wall and wept. A passing nurse stopped to ask her if she could help to which she answered, "No." After she composed herself, she looked in on her mother to find her in the same position, turned and walked down the hall and out the door.

After her teleconference with the doctor, she was sure that her mother would have passed by now, but she also knew that her mother was strong willed and would also fight to live.

The following day she went back again to the nursing home and again put her index finger into her mother's cupped left hand, but this time after she asked her to squeeze, Marion did not.

Danny came into the room as Marie sat in the chair next to the bed. He checked on his mother, turned to his sister, and said, "Come on, we're goin' home."

"But Danny, what if she dies while we're not here?" Marie asked.

He didn't answer her, just took her by the hand and led her out of the room, down the hall, out into the parking lot to her car and said he'd call.

Marie went home and went to bed early seven o'clock. The call from her brother came at 8:30.

"She's gone," he said. "I'm going to the nursing home now to sign some papers and say my goodbyes."

"Not without me, you're not," Marie answered.

When Danny pulled into the driveway, he composed himself before entering his sister's house. He was met by his brother-in-law who said, "She's taking it pretty bad. I think you two need to let me drive you to the nursing home."

"Good idea," Danny said. "Grab something to put my mother's personal belongings in."

The car was unusually quiet as Scott drove them to the home.

Marion was wrapped in a white sheet with arms crossed upon her chest and her eyes closed when Marie entered the room. She bent down to kiss her mother goodbye on the forehead and noticed that her skin felt waxy.

When Scott asked what she wanted removed from the room, Marie walked around her mother's bed to her nightstand, opened the drawer and said, "Only the items in this drawer, not her clothes. Let the staff give them to the needy."

There wasn't much to take. Scott placed the items in a laundry basket he brought with him. The items didn't fill it.

Once more, Marie kissed her mother, took her husband's hand, and turned to walk out the door and into the hall. She didn't stop to look right or left at anyone she passed.

"What about a funeral?" Danny said when they returned to Marie's home.

"We bought a funeral package that included a viewing, but I don't want to have one," Marie said. "I mean she had no friends, just her children. We were her life, Danny, so I think the service should be private with only our friends invited."

"What about the service?" Danny asked.

"Once a priest, always a priest. Isn't that what Melchedesh said? And isn't that what mother believed?" Marie answered. "Say Mass on my dining room table for her at a time to be determined and after we receive her cremated remains."

"I don't have my faculties yet," Danny said.

"Oh! Stop. As far as mother is concerned, you never lost them and I feel the same about it. We don't need robes and all the other paraphernalia you wore when you offered the sacrifice of the Mass. I'm sure God won't care and will shine His light down upon the family throughout the ceremony."

"What about a eulogy?" Danny asked.

"That I will take care of," Marie answered.

SEVENTY

Marion's remains were delivered to Marie's house seven days later by the funeral home director. Waiting for the delivery before the service could begin were family and a few friends. The dining room table was cleared and a white linen table cloth was placed on it. Also placed on the table was Danny's chalice with a picture of Marion next to it.

Marie kept looking out the window for a sign of Cheryl. She had told her son of the day and time of the funeral service believing that her daughter would certainly attend her grandmother's funeral, but there was no call nor was there a showing, at least before the service began.

The doorbell rang. When Marie went to answer it, a middle-aged, grey haired woman in a dark blue suit stood outside and said, "Nicholson?"

"Yes," Marie answered.

"Here," and the woman handed Marie a brown paper bag and turned to walk away.

"What?" Marie said.

Danny hurried over to his sister and said, "It's mother's remains."

"In a brown paper bag?" Marie asked as she held the bag against her chest.

"Yes, and inside the bag is a carton with a plastic bag with mother's remains in it."

Marie pushed by her brother, ran into the kitchen with the bag and out the sliding glass door to the patio where she took a seat on one side of the chaise lounge. She rocked back and forth crying as she held the bag tightly to her chest. Jackie, Marie's best friend, started toward the kitchen when Danny stopped her and said, "She needs to do this. Leave her alone."

After a few minutes, Marie stopped crying, stopped rocking, stood up and headed toward the door where her brother was standing. Not saying a word, he opened the door to the house and escorted

Marie into the dining room where he asked her to give him the remains.

"No," Marie said.

"Please, Marie," Danny said. "We need to start the service now."

"Did Cheryl come?" Marie asked wildly looking around the living room for her daughter.

"No," Danny said.

"Did she call?" Marie asked.

"No," Danny said sadly.

"Wha…?" and she couldn't finish the sentence.

Danny offered a funeral Mass for his mother and distributed communion in the form of pieces of bread. Red wine was sipped from his chalice by each communicant.

When it was time for the eulogy, Danny nodded to his sister, at which point Marie put the tape in the recorder and turned it on. What the attendees heard next caused tissues to be taken from the box near the end table for the voice they heard was that of the deceased, Marion, when she wrote her memories for her children, leaving them a message:

"Hold no grudges and have no discontent. The worst thing is that sometimes we don't have understanding among each other. We say things that could offend, not realizing. Instead of staying away, being pouty, talk to one another because a close family stays together and loves one another and helps each other."

There wasn't a dry eye in the room. When they composed themselves, the friends one by one asked Marie, "My God, how could you do that? Doesn't that make you sadder than if you hadn't heard it?"

"No," was Marie's reply. "It helps me with my grieving. I find it to be very healing to hear her voice."

Once again, Marie looked around and noticed that her daughter had not arrived. She inquired but was informed that Cheryl had not called. She didn't know if she could ever forgive her for not attending her grandmother's funeral. With the passing of time, there would be much more that Marie would have to forgive her daughter for.

One of the friends who attended the memorial service came to Marie when it was over and said, "I answered your phone during

Mass. A woman identified herself as the owner of a floral shop. She asked if the service had started yet and when I told her that it had, she said, 'Oh, dear, I don't know what to do now. I had an arrangement to be delivered but only at the start of the service' and she hung up."

"Who would send flowers to be delivered only at the service? And would they remove them at the end?" Marie questioned no one in particular, but her friends knew that Marie considered that it might have been her daughter.

Knowing she was devastated over the loss of her mother and was in grief, Marie's friends didn't want to discuss Cheryl's heartlessness in front of her, so they kept their feelings to themselves discussing it only when they stood on the sidewalk saying their goodbyes in front of the house after the service.

"I've known that girl since when she was in the hangar, and I never expected that she would treat her mother and the family like this," Mary said. "It's revolting. I've lost my respect for her. What I don't understand is why."

Jackie added her two cents saying, "I think it has to do with Cheryl's husband. I know how manipulative men can be, and trust me, this one Cheryl's married to is real slick even to the point of being sneaky about it. Marie told me that Derek and Cheryl went to the movies when Derek was visiting and while Ronnie was hunting. When Ronnie came home and found Cheryl gone, he pitched a fit driving around and searching for her before finding her in a restaurant with her brother whereupon he approached them and admonished her for going out without telling him, and to boot, he never even acknowledged the fact that Derek was sitting next to his sister."

"Yeah, but . . ." Mary said.

"Trust me. He'll bring about breaking her away from her family to have her all to himself before this is over. God, I feel so sorry for Marie. She and Cheryl were tight, very close. It's apparent to me that this breakdown all started, albeit slowly, right after Cheryl married Ronnie."

Although heartbroken, Marie decided to let sleeping dogs lie for she had neither the emotional strength nor the desire to confront her daughter while she was grieving.

The celebration of a first Mass for Danny after years of working in a civilian environment was realized after his mother's death. The paperwork establishing his priestly faculties was signed and passed through Rome, but a condition of reinstatement denied Danny pastor hood, but he could be an assistant pastor. He gladly accepted the demands of the hierarchy of Rome and was assigned a church in a little town north of Orlando, twenty-nine miles west of Selena Beach.

Danny wanted to buy a small condo on the ocean where he could get away on his days off. He found an efficiency apartment facing the ocean in Selena Beach which was located beachside, bought it and enjoyed the ocean air and sun two days a week allowing his family to take pleasure in using it when he wasn't there.

SEVENTY-ONE

The call came in early evening the following February.

"Cheryl had a baby boy this morning," Derek told his mother.

"Does she want me to come?" Marie asked.

"I don't know, but I don't think so. She didn't ask me to tell you. It was my idea. I thought you should know that you became a grandmother. I'm sorry, Mom."

"I guess I'll leave it up to her to call me then," Marie said weeping, and she hung up.

Scott tried and tried to comfort his wife for this happy but very painful moment in her life, but to no avail. She retired to her bedroom, shut the door, sat on the bed, and cried. Scott listened at the door but lightened his step as he walked away, saddened by the hurt he knew his wife was feeling.

Months went by, but Marie didn't get the call from her daughter she prayed for and then one day, she and Scott heard the fire truck's siren, looked out the window, and saw the smoke coming from their next door neighbor's home. They rushed out the front door to see if they could help. The mother, Mrs. Davis, was running frantically around the front yard calling to her daughter while at the same time, the daughter, Lisa Davis, was running around the back yard calling to her mother.

Marie ran to Mrs. Davis while Scott started toward the back of the burning house to bring Lisa away from the smoke pouring through the roof to the safety of her mother. Both crying hysterically, mother and daughter embraced each other commenting, "You're alright, thank God." and "I love you, Mom," while the father was being escorted by the EMTs to a waiting gurney to have his vitals evaluated

Marie led the women to her garage and offered chairs where another EMT checked the vitals of the mother. They decided that because her blood pressure was high, she needed to go to the hospital. Her daughter and husband accompanied her in the ambulance.

The fire was contained within minutes after the firemen arrived. They put the hoses and other equipment back onto the fire truck and left.

The scene had a profound effect on Marie who, after it was over, turned and walked into her home and while shaking, dialed the number.

"Hello," was the female voice on the end of the line.

"Cheryl, it's your mother. Please don't hang up until you hear me out."

She didn't give her daughter a second to say a word before she continued.

"I just witnessed a fire next door and a mother and daughter clinging to one another after they found out that they were both safe. It was a sight that I'll never forget and that caused me to call you and tell you that I love you. That's all I wanted to say."

There, she'd said it and felt relieved.

"I know," Cheryl said. "I want to see you. Bring the baby around. He's seven months old now and creeping. Let's see. This is Sunday. How about I come on Tuesday? Would that be okay?"

"Would that be okay?" Marie said. "Bring him any time you can. I can't wait to meet him, but yeah, bring him on Tuesday."

When Marie hung up, Scott was standing by her side. She turned to him and looked up at him with tears in her eyes. He embraced her and led her to the sofa where they discussed the event that might bring her daughter back to her.

When Tuesday morning came, Marie was fussin' around the house trying to waste time before she would get her first look at her grandson.

The phone rang. It was Scott. "Is she there yet?"

"No, not yet," Marie answered.

"Are you nervous?" he asked.

"Scared is more like it," she said. "But I can't wait to see him."

"Call me after she leaves," Scott said and hung up.

The phone rang once more.

"Mother, I can't come today. The car is in the garage and Ronnie needs the truck."

"That's okay," Marie answered. "What about tomorrow? Will it be in working order tomorrow?"

"I think so," Cheryl said. "I'll come tomorrow."

Marie was suspicious but kept her mouth shut.

The next day, the phone rang again.

"Mother, now the truck's on the fritz," Cheryl said.

"Well, that's okay. What about tomorrow?" she said.

"I think I'll be able to make it tomorrow." Cheryl said.

"Good," Marie said. "See you then."

After she hung up, she recognized her suspicions were accurate. Something was amiss and she believed her son-in-law had everything to do with it. The fact was, as far as Marie was concerned, Ronnie didn't want Cheryl to see her mother and although she couldn't prove it, she believed it to be so, but decided to play his game and wait it out.

The next morning, Marie waited once again looking at the phone and out the window for she didn't know if she'd get another call or see her daughter pull up in the car with her grandson.

She heard a car door shut, ran to the window, looked out and saw her daughter trying to remove her grandson from his baby seat. Marie ran out the door and looked in the car to see the little guy - fist in mouth, smiling brightly, legs kicking wildly.

She hugged her daughter and said, "As much as I want to get my hands on him, I don't want to scare him, so I'll just look at him and talk softly so he won't cry."

Cheryl picked her son up out of his seat and followed her mother into the house. Once in the living room, she placed the baby on the floor. Marie's eyes beheld a toeheaded, blue eyed, chubby little guy who crept to his grandmother when she called to him. His smile was broad and his dimpled cheeks were rosy and full. Marie picked him up off the floor and hugged him asking, "What is his name?"

"Mark," Cheryl answered.

"Well, baby Mark, you can call me Ba Ba," Marie said.

They visited for a while before Cheryl told her mother she needed to get home and prepare dinner.

"I'll call you," Cheryl said.

Not wanting to push it, Marie answered, "Okay," shut the door and turned to call Scott.

As time passed, there was some effort on Cheryl's part to try to reconcile her relationship between her and her mother, but in every phone call Cheryl made to her mother, in the background Marie could hear Ronnie, "Cheryl, get off the phone. I have a business call to make."

Marie wanted desperately to see more of her grandson. He was in a pre-school program, so every Tuesday Marie volunteered to "play" grandma to all the little two year olds in his class. She would drive Markie home from class and stay with him until either his father or mother came home from work. Usually Cheryl arrived before Ronnie which satisfied Marie.

While volunteering at "tiny town" Marie kept getting sick, having to go to the allergist once or twice a month. Dr. Motsky asked her what she had been doing to have to be seen that often and when Marie told him she had been volunteering at the kinder care school, he said, "Not anymore."

Broken hearted, Marie asked why.

"Because these little ones constantly have one bug or another including colds and fevers. When you pick them up and hug and kiss them, you're infecting yourself, which brings you to see me and that causes me to have to prescribe an antibiotic. If this continues, when you need an antibiotic for some illness more severe, it might not be effective, your system could get used to antibiotic overdose."

So, Marie stopped going to "tiny town" and knew that it meant she wouldn't see her grandson as often as she wanted to.

Marie got a call from her daughter shortly after she had to stop going to the kinder care school.

"Mom, would you attend counseling with me?" Cheryl said.

"Where?" Marie asked.

"I've been seeing a therapist who has suggested we come together to help get a few problems straightened out," Cheryl said.

"Sure, I'll come with you," Marie answered. "When?"

"Next Friday morning at eleven. I have the address and I'll give it to you. Do you have a pencil?"

"Go ahead," Marie responded and started writing the address on a pad of paper.

Marie was anxious to go to the counseling session to try to get to the bottom of her problem with her daughter. On the morning of that following Friday, she dressed in a pink suit with white blouse and wore low navy blue heels. She entered the office at the address she was given and took a seat. Shortly after, Cheryl opened the door of the therapist's office and invited her in. At the time, Marie thought it strange that she was not greeted by the therapist, but dismissed the thought. Her need for resolution of the difficulties with her daughter outweighed any uncertainties.

Introductions made, the therapist started the meeting with the statement, "Cheryl, why don't you tell your mother why you have asked her here."

Cheryl looked at her mother and said, "I'm worried about your drinking and have been for a long time. It's the reason why I don't want you around the baby."

Marie was stunned. Her jaw dropped. Her face became drained. She said nothing as Cheryl continued.

"You called me one evening to come and get you because you didn't want to drive home from Dagwoods and I resented that."

The therapist, Ms. Alano, interrupted to say, "While it was very insightful for you to admit that you didn't believe you should drive, Cheryl had a problem with you calling her to come and get you. Go on, Cheryl."

"Wait a minute," Marie said while looking at Cheryl, "Do you think I'm an alcoholic?"

Cheryl didn't answer the question, but asked another, saying, "Do you?"

"No," Marie said.

"Do you mind answering some questions?" Ms. Alano asked.

"No," Marie answered.

"How many ounces of alcohol do you drink a day?"

"Ounces?" Marie said with shoulders shrugged.

"Yes, shot glass ounces, or do you not measure?"

"I always measure. It's a shot glass full."

"How many times?"

"Twice, maybe three."

"Do you buy your alcohol by the fifth or the 1.75 liter?"

"One point seven five liter," Marie answered.

"And how often do you buy a bottle?"

"I don't know. Scott and I both drink it and there's always friends stopping by who drink."

"Would you say you buy a bottle a week?"

"This is getting out of hand," Marie said annoyingly. "I thought we came here to discuss my daughter's and my drifting apart." Marie stood up.

"Realizing that this must be hard for you to talk about, nevertheless this is what Cheryl wanted to discuss," Ms. Alano said.

"What about my thoughts and why we're here?" Marie asked.

"Do you have something to ask?" Ms. Alano said.

"Yes," and looking at Cheryl, she said, "Why didn't you come to your grandmother's funeral and did you call a florist to send an arrangement for the service only wanting it returned after?"

Cheryl didn't answer the first question and only said "no" to the second.

And at that moment, the door opened and Markie toddled into the room with Ronnie behind him. He ran up to his mother with his hands up to her to lift him, Markie turned to his grandmother and said, "Ba Ba," at which point Marie started crying and walked out of the room to the deck outside the office door to sit down.

Cheryl came out behind her mother and said something to her, but Marie was so devastated she neither heard her daughter nor did she want to. So she got up and left the landing, went to her car and drove out of the lot toward home where her husband and brother waited, hoping for good news of reconciliation of Marie and Cheryl.

After Marie told them what had transpired, Scott shook his head in disapproval and put his arms around his wife's shoulders and Danny commented, "In all my years, both in counseling as a pastor and in talking with psychiatrist friends, I've never heard of such an inquisition in trying to help bring about a resolution between a mother and daughter, or for that matter, a resolution between any two parties who are going through the pain and loss of each other. Not only was it unethical on the part of the therapist, but you were attacked while in a unsuspecting state of mind which sent you into an emotional condition of shock and for that, I have reserved feelings for Cheryl. She will live to regret this someday."

"Ya know the hard part of all this, Danny?" Marie asked.

"What," Danny said.

"I know where this comes from. I never told you this because I was so ashamed. Her father called me so many names for so many years, drunk, whore and made fun of my small body shape. Yet, I stayed with him til the kids were just about on their own cause I knew I couldn't make it financially on my own. I put up with his belittling me for years longer than I wanted to. For what? This?" Marie's voice trailed off.

Shortly thereafter, Marie stopped hearing from her daughter as much and when she did hear, it was a cell phone call, and when that ceased, an e-mail now and again until there was no communication at all.

SEVENTY-TWO

A yearly mammogram revealed that there was something suspicious on Marie's left breast. She was scheduled to see a surgeon for a biopsy.

"There are twenty-four different types of breast cancer, Dr. Williams said when he finished examining Marie. "When I do a biopsy, I have to target the center of the mass, not outside of it nor around it, but at the center. We'll schedule your procedure as soon as possible. My office will get back to you on the date and instructions for pre-surgery prep. Try to remain calm. Eight times out of ten, there is no tumor, mostly calcified milk ducts, but we need to know."

Scott accompanied Marie to the hospital north of Orlando for the breast biopsy the following week. While Marie was trying to remain calm meditating, Scott was visibly nervous sitting on the chair at her bedside, legs crossed, moving his foot up and down. To lessen the tension on both of them, she suggested he go for coffee and a cigarette break. When he returned, Marie was being moved to the gurney to be wheeled into the OR. He walked beside the gurney holding her hand and upon reaching the OR, he kissed her.

"It'll be okay, honey," Scott said as the gurney pulled away. Then yelled, "Love you," and he turned and walked away with tears in his eyes.

Marie was wheeled out of the OR when the procedure was over to a waiting husband who was pacing back and forth. She was still under sedation, was coming out of it, acting like she had one hell of a night on the town, laughing, smiling, and making silly remarks.

"He said he's pretty sure it's not cancer," Scott said joyfully, "but what he biopsied has to be sent to the lab to be conclusive. I'm taking you home and we will celebrate. God I'm so thankful, I love you so."

Marie went home as soon as she was completely awake. She had to wear a special bra and decided that she would baby herself for a few days reading and watching television, chilling out.

The morning of the third day after her surgical procedure, while reading the local newspaper, she turned the page to obituaries and felt her heart drop. She wasn't sure she was comprehending what she read, so she read it over and over again until she knew it was his obit. His name, Clark Ross, address, age, birthplace, employer, and survivors all fell in line with what she had known about him.

Just as she was about to call her friend, she remembered that she also knew the name of the secretary who worked with Clark for so many years. Her hands were shaking as she placed the call to Rosalyn.

"I was just about to call you," Rosalyn said.

"Is it true?" Marie asked.

"Yes," Rosalyn answered. "We don't know the circumstances of his death yet. I'm trying to get a call through to Willy. As soon as I do, I'll call you with him on a line so we can have a conference call. Try to stay calm. Is Scott home?"

"No, he's at work," Marie said.

"I'll get back as soon as possible," Rosalyn said.

Marie sat on the sofa, put her head in her hands and cried. As she got up to get a box of tissues, the phone rang. She answered it.

"Marie, I've got Willy on the phone. Go ahead, Willy."

"Marie, Wednesday night, Clark's wife called me to come quickly, that he had fallen on the floor after getting off the treadmill. I rushed to the house just when the EMTs arrived. I drove his wife to the hospital. When we arrived in the ER, she was told he had expired. That he had a heart attack at home and a stroke on the way to the hospital. That's all I know."

"Wednesday night?" Marie asked. "I was in that same hospital that morning for a biopsy. Oh, Willy, you know what we meant to each other and although it never happened, I knew I'd never forget how he was there for me when I needed someone. The last thing he ever said to me when we had lunch three months ago as I was leaving the restaurant was, 'I still love you.'"

"Are you going to the funeral home or the funeral?" Willy asked.

"No, although she never met me, I wouldn't do that to her," Marie answered.

Rosalyn interrupted and said, "Are you going to tell Scott?" to which Marie said, "No," to which Rosalyn remarked, "You need to tell him so you can grieve. If you don't, I will."

"Okay, love you Rosalyn," and hung up.

When Scott arrived home from work that afternoon, he noticed that Marie was downhearted.

"What's the matter?" Scott asked.

"I need to tell you something," Marie answered. "I've already told you that there was someone before you - someone I met in Suttonville, someone who loved me and helped me get through my divorce."

"Yes, I remember," Scott said.

Scott was sitting on the barstool. Marie went up to him and putting her arms around him said, "He died three days ago and I need to grieve his passing. I didn't want to tell you cause I thought you'd read something into it. There's nothing to read and although I've met him for lunch a few times, I've never been unfaithful to you."

"I believe you," Scott said. "What can I do to help?"

"Just accept the fact that I'll be feeling down for a while, but I'll come out of it, okay?"

"Sure, want to go out to dinner?" Scott said.

"Yes," she answered. She grabbed her purse and they went to their favorite watering hole.

SEVENTY-THREE

Holidays, especially long weekends at the Nicholson home, were celebrated with family and friends, cookouts and swimming and, of course, booze. It was a long weekend that Memorial Day. Everyone who usually came to celebrate the holiday had something else to do, somewhere else they needed to go, so Scott thought it would be a good idea to just take a ride.

The couple came upon a small quaint village, northwest of Orlando, called Cassadaga. The village is home to fifty-five residences of spiritualists and mediums whose ancestors more than a century ago left upstate New York near Jamestown and found a location where they would not be ridiculed for their beliefs. The homes in the village were very old and are wood framed. Although the roads are paved, there are no sidewalks. There is a meeting hall or temple and an old two-story hotel that stands in the center of the village. A bookstore across the street from the hotel sells books as well as items such as crystals and candles, cards and DVDs. In the store, there is a whiteboard where one could find the name of a medium who is on call that day to do a reading.

"Look at this," Marie said. "It feels like we're in another timeframe like olden days. I half expect someone to come out of one of these houses dressed like people did in the previous century."

"Do you want to ride around and through the streets?" Scott asked.

"Yes," Marie answered.

They turned a corner and went up a hill. Marie noticed a woman in her yard who was gardening. She was wearing a pink shell with white slacks and had sandals on her feet. She had her back to Marie's view, but Marie could see that her hair was dark brown.

"Pull in here," Marie said.

Scott pulled in and Marie got out of the car and started walking toward the woman.

"Excuse me," Marie said.

"Yes?" the woman said as she turned around.

"Ah, ah, I don't know what to ask," Marie said.

"Do you want a reading?" the woman asked.

"A reading? I don't know what that is," Marie said.

"Let me introduce myself," the woman said. "My name is Helen Bradley and I am a medium. I get in touch with the spirits of those passed over into the next life. A reading is when you come to me for connecting with your departed loved ones. I am the channel between them and you whereby they give messages through me to you."

"Oh, ah," Marie hesitated. "Do you have a card?"

"Yes, follow me and I will get it."

While standing outside the door waiting, Marie thought it silly to drive all the way back to Orlando only to return another day for a reading, if indeed, she was open to one, so when Helen returned, Marie asked, "Do you have time today?"

"I was away but returned cause I knew someone was coming who needed me," Helen answered.

Marie walked to the car to ask Scott, who was leaning against the car smoking a cigarette, if he minded waiting to which he answered, "No, go ahead."

Marie stepped into Helen's library which was decorated in shades of lavender and cream. There was a sofa and a rocker in the room. Books on spirituality covered the shelves against the wall.

"Sit down," Helen said. "I will be right back."

Looking around the room, Marie thought it looked like any other home library with the exception of the titles of the books in the bookshelves, but she did not know any of the authors.

Helen reentered the room and sat on the sofa next to Marie.

"I always leave the room before a reading to ask for guidance from the spirits and protection from God that no negative energy will surround us during our sitting. Please don't say anything to me while I'm giving the reading. A yes or a no to specific questions I ask is all I'll need, but add nothing to it."

Helen closed her eyes and when she opened them she said, "There is the spirit here of a young man, a son, but I don't think it is your son, more of a relative. First letter, M, second letter I, third letter K - Mike. Oh, no, an accident on a rain slicked freeway up north where you come from. Coming off the ramp, the driver went into skid, hydroplaned and ended up in a ditch. Is this a nephew?"

"Yes," Marie answered.

"Because he's telling me that you are his aunt. He knows his mother cries all the time over his death. Wait a minute. He didn't know he was dead and wandered from relative to relative asking where he was, but no one paid attention to him until you. He came to you and you told him he was dead and to go toward the light."

"No, no," Marie said. "I was feeling bad about his death one evening a month after he died, hooked myself up on the headset, had a scotch, neat, and felt something like a dream whereby I mentally saw his presence to the left of me and mentally told him he had died and go to the light, but I thought it was the booze speaking."

"He's telling me you were the one who told him because before that, he roamed around trying to figure out what happened to him," Helen said.

"When a spirit leaves the body suddenly like in an accident, the spirit finds itself incapable of understanding what happened and more often than not, roams among loved ones until someone, like you, or another spirit comes to help," Helen said.

"We have clergy in our family," Marie replied. "Why not go to either one of them?"

""He did," Helen said. "But religion and spirituality are two different things. They are religious, you are spiritual."

"He wants to ask you for something," Helen added. "He needs you to tell his mother that he is okay, has no pain, is happy and watches over her and his father with love. Did he and his mother not always get along?"

Marie started crying and said, "Yes."

"Well, you don't take anger or blame with you when you pass over. It's just the opposite. He is insistent that you contact his mother and give her the message."

"He knows I can't," Marie replied. "The family will call the paddy wagon and drop me off at the loony ward if I did. I don't know anyone who believes in this. Certainly no one in my family."

"Seeing how much she suffers over the loss, he's adamant about telling her."

"I'll think about it, but I don't know," Marie said.

Helen continued the reading mentioning other people who passed, but Marie couldn't believe how a woman who she had never met before would know about her nephew dying.

Ending the session, Helen hugged Marie and wished her well. Marie left and didn't realize how much time had passed until she saw

Scott still standing by the car smoking another cigarette looking at his watch.

"Two hours?" he said.

"Oh, my God," Marie answered. "I didn't know that much time had passed by. It went so fast."

"Well?" he said.

"Let's find the nearest bar. I gotta have a drink after this."

They drove out of Cassadaga, down the highway and found a Holiday Inn where they went immediately to the bar to order a drink. She told Scott what transpired for two hours before. Scott listened to his wife and believed she didn't make the story up, but he was at a loss to understand it so he made very few comments when she finished.

Marie returned to Helen for another reading a few months later. Helen described how a man who once loved Marie and was going to marry her, shot himself in the head.

"He wants you to know how sorry he is for hurting you," Helen said. "He's asking your forgiveness."

"I forgave him a long time ago, even before he killed himself," Marie answered.

SEVENTY-FOUR

Scott's job at the space coast became jeopardized when award of a defense contract, dependent on keeping the company he worked for open, was awarded to a contractor in Texas. Scott knew the plant would shut down, but he waited to be laid off. He didn't have to wait long. Two months later, he received his pink slip.

"I think it's time to sell the house and move," Scott said to Marie.

"What? Why?" she answered.

"The neighborhood is going down. People aren't taking care of their properties any more, letting them run down. I doubt if we can get a good price for the house because of it. It's time to move."

"What about her?" Marie said pointing to Missy who was fifteen years old and who was sitting on the floor looking first from one to the other as they spoke.

Scott didn't speak.

"I hate to leave this house," Marie said. "Are you suggesting we don't take the dog with us?"

Scott turned away. Marie didn't understand his thinking at the time, but the reason would become evident within months.

"She's fifteen," Scott said. "She's had one tumor removed from her side and another is growing. Also, I don't think she could take the change. I'm afraid she's too old."

"What does he know that I don't?" Marie asked herself.

"No, I won't put her down," Marie said angrily.

Scott walked out of the room.

When she chased him onto the patio, he looked at her and said, "I want to enjoy my retirement. You know how much crime there is here. Remember when the house was broken into? If we hadn't had an argument a second time it almost happened and you went to bed leaving me on the couch, I wouldn't have seen some tall kid looking through the window as I slept, woke up and scared him off. It's not safe here."

"Where will we go?" Marie asked.

"Selena Beach," Scott answered.

"What? Why there?" she asked.

"You love it there and go over there every chance you get. The ocean calls and I think you have sand in your shoes," he said jokingly.

"I'll think about it," Marie said.

Marie stopped in the vet's office the next day to have a talk with him.

"We are thinking of selling our home and moving to the beach," Marie said. "What is your opinion about taking Missy? I mean could she take the change?"

"She's quite old now," he said. "I don't think it advisable to take her into a new environment, especially an apartment. Are you buying a home there?"

"Eventually, Marie said, but not immediately. We intend to rent until we find a place to buy."

"Have you checked to see if dogs are allowed where you are going?" Dr. Shepherd asked.

"No," she answered. "We don't know where we'll live at this point and haven't put the house on the market yet."

"It could be traumatic for her in an apartment. She has a yard here to run in. These are just some feelings you need to think about before you make up your mind, but should you decide to put her down, I will abide by your decision although I don't want to tell you what to do. It's up to you and Scott."

While having cocktails that evening, Marie told Scott of her visit with Dr. Shepherd.

"I may have been a little hasty," Scott said. "We have time before we have to decide what to do. I just don't want to stay here."

Marie called their lawyer the following week asking his opinion.

"How old is the house?" Mr. Wright asked.

"Fifteen years old," Marie answered.

"Does it need improvement? By that I mean roof, water heater, air conditioner? Have they been replaced in that amount of time?"

"No, they are probably overdue for replacement," Marie answered.

"Is it your intention to move anyway?"

"Yes," Marie answered.

"Then my advice is to sell it as is, because you're going to have to start putting money in it soon. Are you going to sell it yourself?"

"Yes."

"Don't sign a contract until I look it over."

"Okay," Marie said and hung up.

Marie put an in the local newspaper to be run over the weekend and didn't expect to receive as many calls as she did. The second couple who came to look at the house decided they wanted to buy it on the spot. Marie had a contract drawn up and faxed it to her attorney who viewed it for content and legality before making notes and faxing it back to Marie.

The buyers, Mr. and Mrs. Rodriquez, located a title company nearby, and agreed to have the closing in a month which gave Scott and Marie time to search for an apartment in Selena Beach, twenty miles south of Daytona Beach. They would rent an efficiency in the same complex as Danny after the closing. The plan also included renting a U-haul to move their furnishings and put them in storage in Selena Beach when they moved.

Not wanting to face it, they put off the decision of what to do with their dog, Scott was the one who mentioned it a few days before the closing, after which they would be packed and ready to move.

"We've come to the point where we must decide," he said.

"I asked the condo manager if they accept dogs, and she said they didn't allow renters to have animals, only owners, so I guess we'd better contact the veterinarian for an appointment to have her put to sleep."

"I'll take care of it," Scott said.

They decided that they would put their dog to sleep the day before they moved. Scott made the appointment with the vet to drop her off in the morning of that day. Missy loved plain cooked spaghetti, so the night before, Marie cooked some and fed it to her. She tried not to show her emotions while doing so, but after the doggie ate the spaghetti, Marie took her in her arms, turned on the stereo, put in a tape and danced with her Missy one last time.

The next morning, Marie and Scott took Missy to the vet who was located half a mile from the house. They walked in the door. The vet greeted them and nodded for the tech to take the dog from Scott's arms and carry her to the infirmary where he promised he would do the procedure immediately.

When Marie bent forward to kiss her, Missy didn't turn her head to look at her. She looked straight ahead. Somehow she knew what was coming. The vet told them it was better for all concerned that they leave.

Outside the door, Marie started crying uncontrollably. Scott put his arms around her and with tears in his eyes, he said, "I'm going back to get her."

"It's done," Marie said. "Let's go."

They closed on their house the next morning and returned to what was once their home to drive away. Scott was driving the U-haul which was packed and ready for the move, and Marie was driving their car behind him.

Marie didn't feel bad leaving the city because it was growing in leaps and bounds and was becoming too big for them. They wanted to enjoy their retirement in a small community where traffic was low and they could get around in a reasonable amount of time. Because the traffic was so heavy in "Mouseville," it took a half an hour to get anywhere in the late 90's.

As she drove up the interstate, she was saddened when she passed the town where her daughter Cheryl, lived, but she looked forward to a new beginning with Scott in an entirely new location. She had lost hope that a reconciliation could happen between her and her daughter since the counseling she had agreed to go to. She missed Markie. Her heart held in reserve the last words he had said to her when she taught him to say "I love you Ba Ba." His little voice could only manage to say, "I ya you Ba Ba." He was only two.

It took an hour to drive to their new furnished apartment in Selena Beach, but before they could register, the furniture had to be put in storage. In past trips to the beach, Scott noticed a storage company five miles from their new residence, drove to it and off-loaded the furniture into a bin.

Marie had arrived ahead of Scott and started unloading the trunk of the car that held their clothes and personal items. The apartment/condo they moved into was an efficiency. There was a kitchen, small living area with a Murphy bed that pulled out of the wall for sleeping and a table contained within the same wall that was used to sit and eat at. The hallway into the bathroom had a large closet for hanging clothes and a dresser built into the wall. There was a linen closet in the hallway. A balcony offered the ocean view of the Atlantic where they could watch the sunrise each morning.

The couple treasured beach living and bought a unit in the complex certain that the compactness of the living space would be no problem for them. They desired to play golf and live an uncomplicated life, cruise, and generally settle back to enjoy the luxury of retirement.

Feeling the need to be productive and because Marie was a people person, she took a part-time, two day a week job relieving the manager of a condominium a quarter mile away. Her duties included answering the phone and calling the contracted vendor when the need arose for repairs and maintenance of the property. Because the mail boxes were inside the office, and after the mailman delivered, she sorted and placed the resident's mail inside each box every day, a duty which became bothersome when some of the old timers wanted to chat and spend too much of their boring day annoying her with tales of ailments, pictures of grandchildren and just plain bitching about everything including how the manager ran the community. When she told her boss how annoying the residents could be, he showed her a trick he used when they were overbearing.

"Take the phone," he said, holding it in his hand, "and push this button and the phone will ring. When you answer it, tell them that you need to take this call and go into the back office. They will leave."

"And nobody has figured it out yet?" Marie asked.

"No, not even once," he answered.

They looked at each other and laughed and laughed.

SEVENTY-FIVE

The relationship between Marie and her sister, Margaret, was strained, but then all their lives, it had been somewhat strained, and Marie didn't know why. It became obvious to her when Margaret, who occasionally visited Marie after leaving the convent, came to see her bragging about how she got to see Marie's grandson and how close she had become to Marie's daughter, Cheryl. Margaret showed her a picture of herself and the little guy taken at Cheryl's house. It pained, saddened, and angered Marie to think that her sister could be so cruel knowing that she had not seen her grandson in a long time, but she realized that she would have to accept it.

The two sisters were sitting alone one rainy afternoon in Danny's condo, where Margaret was invited to spend an overnight, having a glass of wine. Suddenly, Margaret started tearing up and came to where Marie was seated. She knelt down on the floor beside Marie and said, "I'm so sorry for what I've done to you. I've knocked you, cut you down for your drinking and hell raising after your left Steve. I called you a slut and a drunk. I talked to your daughter about your drinking, hoping she would see how badly you had behaved, and I don't know how to make amends to you. All I can say is that I was jealous of you. You married and had two children and when it didn't work out, you found someone else to love you."

Marie looked at her sister and said, "I know!"

"You knew all along?" Margaret asked.

"Yes, I suspected, then one of the times that I was in contact with Cheryl, she told me about it and said she was sick of it and didn't want to see you anymore. Said when you came to see her, you couldn't get through the door without trashing me."

"Oh, God, no," Margaret said. "Can you ever forgive me?" she cried.

"Yes, but let me tell you something," Marie said. "You didn't spread your legs and take a man's member into yourself to become pregnant and carry a baby for nine months. You didn't have labor pains for ten hours, nor did you nourish that baby, get up in the night to rock her when she was sick or worry about her during her growing up years. But, what you wanted without having to go through all the years of care and worry was to become her mother, and that, sister of mine, you have no rights to. And know this, although I do forgive you, I don't know if I will ever be able to trust you again. Should you ever be in need, I won't turn you away, so get up off the floor and dry your tears. In time, our relationship will take care of itself."

Marie left Danny's apartment and went back to her own but didn't tell Scott about her sister's confession because she knew he would confront Margaret which could lead to a family feud and having said her piece, Marie just wanted to let it go.

SEVENTY-SIX

In the previous year, Scott and Marie had traveled to her hometown to see her oldest brother. He had been diagnosed with cancer and had just finished his first bout of chemotherapy. In the year following the visit, his condition worsened, and although he nor his wife was not told, it appeared he would not survive.

The call came to Danny at midnight. "He's gone," Jeanie said crying.

"I'll call you back," Danny said. After hanging up, Danny sat on the edge of his bed staring into space remembering how close he was to his older brother. He remembered the wrestling on the living room floor when they were kids.

He called Marie and informed her of her brother's death, stating he would let her know about arrangements as soon as he called Jeanie back.

A funeral was planned in three days. The family would travel to New York and surround each other with the love and compassion they would need to say goodbye to a family member.

Deciding to attend her brother's funeral, Marie started checking flight schedules, but before she picked up the phone to call the airline that offered the best fare, Scott, after leaving the bathroom, informed her that he had just spit up blood.

"I'm not going," she said. "We need to get you checked out, honey."

She could feel the hairs on her arm stand up and felt a chill.

Scott didn't want to see a doctor. He told Marie that the bloody spit-up had ceased. She believed him and didn't further question him, but three months later, Marie noticed that Scott's voice was raspy.

"Don't tell me that you're going to have allergies too," she said to him. Marie had given herself allergy shots while living in Orlando and had taken antihistamines which, since moving to the beach, were not needed anymore. Her allergist, Dr. Motsky, suggested that it was possible the salty ocean air had relieved her of her symptoms.

"Ya know, honey, I think we should call Dr. Motsky and have you checked out," she said to Scott. "If need be, I can give you the allergy shots. I'm a pro at it now."

Marie made an appointment and they traveled to a town northeast of Orlando to have the doctor check Scott out for allergies.

Marie went into the examining room with Scott and noticed that three times during the doctor's examination, he put his hand on Scott's shoulder and remarked, "You know Scott, cigarettes haven't helped you," but she dismissed his comments believing that he was trying to impress upon Scott the necessity of quitting.

"I want you to have a chest x-ray," Dr. Motsky said after completing the exam.

It got Marie's attention, but her attention intensified when they left the examining room and Marie stopped at the reception desk to talk to one of the nurses she knew. She looked toward the kitchen and saw Dr. Motsky with his back leaning against the wall, talking to his wife, the office manager, and both of them were looking at Scott. His eyes were downcast and when he noticed that Marie saw him, he walked into the kitchen, guiding his wife with him, and shut the door.

At that moment, Marie knew what was wrong with her husband.

An appointment was made with a pulmonary specialist the following week, who ordered a chest x-ray. He came back into the examination room, put the x-ray to the light monitor and looked. Pointing at a spot on the monitor, he turned to Scott, who was sitting on the examination table, and Marie who stood aside him, and he said, "There is a suspicious mass in his upper left lung. We need to do a biopsy and the sooner the better."

"Would you hazard a guess as to benign or malignant?" Marie asked. "Malignant," he said. "I'll schedule the biopsy as soon as possible," and he left the room. Just like that. No other words. None of comfort nor of compassion. Marie had the feeling that he hated cigarette smokers and was disgusted with all of them.

Scott stayed sitting on the table and stared ahead. He didn't say a word.

"Come on, honey," Marie remarked. "Let's go home." Every nerve in her body felt like electricity was running through it, but she wouldn't let on to her husband.

Although Scott drove, the ride home was quiet. Neither one had much to say. The fear was too great and comprehension of what was unfolding at the moment held them mesmerized.

Believing she knew what the outcome of the biopsy would be, Marie called Scott's son, Chad, explaining what had happened and asked him to drive her and his father back to the hospital two days later for the biopsy which he willingly agreed to do.

After admission to the hospital, Scott was wheeled into the OR leaving Marie and his son standing and waiting for the answer to their loved one's condition. It didn't take long before the pulmonary surgeon came down the hall and told them, "The results of the biopsy indicate that the tumor is malignant, inoperable and is known as non-small cell adenocarcinoma of the lung but we'll have to wait for the pathology report. If he doesn't get treatment very soon, he could be dead in four to six weeks. He's in recovery now. I've told him his diagnosis, but I don't think he was coherent enough to understand me, so you'll have to repeat it when he is fully awake."

At this point, Scott's son turned and ran down the hall, down the stairs and out of the building leaving Marie standing alone, stunned, crying, trying to absorb what the diagnosis meant.

She didn't remember if the surgeon said something like, "I'm sorry," or not. She couldn't hear anything at that moment. She was shaking and terrified in fear of losing her husband.

When she regained her composure, the doctor asked her if she wanted him to make an appointment with an oncologist to which she answered, "No. We have talking to do." The surgeon turned and walked down the hall and out of sight.

They wheeled Scott out of recovery and toward Marie who was standing, waiting for him. The aide took him to a room where he could fully awaken before going home.

She stood by the side of the bed and took his hand. When he opened his eyes, he looked into her eyes and asked, "Did you hear the diagnosis?"

"Yes, honey, did you?"

"Yes, I know I have cancer and can't be operated on," and he started crying, at which point she put her arms gently on his shoulders, her head lightly on his chest and sobbed in unison with him.

When his son returned and stepped into the room, it was obvious that he had been in tears, his eyes were red and he was blowing his nose. He took his father's hand and when advised by the nurse, he helped him sit up and put his clothes on. A wheelchair was brought to the room, Scott was helped into it, and wheeled down the hall to the elevator and out of the hospital to the car for the ride back to Selena Beach.

Small talk was all the threesome could speak on the ride home - the weather, a golf tournament coming up, but nothing about Scott's condition. After they entered the condo, Chad decided it best to leave the couple alone for a while, so he went to Danny's condo to try to compose himself before he would be alone with his father.

Marie and Scott held each other and cried.

"I'll beat this," Scott said.

"I know you will," Marie answered although she really didn't believe it.

"Did you know something was wrong when we lived in Orlando. Is that the reason why we left? Were you having symptoms then?" she asked.

"No!" he answered strongly, but Marie didn't believe him. His denial was angry and so firm and it was obvious Scott didn't want to discuss it further. She decided to drop it.

"The thing is we have to decide where to go for treatment," she said. "The manager told me that the cleaning lady who cleans here after renters leave, was an RN who had had enough of nursing and started her own business cleaning condos. I thought I saw her van outside. I'll go down to the office and see if the manager can locate her. Maybe she can give us the name of an oncologist in this area."

"Yeah, go see if you can find her," Scott said while staring out the window.

"Do you want me to stop by Danny's first and tell Chad it's okay to come see you now?"

"Yes," Scott said. "We might as well share our feelings about this disease now rather than later."

After telling Chad that his father wanted to see him, she went in search of the cleaning lady.

She found her cleaning an apartment on the second floor, stepped through the open door and said, "Judy," and while trembling, caught herself starting to fall apart.

"Sit down," Judy said as she turned toward Marie holding a mop in her hand. "What's the matter?" Judy asked.

"It's my husband," Marie said with a shaky voice. "He's got inoperable lung cancer. We've been here such a short time. We don't know anyone to call and I thought you might be able to recommend a doctor."

"Yes, I can," Judy said. "He'll need an oncologist and I know just the one, but know this - he's straight forward, shoots from the hip and won't sugar coat his opinion. If you're looking for a doctor who will tell you only what he thinks you want to hear and not the truth, he's not the one for you."

"No, I'm a realist," Marie said. "And even though I may be fearful of the truth, I want to hear the facts of my husband's prognosis."

"Good, then," Judy said. "Do you see a phone book? Oh, here's one. Let me look up his name and number."

Judy's search in the physician's yellow pages found the oncologist's name.

"Here it is. His name is Dr. Robert Reyes. His main office is in Daytona on Kress Street, but he attends patients at the local hospital also two or three mornings a week."

When Marie returned to the condo with the slip of paper noting Dr. Reyes' phone number, she encountered Scott and his son sitting across from each other at the pull down table. They were both crying. As she stepped in, Chad wiped his eyes and said he had to leave.

"I have the name of an oncologist," Marie said. "I'll make the call tomorrow morning."

"Let me know what he says," Chad said and left the condo.

SEVENTY-SEVEN

Although they usually had only two happy hour drinks, Scott and Marie sat on the balcony that evening drinking vodka tonics, too many of them. They didn't talk much, just enjoyed the ocean and the music of the tide coming in and going out to sea. When they went to bed, they held each other and fell asleep in each other's arms.

The next morning, Marie dialed the number given to her by the cleaning lady, the call she didn't want to make. She was put through to Dr. Reyes' nurse, who calmly took the information and made an appointment for Scott to be seen.

Three days later, they were directed into Dr. Reyes' office where he introduced himself. He was a tall, slim man who was balding on the top of his head. His grey hair surrounded the sides and back of his head. He appeared to be in his early fifties. Calmly he went over the report sent by the hospital where the biopsy was performed.

"Although your tumor is inoperable, there is a new protocol that I want you to consider," he said. "I will make an appointment for your with Ms. Bradley, my nurse assistant, who will explain what the protocol entails."

"The doctor who performed the biopsy said if he doesn't get treatment very soon, he would be dead in four to six weeks," Marie said.

"I doubt that," the Dr. Reyes replied. "There's time to decide what the best treatment for you should be. He put his hand on Scott's shoulder and said, "I can give you a year, maybe two, but not five," and he left the room to make the appointment.

Marie and Scott sat in the chairs stunned with the announcement of Scott's time left to live.

When Dr. Reyes returned, he had an appointment card in his hand showing that a scheduled time had been made for a preview of the protocol treatment with Ms. Bradley the following week at Hampden Hospital near Daytona Beach.

They were early for the meeting with Mary Bradley. Mary called them into her office on the hour of the time of Scott's appointment.

Mary was a tall lady who had light brown hair and brown eyes. Over her nurse's uniform, she wore a white coat with her name on it and the name of the hospital. She had an infectious, compassionate smile that made Scott and Marie hem immediately feel comfortable in her presence.

It took an hour for Mary to explain the protocol to be used for Scott's type of cancer. Most of what she said they could not understand, not so much because they were ignorant, but because they were extremely anxious about his condition. She said there would be three different drugs used in his chemotherapy and there were other patients in different parts of the country who would be given the same protocol as Scott. When she finished her presentation, she informed Scott that it was not expected that he would make a snap judgment at that moment.

"It's advised that you take twenty-four hours and talk this over with each other before agreeing to this treatment," Mary said.

"No, I know I want it. I don't need to think about it," Scott said.

"Dr. Reyes will not accept your signed agreement on the same day as our meeting," she answered. "Go home and discuss it and call me tomorrow. Good luck and please try not to worry. You've chosen the right physician to treat you. After working with him for many years, I know he will do everything he can in your best interests to help you."

"I don't want to waste any time getting into the treatment," Scott said to Marie as they left the hospital.

"We'll call tomorrow and inform her of your decision, but for now, let's go to our favorite watering hole and have a couple and some dinner," Marie said.

They sat at the bar of the Walker Inn near the beach and for a few minutes forgot the horrific emotions they were suffering. Marie looked at Scott and commented, "I want you to know that you are the one who needs to make the decisions that you feel are best for your treatment and if you want my opinion, I will always be with you for it, but in the end, it will be your judgment call to make. If you ask, what would I do? I can't answer that because I'm not walking in your shoes, honey. Does that sound heartless cause I don't mean it to?"

"No, I appreciate the fact that you believe in my judgment for my welfare, but I know I'm gonna' need your input. Okay?"

"Absolutely," Marie said.

They ordered dinner and went home, hopefully to find a good night's sleep free of tossing and turning and free from the feeling of terror.

Scott placed the call to Mary Bradley the next morning informing her that he wanted to be a part of the protocol she explained the day before. They set a time for Scott to return to the hospital to sign the procedure commitment papers which, if he wanted to at any time, he could decline, change his mind and withdraw.

The first five would be given at Hampden Hospital. Marie went with him the first time. Scott felt no unpleasant reaction to the chemo and because Marie had made arrangements to fly to Suttonville for a few days for her son's birthday, Scott had encouraged her to do so. He explained to her that there was no need for her to molly coddle him. He had another reason for persuading her to go. He knew that with each treatment, he could get sick and wanted her to get a break away from all the emotional drain she suffered since his diagnosis.

Marie accepted Scott's persuasive approach to her traveling and boarded a plane to see her son in her hometown two days later, a day before Scott's next chemo.

Friends and family were happy to see her which made her relax and find contentment in being with them for a short time.

The short time didn't last long. Two days later, she got a call from her brother, Danny.

"Marie," Danny said. "Scott drove himself to the hospital last night with abdominal pains. I went to see him before calling you. His pain is excruciating. He's being given Demerol and even that's not helping much."

"Oh, God, Danny, Marie said sobbing. "What hospital?"

"The one in Selena Beach, Hart Medical Center," Danny said. "I think you'd better get back as soon as possible."

"Is it the cancer?"

"I don't know," Danny said.

"Do you have the number at the hospital?"

"Yes, here it is," and he gave his sister the number of the ER.

Hands shaking, she dialed and when the call was answered, told the nurse's desk who she was.

"Just a minute," the answerer said.

A nurse came on the phone and said. "Mrs. Nicholson?"

"Yes," Marie said hurriedly.

"Your husband came in last night with abdominal pains. He was diagnosed with a blocked bowel. We have been trying to unblock it with enemas, but so far that isn't working, and a decision has been made to take him to the OR for surgery," she said.

"Oh, no, I'm in New York" Marie said helplessly. "He has lung cancer and had one chemo treatment for it. Does it have anything to do with the cancer? I mean is it cancer related?"

"No, and we have to go to the OR now," the nurse said.

"Can I talk to him?"

"I'll put the phone to his head, but I don't know if he'll recognize your voice. Here we go. Okay, go ahead, Mrs. Nicholson."

"Honey, honey, I'll catch a plane as soon as I can and be there sometime later today. I love you Scott. Can you hear me?"

Scott mumbled. The nurse put the phone to her ear.

"Please, please take good care of my darling," Marie said sobbing.

"I promise. I will," the nurse said crying in unison. "We have to go now."

And she hung up.

Marie's son found a flight that was leaving nearby Scranton in four hours, so Marie packed her luggage, Derek placed it in his truck and drove the hour and a half to the airport. After checking in, Marie said her goodbyes to her son and went to the bar for a drink. The flight was a shuttle flight to Philadelphia with connecting flight to Orlando. Marie had a half hour wait in Philadelphia before boarding her connecting flight, but found herself feeling weak and somewhat dizzy as she wandered the halls of the airport searching for the departing gate. A flight attendant noticed her dazed appearance and approached her.

"Can I help you? Are you okay?" the attendant asked.

Marie looked at the attendant and started crying. "My husband is in a hospital being operated on at this moment. He has lung cancer and I don't know how things are going," she cried. "If I could grab the ass end of a jumbo jet, I would, to get myself there to be at his side when he comes out of the anesthesia, but here I am at an airport wondering if he is still alive," Marie said.

"Come with me," the attendant said and led Marie to the airline's office where the manager in charge asked her what hospital her husband was in after helping her sit down.

"Hart Medical Center in Selena Beach, Florida," Marie cried.

The manager placed a call to information in the area code, got the phone number and dialed.

"This is Mr. Sweet, of US Airways," he said when he was connected to the hospital. "I have a passenger whose husband was admitted to your hospital this morning and was taken to surgery. Could you put me through to the OR nurse's desk?"

"Immediately," the operator said.

"Surgical ward, Ms. Confers speaking,"

Mr. Sweet handed the phone to Marie.

Marie held her breath after asking if her husband was out of surgery and how he was."

"He is in recovery and is doing well," the nurse answered.

"Tell him I'm on my way," Marie said sobbing.

"I will do that, but he might not hear me," nurse Confers said. "He has been given pain medication and is somewhat out of it. When do you expect to arrive in case he is coherent? "

"Sometime late evening," Marie answered. "Thank you for taking care of him."

After hanging up, the manager remarked, "We're going to have you escorted to the plane by one of our flight attendants after the other passengers have boarded. In the meantime, rest here until your flight is called."

Marie was assigned a window seat. After the attendant accompanied her to it, she wished her well and told her to ask for anything she might need from the in-flight attendant as he had been notified of her dilemma.

As the plane taxied down the runway, Marie put her head back and said silently, "Hang in there, honey. I'm on my way home to you."

Danny was at the airport to pick his sister up when her plane arrived. He had arrived early and although it was dark and late and the ride took an hour and a half, Marie couldn't wait to get to the hospital to see her husband.

"Did you see him when he got out of surgery?" she asked Danny.

"For a short time only when he was wheeled to recovery. He was out of it and I don't think he recognized me," Danny said.

SEVENTY-EIGHT

When Danny pulled into the parking lot of the hospital, Marie jumped out of his car and ran in the front door to the elevator punching the up arrow continuously. When the doors opened, she entered and pushed the 2 button to the surgical ward.

"Scott Nicholson," she said to the ward station attendee. "What room?"

"Room 219, down the hall and to your left."

Marie ran down the hall and into the room to find her husband slightly elevated in bed.

"Hi, Mommy," he said.

"Oh my God, you're okay," Marie cried as she wrapped her arms around him.

"Yes, I'm okay," Scott said.

"How long have you had this pain?" she asked. "And why did you let me go to see Derek?"

"I didn't think anything of it until it got so bad I had to drive here," he answered.

"And you drove yourself?" she asked.

"Oh, don't make such a big deal about it. I'm okay. What time is it?"

"Two a.m.," she answered.

"Go home and get some sleep," he said. "I ain't goin' anywhere. I'll see you in the morning."

She kissed her husband goodbye and left him to go to a waiting Danny who was in the lobby. Danny drove Marie home to get some sleep before returning a few hours later.

Marie spent most of the next day with Scott sitting beside his hospital bed, holding his hand and reassuring herself that he was recovering from the surgery. He convinced her to go home at the end of the afternoon commenting, "Why don't you stop for a nip and eat on your way home and don't worry about coming back to see me tonight, okay?"

She yielded to his suggestion and stopped at Walker Inn, sat at the bar and ordered a vodka, rocks with a slice of lemon. The bartender, Jerry, asked her how Scott was and remarked that if he could do anything to help, please call, and he gave her his home phone number.

Marie went home, poured herself a couple more drinks and went to bed at ten o'clock. She wasn't asleep an hour when the phone rang.

"Mommy (his pet name for her)" Scott said. "There's people talking in the hall outside my door and I heard one of them say that a guy named Big D was gonna get me tonight."

"What?" Marie said.

"Yes, someone named Big D is coming for me tonight," Scott said. "I'm afraid to be in this room."

"I'll call the nurses' station," Marie said.

"Okay," Scott said. "Call me back," and he hung up.

When she reached the nurses' station, Marie asked, "What's goin on?"

"I don't know what you mean," was the reply.

"My husband just called me and told me that he heard that a guy named Big D was going to get him tonight."

"Oh, that," she answered. "We've moved him to another room because he told us the same thing. We believe he's hallucinating."

"He didn't sound that way to me," Marie said.

"Well, we're pretty sure that's the problem," the nurse said.

"I'm on my way," Marie said and hung up, but before she could grab her keys, the phone rang again.

"Mommy," Scott said. "He's outside my window looking through the blinds."

"I'm on my way," Marie said.

Not wanting to waste a second waiting for the condo elevator, Marie raced down the stairs, jumped in the car and headed out of the lot toward the hospital.

She pulled into the hospital parking lot, parked the car, ran into the hospital and headed to the elevator.

Pushing the UP button, the elevator door opened almost immediately. She stepped into the elevator and kept her finger on the arrow until the doors closed. When the doors opened on the second floor surgical ward, she stepped out of the elevator. Walking toward the nurses' station she said, "What kind of a fuckin' rinky, dinky, god-damn hospital is this anyway?"

The ward nurses turned toward the potty mouthed woman and gasped at her arrogance, but no one said a word.

"What room have you moved my husband to?" she asked.

"Room 234, across the hall from where he was," one of the nurses answered.

Marie ran down the hall to Scott's room. He was sitting up in his bed staring toward the window. Not knowing what to do next, Marie remembered that Mary Bradley, the oncologist assistant to Dr. Reyes, had given Marie her home phone number, so she placed a call to Mary explaining what had happened.

"Go to the ward desk and ask to see the head of nurses," Mary said. "Then call me back."

Mary hurried back to the nurses' station and requested they contact the head of nurses immediately.

No one wanted to get in this seemingly crazy woman's way. A call was placed and within fifteen minutes the head of nurses came to the surgical ward.

When Marie explained to her what had transpired, the head nurse suggested that since a partner of Dr. Reyes, a Dr. Sorento, was in-house, they contact him for an evaluation of Scott.

Dr. Sorento arrived in room 234 within a short time and questioned Scott asking, "Who is the president, who won the World Series, who won the masters, what year was this, what city was this, and on and on, to which Scott answered each question correctly and matter of factly.

"He has been on a tremendous amount of pain medication since before his surgery and after. In my opinion, he is having hallucinations from the effects of the drugs," the doctor declared.

"But he answered all your questions correctly," Marie questioned. "How could he be hallucinating and still seem so lucid?"

"It happens, so what I'm going to write orders for is to reduce his pain medication and he will come around within hours."

"I don't know," Marie said. "Something strange is goin' on here and I don't like it."

Realizing that it would be useless trying to pacify her, Dr. Sorento turned and walked down the hall away from Marie toward the ward station.

Scott seemed so fearful and she wanted to calm him, so noticing a "rent-a-cop" sitting at a small desk down at the end of the hall, she went to talk to him.

He looked up from his magazine as she approached. He appeared to be quite old, at least in his seventies, had fine grey hair, was skinny and stood five-five.

She explained her dilemma to him and asked him if he would follow her to her husband's room to which he agreed. When they entered the room, she said, "Honey, look, I've hired a guard to stay outside your room tonight. No one will enter your room without his knowing, stopping and questioning that person. Will that make you feel more at ease about Big D?"

"Okay," Scott said. The old guard left the room and went back to his desk.

Then Scott added, "Listen, do you hear that?"

"What?" Marie asked.

"That, hear it? Someone's playing Amazing Grace on an organ in a room down the hall."

Marie froze. She couldn't answer him. She then believed that her husband was suffering hallucinations from the pain meds. She knew she made an ass out of herself barging through the elevator doors, cussing at the nurses, questioning the doctor and she was so regretful for her actions, that she didn't know how to make amends.

She hurried to the ward station and found Dr. Sorento sitting at a desk filling out patient orders. She approached him timidly, cleared her throat and said, "Dr. Sorento, please forgive me for the way I acted. I've just realized that your diagnosis is accurate and I am so sorry for offending you."

"It's okay," Dr. Sorento answered. "He's your husband and you love him…want the best care for him. I understand."

The nurses at the station were watching her as she apologized to the doctor. She turned to them and said, "I'm so sorry. Please forgive me." They nodded and turned back to their duties. One of them came to her and remarked, "We'll call you if there are any changes. Why not go home now and get some rest."

Marie went back to her husband's room, found him dozing, kissed his cheek, and left the hospital.

At three o'clock, Marie's phone rang.

"It's the surgical ward of the hospital," a voice said. "I've called to tell you that we've moved your husband to another room in the front side of the hospital so Big D can't get him." "Do you want me to come and stay in his room with him?" Marie asked.

Good God! No! We don't need that crazy woman back here tonight, the nurse thought, but said, "No, we just want to inform you of his whereabouts."

Scott remained in the hospital for five days before he could go home. During that time, he started losing his hair. Each day, he swore he heard someone playing Amazing Grace on an organ in a room down the hall. Marie brought a potted plant to the nurses the day Scott was released. The card attached to the holder stuck in the soil of the pot read "I'm sorry." Before leaving, Scott asked Marie to push him in the wheelchair around the entire floor of the surgical ward so he could prove to himself that it was just a figment of his imagination. Finding no organ, hearing no music, he finally accepted the fact that there never was an organ that the one he heard was in his mind only and that no one else heard it.

When Marie's mind became uncluttered with anxiety over Scott's surgery, she had to laugh when she realized that if Scott saw Big D through the window of his second floor room, Big D had to be sixteen to twenty feet tall but the thought never connected when Scott first told her he saw him.

Scott's chemotherapy resumed two weeks after his surgery. Marie accompanied him on the first day. Dr. Reyes was in his office off the chemo area when Marie went to the door and asked him if he had a minute.

Turning around and recognizing Marie, Dr. Reyes answered, "Sure, come in and sit down. What's on your mind?"

"I guess you know by now what happened when Scott had his surgery. I mean about me barging into the surgical ward and raising all kinds of hell," she said.

"Yes, I heard about it," Dr. Reyes said with a twinkle in his eyes. "The whole hospital heard about it. As a matter of fact, the consensus of opinion between the staff of doctors and nurses was that they'd sure like to have someone like you on their side if the need ever arose. However, a couple of the nurses made the comment that they'd get in line to catheterize you if you needed it."

"Ouch!" Marie replied. "I just wanted you to know I'm sorry."

"Don't worry about it," Dr. Reyes said. "We know you and Scott are under a tremendous amount of stress."

"How's he doing?" Marie asked.

"There's been some shrinkage but not as much as I hoped for," he answered.

SEVENTY-NINE

After the second chemo treatment, Scott drove himself to the hospital but asked Marie to drive for his third. During this treatment, Marie walked into the reception area searching for something to read to distract her from the anxiety she was experiencing.

She was approached by an oncology nurse named Polly, who while talking to Marie asked, "Are you angry?"

"What?" Marie asked.

"Are you angry?" the nurse repeated.

"I don't think so," Marie answered.

"Can you wait here a second? I have someone I'd like you to meet," nurse Polly added.

"Okay," Marie said inquisitively.

When Polly returned in five minutes, she brought with her a woman who was five feet seven, had brown hair, grey eyes and a warm, kind smile.

"Marie," Polly said, "This is Barbara Barkley, who is the psycho social counselor for the hospital. She helps patients and their families deal with the emotional pain of their disease."

Marie and Barbara shook hands. When Barbara asked her if she would like to step into her office, Marie said "yes" and followed her down a corridor into an office that was decorated in neutral colors of tan and light green. The lighting was low and soft music could be heard playing on a CD on Barbara's bookcase shelf.

Barbara asked Marie if she wanted to share her thoughts about her husband's cancer.

"Well," Marie responded, "I want to face the possibility that I may lose him to this dreadful disease, so I walk the beach every morning around nine. No one can hear me if I want to scream and cry, but more than anything, I have begged God not to let Scott suffer, telling Him that I can let Scott go, but please don't let him suffer."

"Does that comfort you, help you carry on through each day?"

"Yes," Marie answered. "I have the utmost trust in God's Will or I couldn't get through the day if I didn't, but sometimes, emotional weakness surrounds me and I give in to the thought that I might not have Scott too much longer."

"What do you do?" Barbara asked.

"Get mad? Oh! My goodness, how did Polly know?" she asked.

"Because you wouldn't be human if you didn't feel some anger over his sickness," Barbara responded.

They had three more appointments before Barbara asked Marie about her parents… growing up years with her siblings.

"Great parents," Marie said.

"Red flag," Barbara remarked.

"What? No, really, I had a good childhood…loving mother, caring brothers and sister."

Barbara lowered her voice and although she never displayed a boisterous one, it became softer and softer, lower and lower, until Marie found herself talking about something that had happened to her when she was a child.

"I saw an ad in the newspaper for summer job as an apprentice florist when I was thirteen," Marie said. "I showed it to my mother and asked her if I could call and she thought it was a good idea. The florist who answered the phone said he would like to meet my parents after interviewing me, so he talked to me at mother's apartment."

"He was an older man, maybe fifty, who was pudgy and had grey hair, but was polite and neat in appearance. He said his shop was in a town outside of Suttonville… a town called Pine Creek, but that he would come pick me up on the days I worked for him learning how to design floral arrangements. I was so happy because the work was creative and mother, after meeting him, agreed that I could accept the position."

"The shop was in the basement of his house. His wife was upstairs. In the beginning of my apprenticeship, he had me helping him with funeral arrangements. He called it "screwing roses" which meant cutting the rose off where the stem met the flower and inserting a pipe cleaner in the rose which made it easy to place the roses and other floral items in the star foam holder in the container that would hold the arrangement."

"He asked me if I wanted lunch one day and when I answered 'yes' he left to go upstairs to the kitchen to fix a sandwich and a coke. When he returned, he had a bottle of whiskey with him. After he poured the coke into a glass, he added whiskey and handed the glass to me. I didn't like the taste, but drank it anyway. A few minutes later, a comment was made about my breasts being small. He moved toward me and placed his hand down my shirt. He fondled and massaged one of my breasts. I moved away from him after that and can only remember that he said that I would have big breasts if that were done often."

"I was afraid and asked him to take me home which he did, and I never went back again, nor did I tell my mother."

"Do you know why you didn't tell her?" Barbara asked.

"How could I? I thought it was my fault. If I told her, would she believe me? Would anyone in the family ever believe me? I didn't think so."

"You kept it inside all this time?"

"Yes, I had forgotten it," Marie answered.

"May I suggest that you didn't forget but put it on a shelf in your subconscious until now?" Barbara said.

Marie looked at Barbara and said, "You hypnotized me, didn't you?"

Barbara sat and smiled without answering leaving Marie in awe of the experience, but not angry.

"Do I have to talk about this in more detail again?" Marie asked.

"No," Barbara said. "Not unless you feel it necessary."

The two women formed a trusting bond that Marie would come to have the need for again in the future.

EIGHTY

After Scott had five chemo treatments, Dr. Reyes told the couple it would be all right to take a vacation, so they cruised to the Caribbean and enjoyed themselves. Too much rich food and alcohol didn't prove to be difficult for Scott. He danced with Marie to the disco music being played on deck in the late afternoon. Marie noticed that he didn't seem short of breath after dancing a set so she relaxed, confident that the possibility existed that he might be able to beat this horrible disease.

When they returned from the cruise, Scott was informed that the tumor had shrunk a bit, although not as much as Dr. Reyes had hoped, so more chemo was ordered, but this time, Scott became sick. Thrush had invaded his mouth. He shivered and complained of muscle pain and when it happened, Marie wrapped him in blankets and lay with him on the bed. The diarrhea assaulted his intestinal tract and left him weak, but worst of all, he started vomiting and couldn't keep anything in his stomach.

Marie had heard that marijuana helped those who were going through chemo, so after watching her husband run to the bathroom so many times, she called the doctor.

"Let's put it this way," Marie said when he took her call. "If I can't get it any other way, I'll find someone who will sell it to me on the street, but I will not watch him go through any more vomiting without some kind of help."

"I don't want him smoking it," the doctor said. "I can help him by prescription. I'll call it in to a nearby drug store, the only one in your city who stocks it, and you'll have to go pick it up and show identification of who you are."

"Do it," Marie said. They never mentioned what IT was.

Marie got in the car and drove to the drug store located in the center of the city and after showing identification, picked up the script. She took it to the car and opened the bottle to find a number of tiny B-B sized brown pills in the bottle. When she looked at the label, she discovered that the drug name was Marinol.

Racing home to her sick husband who she left sitting in a chair near the bathroom, she climbed the stairs and opened the door.

"Honey, I've got the prescription," she commented.

"I don't know," Scott said.

"What?" she exclaimed.

"Well, if that's marijuana, then it's illegal, isn't it?" he asked.

"Not if it's prescribed by a physician," she answered.

"What will happen after I take it?" he questioned.

"Oh, shit, Scott, you'll probably roll on the floor laughing and then get up and eat every snack in the cupboard," she claimed. "I tried it once a long time ago. Everyone in the room was laughing hysterically, but me, so I decided not to try it again and I had had a couple of scotch and waters beforehand."

When the chemotherapy ended, it was decided to start Scott on a treatment of radiation. He had four treatments, but the tumor had not shrunk. During this time, the couple traveled around the state lodging in luxurious vacation spots. Scott had gained weight…weighed more than he had before the cancer was detected. He continued golfing in the men's league at the local golf course. His stamina was beyond what his doctor expected.

He started crashing twenty months after the discovery of his cancer. His lung filled with fluid and had to be tapped. This procedure had to be done without anesthesia because anesthesia could have caused him to die, so injections of Lidocaine were positioned around the site where the surgeon cut to drain the lung. Knowing how painful the procedure would be and thankful that the surgeon was detained, the assisting nurse suggested that Marie go home and she would call her when the doctor arrived, but she waited until the procedure ended before making the call to Marie. The nurse never told Marie how her husband cried out in pain and Scott didn't want Marie to know that, although he was given so many shots of Lidocaine, it wasn't enough to deaden the pain he experienced.

After he was released from the hospital, Scott laid low for a while trying to recoup the energy he lost during the tapping of his lung but once more bounced back.

Marie continued to work at the condo community. Her boss, knowing that she and Scott lived in an efficiency, tossed a key to her one day.

"Go look at 216, but don't look at it," he said. "It's a one bedroom, bath, kitchen, dining area and living room."

"What? Why do I go and look but don't look," Marie said.

"Because I know what you can buy it for. All it needs is cosmetic surgery which I believe Scott's capable of doing. Go on. I'll tend the office."

Marie went to view the condo. When she opened the door and saw the burnt orange stained rug, hanging dining room light fixture literally hanging, the card table that she guessed was a dining room table, the pea green kitchen appliances and the holey furniture, she turned and walked out the door, down the steps, across the parking lot and to the office.

"You've got to be kidding," she said to Tommy, her boss. "It's a shithouse up there. No wonder it hasn't sold. Who'd want it?"

"Call Scott, see what he thinks," Tommy replied. "I know you can get it for 57K, which on the ocean, is a steal. It just needs some beautification, new appliances, paint, that's all."

She called Scott who arrived within minutes. He went to the condo, came back and said, "We'll take it."

Is the glass half full or half empty. It was half full in Scott's opinion.

The bank approved the loan for the new condominium. Marie put an ad in the Orlando newspaper and sold the efficiency in two days. The new owners would take possession in four weeks, during which time Scott would remodel their new residence. He made Marie promise that while he was remodeling, she would not be the overseer and was only allowed to bring his lunch to him while he worked on it.

Scott had never laid tile floors, but he learned how. He patched and painted the walls and installed new cabinets. He removed all the electrical fixtures and replaced them with new ones Marie picked out. They bought new appliances and purchased wall-to-wall carpeting. By the time the four weeks had passed, the Nicholson's were ready to move into their new home.

They celebrated Christmas in the condo with a couple of family members. That New Year's Eve was chilly enough for hooded wind breakers, but they didn't let that stop them from sitting on the deck on the ocean with a glass of wine in their hands to welcome in the New Year.

Scott's outlook was positive even though he started losing weight and started to become short of breath at times. As much as possible, he kept breathing problems from Marie. He wasn't able to ride a bike on the beach with her. Instead of telling her why, he told her he wasn't interested, and that it was too cold. If she caught on to the real reason why, she didn't mention it.

In March, Scott signed up for a two-day golf tournament and was able to complete the first day.

"I can't play tomorrow," he said to Marie as they were having the happy hour.

"Why, what's wrong?" she asked.

"I couldn't make it up the incline to the green to putt," he sighed and turned his face away from her in tears. He knew he was going down, and all the positive thinking in the world wasn't going to prevent what was coming for him.

Marie got up from her chair, sat on the armrest of his chair, and buried her forehead in his neck. Saying nothing, she hugged him and for a moment they were suspended in their own time.

Dr. Reyes evaluated Scott the following week and suggested three more rounds of chemo.

"Why?" Marie asked aside from Scott. "He's losing weight and his pallor is grey. He's getting weak and isn't eating very much solid food. How can he withstand more chemo?"

"This is a lighter side and not the same protocol as he was given before, and it will help him," the doctor said.

"It's up to him," she replied.

In hope, Scott agreed to three more treatments and started them the following week. He needed Marie to drive him to the hospital, but it was decided the treatments would be given at Hart Medical Center in Selena Beach. The first treatment had no serious side effects, but when she took him back for his second one, the oncologist nurse walked toward him, gave him a hug and remarked, "Little feverish today? Let's take your temp and see. A hundred and one," she exclaimed after removing the thermometer.

"Did I see Dr. Reyes in his office while passing through?" Marie asked.

"Yes," she said. "Do you want to see him?"

"Please," Marie answered.

"I'll take you to a room with a bed," she said. "Wait here. He'll be in shortly."

Scott sat on the bed and stared ahead. Marie knelt behind him and put her arms around his chest, her face on the back of his neck.

"Don't leave me, honey," Scott said.

"I will never leave you, never," she cried.

Dr. Reyes opened the door and stepped in.

"Not feeling too well?" he asked Scott.

Scott didn't answer. Didn't even look at him.

"I need to admit him," Dr. Reyes said to Marie after checking his chart.

"Not in this hospital. There is no oncology ward; just a treatment room."

"Then take him to Hampden Medical. I'll write orders including admitting orders. Take him to the oncology ward and don't stop. They'll be expecting you. And, Marie?"

"Yes, doctor."

"Don't go home for a toothbrush."

Marie told Scott to wait at the entrance while she went for the car. He didn't give her any flak about it. He was too sick.

Although she was scared, Marie didn't drive over the speed limit to the hospital in Daytona. It took half an hour to get there. When she pulled up to the entrance, she put the car in park and went for a wheelchair.

"Are you Mrs. Nicholson?" a male voice said.

"Yes," Marie answered.

"We're ready to take Mr. Nicholson to his room," the orderly in scrubs replied. "No need to stop at admitting."

Scott was wheeled past admitting and into the elevator which stopped on the sixth floor oncology ward.

He was greeted by a nurse and shown to a private room where he disrobed and put on the hospital gown.

Although she was fearful, at the time Marie wasn't attentive enough to recognize that Dr. Reyes instructions to her to get Scott to the hospital without stopping home was indicative of a grievous situation. She only wanted her husband safe and in the hands of medical supervision where he could receive the best possible treatment.

"You need to get some rest," Scott said to his wife after he climbed into bed. "Go home and don't come back tonight. I'll be alright and I'll call you."

"Are you sure?" she asked.

"Yes, there's nothing you can do here. I'll call you, honey… promise."

Marie left the hospital and cried all the way home. Pulling over half way home, she asked, "Is this it, God?" she asked. "Are you going to take him now? Please let me be ready for this and accept it."

Scott remained in the hospital while the infection diagnosed in his lung was attended to. Marie went to see him each day and took him home on the sixth day.

"I received the last of the three chemo treatments while I was there," he told Marie.

Although she wanted to scream about another treatment, she said nothing because they had made a pact that Scott would take control of his decisions regarding the treatment of his lung cancer. Her own energy was running low with worry trying to accept that he wasn't going to make it.

EIGHTY-ONE

Scott had no appetite, so Marie made him milkshakes from dairy energy drinks and put three scoops of ice cream in them. One evening shortly after leaving the hospital, he asked her, "happy hour tonight?"

"What do you want?" she questioned.

"Vodka tonic," he replied.

They sat on their condo deck looking out at the ocean and sipped their cocktails. Now and again, Scott would get up and spit up blood over the rail to the bushes below. It seemed strange to Marie that it didn't faze her.

She went in to make a hamburger and fix his shake. He came into the kitchen and asked, "Do you think you could make me one too?"

"Certainly," was her answer and she grilled two burgers for them. He was able to get the burger down and smiled commenting, "That sure tasted good."

Sitting and watching television later that evening, Scott looked at Marie and said, "I think you should go to bed early, honey. You've been giving me my medication around the clock. You need sleep. I'll call you if I need you."

She couldn't argue and headed down the hall to the bedroom to sleep, closing the door behind her.

At eleven o'clock, Scott kicked the door open and said, "Call 911. I can't breathe," and went to sit on the sofa.

Marie scurried out of bed and ran to the phone. Shaking, she dialed the number. "My husband has lung cancer and can't breathe," she said and gave the address.

"Is he turning blue?" the operator asked.

"No, he's sitting on the sofa," Marie said.

"Help is on the way," the operator said and signed off.

Five minutes later, the fire truck arrived. Two minutes after, the ambulance came and the EMT found Scott still sitting on the sofa.

"Do you have a DNR?" the fire fighter asked Marie as he looked toward the kitchen.

"No, I think he was going into hospice tomorrow, but I have power of attorney, health care surrogate, and he has a living will," she said trying to keep herself composed.

"Get the documents. They'll need them at the hospital," the fireman said.

While she went to get the papers, the EMTs were talking to Scott, checking his vitals.

When she returned from the bedroom, she heard one EMT asking, "How you doin' buddy? We're gonna take you to the hospital. Get you checked out, okay?"

Scott shook his head up and down, but didn't say anything.

"Get the gurney," another EMT said.

"No," Scott said firmly. "I can go down the stairs by myself."

And he got up from the sofa and started toward the open door and proceeded down the stairs to the waiting ambulance. When he reached the bottom of the stairs, he got on the gurney… the driver placed it in the ambulance.

Marie stood there looking at the fireman and said, "Where he goes, I go."

"I'm not supposed to put you in the ambulance, but if you'll agree to be good, I will."

"I'll be good," Marie said.

After Marie climbed in the passenger side of the ambulance, the fireman pulled the seat belt across her chest, fastened it and said, "Good luck." He closed the door and walked to the fire truck.

When the ambulance driver opened the door and saw Marie sitting in the passenger side, he said, "You can't ride in here," to which she said, "Try pushing me out cause I go where he goes."

"Okay Ma'am, but you gotta be good," he replied.

"I'll be good," she said. "Do you have to turn on the siren. I mean it will scare him."

"Ma'am, there's no traffic beachside at this time of night and all the snowbirds have left, so, no, I don't need to turn on the siren, but I need to keep the flashing red light on."

"Thank you," Marie said.

The ride to the hospital took five minutes and during that time, the EMT was in contact with the ER.

"The wife's in the bus with me," he said. She has power of attorney, health surrogacy, and his living will with her. ETA two minutes."

Marie kept quiet and stared ahead.

The ambulance crossed over the bridge to the mainland and turned left at the first light and into the portico where the medical team removed Scott and took him into a curtained area in the ER. Marie was advised to go to the ER admitting office to fill out paperwork.

Hands shaking, Marie signed the necessary paperwork and gave the documents she brought with her to the admitting clerk, who after copying them, handed them back to Marie.

She was told she could sit with him while he was being evaluated. While the doctors were assessing his workup, Marie asked if she could use the phone to call her brother.

"Danny," she said when he picked up the phone. "I need you to come to the hospital. It doesn't look good."

"Okay," Danny said. "I'll be there soon."

Marie turned away from the desk outside the room Scott was in. The ER nurse was waiting for her to finish her call. She had a plastic container in her hand.

"Do you know what this is?" the nurse asked.

"No," Marie said. "It looks like a cooked elbow macaroni."

"It's a piece of his lung he coughed up. He's not gonna make it. Do you have power of attorney?" She had a clipboard in her hand with a DNR document clipped to it.

"Yes, but he's sitting up and very aware," Marie said. "I can't believe he's gonna die tonight."

At that moment Danny came through the ER doors and walked up to his sister. He knew the drill, as he had given the last rites thousands of times during his years as a priest. He went into the room to see Scott and when he came out, he said to his sister, "Sign it."

As Marie looked at her brother, the tears started.

"Go ask him," the nurse said.

"What?" Marie ask surprised at the request.

"He's lucid enough to make the decision," she said.

Danny shook his head up and down when Marie turned to him.

The medical team left the couple alone when Marie went to ask him.

Slowly, Marie walked into the room where her husband was. She kept her composure as she said, "Honey, do you want to be intubated?"

"For how long?" he asked.

"Forever," she sighed.

"No! Am I gonna' die tonight?" Scott asked.

"Only God knows," she said.

"I'm gonna miss you," he cried. "Go, go on, out to Danny, go on."

"But Daddy" (her pet name for him), she said.

"Go on," he said.

As she started to walk away from him, she took three steps and thought to herself, *I didn't come this far to walk away from him now.*

She turned and walked back to Scott and reached his bed just as he went into a seizure, his arms moved up in front of him and shook violently. His eyes rolled back into his head and just as he slumped forward, Marie caught him in her arms and yelled for help.

The medical team ran to him. The nurse gave him a shot and he relaxed as he was gently laid back onto the pillow. Marie looked at the monitor and saw that it had not gone flat line, so she started whispering in Scott's left ear.

"Go, honey, go into the light. It's okay. I'll be okay. Remember when you told me that you had a dream that Missy would come for you? Well, she's coming for you now. See her coming over the hill, tail wagging. Go to her. I love you, and I'm not that far behind you."

Scott let out a breath, the monitor showed a flat line and she knew he had passed. When she turned around, the attendees were standing at the end of his bed. They had tissues to their eyes.

"Who's Missy?" one of the nurses asked.

"Our doggie who died two years ago," Marie said.

She stayed with him for a short time before Danny came in and gave him a blessing.

"Come on Marie," Danny said. "Let's go home."

A directive was given for removal of the body to a crematorium by Marie.

A doctor asked Marie if she wanted anything Scott was wearing. He had on green shorts and rubber flip flops.

Marie looked at him and said, "I want the wedding band."

He removed the band from Scott's finger and gave it to Marie, who clasped it in her hand and held it to her heart.

She was told she could stay if she wanted to.

"No," Marie said. "His spirit has left the body."

Danny took his sister by the elbow and escorted her down the hall and out the doors of the ER to the parking lot... his car and home.

Marie knew she had to place a call to Scott's son. When his wife picked up the phone and heard Marie's voice, she said, "Oh, No," and handed the phone to her husband.

"Your father passed early this morning," Marie said crying.

"Why wasn't I called?" Chad asked.

"It wasn't expected until the nurses showed me what he spit up and informed me that he would die soon," she answered. "You couldn't have made the five hour drive within that time. Besides your father asked that I call you after he knew he was dying."

"I'll have to call you back," he said, and hung up.

The next call she made to Jackie.

"He's gone," Marie said when Jackie answered the phone. "I don't want you to drive over in the dark but will you come when the sun comes up?"

"I'm sorry," Jackie said. "I'll come this morning."

Still in shock and in a fog, Marie paced through the condo looking at items that belonged to Scott that she knew she would have to get rid of. Mid-morning, she heard the knock on the door. When she went and opened it, Jackie was standing there. She put her arms around Marie and held her friend, crying as Marie asked her to come into the condo.

Marie repeated the story of Scott's passing and as she told it, she couldn't believe she was hearing herself saying the words. It seemed like she was talking about someone else's husband, not hers.

"I need you to help me with his clothes," Marie said. "I can't leave them in the closet. I'll start wearing his shirts and smelling his jackets and I know I'll never be able to get over his death if I do."

"What do you want me to do?" Jackie asked as she followed Marie to the bedroom.

"Search the pockets for anything left in them," Marie said.

"Do you want me to put the clothes in my car?" Jackie asked.

"Would you?" Marie requested.

"Of course I will," Jackie answered.

After the friends/sisters finished searching through Scott's clothes, Marie and Jackie took them to Jackie's car and placed them in the trunk.

"What do you think I should do next?" Marie asked Jackie.

"Has the crematorium called you?" Jackie asked.

"No, not yet," Marie remarked.

"Let's go to your computer and I'll help you write an obituary for them. Then we'll call them, after which I'll take you up so you can sign the papers. Okay?" Jackie asked.

They sat at the desk and Marie started writing the names of survivors.

"Should I include Cheryl?" Marie asked.

"I would. I don't care if she didn't go see him when he asked for her. She's still his step-daughter and he was good to her," Jackie said trying to hold back her irritation with Marie's daughter.

Jackie drove the seven miles to the crematorium office where they met with a specialist who accepted the typed document Marie handed her and made suggestions to complete it for issuance to the newspaper.

"Your husband's remains will be ready to be picked up in five days," the woman said.

"Why so long?" Marie asked.

"We're backlogged. Lots of people have chosen to be cremated nowadays. We'll call you when they are ready. Is there anything else I can do for you?" she asked.

"No," Marie replied.

"Then I'll let you go. I'm sorry for your loss," and the woman exited the office leaving Marie and Jackie sitting there.

"Does it sound like an assembly line of bodies waiting to be processed to you, or is it me?" Marie asked her friend.

"It does indeed," Jackie answered.

They left the office. Jackie drove Marie home and sat with her a while before leaving her.

"Call at any time if you need me," Jackie said.

She hugged her friend and walked out of the condo, leaving Marie sitting in the rocker staring at the front door.

He's never coming through that door again, Marie thought, and she started crying.

EIGHTY-TWO

Marie knew that Scott wanted to be buried at sea, so when she called his shipmates to tell them of his death, she asked if they would escort him out to sea. They all said they would be honored.

Marie remembered that at one time Scott told her that of all his Navy documents, the one most necessary to keep was his DD214. "I can't even get into heaven without it," he commented jokingly.

Driving to the Coast Guard station three miles away, Marie carried with her a file full of papers she thought might be necessary. After offering her a seat, the senior chief spoke his condolences and took the file offered to him to search for what he needed to set up a burial date.

"Usually, we take cremated remains out when we have more than one, but we also offer a service of allowing survivors to escort the remains of just one. However, I can't give you an escorted date for four weeks especially since you need to schedule the sea burial on a Saturday to accommodate his shipmates."

"Okay," she said. "That will be fine."

The senior chief accompanied her to the door and added, "I've set his service on June 6th at 11:00, after which the cutter will take the remains out to sea."

Marie received the call from the crematorium five days later. Her ex-sister-in-law, Linda (who would never be an ex to Marie) had flown in to show support for Marie.

"I'm driving to pick up Scott," she said when Linda called her.

"You need Danny and I to take you?" Linda asked.

"No, I have to do this myself," Marie answered.

At that point, Danny took the phone and said, "Marie, I think we should take you."

"No, Danny," she answered. "I want to do this alone."

"Then, call when you get back…will you?"

"Yes," she said.

Marie drove to the crematorium. An assistant undertaker retrieved Scott's remains from another room away from the reception area and handed them to Marie. The remains were in a plastic bag in a brown cardboard box much the same as Marie's mother's were when delivered.

"Do you need help?" he asked.

"No, let me sit a while," Marie said.

"You can sit on the sofa," he commented and guided her to an ice blue crushed velvet sofa at the end of the room.

"Stay as long as you need," he said. He left the room.

Sitting on the sofa, Marie held the cardboard box to her breast and cried, "Oh, Daddy, why did you leave me?"

After a few minutes, she got up and walked out the door still holding her husband's remains to her breast, got into her car and gently set the box on the passenger seat. "We're goin' home one last time, honey," she said. Putting the car in reverse, she backed out of the parking space and drove out of the lot toward US 1 and home.

She remembered that she needed some vegetables as she drove and pulled into the parking lot of the fruit and veggie stand. Looking at the box, she said, "I have to go get some lettuce and tators, but I'll be right back, honey."

After making her purchases, Marie came back to the car, opened the door, got in, put the key in the ignition, and said, "Now we go home, Daddy," and drove another three miles to her condo.

When she arrived home, she gently picked up the box containing Scott's remains and brought it into the condo.

"Where shall I put you until you go out to sea?" she asked while looking at the box.

Before she finished the question, she knew where the box should go, so she walked down the hallway and into the pantry where she placed the box on the floor in the corner and put Scott's driver golf club on top of the box.

In between the time she picked up Scott's remains and the burial day, Marie found herself remembering happy times with her husband. They made her smile. Then she remembered sad times, times when they had an argument, times he almost always let her win, and she would cry asking him for forgiveness for being such an ass, for she knew that those times were not worth the pain caused to each other in view of now and being without him, but then hindsight is …

She bought a long dress for the memorial service that was held at the shore of the Coast Guard Station. Jackie picked her up and drove her to the service. Marie didn't expect to be given the folded American flag that was presented to her by the chief, so she looked puzzled when he stood on the deck and gave her the speech as he held the flag in his hands. Scott's buddy took the flag and gave it to her, telling her in layman's language what it meant. She accepted it and buried her face in it and cried.

Scott's shipmates boarded the cutter and stood on the back deck.

"Are you coming aboard?" someone said.

"What," Marie answered. "No," I can't," she answered.

She knew she could do everything necessary for him while he was alive, but this was too much for her to endure… she was afraid she would slip in the water behind her husband when his remains were spread into the ocean, so she declined boarding.

She had made a paper WELCOME HOME band with the colors of the Vietnam service ribbon in the background and had secured it around the cardboard box that held her husband's remains.

Scott's friend, remaining calm said, "Marie, give me the box."

"No," she replied.

"Marie, please…give me the box. It's time to take him home to the sea." He had tears in his eyes.

"Okay," she said, and handed him the box with the ribbon still surrounding it.

The cutter got underway, leaving Marie standing alone on the deck as she watched it glide away from the dock. She had hired a bagpiper to play. He played *Amazing Grace* while standing on a plot of land that jetted out on the water as the cutter passed him and went out into the ocean.

"Oh, Daddy," she cried as she watched her beloved slip away from her for the last time, and then she felt a hand on her shoulder. When she turned her head, she saw Jackie, who then embraced her, and the two girlfriends fell into each other's arms crying.

When the cutter could no longer be seen, the piper played *Anchors Away*. It made Marie remember not only her husband, but her father who had been a sailor in WWI.

Marie had invited Scott's oncologist and the nurses who attended him to the memorial service. While his doctor could not attend, three of the nurses did and made the comment that they had not witnessed a more emotionally moving service since they became oncologist nurses. One mentioned that Dr. Reyes was honored to be invited as many of his patients were angry at him because he did not save their loved ones.

"It was not his fault," Marie said. "He did what he could for him and gave us twenty-two months together. Tell him I bear no ill feelings toward him, but thank him for all he did."

Jackie took Marie by the arm and led her to her car. She drove to a restaurant Marie had reserved for a reception. Hors d'oeuvres were placed on tables. Marie made an arrangement for an open bar. The bartender was told to let Marie know when the tab reached a certain amount as she did not want to go over what she had planned to pay.

Marie ordered a scotch/rocks with a splash and drank it down. Then she ordered another. The mates who escorted her husband came through the door a half hour later. One went up to Marie and said, "It was the strangest thing. When the cutter stopped and the chief advised that the remains should be put into the sea, Tom opened the box, opened the plastic bag and let the remains go, whereupon the chief said, "Let the ribbon attached to the box go also."

Tom said, "But it's paper. I thought we could not do that."

"Let it go into the sea," the chief said.

Finishing his story, the shipmate said, "So, Tom slipped it into the sea whereupon it followed the whirlpool made where Scott's remains sank. The ribbon came upon the whirlpool and was swallowed up in it, and we never saw it again."

Marie looked at the bartender and said, "I'll have another."

Danny drove his sister home, gave her a peck on the cheek and told her to try to get some rest…he would call her in the morning.

EIGHTY-THREE

She didn't think she could get through one more day without him...her heart was empty. Every card Scott had ever given her was always signed, *Yours Forever, Love Scott,* and she had kept every one of them...tied them in a ribbon and kept them in her bureau drawer. Now that he was gone, she read and reread them every day, but it didn't help the pain of loss she felt.

She went to the golf course where she and Scott were members and played frequently. The staff showed their compassion for her loss by not asking any questions. Marie did have one request that was granted.

"Will you allow me to go play nine holes alone just one time," she asked John, the pro.

"You can go right now," he answered. "And I'll hold up anyone who comes to play after you for a few minutes."

Marie retrieved her clubs from the trunk of her car and headed to the first tee.

"Well, honey, let's see how I do without your instruction and encouragement," she said to Scott.

Yes, she said it to Scott, her dead husband, for Marie believed that he was with her and would remain at her side until the day they would be together again in eternity. It wasn't her intent to break any records that day and she didn't ... didn't even count her strokes. She only wanted to be in a place where he loved to play. It surprised her that she hadn't fallen apart and broke down as she was finishing the ninth hole and she thought she heard him say, *"All right side. You can't get the ball up in the air. Your left side gets it there. You can do it."*

Danny knew that his sister suffered. All he could offer to help ease her pain was to call her every morning and ask her if she wanted to go have a drink and eat. They went to watering holes she and Scott had frequented. When the bartenders who knew Scott...knew he had died asked her how she was doin', she composed herself enough to let them think she was doin' good...they knew it wasn't so, but allowed her her privacy.

One day three months later, Danny called Marie and said, "Want to go and help me pick out a puppy? I got the name of a Shih Tzu breeder."

"What?" Marie asked. "They have personalities like humans do," she added. "All you need to do is watch as they play with each other. You'll notice the quiet ones as well as the frisky ones and can make a choice while watching."

"Ah, come on," Danny said. "I'd like your advice."

After picking up Marie, Danny drove to the breeder's residence and knocked on the door.

"Come in," the breeder said. "The puppies are on the patio. I'll let them in so you can meet them."

In scampered four little pups, three of which started frolicking around Danny's feet after he sat down.

"So what da ya think?" Danny said as he looked at his sister.

"Well, that one there, is full of piss and vinegar," Marie commented smiling and pointing at one of the pups.

Marie looked around and noticed one of the puppies quietly sitting under an end table, and said, "What's the matter with that puppy?" Her color was in equal parts of black and white with a white streak from her nose to the top of her head. The black around her eyes made her look like she had a mask, but her mouth was white. She had a button nose peeking out of the middle and above her mouth.

"Nothing," the breeder said. "She's just quiet."

"She sick?" Marie asked.

Sound familiar???

"No, just quiet. She's the runt, the last one born and usually they have quiet dispositions."

Marie turned her head back to her brother who was still trying to decide which one to choose. Out of the corner of her eye, she noticed that the runt puppy had moved and was sitting under the coffee table staring at her.

She went over and commented, "What's the matter, little one? Are you sicky? Poor little thing."

Marie picked the puppy up, held it to her chest and walked back to the sofa. By the time she sat down, the pup had nestled in the crook of her chest and shoulder and had fallen asleep. When she looked down, the puppy's back was moving up and down with each breath, but her eyes were closed.

Oh, Oh! She thought.

Danny picked up a female and said, "I'll take this one."

Marie looked at the breeder and said, "I'll take this one."

"Are you getting one too?" Danny said.

"Looks like I am," Marie said. "Look Danny, she fell asleep."

Someone have a hand in this?

"You can't take them for another week," the breeder stated.

"That's okay," Marie said. "I have to go buy doggie items for her, so I can't take her today anyway. Take good care of her please until I come back for her."

She kissed the pup on the top of her head and handed her back to the breeder.

Marie went to the local pet shop and bought a cage. She called it a housie, toys, dishes, cookies, food and some mesh wire to cover the balcony outside her condo. There was a lift in her spirit in knowing the little one would be hers soon.

Could it be that her brother knew what he was doing in asking her to go with him?

The following week, Danny and Marie went back to the breeder to pick up the puppies and take them home. Danny stapled the wire mesh around the inside of the porch on Marie's balcony so Marie could let the little one out to be trained to piddle on newspapers.

"Well, little one," Marie said holding the pup after her brother left, "It's just you and me. Welcome to your new home." and the puppy licked Marie's face.

What to name her. Many cute names came to mind, but Marie couldn't get past the name she loved so much, so she called her "Missy."

She listened to jazz music on tapes in the evening while having a Vodka Martini. She never drank them before her husband died, but grew to like them after a friend introduced her to them. She picked the little doggie up and danced with her, sometimes crying into the doggies furry back. She missed Scott so much, and even though five months had gone by since his death, the grief hadn't subsided. When the music Scott and she danced to played on the FM station she liked so well, she'd run to turn it off, the memory of them dancing would encompass her every thought.

When Marie opened the door to the pantry one evening, a golf ball she hadn't noticed before fell off the shelf and onto the floor. It was one of Scott's. She'd had too many Martinis. She sank to the hallway floor, picked up the golf ball and threw it down the hall screaming, "I hate you, God. You took him away from me," after which Marie fell over on her side and sobbed, "I didn't mean it, God. Please forgive me." She lay on the floor crying until she felt a sticky little tongue on her cheek, looked up and saw her Missy licking away the tears on her face and at the same time, wagging her tail in uncertainty of what was happening. Marie knew at that moment she had to find a way to deal with her loss of Scott for even her little baby angel was trying to comfort her.

Feeling that she had hit rock bottom after she cursed her Creator, Marie signed up for an aerobics class at a nearby gym and found that the music was of the disco age that she enjoyed so much. She met new friends and looked forward to the delight of being with them three times a week.

EIGHTY-FOUR

Two months after adopting the puppy, Marie started to feel a stinging pain on the outside edge of left foot, but it wasn't enough for her to be overly concerned, so as she walked, she turned her foot inward to relieve the pain. She went to the pool one morning. Starting down the steps that led into the shallow end, Marie slipped into the water, tried to stand up and realized the pain was sharp, so she got out of the pool, dried herself and made her way back to her apartment. A retired nurse lived in the next-door condo. Her door was open and she was visible sitting in her easy chair. As Marie reached the top step, she let out a yell and the neighbor came to the door.

"What's the matter?" Edwina said.

"I don't know," Marie said, and told her about the foot.

"Let me see," Edwina said. After examining her foot, Edwina commented, "I think we'd better go to the hospital."

"What? No," Marie said.

Edwina insisted and drove her neighbor to the hospital to be evaluated. "The fifth metatarsal is broken," the ER nurse commented after the doctor reviewed an x-ray, "and we don't have a boot that small to fit you."

Why is it that ailments always happen on a weekend?

The staff placed a temporary cast on Marie and sent her home. The problem now was how she would get around the condo and take the doggie out for a walk.

Marie sat in her apartment looking at Missy and commented, "Well, little girl, it's a good thing you are trained to go on the porchie cause Mommy can't take you down those fourteen steps with a broken foot." Missy sat and looked cocking her head at her master's declaration.

She knew she had to devise a way to get around the condo. Looking at the secretary chair that had wheels on it, she likened it to a wheel chair she could push through the condo with her other foot.

She could sit on it and lower it to get into the fridge and heighten it to get to her upper level needs. No problem. In three days, she would be fitted for a boot.

The following Monday, she left the osteopathic doctor's office with a boot on her foot that allowed Marie to stand on it and even walk her doggie with no difficulty. She wore the boot for five weeks. Nearing the end of the fifth week, Marie was coming back from a walk with Missy. She looked up at the stairs leading to her condo and asked herself, "What happens if I break a hip?" and immediately knew the answer to her own question.

She called her brother, Dan, and asked his opinion.

"I think I'm gonna put my condo on the market," she said. "It's a seller's market and I know I can get a good price for it. I'm concerned about climbing the stairs as I age plus those damn kids in the pool screaming Marco-Polo all day long drives me nuts."

"How much are you gonna ask?" Danny said.

"I'm going for two hundred eighteen thousand," she replied. "I'm gonna sell it myself. I'll put in the Orlando newspaper on a weekend and see what happens. I don't have to move, so I can wait if it takes a while to sell."

The advertisement was in the following weekend newspaper. Marie received twenty calls the first day. A couple wanted to see it as soon as possible that Saturday. They made an appointment to view the condo at 1:00, showed up at 12:30 and were so impressed, that they counter offered. Marie settled on two hundred sixteen thousand and was given a check for $5,000.00 as good faith down payment with the entire amount due at closing. The buyers accepted a title company Marie suggested.

Marie was elated. She was gonna make four times what was paid for the condo and figured it would give her a goodly amount to buy a home.

The closing was in two weeks. Marie was told to take her time moving as the couple were going to use the property as a weekend getaway. Marie declined their generous offer. There wouldn't be much to move since the appliances and furniture were included in the sale.

Danny had moved out of his garden villa in Selena Beach a month before Marie sold her condo. As hospital chaplain, he needed to be closer to Daytona where he ministered to the sick and dying as well as said Mass at the local church and nursing homes.

"You haven't any time to look for a place to buy," he said to Marie, "so why don't you move into my place until you decide what you want to do?"

Pleased at the offer, she accepted. After the closing, she and some friends helped her move into her brother's home.

After staying two weeks, Marie decided to buy the villa. The closing was in a week, as Marie decided to pay cash for the property. She didn't want a mortgage.

The first week of August, Hurricane Charley grew out in the Atlantic and was nearing the southeast coast of the United States. A warning for beachside residents to evacuate their homes and find shelter inland was cause for distress for Marie. She packed some belongings, including legal documents, and headed to Orlando to stay with her friend, Jackie. Missy was so tiny that Marie put her in a cardboard box, nested it with towels, and placed it on the floor beneath the passenger side of the car.

Sitting glued to the television for updated reports of the whereabouts of Charley proved to cause too much anxiety for Marie, so she retired to the guestroom with Missy and find some peace.

When the storm passed and Marie returned home, she was apprehensive driving down her street wondering if she would find her home still standing. As she pulled into the common driveway that aligned with the five patio homes, one of which she owned, she looked around and saw that her home was still standing and appeared to be undamaged by the wind and rain of the tropical storm. She silently thanked God.

Seventy-five percent of the residents of the little beachside community returned to find their homes damaged by the wind. Roofs blew off allowing the torrential rain to find a way through the uncovered homes. Furniture had to be hauled away, mold had already started to gather in the walls of the homes that had none or very little roofs left. Special mold searching machines were brought in to look for and find the mold in order to evaporate it. It would take days and months before the residents could move back into their dwellings.

The worse was yet to come. Two weeks later, Hurricane Frances paid a visit to the beachside community...the eye passing directly over it. The eerie frame of neighbor's minds in the silence of the eye before the storm struck was cause for a hurricane party, so they brought their bottles of booze and settled in one house with the television turned on for twenty-four hours. Marie decided again it was too much for her and went home.

What damage Charley didn't find, Frances did. More homes were damaged and it still wasn't over, for two weeks later Ivan came across the Atlantic and covered the entire peninsula with howling winds and rain. Marie stayed in her bathroom during this storm. She placed towels in the bathtub for Missy to be safe, retrieved an ice bucket from the cupboard and filled it with ice, grabbed a bottle of vodka and a lemon, and some crackers and cheese. Having a battery operated radio sitting on the counter allowed her to stay tuned to the latest updates on the storm. There was a local number she could dial to inquire if she could open her door and peek out before moving about outside. She was told not to the four times she called it. On the fifth time, she opened the door anyway expecting to find the driveway flooded, but saw no standing water, so she stepped outside and looked around. It was as though no storm had passed through her street at all. She sighed a sigh of relief, went back in the house and closed the door.

It still wasn't over. Hurricane Jeanne followed ten days behind and once again struck the small community with a vengeance. Trees fell down in the streets and onto already missing rooftops with the weight of their roots being soaked through three other storms. Residents fled inland once more and worried about returning to the emptiness of finding there was no place to live.

When it was over, it would take a year to clean up and repair/remodel the properties of the island population. Homes had blue tarps on their roofs for months. Roofers were in demand and couldn't accommodate everyone in need in the immediacy of their needs.

Hurricane Charley caused the roof to fall in on the bed in the condo Marie sold to the young couple. She found out later that they had not purchased insurance for damage within their living quarters. Marie's villa remained undamaged.

EIGHTY-FIVE

A retired army officer who worked out at the gym Marie frequented stopped her one day asking, "Did I hear you say that your husband was in Vietnam?" to which she answered, "Yes."

"Are you aware that you may qualify for a VA entitlement as a result of his serving in Nam and being exposed to agent orange? That his exposure and eventual demise is considered a service connected death?" the officer asked.

"No," Marie answered.

"I have an article I received recently. I'll bring it to you next time I come and you can decide if you want to pursue it."

"Okay," she remarked.

Two days later, the officer handed Marie the article. She called the Veteran's Administration in St. Petersburg, Florida, and talked with the veteran's service center director who sent her a list of veteran's representatives in Florida. She called the service representative in Orlando and made an appointment with him to find out if she qualified. He told her to bring all the medical records she had documenting her husband's lung cancer. Marie had saved every explanation of benefits Scott had received from the beginning of his diagnosis of cancer to the last one at the time of his death.

"I think you qualify for entitlement," the retired senior chief representative said after filling out the paperwork, "but these records and documentation have to be sent to the VA for final authorization, and it will probably take six months before you hear. At the present time, I can't quote the exact monthly entitlement for a widow, but like social security, the amount is raised every year."

Marie swallowed hard and didn't know what to say, but she knew she could use the extra money to help her live a comfortable lifestyle, for she had no desire to marry again. Every card Scott gave her was signed, "Yours Forever, Love, Scott," and she believed that one day, they would be together again.

When she told Danny, he commented, "He's still taking care of you." Marie believed that also, especially since she had recently found the last anniversary card Scott gave her that was signed, "Yours Forever, I Will Always Be With You." It took her breath away…she had reread it five years after his death.

Within three months after applying for the VA benefits, Marie had a letter stating that she qualified for widow entitlement. The reason stated Scott's death was service connected as a result of inhaling Agent Orange while serving as a river rat in Vietnam. Marie was elated for realistically speaking if she could no longer share life with Scott, she would enjoy what she had left of her life alone.

Marie wanted to share her claim with other widows, so she tried to get the word out, even to the extent that she began to read obituary notices in the local paper, and, if she noticed that the deceased was a Vietnam vet, she called the funeral home, asked for the directors and advised them of the right of the survivor to file a claim. Marie received two calls, both from widows who thought they would be capitalizing on their husband's death and couldn't possibly consider filing a claim, so she decided that she would only offer her knowledge of the benefit if she was asked.

Five years after Scott's death, Marie had not had a date. Hadn't even thought about dating. She saw her brother often and the two of them enjoyed going to happy hour, so she found no need for a man in her life. She often remembered when she and Scott had an argument, he would comment, "You'll never find anyone who loves you more than I do," to which she answered, "Who's looking?" They'd laugh, fall into each other's arms and end up in the passion of once again exploring each other's sexuality. They were never disappointed after their love making even after all the years together.

EIGHTY-SIX

Marie had had bouts with diverticulitis which necessitated an antibiotic as well as pain prescriptions. The pain medicine was so strong that Marie, once she took it, would not leave her home or drive her car, her brain was too anesthetized. It was after having taken a pain pill early one morning in October of 2006 that Marie received a phone call. Looking at the caller ID, she saw a county number, so she picked the phone up off the cradle and answered it.

"Is this Marie Nicholson?" a voice asked.

"Yes," Marie answered.

"This is Deputy Jensen of the Volusia County Sheriff's Office. Do you have a brother Danny Maxwell?"

"Oh, God, No," Marie cried.

"He's okay, ma'am. There's been an accident where he is involved. He has been taken to the hospital in an ambulance, but his little dog was with him. We need the dog picked up and the car moved. Can you come and get both?"

"Dear Lord," Marie exclaimed. "I just took a pain pill and wouldn't back my car out of the driveway with the buzz I'm feeling."

"Well, ma'am, someone has to come and take possession of the vehicle and get the dog," the deputy stated.

"Let me think," Marie said. "Okay, I know, call my sister who lives in the next county just over the line and ask her to come," and she gave the officer Margaret's phone number.

Margaret drove to the accident site and retrieved the doggie. She asked the deputy if she could park the car in a nearby lot until she found someone to help her move it, to which he responded, "Twenty-four hours or we'll impound it."

Margaret took Danny's dog to her apartment and headed back to the hospital where she inquired about her brother's condition in the ER.

She saw him laying on a gurney. His eyes were closed and he lay motionless. Standing by his side, she said, "Danny, it's Margaret." He made no response to her presence.

Dr. Ghan, a neurosurgeon, had been standing on the other side of the gurney when Margaret approached.

"Doctor, what's wrong with him?" she asked.

"He has two subdural hematomas of the brain, one on each side of his temple. Your brother has taken many falls. His body has old bruises all over it. I have to go in to repair the damage. What I need you to do is to keep him awake, shake him - talk to him, but keep him awake until I can operate. If he falls asleep, he could go into a coma. The biggest problem right now is that he is on a blood thinner, and I cannot operate until we can coagulate his blood or he'll bleed to death. I can't promise anything."

The wait for his blood to thicken seemed like hours. It happened faster than expected. When Danny was taken into the OR, Dr. Ghan told Margaret, "Go to your sister's and I'll call you there when the surgery is over. There's nothing you can do here.

When Margaret pulled into her sister's driveway, Marie was waiting for her. They stood in the kitchen while Margaret told her sister what was happening. They looked at each other and hugged, crying, remembering another time when they were little girls and their mother was taken to a hospital for surgery and they knew not whether she would return. They shared the same anxiety on this morning that they did so many years ago.

Dr. Ghan called after the surgery to inform them that Danny made it through the surgery, although it would be still touch and go for seventy-two hours.

Marie called Linda and asked her to fly down.

"I don't think he'll make it," she said crying, "and I'm gonna need you. Will you come?"

"I'll catch a flight as soon as I can," Linda responded.

"You can only stay a few minutes," the nurse in recovery said to Marie. "He's out of it and will be for a day or two. Don't be afraid of what you see. The doctor had to make an incision from one ear across the top of his head to the other ear."

When Marie stepped to the side of her brother's bed she was aghast. There was a tube coming out of the top of Danny's head. He looked like a teletubby. He didn't open his eyes when Marie said, "Hey, Unc, how ya doin'?" and she bent down to kiss his cheek. Margaret and Marie stayed a short time, only leaving after they recognized the fact that Danny was "out of it," and they needed to get to the airport to pick up Linda.

Linda wanted to go directly to the hospital when she arrived.

"I have to see that he's alright," she stated.

His condition hadn't changed when they walked into the room. They stayed a short time before going to Marie's house for the "wait."

The next day when they went back to the hospital, Danny was semi-conscious.

"Linda, is that you?" he called out.

Linda went to his bedside and bent over to kiss her ex-husband's cheek.

He looked up and asked in a low voice, "Did you bring your wedding band?"

The women went to Danny's trailer to check it out for temperature and to find paperwork he may need concerning insurance claims. When they opened the door and stepped in, Linda looked into the bathroom and saw bloodied towels in the sink and on the floor.

"My God," she said. "He must have fallen the morning before he went to the beach to say his brievery and went anyway. There's a lot of blood on these towels."

Linda retrieved a garbage bag and put the bloodied towels in it.

Danny remained in the hospital a week before entering a rehabilitation facility near the hospital. He was taught how to walk, get into a car, back into a chair by feeling the edge of the seat on the backs of his knees before sitting down. Visiting hours found the hallway outside Danny's room lined up with parishioners waiting to see him which caused concern in the nursing staff. Danny's visits were sapping his energy and he needed that for physical therapy. After a consult with Marie, who had Danny's power of attorney, it was decided to place a sign on his door stating that any visitor must check with the nurse before entering, but it didn't stop the visits the people snuck in anyway, much to the consternation of both the staff and Marie.

Danny had two insurance policies. It seemed to Marie that the administrator was keeping her brother longer than necessary. Marie felt that in six weeks of therapy, Danny was improving to the point of being able to be released and Christmas was seven days away.

"Oh, no, he's not ready to be released," the administrator said. "He needs at least two more weeks."

"Tell you what," Marie answered boldly. "I'm coming for my brother on the 24th and taking him home whether you agree or not."

And that's just what she did.

After a period of recuperation, Danny started to return to his priestly duties. The single- wide trailer he lived in near the church allowed him to walk to say Mass, but he started acting strange in that his memory seemed to fail him. When he walked, the gate of his steps became shuffled. He wasn't picking up his feet. The sisters were concerned about his driving and approached him.

"No, no, I'm alright to drive," he commanded, but it was becoming evident that he was not. It was noticed in the church parking lot by the staff one day. He was standing by his car staring into space, seemingly confused as to where he was, which caused the secretary to call the 800 number to report him to the DMV.

When he received his notice for driver's examination, in it he was also informed to bring someone to drive him home in case he didn't pass the exam. He called Marie and asked her to meet him at the DMV at 9:30. When Marie arrived, Danny was sitting on a chair studying the handbook given to him when he arrived. He didn't tell her that he had already failed the first written exam, but that he was just waiting to go in for it. Examinees came and went as Marie sat in the waiting room, but her brother was taking a lot of time with his written/computer exam. She got up and peeked through a small window in the door leading to the examining room. She noticed Danny sitting and staring at the screen, and she knew he probably wouldn't make it, so she stepped outside.

Noticing an examiner walking toward her, she stopped him and asked him if he had a minute.

"Sure, how can I help you?" he asked.

"This is the hardest request I've had to make, but I need to do it anyway," she answered.

"My brother is in there taking the written exam. The family doesn't think he should drive any longer. He won't listen to anyone," she exclaimed with tears filling up in her eyes.

"I'll check it out and get right back to you," the examiner said.

"Please, please don't let him know I stopped you. He'll never forgive me," Marie said as she held a tissue to her eyes.

"He'll never know," he said and disappeared through the door.

When the examiner returned, he said, "He's been here since 7:30 this morning and failed the test twice. He can't take the driving test unless he passes the written one. He has one more chance to pass or his license will be surrendered. I wouldn't worry. I hope I've helped."

Danny passed the written test on the third try but failed the driving test, so his license was surrendered to the Dept. of Motor Vehicles. He was devastated when his sister drove him home.

The next seemingly insurmountable issue for Marie was to talk to him about was living alone, but she waited until he could digest the loss of his driver's license before approaching him.

Her stomach was tied in knots the day she set about discussing his situation with him.

"No," Danny said. "I'm okay to live alone. I don't want to go to a nursing home."

"Not a nursing home," Marie answered. "An independent living facility."

"Where?" he asked.

"Well, I've gone with you when you've said Mass at many places, but to me there's no place as first-class as Glendale in Daytona Beach.

"We can't afford the monthly rent there," he stated.

"Yes, we can. You don't worry. I'll get it for you," Marie said.

When Danny had his brain surgery, Marie had a call from the bishop asking if the diocese could do anything for Danny. She told him if the time came, she would call and ask him for it. The time was now. Marie prayed for guidance for that which she was about to do.

"I'm Fr. Danny Maxwell's sister," she said when the phone was answered by a sister someone. "Bishop Kelly asked that I call him in regards to my brother's condition. Is he available and would you put me through to him please?"

"Marie," Bishop Kelly commented when he took the call. "How's Danny?"

"That's what I'm calling about," Marie said. "Remember when you said if needed, I should call you?"

"Yes, I do," he replied.

Marie took a deep breath, and said, "I need a thousand dollars a month for him to go to a facility because he can't live alone anymore." She held her breath and closed her eyes waiting for a reply.

"I can't make that decision. I have to put it before the board of priests who will confer and make a determination. Is the facility a first-rate one?"

"That's why I need the money. It is."

"I'll get back to you in a couple of days after the board meets," he said.

Danny was surprised when Marie told him that she made the call to the bishop, and he didn't really believe the money would be forthcoming.

The next day, the two sisters accompanied Danny for his last visit to the neurosurgeon. While they were meeting, Marie's cell phone rang. When she looked at the caller ID, she saw that the screen showed the area code where the chancellery was located.

"I have to take this call," she said, and was shown a room by the nurse where she could have some privacy.

"Marie?" she heard when she pushed the talk button. "It's Bishop Kelly calling. You've got your money. It will start coming next month. Shall I send it to you or to your brother's account?"

For a second, she couldn't talk, she was crying. She quickly composed herself and answered, "My brother's account. God bless you bishop for this gift to him to live out his last days in a superior residence."

"If he doesn't receive it, call me," he added.

"I will," Marie said.

"Oh, I know you will," he said with a smile in his voice. "I'll be in touch soon," and he hung up.

Bishop Kelly called Marie two weeks later.

"I have a couple questions to ask you," he said. "Do you know how long residents live after they go to a retirement facility?"

"Well, according to a long-term policy I bought five years ago, the average time of residency is three years, but then the place Danny lives in has four levels of care: independent, assisted living, congregate, and nursing," Marie said.

"Okay," Bishop Kelly said. "I have another sensitive question to ask you. Did your brother share with you the fact that he cannot be buried in this diocese? That in this diocese he cannot say Mass nor hear confessions, nor baptize, nor exercise any other priestly duties he performed before he left the priesthood?"

Marie felt her blood pressure increase, felt the anger rising within her, and although she wanted to tell him to go to hell, for her brother's sake, she kept level-headed. She answered that she had not been told, which was true. She figured Danny was too ashamed to tell her.

"As far as burial, his cremated remains will be taken out to sea by the Coast Guard," she answered. "I have purchased a pre-need funeral service package for him, me, and my sister, so there's no worries there."

"Sounds like you have everything under control," the bishop said.

"I do," she answered.

"Good, then, God Bless," he said and rang off.

Spittin' mad was the only way to describe Marie's frame of mind. She stomped her right foot, banged her fists on the kitchen counter, and yelled, "Son of a bitchin' Catholic church. I guess it would be okay if he liked little boys. Then you could send him out west where nobody knew him. Bet you'd let him perform his priestly duties then, wouldn't you. All he did was fall in love with a good woman. God damn hypocrites." And the tears ran down her face as she poured a vodka/rocks and sobbed. She didn't blame the bishop, as he seemed like a good man, but she decided that she would not further embarrass Danny by letting him know what she was told.

Danny seemed to thrive living at Glendale. He was able to say Mass in one of the two chapels, and he found comfort in knowing that he was valued by both the residents and the staff. One morning after Danny was a resident for two years, the chaplain placed a call to Marie stating that, in his opinion, he thought Danny should be moved to assisted living. He had fallen in the parking lot and did Marie know that he had been taken to the hospital to find out if he broke his arm.

"No," she answered. "When was this?"

"Two weeks ago," the chaplain answered. "I think you need to talk to the administrator to see if he should be moved."

When Marie conferred with Marlene, the administrator, she was advised that the staff was keeping an eye on Danny, and should it become necessary, they will contact his doctor for his evaluation of moving Danny to ALS. In the meantime, she didn't feel it was necessary. Somehow Danny found out about the confidential meetings and blamed Marie.

After his brain surgery, Marie used her power of attorney and withdrew money from his bank account to hide for him in case he had to deplete all his assets for costly assisted living or nursing care. She wanted to ensure that he would have "pocket" money to spend, and she informed him of her action. He agreed that it was a wise decision. But now, angry with what he thought she had done, he took away the power of attorney as well as the healthcare surrogacy he gave her years before.

Marie was devastated when Danny called one evening and angrily said, "I want my money."

"Okay," she said. But she couldn't believe that he didn't trust her by asking for it, so she didn't immediately do anything about it.

Two days later, Danny called again and asked, "Where is my money? I want it now."

Distraught, Marie called a priest who was a buddy of Danny's.

"Don't give it to him," he said.

"I don't know, father," she said. "I've never seen him this mad. I tried to do something I thought would benefit him. What hurts is that he doesn't trust me and I'm so saddened. We've been so close. I don't understand. I think I'll get it for him. The hell with it."

"Marie," the priest said. "He's not well. His dementia is getting worse. Those who suffer from this disease usually go after the one who's closest to them."

"I can't take anymore," Marie said.

The next morning she went to the bank, drew out the money, had a certified check made out to Danny and mailed it certified, return receipt requested. She went home, had a glass, maybe two, of wine and cried herself to sleep sitting on the sofa.

EIGHTY-SEVEN

Marie continued to work out at the gym and befriended one of the woman trainers, Mary Ann, who was Cheryl's age. One morning after an aerobics workout, two of Marie's friends approached her about going to Cassadaga.

"We understand that they have some sort of service on Wednesday nights in their temple," Rose said. "A bunch of us would like to go over and see what it's all about. Wanna come?"

Marie had traveled to Cassadaga many times after Scott's death for a reading with Helen Bradley and had received many messages from "the other side," so she knew a lot about mediumship and enjoyed her visits with Helen.

"Yeah, I'd like to go with you guys," Marie answered. "I don't drive at night, so could I ride with someone?"

Mary Ann offered to pick Marie up and drive her to the Wednesday night meeting at the temple of the mediums who lived in the small community of Cassadaga.

When the women entered the temple, they saw that it compared to an auditorium, with a stage in front and folding chairs affixed in a semi-circle in front of the stage. A welcome was given to all who attended and a speaker was introduced who gave a short description of how a medium can help believers connect with friends and relatives who have passed over to the next dimension. After the speaker finished a local medium gave readings to the audience. After each of the forty attendees had a brief reading, the rest of the service was turned over to the practice of Reiki healing.

Marie looked at Mary Ann and asked, "What are they talking about?" to which Mary Ann said, "Just watch."

Four Reiki practitioners (healers) came from the audience to the front of the temple bringing with them stools or chairs which they placed below the stage. At this point, attendees, one at a time, came forward and sat down on the stool. The Reiki practitioner asked their names and told them to sit quietly, after which the healer either laid her hands on various parts of the body, or held them just a couple inches above. It is believed that the person receiving Reiki will draw needed amounts of energy from the practitioner who has been attuned or initiated by a Reiki Master to transfer the magnetic energy of the universe.

Mary Ann looked at Marie and commented, "There's a position open to your left. Would you like to go for a healing?"

Confused, Marie got up and went to a stool in the left of the lecture theatre. When she arrived, she accepted the invite by a tall, middle-aged, grey, long haired woman to sit down on her stool. Marie had practiced meditation for years, so she decided to assume the position and placed her hands on her lap and closed her eyes. She didn't know how long she sat there and didn't see what the woman was doing during that time, but when she was told she could leave, she went back to her place and sat down next to Mary Ann.

"She spent a lot of time around your heart," Mary Ann said.

"What does that mean?" Marie asked.

"You were taking in a lot of energy in the heart chakra," Mary Ann answered.

"Energy?" Marie asked.

"Later, I'll explain," Mary Ann replied.

In the half hour ride back to the beach, Mary Ann explained that Reiki is not a religion. It is the Japanese declaration for universal life force energy and that we all have energy. What makes Reiki different is the attunement or initiation process the student encounters in the levels of Reiki lessons.

"How do you know…Oh! You are one?" Marie asked.

Mary Ann smiled and moved her head up and down.

"How come you didn't tell me?" Marie asked.

"There are those who laugh and make fun of this kind of healing," Mary Ann said, "so I don't broadcast it, but I know it works."

"Will you perform a healing on me?" Marie asked.

"When would you like me to come to your house and give it?" Mary Ann asked.

An appointment was made the following week. Mary Ann arrived with a massage table that was folded in half. She set it up in Marie's living room, put on some soothing, transcendental music and asked Marie to lay on her back on the table. Beginning at Marie's head, Mary Ann placed her hands on various parts of her body, being careful not to engage inappropriately any private parts, and moved down Marie's body to her feet. When she lay her hands on Marie's solar plexus, Mary Ann's hands vibrated which made Marie wonder if she was going to pass out.

"If she does, I'll get off the table and dial 911," Marie thought.

The vibration stopped before the healing was completed, but before Mary Ann completed the healing, Marie had a dream, possibly a vision, of a white dove flying toward her. Marie awakened feeling calm, peaceful and refreshed. She couldn't describe the experience to her friend except to ask if others Mary Ann had performed Reiki on described dreams or visions as a result of the healing.

Mary Ann replied, "It's common for that to happen, not all the time, but yes, it happens."

"I want to know more about it," Marie said.

"I'll give you some literature to read," Mary Ann said.

Mary Ann brought into the gym three books about the practice of Reiki healing and Marie, fascinated by her interest in it, closed her mind to everything around her while reading them. She decided that she wanted to become a Reiki practitioner. When she told Mary Ann about her decision, Mary Ann accepted her as her student and began her training to level one healing.

The laying on of hands of level one allows the healer to transfer energy to either oneself or another while level two allows the healer to transfer energy to someone in the next room or across the world. Level three is Reiki master who has been attuned to not only to level one and two, but is a teacher to the first two levels to open the student up to become channels themselves.

After her attunement to level one and two, Marie let the word out that she was a Reiki practitioner. She bought a used folding massage table from her acupuncturist to use for treatments.

Her first healee was her dear friend, Jackie. The vibratory sensations Marie felt while placing her hands on her were not as scary to Marie as they were to Jackie, for Jackie didn't know what was going on.

"All it is is the energy of the universe passing through me to you," Marie said. "The energy goes where it is needed in your body for both physical as well as spiritual healing."

When Marie placed her hands on another friend, Anna, the vibrations materialized on both the front as well as the back side of her body. Anna called the next day stating that little blister-like eruptions lined the area on each side of the three year old incision of her left knee. After discussing it with Mary Ann, Marie told Anna that the eruptions were nothing to worry about. The incision had not fully healed.

Although she wanted to share this gift, there were those who smiled and said, "Uh Huh," when Marie talked about being a Reiki practitioner, and she knew she was being ridiculed for her belief, so she stopped mentioning it, allowing word of mouth to be the only public statement she could accept.

Instead of charging for her service, Marie asked that her clients make a donation to the local Human Society and had a jar sitting on her counter for her patrons to fill. She never paralleled herself to the scriptures with reference to the laying on of hands, for she knew she was only the conduit through which the universal energy flowed. Before she started every Reiki healing, she called upon God, His Son, and the Holy Spirit to guide her.

While surfing through the internet one day, Marie came upon a January 2010 article that was in The Reiki Digest which stated: "Try Reiki," Dr. Oz tells millions on TV. Dr. Mehmet Oz, a renowned cardiovascular surgeon and host of the third (or possibly second) most popular syndicated television program in America, this week introduced millions of viewers to the natural healing practice of Reiki as part of a program on alternative and natural remedies."

The article continues with Dr. Oz stating that he has allowed a Reiki practitioner in the operating room.

At the show's conclusion, Oz did his usual "Oz's Orders" segment: "Here are the three things I want you to remember from today's show. First off, try Reiki. This alternative medicine treatment can manipulate your energy and cure what ails you." And he recommended that viewers boost their metabolisms and check their blood pressures. "Those are my doctor's orders."

Thank God that a man of science is accepting of something that is so foreign to the layman, Marie thought after reading and printing the article.

EIGHTY-EIGHT

Marie had to go into Orlando to seek a second opinion for a non-emergency medical problem she was having. Her young neighbor, Jimmy, offered to drive her, expressing his need to purchase an item he could not find in the Daytona area.

After leaving the doctor's office, Jimmy drove south on the interstate exiting on Green St. Marie was becoming anxious during the ride for she knew it would take them near a place she hadn't been in years.

"Turn right at the next street," she said.

"What?" Jimmy asked. "Why?"

"Just please do it," she answered.

Jimmy turned right onto Franklin St.

"Turn right again," Marie commanded.

"Where are we going?" Jimmy said as he pulled into the front of a small house.

"I'll be right back," she said as she got out of the car.

"It's now or never," she thought to herself.

Marie walked down the sidewalk as a woman was getting out of an SUV.

"Are you Marie?" the woman said.

"What?" Marie answered.

"Are you Marie?" she said.

"Yes," Marie answered.

"Come on in," the woman said.

Marie stepped into the building, walked toward a table near the door and turned her back.

"I need to leave," she said.

"Sit down," the woman said softly.

"No, I want to go," Marie said.

"Are you ill?" the woman asked.

"No," Marie said shaking. "I just want to go. I made a mistake and I want to go."

"Please sit down, Mother," the woman said.

Marie turned around and faced the woman, exclaiming, "Cheryl?"

"Don't you know me?" Cheryl said.

"No," Marie said.

Cheryl pulled out a chair and helped her mother to it.

"I want to ask you to my seventy-fifth birthday party," Marie said. "Will you come?"

"I'm sorry Mother, when is it?' Cheryl said.

"December 24th," Marie answered. *"Oh, my God, she forgot my birthday," Marie thought.*

But then it had been fifteen years since they had seen each other.

"What is your phone number?" Cheryl asked.

Marie gave it to her daughter.

Cheryl asked about her Uncle Danny and Aunt Margaret.

"The boy," Marie asked. "Do you have a picture of him?"

Marie hadn't seen her grandson since he was two. He was now eighteen.

"Yes," Cheryl said and invited her mother into her office space where pictures of Mark covered the wall.

"He's going to college?" Marie asked.

"Yes, on a full scholarship," Cheryl answered.

It was becoming extremely unnerving for Marie She could feel her heart beating fast, so she told Cheryl she needed to leave. There was one more thing Marie had to do, so she put her arms around her daughter and said, "Cheryl, if I have done anything to hurt you, I am so sorry."

Cheryl hugged her mother, but said nothing.

"Jimmy's waiting in the car for me," she said. "Would you like to meet him?"

"Yes," Cheryl said. "Who is Jimmy?"

As they walked out of the building, Marie told her what a wonderful young man Jimmy was and how kind he had been to her, helping her when she needed him.

Introductions were made aside Jimmy's car. Cheryl and Jimmy exchanged greetings and shook hands.

Marie got into the car, Jimmy backed out and drove down the street toward the interstate while at the same time, handing Marie a box of tissues he kept in his car.

Marie stopped crying and shaking a few minutes after Jimmy entered the interstate. Jimmy knew about the estrangement of his neighbor and her daughter but not every detail. When she arrived home, Marie was spent and sat down to compose herself and tried to digest what had happened. She knew she hadn't intentionally gone to her daughter's office, had no idea she would end up there, but even if it didn't work out, she was glad she had made the effort to mend her relationship with her daughter.

Marie called her son, Derek, after she had time to calm down.

"Mom," Derek said. "I'm so proud of you. It took a lot of courage to confront her like you did."

"Courage?" Marie questioned. "She's my daughter. How can that be courageous?"

"I just meant that"....and his voice trailed off.

"It was traumatic for me," Marie commented. "It took a lot out of me and I can't go through that again."

One week later, Derek called his mother.

"Mom," he said sadly. "I'm so sorry. Cheryl called and said, 'I want to end this once and for all. I don't want anything to do with her.'"

"It's okay, son," Marie said. "I had some hope, but somehow that wasn't the only reason for going to her."

"You wouldn't want to walk around on eggshells, would you?" he asked.

"No," Marie said. "I need to go."

"See ya, Mom."

Marie's birthday party was held at a nearby restaurant. Twenty-two guests arrived to wish her well. A buffet and an open bar was set up for friends and family. She didn't want any gifts. Her invitations stated that their presence was gift enough for her.

EIGHTY-NINE

Time passed and Marie continued to walk the beach finding it comforting to watch the ocean waves kiss the shore at low tide. She thought of Scott as she walked and wondered when she would be with him again. Many was the time since his death, she thought she heard within, his voice, saying, "Soon."

It was one such day when she walked the beach that she started to feel heaviness in her chest. A pain started at her shoulder and ran down her left arm. Fearful, she sat down on the sand and within seconds, fell over on her side clutching her chest.

It was spring break for the college kids who like to party on the beach. A group of young men were walking behind Marie when they noticed her sit down, then fall over. They ran to her side and knelt down. One young man yelled to another, "I think she's having a heart attack. Call 911!"

When the ambulance arrived and as they were attending her, an EMT asked the young men if anyone knew the old woman. She had no identification.

"Wait," the medic said. "There's a cell phone in her pocket with her name on the back. It's pretty worn, but I can read a name, Marie Nicholson," he said. "And there's a phone number."

"Oh! My God!" one of the young lads said. "I think it's my grandmother."

"Think?" the medic questioned.

"I haven't seen her since I was a toddler," he said.

The young man whipped out his cell phone and called his mother. He told her how it happened, how he came upon this old woman who passed out on the beach. Cheryl told him that she believed it was his grandmother. She gave him instructions…things to say that would allow her mother to recognize that he was her grandson.

As the medical technicians were transferring the old woman from the beach to the ambulance, the young man asked, "Can I go with her?"

"We usually don't allow a rider, but in this case, I think it's a good idea," the medic answered.

Mark climbed into the ambulance and was allowed to sit aside his grandmother whose eyes were closed. He took her small, boney hand and said, "I'm here Ba Ba. I ya you."

Marie opened her eyes and in her heart, she saw not a young man, but a little toe haired toddler with blue eyes. She smiled, pulled off the oxygen mask, and said, "An-mal crackers!"

The ambulance driver, who was traveling at a fast rate of speed with the siren blaring and red light circling above, drove over the bridge, turned left, and stopped in front of the ER entrance of the hospital where Marie was taken into the emergency room with her grandson running behind. The automatic doors leading to the emergency room slid shut just as the Florida afternoon monsoon rains started falling down.

EPILOGUE

In all probability, the reader of this chronicle might wonder, how another would know so much about Marie's life. I am the narrator of this story and have been with Marie since the moment she was born. I am her guardian angel, or as she likes to call me, her spirit guide. My name is Lydia.

CPSIA information can be obtained at www.ICGtesting.com
Printed in the USA
LVOW090250031011

248819LV00003B/5/P